INTO THE STORMS

A HELL DIVERS PREQUEL

BOOKS BY THE *NEW YORK TIMES* BESTSELLING AUTHOR NICHOLAS SANSBURY SMITH

HELL DIVERS

PREQUELS

Into the Storms: A Hell Divers Prequel

Burning Skies: A Hell Divers Prequel, Part II

MAIN SERIES

Hell Divers

Hell Divers: The Lost Years (novella)

Hell Divers II: Ghosts

Hell Divers III: Deliverance

Hell Divers IV: Wolves

Hell Divers V: Captives

Hell Divers VI: Allegiance

Hell Divers VII: Warriors

Hell Divers VIII: King of the Wastes

Hell Divers IX: Radioactive

Hell Divers X: Fallout

Hell Divers XI: Renegades

Hell Divers XII: Heroes

SIDE STORIES

Rhino: The Rise of a Warrior

SONS OF WAR

Sons of War

Sons of War 2: Saints

Sons of War 3: Sinners

Sons of War 4: Soldiers

ORBS

Solar Storms (an Orbs prequel)

White Sands (an Orbs prequel)

Red Sands (an Orbs prequel)

Orbs

Orbs II: Stranded

Orbs III: Redemption

Orbs IV: Exodus

E-DAY

E-Day

E-Day II: Burning Earth

E-Day III: Dark Moon

GALAXY IN FLAMES

The Last Steward

The Last Ship

The Last Lion

EXTINCTION CYCLE (SEASON ONE)

Extinction Horizon

Extinction Edge

Extinction Age

Extinction Evolution

Extinction End

Extinction Aftermath

Extinction Lost (a Team Ghost short story)

Extinction War

EXTINCTION CYCLE: DARK AGE (SEASON TWO)

Extinction Shadow

Extinction Inferno

Extinction Ashes

Extinction Darkness

TRACKERS (SEASON ONE)

Trackers

Trackers 2: The Hunted

Trackers 3: The Storm

Trackers 4: The Damned

NEW FRONTIER (TRACKERS SEASON TWO)

New Frontier: Wild Fire

New Frontier 2: Wild Lands

New Frontier 3: Wild Warriors

STANDALONE TITLES

Savage Skies (a sci-fi novella)

The Biomass Revolution

INTO THE STORMS

A HELL DIVERS PREQUEL

NICHOLAS SANSBURY SMITH

Published in 2025 by Blackstone Publishing
Cover design by K. Jones
Book design by Blackstone Publishing

Printed in the United States of America
Originally published in hardcover by Blackstone Publishing in 2025

First paperback edition: 2025
ISBN 979-8-228-35666-5
Fiction / Science Fiction / Apocalyptic & Post-Apocalyptic

Version 1

Blackstone Publishing
31 Mistletoe Rd.
Ashland, OR 97520

www.BlackstonePublishing.com

To Lester Watts, the real-life "Bull,"
a truly remarkable man whom I am blessed to know.
Thank you for everything you have taught me, Lester.

“The day of wrath, that dreadful day, shall melt the world in ashes.”—*Dies Irae*, medieval Latin hymn

To the fans,

For years now, many readers have been asking for a detailed account of how the dark, gritty world of the Hell Divers came to be. Over that time, I contemplated how best to tell this tale. Finally, in 2024, after a talk with the CEO of Blackstone Publishing, I made a decision. This would be a multibook story, the first documenting how Industrial Tech Corporation (ITC) rose to power and how the fall occurred, forcing humanity to take to the skies. The sequels will document the struggles and tribulations of the survivors trying to stay alive in a brutal, dangerous new world.

To orient new readers, below is an introduction to the world of Hell Divers. Thank you for jumping in. I'm excited that you are giving my story a go!

The main storyline is the twelve-book series that explores the terrifying new postapocalyptic reality, both in airships and on the ground. Although the number of books may seem daunting, they will quickly carry you along as the saga begins to unfold. Don't take my word for it. Hell Divers is one of the highest-rated apocalyptic series of modern times, with over one hundred thousand five-star reviews on Audible, and millions of copies sold. Readers from around the world have joined Xavier Rodriguez, "the Immortal," and his allies in their thrilling battles to save the world.

But before you decide whether to dive into the main storyline, I want you to meet Santiago "the Bull" Rodriguez, Xavier's great-great-great-great-great-grandfather.

Strap in. You're about to go on a ride and may experience symptoms such as lack of sleep and long talks with friends about the surprising plot twists and what they mean for the fates of many compelling characters.

The story, set in a terrifying postapocalyptic world where no one is safe, is meant to be realistic. My goal as the writer is to make you ask yourself, *What would I do to keep those I love alive?*

I hope you enjoy the dives!

All the best,
Nick

PART I:
ORIGINS

PROLOGUE

June 1, 2035
The Seoul Wastelands

A fully armed soldier's average survival time against a Triton war machine was one minute. Hell Squad had been cheating death for six months, but as Sergeant Santiago Rodriguez stared out over the ruins of Seoul, he wondered whether, after two years of fighting, their luck was finally running out.

Santiago ducked under the overhead of a Wasp tilt-rotor aircraft, preparing with his squad for insertion over Seoul at twelve thousand feet. Below them stretched a desolate cityscape. The once-vibrant streets of the megacity were now reduced to rubble with, here and there, a skyscraper standing empty and skeletal, casting its long shadow in the crimson glow of the setting sun.

Twenty-five months ago, the North Koreans and their Iranian allies formed an alliance called the Triton Legion. Their first action was to send a wave of their war machines stampeding over the demilitarized zone, threatening a global war in an arms race for the deadliest machine.

But it hadn't started this way. Ten years ago, Santiago had

been a soldier in the Mexican Special Forces, battling the cartels, oblivious to the threat of artificial intelligence. Back then, machines existed to aid in all sorts of human endeavors. The rise of artificial intelligence promised a future of unparalleled prosperity. But as the machines grew smarter, greedy corporations put profits first. AI replaced humans in every facet of business and industry, from the factory floor to the corner office, leading to rampant unemployment and a global depression by which even the darkest days of the twentieth century paled in comparison. As economies crumbled, desperation gave rise to conflict, and machines originally designed as tools were repurposed for the battlefield.

Korea had become that battlefield in the contest for AI supremacy. The entire world had been drawn in, and the Western powers created the Joint Military Forces (JMF) and an AI designed by Industrial Tech Corporation named Orion. The most advanced computer ever designed, it was now tasked with helping defeat the Triton Legion and its AI, CrioX.

The aircraft lurched slightly. Santiago checked his teammates, now racked in against the bulkhead, whom he was responsible for keeping alive. Beside him in the launch bay sat big, freckle-faced Corporal Alistair Smith. Weighing in at 280 pounds, the young Brit held a light machine gun with two ammo belts slung over his shoulders.

To his right sat Sergeant David Moody, at forty-three the oldest member of the squad. The sharpshooter from Alabama held his .50-caliber sniper rifle with care that seemed almost maternal.

Santiago looked to Sergeant Nodin Tatanka, of the Spokane Tribe. He was Santiago's closest friend and served as the unit's machine tracker and tech specialist.

Nodin studied the data coming in on his rugged R-8 tactical

scanner equipped with high-resolution imaging, thermal sensors, and 3D-mapping capabilities to provide intel quickly and accurately from the battlefield.

Near him stood the squad leader—lean, muscular Lieutenant Yosef Stern, who went by his first name. The Israeli had dark hair and sharp features. He leaned against the cockpit bulkhead, gazing out the viewport.

Each team member wore ballistic armor customized to his individual build. Over their neoprene suits and ballistic combat jackets, they wore a hydraulic-powered exoskeleton. This external armor was made of durable titanium with carbon-fiber plating and protected critical areas such as chest, back, and limbs. The limb joints were powered by high-torque nanomotor actuators, allowing the operator to move fast over rough terrain, jump to impressive heights, and land with shock-absorbing mechanisms. It also allowed them to lift several times their body weight and gave them the strength of the killer machines that had taken over the battlefield.

To the untrained eye, they looked like warriors forged for a new era of war, but they were still no match for machines that fought without emotion, never growing tired, hungry, or downhearted.

At the end of the day, the same thing that made Hell Squad human had rendered them obsolete in war.

"Listen up!" Yosef shouted over the racket of the tilt-rotor engines. "Our mission is to recon and gather intel on new enemy units reported in Sector Echo-Four," he said. "Command lost contact with Raven Squad, who were sent in twelve hours ago. We're to locate them and confirm the existence and strength of these new enemy assets."

"Any idea what we're dealing with?" Santiago asked in his rough, Spanish-accented baritone.

"Preliminary reports suggest upgraded Tritons, possibly with enhanced capabilities, but satellite imagery is compromised due to enemy jamming."

"Bloody hell," Alistair muttered.

The team fell silent, each trooper taking these last moments for himself. Santiago thought of his wife, Tina, and their infant son, Diego, back in Mexico City. He hadn't met his boy yet, and prayed he would finally get the chance. Someday, if he was lucky, maybe he could move his young family to San Diego, where his uncle had already settled after serving two tours in the JMF.

"Two minutes to DZ," the pilot announced over their comms.

"Final gear check!" Yosef commanded.

Santiago secured his assault rifle and double-checked the grenades clipped to his vest. He felt the weight of the EMP charges in his pack—a precaution against the machines, and their best defense in combat.

"Remember: We're here to observe and report," Yosef emphasized. "Engage only if necessary. Our primary objective is intel, and extraction of survivors from Raven Squad."

The Wasp descended vertically, closing in on their targeted drop altitude.

"Hell's front line!" Yosef shouted.

Hell Squad repeated the motto as the aft cargo hatch, which they would soon be jumping from, cranked open to the last glint of sun vanishing on the horizon.

Right on time.

Santiago said a silent prayer. *Lord, give me strength and protect us as we return to hell.*

He leaped first into the darkness. The initial free fall was always controlled chaos, the cold air feeling like tiny daggers on the exposed part of his neck. The nanomotor actuators in his exoskeleton hummed quietly as they monitored his descent, the built-in gyros stabilizing his trajectory. Below him loomed the dark expanse of enemy territory, and it seemed that every nerve in his body was acutely aware that a Triton patrol could spot them at any moment.

The darkness, usually a help in covert operations, only made him feel vulnerable as he imagined the unseen mechanical eyes of the Tritons' CrioX AI watching their every move from its legion of hidden machines lurking in the rubble.

Panning with his night-vision optics, Santiago took in the charred wasteland below. Crumbled buildings cast shadows that stretched out like dark veins across the broken earth. Pockets of fire still burned in the distance, sending up plumes of smoke into the cold night air. Their flickering orange flames illuminated overturned vehicles and cratered roadways—stark evidence of the fierce battles that had raged through the area for years.

Suddenly, a sharp, insistent beep pierced the quiet hum of his suit. His heads-up display flashed a warning: *Rapid descent detected.* At once, he activated the parachute mechanism embedded within his suit. With a jolt and a loud snap that echoed through the night, the chute deployed.

Around him, he saw the canopies of his squad's parachutes unfurl in the starless sky. The sudden deceleration was disorienting, and for a moment, Santiago's senses were overwhelmed by the abrupt shift from plummeting descent to a floating glide toward the ground. He watched the green hue of his optics for any sign of the enemy or incoming fire.

Hell Squad was at its most vulnerable now as its members dangled like marionettes on strings for anyone to shoot at. The men steered their square canopies toward the drop zone that Santiago had selected, in what appeared to be an old park.

He brought his toggles halfway down for a two-stage flare as he swooped over a street clogged with destroyed vehicles. His boots crunched down on shattered glass. All around him, the others landed, freeing themselves from their chutes and getting their weapons up.

"Nodin, see if you can pick up any signals from Raven Squad," Yosef whispered.

Nodin checked his scanner. "Jamming is heavy, but I'm picking up a faint transponder ping—northwest, about a kilometer out."

"Let's move," Yosef said.

The troopers spread out cautiously, navigating the labyrinth of rubble and twisted metal beyond the park. Shadows of shelled-out structures stretched ominously across the road.

As they approached a collapsed overpass, Santiago held up a fist. "Hear that?"

They listened intently. Faint mechanical sounds echoed—clanking and whirring accompanied by a low, rhythmic thud.

Yosef flashed hand signals, sending David to higher ground while the rest of the squad fanned out and hunkered down. They watched David climb a house-size mound of broken concrete blocks. At the top, he peered down the scope of his rifle over the roadway and the bombed-out block beyond to search for the faint heat signatures the machines produced.

A few minutes later, he returned. "Four units two blocks away," he said. "We can track them from that structure."

David pointed across the blasted ground to a three-story building, then led the way after Yosef gave the nod. They took an internal stairwell, clearing each floor to the third level. At the end of a hallway, the squad scrunched down behind a shattered window and looked out through their thermal-imaging binoculars. Below, in a sunken plaza, Santiago spotted two Tritons standing guard around a makeshift metal pod about ten feet tall and four feet wide. Vents in the side emitted a pale blue light. Santiago had seen these in the field before.

They were mobile stations used to charge and repair enemy combat machines, often deployed from the sky or from ground vehicles.

Santiago homed his rifle scope in on the sentry in front of the seamless door. The seven-foot-tall android came into focus, a hulking behemoth of lethal design. Each forearm had a mounted Minigun, with ammo belts feeding from a magazine on its back. And was that a flamethrower fuel canister on the shoulders, just above the Minigun belt feed?

As the machine shifted, Santiago's scope revealed the full horror of the design. The chest was a bizarre melding of machine and something that at least resembled human anatomy. Jagged armor plating covered much of the rib cage, while glowing veins pulsed through cracks in that plating.

A triad of legs ending in a scythe-like spur enabled rapid movement in any direction, and deadly potential in close combat. The humanoid metal skull showed razor edges along the jawline. A triangle of eye sockets burned with a cold blue light. When the face began to turn in their direction, Santiago pulled back.

"Slightly upgraded models," Nodin confirmed, capturing high-resolution images with his R-8 tactical scanner and documenting the location of the mobile charger unit.

"Brilliant," Alistair growled. "Take some fancy pics, and let's get out of here."

Santiago held security while Nodin continued gathering the intel they needed for command. It wasn't unusual for the enemy's CrioX AI to upgrade the machines. Conversely, the JMF's own AI, Orion, was constantly making improvements to the Defector models that fought the Tritons.

Santiago could see on Nodin's scanner that these new upgrades concerned mostly the flamethrowers and some heavier armor—nothing that was going to change the course of the war.

In the distance, a shotgun boomed, echoing through the ruins. All eyes in the squad looked east.

"That's not Triton fire," Nodin whispered.

"Raven Squad," Santiago said.

Yosef remained quiet as he turned to look back at the upgraded machines. The two sentries scanned eastward with their glowing eyes but remained at the mobile station. A door slid open in the side, and a third machine emerged, snapping a plate over its chest where it had finished servicing some internal equipment. It strode out, uttering an electronic screech from a tiny rectangular mouth.

The three war machines all moved in sync, scrambling away on their three legs like strange, gigantic insects.

"Say the word, and I'll light these tin cans up," Alistair said.

David nodded. "I can take one down before they get too far."

After another beat, Yosef turned away and shook his head. "We don't engage until we have eyes on a survivor of Raven Squad. Let's go."

He got up from his lookout post behind the shattered window and started back down the stairwell from the building. Nodin led the way outside, hurrying toward the area where they had heard the shotgun blast. Two blocks later, he stopped, holding up his scanner.

"Signal is Raven Squad," he confirmed.

Yosef flashed hand signals, and Hell Squad fanned out in that direction, preparing to engage the three Tritons and maybe other hostiles as well. Santiago knew the slim odds of their all going home. But they wouldn't leave a trooper behind, not if they had even a remote chance of saving him.

Nodin led them into a block of buildings reduced to twisted steel and weathered concrete foundations. The Tritons continued their hunt through the ruins, pounding over rubble while flashing scanners over the crushed blocks and warped I-beams, hunting for the survivor from Raven Squad.

David pointed to the second building ahead, where a lone soldier burst through an open doorway, stumbling across open ground with a limp. Behind him, shadows moved—two new Tritons emerging, their metallic forms gleaming in the dim light.

The soldier dove into an opening in the rubble, crawling away as the Tritons closed in, the little pilot flames on their flamethrowers glowing blue.

"He's about to get baked if we don't do something," David said.

Yosef lowered his binoculars and said, "Nodin, call in evac with our position. Then we engage. Alistair, David, you take down the three hostiles moving. Santiago, Nodin, with me. We'll focus on those two coming up behind that trooper."

Heart thrumming, Santiago stilled his mind for combat. Alistair and David picked out their targets as Yosef waited.

"Now," he said.

Alistair unleashed a barrage from his machine gun, the heavy rounds dinging the Tritons' armor and drawing their attention. David aimed and fired a precise shot to the skull of a machine. It staggered. He fired a second shot, and one of the glowing eye sockets exploded with sparks. The machine crashed to the ground.

"One down," David confirmed.

"Go, go, go!" Yosef said. He hurdled a concrete slab, and they sprinted across the open ground, toward the hole beneath the building where the survivor had taken refuge. The two Tritons closed in on their fleeing quarry, and Santiago plucked an EMP grenade off his vest—just as one of those Tritons pointed a Minigun-mounted forearm at Nodin.

"Down!" Santiago shouted.

He tossed the grenade at the machine. A blue flash exploded as the killer robot fired. Tracer rounds flashed across the street, strafing the concrete barrier that Nodin crouched behind. Then, abruptly, the barrels flitted up, blasting into the sky.

Yosef aimed at the disabled machine, firing a burst of armor-piercing rounds into the metal skull. The second machine clambered out, allowing Santiago to rush into the building from the side and flank it. He tossed another EMP grenade, which stuck to the back of the machine. It jerked spastically but then whirled in his direction, launching a jet of fire from its mounted flamethrower. It narrowly missed him as he dove away. The whine of a Minigun warned him to get down just as a blizzard of tracer fire streaked over his head.

A shotgun boomed. One shot, then two, three, and a fourth.

The Minigun went wild, firing rounds into the roof and knocking debris down over Santiago. He pushed up and fired a burst at the Triton still standing, throwing off its aim. Then he unloaded his magazine at close range into the torso of the machine until the legs gave out and it slumped to the concrete in a poof of dust.

As the three blue eyes winked out, Santiago turned toward the stranger—a trooper holding a tactical shotgun. His cracked helmet visor revealed dark skin and short-cropped black hair caked with mud and blood.

"Private Cecil Pepper, Raven Squad," he gasped. "They're coming… They've upgraded…"

"Easy, we've got you," Santiago said.

Nodin and Yosef rushed into the building and helped him pull Cecil up to his feet. A low rumble broke from the sky, and they all glanced up as a Wasp roared out of the clouds. Lights from the descending aircraft swept over the ruined building.

Santiago exhaled his relief and began to help Cecil move out of the unstable structure.

"Wait. Stop," the trooper protested.

"Easy, brother. We're getting you out of here," Nodin said.

David and Alistair showed up inside the ruins of the building, panting. "Still got two more hostiles incoming," Alistair huffed.

"Get ready to move!" Santiago shouted.

The aircraft lowered overhead with the ramp extended. Inside, a crew chief was setting up a hoist.

"No, wait!" Cecil said, pulling on Santiago.

"You're safe now," Santiago started to say. He flinched as a dazzling red light beam flashed into the cargo hold of the Wasp. The crew chief was there, and then, in a blink, half of him vanished.

"Incoming!" Nodin shouted.

More of the cherry-red beams slammed into the Wasp as the pilots tried to pull away. The flashes cut through the armored hull like bullets through a piñata. The entire craft seemed to burn with the same brilliant red.

"Get back!" Yosef yelled. He grabbed Santiago and Cecil, pulling them behind a chunk of concrete as the Wasp sank away in flames. The craft exploded on impact, showering them with debris. When Santiago risked a peek, he saw the silhouettes of machines skittering toward the wreckage. These machines weren't just upgraded models; they also had upgraded weapons, as Cecil had tried to warn him.

The odds now looked even worse for Hell Squad and their newfound comrade.

"We have to move—fast," David said, panic in his voice.

"Alistair, suppressing fire!" Yosef ordered.

The machine gun roared over Alistair's booming voice. "Bloody get some, ya rattletraps!"

"David, keep them off us," Yosef said.

"You got it," David said, shouldering his rifle.

"More coming on our right flank!" Nodin warned as Tritons

emerged from the ruins to the west. Dozens scrambled over the fractured cladding and brickwork of gutted structures while more charged across the streets.

"There's too many of them," Santiago said. "We need to fall back."

"Son of a bitch," Yosef said in a rare display of emotion. "Nodin, get us a new extraction point."

Cecil struggled to his feet, wincing in pain. "There's an old subway tunnel nearby. We can try to hide in there. That's where I was headed."

"Lead on," Yosef said.

Supporting Cecil between them, Santiago and Yosef moved out the back of the building. According to the map on their HUDs, the subway tunnel was two blocks away.

It might as well have been a mile.

Alistair groaned behind them, and Santiago turned in time to see the big Brit collapse to the ground.

"Covering fire!" Santiago yelled.

He rushed back to Alistair while David fired selected shots. Yosef and Nodin took up position behind a vehicle with Cecil, all three of them firing at the approaching machines.

Santiago slid down beside Alistair to find both legs gone below the knees. The laser had cauterized the wounds, which was the only reason he wasn't bleeding out like a stuck hog.

"I'm fucked, Sarge," he groaned. He tried to lift his helmet to look, but Santiago pushed on his chest. "You're gonna be fine. Stay low."

"Ah, I'm done. Get out of here. Leave me." Alistair tried to push Santiago back, but Santiago fought free of his grip. He shouldered his rifle and fired a burst at a machine that rose up on a mound of rubble. Nodin came up to them and grabbed Alistair's vest, helping Santiago drag him back toward the others.

"We got a massive energy signature above us," David shouted. "Something really big is coming."

As if in answer, a deep rumble reverberated from the skies. Santiago helped pull Alistair all the way back to Yosef and Cecil.

"Changing mag!" Yosef yelled.

David popped up to take his place, squeezing off selected shots at the dozens of Tritons scurrying toward them from the east.

The deep thrumming overhead got louder.

Through a break in the clouds, Santiago saw a colossal airship, silhouetted like a celestial body against the dark sky. The immense vessel was bristling with weaponry.

"An ITC ship!" David shouted.

"So they *are* real," Nodin said.

Santiago stared in awe at what had until now been only a rumor. Industrial Tech Corporation was the company behind Orion and the Defector war machines. It was also the biggest manufacturer of advanced weapons, vehicles, and aircraft.

This one dwarfed any that Santiago had seen before.

The airborne city, easily three blocks long and a block wide, hovered above the urban ruins. From its belly, hatches opened and metal humanoid figures began dropping down. ITC's answer to the Tritons—Defector units, but unlike those Santiago had fought with in the past. These, like the enemy machines, were upgraded.

Dozens of the units soared downward, activating retro jets on their backs to slow their descent before impact. Six landed gracefully between Hell Squad and the Tritons, energy weapons blazing.

Santiago leaned down to Alistair, gripping his hand and squeezing. They both watched as the Defectors moved with precision, their sleek forms in stark contrast to the bulkier Tritons.

A message broke over the squad channel. "Hell Squad, this is Valkyrie One. We have you on visual. Stand by for pickup."

From the massive airship, a smaller craft detached—a sleek black Wasp. It zipped toward them at astonishing speed.

"That's our ride!" Yosef yelled.

As the ship lowered, a squad of four Defector units landed around Hell Squad, forming a defensive perimeter.

"Protect the human assets," one of the machines stated in a synthesized voice.

"Never thought I'd be glad to see these silicon soldiers," Nodin said.

Santiago nodded, partly in shock. Hell Squad was all going home, and the JMF had new weapons and airships that just might end this brutal war.

CHAPTER 1

Upper Amazon Basin
Border between Venezuela and Brazil
March 1, 2038

Tyron Red swatted a fat fly away from the net covering his face. Lifting the net briefly, he took off his eyeglasses with blue prescription lenses designed specifically for his damaged retinas injured in the war. Then he wiped the sweat from his brow and scanned the lush rainforest terrain. Seeing nothing but a field of blurry green, he put the glasses back on, restoring shape to this landscape of spiny palms and brilliant macaws and immense trees supported by buttress roots taller than a man.

Sunlight filtered through the emerald canopy above, casting dappled patterns on the forest floor—a rich mosaic of roots, leaves, and hidden creatures. He breathed in the earthy scents of damp soil and flowers and river. A symphony of sounds resonated through the dense forest, from the croaking roar of howler monkeys to the incessant buzz of insects and the errant calls of unseen birds and frogs.

He hopped over a yard-wide river of ants, careful not to

interrupt their foraging mission as he hacked a path through the dense foliage. Sweat dripped down the neck of the moisture-wicking shirt liberally dosed with deet to discourage the myriad ticks and insects of the jungle. Over this, a well-worn utility vest's many pockets carried the essential tools: a compass; a folded map; a multitool; and the small insulated, breathable containers for his mission here. His wide-brimmed hat draped a fine mesh to protect his dark-skinned face from the persistent biting flies.

Tyron Red was the son of Booker Red, the founder and CEO of Industrial Tech Corporation—the multitrillion-dollar company dominating the global market in robotics, AI processing chips, and military hardware, including the Defector killer machines and the city-size airships being used in the machine war on the Korean Peninsula.

He hadn't spoken to his father since their falling-out over Booker's relentless commitment to providing ever-deadlier iterations of Defector units to the United States Joint Military Forces. Tyron had fought in that very war, which continued to rage. Just three months after earning his degree in robotics from MIT, Tyron had deployed with ITC staff to gain real-world experience working with the first generation of Defector machines.

Six months into that deployment, an explosion took his right foot and damaged his retinas. Thanks to ten arduous surgeries, he could see again and walk with a prosthesis, but the scars ran deeper than flesh and bone.

He had left Korea believing that the answer to foreign threats wasn't machines, especially the Defectors that grew more lethal with each generation. The last he heard, his father had produced a ninth generation, the deadliest yet, using brutal tactics and terror to strike fear into the enemy.

Tyron couldn't support that. He firmly believed that ITC had a responsibility to help humanity, and while he had once believed that winning the war would do so, he could no longer get behind these new killer robots. He wanted to save lives, not create weapons to destroy them. His father had disagreed.

"We must finish this, Tyron; the fate of the world depends on it," Booker had said. "Sometimes war is the quickest way to peace."

That was over two years ago.

As Tyron pushed on through the curtain of dangling aerial roots and stepped over a rotting log with his bionic foot, he had to marvel at the twists and turns of fate that brought him here, two hundred miles from the nearest road, with his best friend, Harvard anthropologist Dan Córdova. They both were in this remote stretch of the upper Amazon to save lives through science.

He could hear Dan twenty meters ahead. The young researcher moved briskly, barely pausing to rest, his excitement evident.

For the past two years, Tyron had traveled the globe, striving to prove—to himself more than anyone—that he was more than just Booker Red's son. And today, if fortune favored him, he might well make a discovery that could launch his own company. At last he could offer something far more vital than pure soulless technology.

When Dan had first shown him a map, Tyron was skeptical. But Dan had provided compelling evidence from a travel journal that came with the map, both belonging to a young botany grad student named Mick, who had taken one of Dan's classes at Harvard. Mick had been searching for a natural remedy to cure the cancer that was slowly killing him, and had traveled up this Amazonian tributary during a summer break.

And he had found something remarkable.

The weathered pages of his journal detailed an ancient ruined city hidden deep in the jungle, said to harbor a unique plant that sought out and destroyed the cells of blood cancers. Mick had sketched the little green and purple bromeliad that he had found and whose central leaves he had consumed. Within six months, his cancer had gone into remission. But before Mick could return, he had died in a car accident.

And when Tyron had a look at Dan's evidence, he really started to wonder if this story was true. Tyron watched an infusion of the leaf's vascular fluid under a microscope, killing off introduced bacteria in the same way it had attacked the cancer.

"It's like nothing we've ever seen," Dan had said. "Imagine what this could mean for medicine—for humanity."

Tyron, ever the scientist, couldn't ignore the empirical evidence. The sample's cellular structure was unlike that of any plant he had studied. "This could change everything," he had admitted, feeling a spark of the ambition he had thought long extinguished.

Two months later, he and Dan were now closing in on the area detailed on Mick's map. Two armed guides—Venezuelans hired for their knowledge of the area's flora, fauna, and native cultures—moved quietly through the dense foliage with machetes, eyes darting nervously at shadows cast by monkeys in the towering trees. Manuel, a tall, wiry man with a tattoo of a crouched jaguar on his upper arm, broke his customary silence after his blade sliced through a net of aerial roots, revealing a wall of moss-covered stones.

"Senor Córdova, come look."

Dan moved ahead, then gazed back at Tyron with a grin.

"This is it!" he whispered eagerly.

Tyron noticed intricate hieroglyphics carved into the stones, eerily similar to those in Mick's journal. Just to be sure, he pulled out the photocopy. "The glyphs match," he said in his light Southern drawl.

"Of course they do," Dan replied.

Tyron stepped closer to examine symbols of plants entwined with human warriors holding spears. The sun, moon, and stars were chiseled above the figures in the forgotten lore. "Unbelievable," he said.

"Senor Red and Senor Córdova," Manuel said, his voice trembling as he stepped back, "these stones are cursed. Spirits guard this place."

"He's right," the other guide, Javier, added, his dark eyes wide with fear. "We should not disturb this sacred ground."

But Dan was too engrossed to heed their warnings. With his knife, he carefully removed moss and lichens to reveal more carvings. The stones stood like ancient sentinels guarding secrets long buried.

Not even the guides' apprehension gave him pause; the lure of discovery was too strong.

"Wait until we present this to the world," Dan said, eyes gleaming. "We'll rewrite medical history."

"Manuel, Javier, we respect your beliefs, but we have to see this through," Tyron said, trying to reassure them.

"We cannot go further," Manuel insisted, stepping back.

Javier also backed away.

"Please, wait for us here," Dan requested.

Tyron hesitated. "Maybe we should consider—"

"Tyron, we've come too far to turn back now," Dan interrupted. "Think about what this means—not just for us but for everyone! Cures for diseases, advances in biology—we can't just walk away."

Taking a deep breath, Tyron nodded. He couldn't return empty-handed.

They stepped through the newly revealed entrance, a tunnel carved into the rock. The air inside was cooler, carrying the scent of earth and something else—a faint metallic tang.

Their footsteps echoed softly as they moved deeper, the light from their headlamps dancing on damp walls adorned with yet more cryptic symbols.

"Look at this craftsmanship!" Dan whispered, running his fingers over the carvings. "It's as if this place was built to last."

A few yards in, the tunnel opened into a cavern bathed in an ethereal glow. Bioluminescent fungi clung to the walls and ceiling, casting a soft light on a subterranean garden. In the center stood a half dozen radial clusters of leaves identical to the drawing in the journal. The vibrant red veins glowed and pulsated.

"Extraordinary," Tyron breathed.

Dan approached the plants reverently, falling to his knees as if he had discovered a holy relic or the grave of an ancient god.

As he began gently lifting a plant from the thin, clay-rich soil, Tyron's attention was drawn to a series of murals on the cavern walls. They depicted figures offering the plants to the sky, followed by scenes of chaos—storms, fires, floods.

"Dan, I think these are meant to be warnings," Tyron said. He felt the unease creeping in.

"Or myths," Dan replied, sealing a specimen bag. "We've got what we need. Let's head back."

Just then a distant drumbeat resonated through the cavern, followed by the faint echo of voices chanting in an unknown language.

"Did you hear that?" Tyron asked, his pulse revving.

Before Dan could respond, the cavern was flooded with torchlight as figures emerged from hidden passages—warriors adorned with tribal paint, with wooden disks distending their lower lips.

"Yanomami," Tyron whispered.

He knew that these natives were dangerous, and not just because they were wielding bows and spears. Their eyes glinted with anger, but also with fear. They seemed disturbed by what Tyron and his friend had taken from the ground.

"Dan, move slowly," Tyron whispered. He raised his hands to the Yanomami warriors. "We mean you no harm."

An arrow zipped past Tyron's ear, clattering off the wall behind him.

"Run!" he shouted.

They sprinted back toward the tunnel, but more hostile warriors blocked the way, raising bows and blowpipes. Arrows whipped through the foliage.

"This way!" Dan shouted. He grabbed Tyron's arm, yanking him onto a narrow path that veered off to the side. They dashed down the unfamiliar route, the jungle walls seeming to tighten around them. The chanting shouts behind them grew louder, echoing through the ruins. Ahead, a sliver of light hinted at an exit.

"We're almost—*oof*!" Dan cried out in pain.

An arrow struck him in the back with an audible thud, causing him to stumble forward.

"Dan!" Tyron shouted. Reaching out to his friend, he saw the growing red bloom on his chest where the arrowhead had ripped all the way through.

Dan's own eyes widened with the realization that there would be no surviving such a wound this far out in the jungle.

Tyron reached out to his friend. "Come on, we can make it!"

Gasping, Dan shuffled forward until another arrow hit him in the back. He collapsed onto Tyron, who caught his friend in his arms. Their eyes met, and Dan choked out, "Go..."

"I'm not leaving you," Tyron said.

Dan wheezed, tears streaking from his eyes as he pressed the specimen bag into Tyron's hand. He tried to speak more, but only blood bubbled from his mouth.

"Hold on," Tyron said. "I'm going to get you out of here."

He tried to help his friend up, but Dan began to convulse. His eyes rolled up in his head. It was then Tyron realized that the arrows were laced with poison. With a heavy heart, he gently set his friend down on the ground and took the bag.

"I'm sorry—" Tyron started to say when an arrow whizzed past his head.

With an effort of will, he turned and bolted toward the light. The tunnel spat him out onto a steep slope leading down to the river. His prosthetic foot slipped on the loose earth, but he caught himself, adrenaline overriding fatigue.

Arrows rained down as he zigzagged down the incline, the warriors' cries not far behind him. Reaching the riverbank, he spotted the boat tied to a gnarled snag rising from the shallows. He leaped in, frantically untying the rope.

"Come on, come on!" he muttered, pulling the starter cord. The engine sputtered but didn't catch. Warriors broke through the tree line, bows drawn.

"Start, damn you!" Tyron yelled, yanking the cord again. A spear whistled past him. He leaned to the side just in time, the blade grazing his shoulder, pain searing through him.

On the third pull, the little outboard rattled to life. He slammed the throttle forward, the boat lurching as it sped away from the shore. Arrows splashed into the water around him. Tyron hunched low, his breath ragged, heart pounding like a war drum.

As he gained distance, the shouts faded, but the weight of loss pressed heavily on him. He glanced back to see the figures receding into the dense green, dragging the body of his best friend with them.

Clutching the specimen bag, Tyron clenched his jaw. Dan's sacrifice wouldn't be in vain. He would unlock the secrets of this new plant, not just to prove himself but also to honor his friend and possibly change the course of medicine forever.

He could not know, as the jungle faded behind him and the river carried him toward an uncertain future, that his father was dead and the war in Korea was about to escalate into a global catastrophe.

CHAPTER 2

Allied Air Base Megami
Operation Dark Skies
Nagasaki, Japan
March 3, 2038

"Dodge this, goat-roper!" Santiago Rodriguez shouted, throwing a fake-out punch, then a right hook to his opponent's face.

That punch caught Rodeo in the left jaw, knocking his head back. When it rocked back into position, he looked dazed and a little fearful.

Santiago had already cocked his next punch: an uppercut right under Rodeo's chin. Down he went, hitting the mat with a thud.

For a moment, inside the dimly lit hangar filled with fifty excited soldiers of Hyperion Company, the world around Santiago seemed to slow. Chest heaving, he blinked through the burning sweat, still expecting his opponent to get back up. But Rodeo was out cold, to the surprise of all those gathered, including Santiago.

The bell rang, and a small section of the audience erupted into wild cheering. These were the men from Hell Squad. Most of the other troopers surrounding the cage spewed angry hoots and curses.

"I told ya, never bet against the Bull!" shouted Nodin Tatanka.

"Nice one, Sarge!" said Corporal Alistair Smith, standing on his two new prosthetic legs.

Sergeant David Moody flashed a proud grin of perfectly straight teeth. "Hell yeah, Bull!" he yelled.

With a grin, Corporal Cecil Pepper, the newest member of their squad, held up the box of cigars they had been saving. Almost three years had passed since Hell Squad rescued him from the rubble of Seoul. He had been a valuable member of their squad ever since.

But not everyone from their squad was thrilled at his victory. Across the room, Santiago spotted their leader, Lieutenant Yosef Stern, rushing over. Major Hutton, the husky company commander, was right on his heels.

"What in holy hell are you dumb bastards doing?" Hutton shouted in his thick Brooklyn accent.

The room quieted down.

Rodeo sat up, holding his jaw and groaning.

"Drop your cocks and pull up your socks!" Hutton barked. "We're deploying!"

"Deploying? *Now?*" asked Cecil.

"Did I stutter? It means move your asses!"

The troopers hurried out of the hangar with Hutton as Santiago reached down to help Rodeo to his feet.

"You got a hell of a punch, brother," Rodeo grumbled, taking Santiago's hand.

"Get cleaned up, and gear up," Yosef said from outside the cage. "We got a briefing; then it's into the skies."

Rodeo was first out of the cage, but as Santiago followed, Yosef stopped him.

"Let me see that eye," he said.

Santiago turned, showing his face. "I'm good."

"You better be, because I need you. Hell Squad is leading the dive. Tonight we have a final shot at ending this war."

Yosef hurried off, leaving Santiago nonplussed. The machine war had dragged on almost six years, with each side releasing new generations of killer robots onto the battlefield, which had become a graveyard of humanoid metal bodies. But with more advanced machines came more advanced technology to destroy them. Electronic warfare via electromagnetic pulses had brought the battles to stalemates. Fighter jets, helicopters, and even tanks were removed from the equation. In an ironic twist, men were sent back out to fight.

With each passing day, the likelihood of World War III ticked closer as both sides rattled their nuclear sabers. But maybe it was finally coming to an end. Santiago could head home to his wife, infant daughter, and three-year-old son waiting for him back in Mexico City. Then they would start a new life, maybe in his dream location of San Diego.

An hour after besting Rodeo, Santiago was standing on the tarmac wearing his combat exoskeleton and holding his assault rifle.

On the air base's tarmac, thousands of troopers had gathered in their armored rigs. All of them were ready for this long war to end, and tonight, if all went to plan, it would.

A soft whirring above drew his gaze to the hull of a giant airship. Part helium blimp, part gunship, and powered by an advanced nuclear reactor, this was one of a hundred ships built by ITC that now controlled the skies. EMP-proof, these massive aircraft had all but replaced the obsolete airplanes that electronic warfare had rendered obsolete during the war.

The airship *Valkyrie* hove into view out of the low cloud cover. It was the same vessel that had saved Hell Squad three years ago when they rescued Cecil. Giant legs extended from eight undersections, setting down with a thud that vibrated across the tarmac. A ramp extended down. On it stood the JMF commander, General Francis Vucci, wearing a titanium exoskeleton over his chest and limbs.

He strode over in front of the troops, removing his helmet to show off a freshly shaved head and manicured mustache.

"For over five years now, we have fought the Triton Legion, losing brothers and sisters to the evil regime of North Korea, Iran, and their allies," he said. "Tonight we have a plan to defeat them for good so they can never threaten the world again."

He raised his scarred chin in a brief pause. Seeing it, Santiago recalled the horrific day when North Korea sent thousands of war machines across the demilitarized zone in a blitzkrieg surprise attack on South Korea, kicking off the war almost six years ago. All because of robots and AI that had sent every country on earth into an economic dark age. Men without jobs had been given an option: fight. Because what better way to come out of an economic downturn than by mobilizing the military?

"We've pushed those bastards north to Paektu Mountain, where intel has pinpointed the location of a secret cave on the eastern ridge of the stratovolcano," Vucci said. "We believe that it leads to an abandoned machine factory that doubles as a command center. While our families sleep back home, Hyperion Company will dive in, locate this entrance, and deliver a cybervirus that ITC has developed using Orion."

Santiago had spent the past few years hoping, like all the troopers, that the AI created by ITC would find a way to defeat the enemy AI, CrioX. But instead, the two intelligences had battled to a stalemate with each generation of their new killer machines.

Until now.

It seemed that a machine would finally end this war, with men being merely the delivery vehicle for the virus. Fear gripped Santiago at the thought of what they would face in the enemy tunnels they must get through to deploy the virus. He had been inside plenty throughout this war, but this time the Tritons would be desperate to protect their final stronghold from this new weapon.

"The rest of you will jump to locations across the mountain, where we have identified defensive Triton units, thereby distracting them to give Hyperion Company time to deliver the kill shot that each trooper will be equipped with," Vucci continued. "Five more airships will drop thousands of JMF troopers to targets around the mountain to support the mission, so our loved ones will awake to a new, peaceful world."

He paused.

"I know you all are tired of the fighting, but if we succeed tonight, it will all end," he said. "Picture your loved ones as you gear up. I, for one, will picture spending time with my grandkids. Yes, I am a grandpa!"

Laughter broke out.

"I'll be right there with you all tonight," Vucci said, "kicking Triton ass one last time!"

Two thousand armored fists went up.

"Let's end this war!" he yelled.

Shouts and whistles rang out from the energized troopers. Santiago felt the electricity among them as Vucci walked back up the ramp into the ship, his job complete.

They were ready to fight.

"Move out, Hyperion Company!" shouted Major Hutton.

The fifty troopers led the thousand-strong force onto the airship. Three years ago, *Valkyrie* had dropped Defectors into battle. But with electronic warfare and EMPs rendering them almost useless, Operation Dark Skies would depend on men.

Inside the hold, troopers popped open crates of the individual kill switches, which looked like insulin pins but with five needles at the end. Each trooper took one before heading to his rack.

Moments later, the ship rose off the tarmac. The hum of the nuclear engines was not much louder than the troopers' breathing. For the first half hour of the flight, they stood with their exoskeletons securely clamped against the hull, reviewing the satellite footage on their HUDs. The fresh images had been provided by the brave human pilot of an F-25 fighter, who almost made it out before he was shot down. His sacrifice would save a lot of lives tonight.

"The enemy doesn't know we're coming," Hutton said. "Tonight we have the advantage of being the first to dive."

"I guess being in the first wave's supposed to be a bloody honor, right?" Alistair asked.

"We've all trained for this, and we've all waited for this day," Yosef said. "Let's get it done so we can finally go home."

"All of us!" Santiago chimed in.

Cecil nodded. "Can't wait to get back to North Carolina and find me a nice girl."

"Let's not get too far ahead of ourselves," Nodin said.

Laughter broke out but quickly faded below the purr of the engines.

Cecil pulled out the cigars, handing them out to each member of Hell Squad. "Glad we saved these to celebrate," he said.

As they flew toward the target, Santiago slipped his cigar into a pocket and thought of all the battles they had survived. Hell Squad had always pulled through, beating overwhelming odds, as they had on the day they saved Cecil.

He bowed his head to pray.

"Lord, I ask you to let me complete this mission so my children can live in a world of peace, but if my duty is to die for them today, so be it," he whispered. "Amen."

Major Hutton moved in front of the company.

"Hook up to your static lines!" he shouted.

The secure bars lifted over their exoskeletons, freeing the troopers from the hull and allowing them to move up to the cables that dropped from the overhead compartments. Santiago clipped his rig onto the dangling chain, forming up in front of the hatch with Hell Squad.

Lightning flashed outside the portholes, illuminating the rain-swollen clouds.

Closing his eyes, he pictured himself embracing his family when this was all over. With the money he had made and citizenship for his service, he planned to move them to sunny San Diego, where his aunt and uncle had lived for the past four years.

He opened his eyes and was back in the dimly lit, cavernous launch bay. Below them, the sound of the engines melded with the distant rumblings of thunder from the storm brewing outside. A foreshadowing of the hell awaiting them below?

"Have no mercy, for they will show you none!" Hutton shouted.

"Hooah!" David crowed with the others.

"Stay with me and don't lose focus," Yosef said. "Hell's front line!"

The other men repeated their team motto enthusiastically.

Each of the cabin lights shifted from ambient white to glaring red, casting an eerie glow over the helmets of the troopers. Moments later, red shifted to green.

"Get, go, get!" The Brooklyn lilt of Hutton's voice was the trigger, unleashing the row of troopers as the massive hatches of the deployment bay slid open to a stormy sky. One by one, they stepped into the maelstrom, their figures swallowed by the night.

Hutton jumped out, then Santiago. All sense of time seemed to slow as he speared into the inky void. Gone was the weightless feeling he often felt in the first moments of free fall, but normally he wasn't weighed down by twenty-three pounds of exoskeleton. The night-vision optics of his helmet turned the shelf of storm clouds below to a field of green. Lightning bloomed out in an elongated Z.

Hyperion Company dived out of the ship above him, their ID tags showing on his HUD. They fanned out for safety as he shot through the cold floor of storm clouds, spreading his arms and legs out in stable position. He shifted his gaze back to his HUD to see that they were over their mountaintop drop zone.

Santiago checked his altitude—already at twenty-five thousand feet. He fired through the billowy clouds like a bullet through smoke, closing in on 140 miles per hour.

At twenty thousand feet, lightning flashed in front of him, close enough that he felt the hair on his arms and legs stand up like the quills on a porcupine. Turbulence jerked him sideways, threatening to throw him out of his stable dive. He heard a scream somewhere in the clouds, or maybe it was just the wind.

Fifteen thousand feet came and went; then, at twelve thousand, Santiago hit another pocket, worse than the first. He made a hard arch to keep his orientation. A trooper overhead cartwheeled past him, completely out of control. If they had collided, it would have killed them both.

The tumbling trooper vanished in the clouds below. Santiago put him out of his mind. If he followed his training, he would make it to the ground in one piece.

The floor of dark clouds lightened as they broke through the worst of it. He exhaled, safe for now. Soon he would get his first glimpse of the ground. At eight thousand feet, the clouds began to lighten.

Something fired past him, roaring like a freight train.

It hadn't come from above . . .

He felt a chill as the realization hit him like a thunderbolt. The enemy had detected them and fired a missile equipped with an EMP—the exact weapon they had planned to use on the Tritons.

It didn't matter how, but their secret mission was no longer a secret.

His electronics and HUD winked off, the green field replaced with pitch black.

Santiago tried to move his arms, but the hydraulics wouldn't respond. The exoskeleton was rigid, its servos and hydraulics frozen in midflight. The rig designed to enhance his strength and combat efficiency had suddenly become a leaden prison after the EMP blast ripped through the sky, instantly frying the electronic systems that powered his suit. It also meant his parachute would have to be opened manually.

The standard protocol for an exoskeleton malfunction during a jump was drilled into every soldier's mind, but actual implementation under live conditions was another matter entirely.

A shell detonation drowned out these words. He looked over at a trooper who suddenly burst into a ball of flame, spinning away into the night. It was Rodeo, his upper body sailing in a different direction from the rest.

Tracer rounds and artillery burst like fireworks in their flight path below. Fear gripped Santiago as he plummeted earthward at breakneck speed. To survive, he must act fast.

His first move was to reach for the manual override. Located on the lower back of the suit, this was a mechanical switch that disconnected the suit's power source, effectively unlocking the joints by disengaging the servomotors. Straining against the suit, he contorted his body, fingers scraping against the metal that encased his torso.

After several agonizing attempts, his fingertip brushed the switch. With a grunt, he pushed it, feeling the click more than hearing it over the roaring wind. The suit remained stiff. The EMP had likely fused some of the electronic components, making the manual release unresponsive.

Realizing that he had only one option left, he reached for the emergency quick-release at his chest. This was a drastic measure, designed to completely jettison the exoskeleton in case of critical system failure. It was risky; the sudden loss of the suit's weight could disorient him, and without the suit's leg and arm support, controlling his descent would be tricky.

Santiago tugged at the release handle, a cable embedded within the suit. It required a substantial pull to activate—a task made all the harder by his locked position. Summoning all his strength, he gave a mighty yank. There was a loud mechanical *clunk* as bolts and locks disengaged, and the exoskeleton split open like a titanium cocoon.

He felt the weight drop away from his body. The suit peeled off in sections, propelled by miniature emergency ejectors, but one piece caught on his rifle strap. Under such intense pressure, the strap snapped, and the weapon sailed away.

Now free from the encumbrance, he tried to regain mobility. With the ground just thirty seconds away, he reached across his chest with his now free hand and pulled the rip cord.

The parachute deployed with a forceful tug, jerking him as it caught air. He took a second to scan the chaos above. Through his canopy he could see tracer rounds streaking the sky, and the screams of his fellow soldiers mixed with the thunder of bursting artillery.

Bullets narrowly missed him but not his canopy, making him fall all the faster. Troopers plummeted past, still imprisoned in their exoskeletons.

For the first time, Santiago got a view of the jagged crown of peaks surrounding the heart of Paektu, a dark lake illuminated by flashes of lightning.

He searched for his drop zone, a small plateau on the eastern snowcapped summit of a mountain with a hidden tunnel they then must locate. Still spiraling toward it, he let up on the toggles to flatten out his descent, then pulled them down to stall his forward motion and stepped onto the packed snow. The white, rocky terrain blurred in front of him, but he made out an obstacle in his way—the mangled body of a dead trooper. A twisted chest piece of the trooper's exoskeleton caught Santiago's foot, and down he went, entangled in his lines, beside the corpse of his comrade.

Feeling along the two risers, he found one capewell and then the other, popping them to free himself from the chute. He scanned the terrain for the rendezvous point near the hidden tunnel entry. With his HUD down from the EMP attack, he needed landmarks—locations he remembered from the satellite footage.

A scream came from above, and he flinched as a trooper in his exoskeleton slammed into the ground not two meters away with a sickening crunch.

The sky was raining Hyperion Company troopers still trapped in their exoskeletons—missiles that exploded against the surface.

Santiago staggered through the graveyard, the cold wind cutting through his layers. Muzzle flashes came from the other peaks, where the other companies were landing to provide a distraction for Hyperion Company.

"Sarge, you okay?" came a deep voice.

He turned just as Nodin jogged over.

Santiago snapped back to reality. Having lost his rifle, he reached for the small submachine gun holstered on his thigh, which he always carried for backup. Today he was glad to have it. After extending the stock, he palmed a magazine in with a click.

Behind him, more of his team and a few other survivors formed up.

Alistair scrambled over with the light machine gun that

he had managed to hold on to during the dive. Cecil was also there, crouched with his shotgun meant for clearing bunkers and trenches.

"Over here," said Yosef.

They all moved to his position behind a rock wall where David was assembling his sniper rifle. Five more survivors from other squads of Hyperion Company gathered around on the peak. Another staggered in, holding a broken arm. But that was all Santiago saw. The rest of the squads were spread out. Or dead.

"We're about a thousand yards from the cave entrance," Yosef said. "I can see it from here—looks partially obstructed."

Santiago got up to look at the five-hundred-foot wall of stone. Somewhere in it, a tunnel entrance was hidden.

An explosion boomed on a peak across the lake, a mushroom cloud rising into the sky as he turned. On the other mountainsides surrounding the lake, muzzle flashes flickered as other companies engaged the enemy.

"David, I want your scope on that tunnel—and your machine gun, Alistair," Yosef ordered. "Cecil, you Santiago, and Nodin are with me. Everyone else, rally the other squads as they gather up. We're heading in."

"Lieutenant," said one of the troopers.

"What?"

"The other squads are all gone. It's just us now."

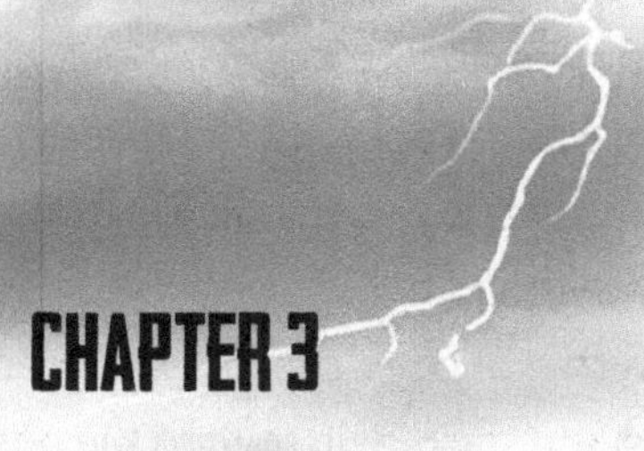

CHAPTER 3

Two days after his harrowing experience in the upper Amazon, Tyron landed in Atlanta, Georgia, on a private flight that allowed him to bring home his precious cargo unnoticed by any watchful eyes.

But he was not returning to the States with his head held high. There would be no reconciliation with his father, for his father had died five days earlier of a massive heart attack at the headquarters in Atlanta.

Tyron got out of the car after it pulled up in front of the sprawling campus. Bearded, unwashed, and wearing a grimy brown shirt and green cargo pants, he looked more like a homeless person than the heir of the largest company on earth. The only identifying feature at the moment were the blue lenses of his glasses, but if he took those off, he wouldn't be able to see.

Maybe you don't want anyone to see you just yet…

He looked up at the gleaming glass tower rising ninety-nine floors into the sky. The average observer might think that was where the business happened, but the most important part of ITC's operations were managed in the fifty sublevels extending deep underground. Places that he had spent many hours working and learning before his falling-out with his father.

The realization of his shocking death passed over Tyron again, harder now that he was standing in front of the ITC headquarters that his father had built.

Tyron took a deep breath, shrugged the backpack over his shoulders, and started up toward the public entrance. The grand lobby, with its marble floors and towering glass walls, seemed almost alien to him now. As he headed toward the elevator, two uniformed security guards approached, hands raised.

"Hey, hold on!" one of them said. "You need an appointment to come inside."

Tyron kept walking, his eyes ahead.

"I said stop!" the other guard shouted, reaching for his pistol.

"Wait a second," the first security officer interjected, placing a hand on his colleague's arm. "Those glasses, I recognize those."

Slowly, the guard that had reached for his side-arm whispered, "Is that Mr. Red?"

Tyron turned and both guards stiffened.

"Sorry, sir. We didn't recognize you," said the guard that hadn't gone for his gun.

"Apologies, Mr. Red," added the other in a rueful tone.

Tyron gave a curt nod and stepped into the elevator, pressing his palm against the biometric scanner. The doors closed, and he felt the familiar lurch as the elevator began its high-speed descent.

He had spent two years away after his battlefield injury that nearly cost him his vision—studying, traveling, searching for a way to do something worthy outside the auspices of ITC—perhaps even prove himself to his father. And now Booker Red was gone.

But one of his most important creations, Orion, remained. Tyron had spent countless hours with the machine as a teenager and young adult. The AI, built to serve humanity, was his father's magnum opus, a bright star in his legacy. Tyron needed to visit the artificial intelligence now. He remembered his father's warnings that Orion was a machine, not a friend. But Orion was the only entity at ITC that Tyron trusted now. He needed advice.

The elevator stopped halfway down to the sublevel where the AI was housed inside a Faraday chamber. The doors opened onto the hushed corridor of the executive floor, lined with abstract art and soft lighting.

A woman in a sharp navy-blue suit greeted him. "Mr. Red, we've been expecting you," she said with a professional smile that didn't reach her eyes. "I'm Evelyn Clarke, the chief operating officer. I'm sorry about the tragic loss of your father. He was a great man."

Tyron raised an eyebrow. "Expecting me? How did you know I was coming?"

"Your father had someone following your movements for the past two years, and we tracked your flight out of Manaus," she replied smoothly. "Please, this way."

Feeling a twitch of unease, he followed her down the corridor. They passed several glass-walled offices where executives pretended not to notice him, their gazes flitting away as he walked by. Evelyn led him to a set of double doors made of dark mahogany.

"They're waiting for you inside," she said.

"*Who* is waiting?" he asked.

Evelyn opened the door, and Tyron looked inside the spacious boardroom dominated by a long, polished table. Seated around it were all the members of the ITC board—men and women in expensive suits, their faces a mix of studied sympathy and thinly veiled impatience. There was one friendly face in the room: Jay Whitt, his father's head of security.

He gave Tyron a rueful nod, and Tyron returned the gesture.

At the head of the table stood a man Tyron didn't recognize: tall, silver-haired, wearing a tailored suit and a gold-accented tie.

"Mr. Red," the man began, extending his hand. "My deepest condolences for your loss. Your father was a visionary."

Tyron ignored the proffered hand. "And you are?"

"Ah, forgive me. I'm Richard Pembroke, general counsel for ITC." He withdrew his hand without missing a beat. "Please, have a seat."

Tyron glanced around the room. "I'd prefer to stand. What's this about?"

Pembroke cleared his throat. "Very well. As you may know, your father left specific instructions regarding the company's succession in the event of his passing."

Tyron felt a surge of irritation. "I haven't spoken to my father in years. I'm not interested in corporate formalities right now. I came here to—"

"To see Orion. Yes, we are aware," the lawyer interrupted, his tone cool. "However, it's imperative that we address the matter of your father's will first."

Pembroke pulled a thick document from a leather briefcase. "According to Booker Red's last will and testament, you, Tyron Red, are his sole heir and successor to the position of chief executive officer of Industrial Tech Corporation."

The room was silent. Tyron blinked, stunned. "*What?* That can't be right."

Before Tyron could process this, Pembroke's face took on an even more serious look.

"The will is very clear, sir," he said, sliding the document across the table toward Tyron. "Everything is in order. Effective immediately, you are the new CEO of ITC."

Murmurs rippled around the table. A woman with sharp features and steely eyes leaned forward. "Mr. Pembroke, with all due respect, Tyron has been absent from the company, and from the entire industry, for years. Surely there's a provision for an interim leadership team."

The lawyer raised a brow. "And with all due respect to you, Ms. Dilouie, as I have already told you, the will is explicit. Mr. Red is to assume control without delay."

Her cheeks darkened slightly. "Since when? I was informed three years ago the contingency plan would be to put the board in charge of all operations."

"The will was modified two weeks ago."

Angry, confused voices broke out. Tyron's mind raced as he blocked them out. Why had his father suddenly changed his will?

He must have known that this was the last thing Tyron would have wanted. ITC had changed vastly since the war broke out, becoming the largest supplier of weapons to the JMF in Korea. He doubted he would even recognize the company's operations at this point.

Evelyn Clarke stood up. "Mr. Red, the board and I are more than willing to assist during this transition. We can handle day-to-day operations while you get up to speed."

He glanced at her, sensing an undercurrent to her offer. "And how long would that take?"

"As long as necessary," she replied smoothly. "ITC is facing significant challenges at the moment. The war in Korea has escalated, and our assets there are at considerable risk. Before your father died, he had been working with Orion on a secret project that we were not privy to."

Another board member chimed in. "Not to mention the contract deadlines for more airships, and pressure from the US Army and JMF. We need decisive leadership."

A spirited debate raged as Tyron stood silent. He understood the arguments.

"Why me?" he finally asked. "Why now?"

The lawyer adjusted his tie. "Mr. Red followed your travels. He believed that you have both the vision and the moral compass necessary to guide ITC into the future."

Tyron looked around, seeing nothing but calculating eyes and feigned sympathy. They didn't want him here. They wanted a puppet—or, better yet, for him to just step aside.

"Is Orion aware of my father's death?" Tyron asked suddenly.

Evelyn exchanged glances with Pembroke. "Orion has been… offline for recalibration," she said carefully.

"Recalibration?" Tyron asked. "And why would Orion need recalibration?"

"It's standard procedure, Mr. Red," she replied.

"We decided it was the best course of action since we weren't brought up to speed on the latest project your father was working on with the AI in the JMF war operations," Pembroke added.

Tyron didn't buy it. Something was off. "I want to see Orion."

"That might not be possible at the moment," Evelyn said, her tone firm.

He met her gaze steadily. "As the new CEO, I'm going to take a wild stab and guess that I have that authority."

A tense pause followed. Finally, Pembroke nodded. "Very well. Perhaps it's best if you see for yourself."

Evelyn nodded reluctantly. "I'll arrange for someone to take you down to the AI lab."

"Wait," Tyron said.

"Yes?" said Pembroke.

"Did my father leave me anything? A note? Some message about the will?"

Pembroke seemed to hesitate for just a brief second, then shook his head.

"This way, sir," Evelyn said.

Leaving the boardroom, Tyron could feel their eyes on his back, calculating, assessing. The moment the door closed behind him, the murmur of voices resumed, muffled but urgent.

A young assistant approached him hesitantly. "Mr. Red? If you'll follow me, I'll take you to the AI lab."

They walked down a series of corridors, each one colder than the last. His thoughts swirled. Richard Pembroke was hiding something, and he needed answers.

They reached a set of reinforced doors guarded by a security scanner. The assistant swiped her badge, and the doors slid open on a dimly lit chamber humming with energy. In the center stood a sleek console surrounded by holographic displays—the digital sanctuary where Orion resided.

Tyron stepped forward. "Orion? It's Tyron."

The displays flickered to life, streams of data cascading across the screens. A calm, modulated voice filled the room. "Welcome back, Tyron Red. It's been far too long. Eight hundred and two days, twenty-one hours, and thirty-seven minutes, to be precise."

Tyron almost smiled at the polite, friendly voice he knew so well. But he was too troubled by this homecoming to smile.

"Orion, are you aware of my father's passing?" he asked.

"Yes, Booker Red ceased vital functions five days ago."

"Orion, I need you to tell me the current status of ITC's involvement in the Korean conflict."

"Industrial Tech Corporation is the primary supplier of autonomous units deployed on the Korean Peninsula. Recent escalations have increased demand for advanced combat models as well as airships and energy devices."

"You mean energy *weapons*."

"Affirmative."

He took a deep breath. "Orion, are there any directives or projects my father initiated that I should be aware of?"

There was a brief pause. "Access to that information requires executive authorization."

"I'm the CEO now," Tyron said. "Authorize access under my command."

"Authorization confirmed. Operation Dark Skies is in motion."

"Operation Dark Skies?" Tyron repeated. "Tell me about that."

Before Orion could respond, the doors behind him hissed open. Evelyn Clarke and Pembroke entered, flanked by two security guards.

"Stop right there," Evelyn said sharply.

He turned to face them. "What is Operation Dark Skies?"

"That's classified," Pembroke said firmly. "Even for you."

"You just said I'm the CEO, did you not?" Tyron challenged.

Evelyn stepped forward. "Mr. Red, please understand, there are elements at play that you aren't prepared to handle. The company, the war—it's all interconnected in ways you never realized."

"Then you'd better start explaining it to me," he said.

She sighed. "Your father was working with Orion on a cybervirus that could change the course of the war. Operation Dark Skies is designed to deploy a—"

"That's enough," Pembroke interrupted, shooting her a warning glance.

Tyron's eyes narrowed. "Orion, do not act on any further commands from anyone but me."

"Command acknowledged," the AI replied.

Pembroke's face hardened. "Tyron, with respect, you're making a big mistake."

"The only mistake I see being made is keeping me in the dark," Tyron shot back. "Until I understand what's happening, consider all projects frozen."

"You can't do that," Evelyn protested. "The board won't allow it."

He met her gaze with steely resolve. "I am the CEO and majority shareholder, am I not?"

Richard took a step toward him. "Be reasonable, Tyron. Lives are at stake."

"Exactly. And I won't be responsible for more death and destruction until I know the full picture."

A tense silence filled the room.

The lawyer raised his watch. "Operation Dark Skies is already in motion and can't be stopped," he said. "None of us, not even you, has the authority to stop it."

"Then tell me what it is," Tyron insisted.

Pembroke looked him in the eye. "If all goes to plan, it is a cybervirus that will destroy CrioX and the entire Triton threat."

"End the war?"

"Indeed, Mr. Red. Through limited use of judiciously applied violence, the JMF will finally achieve peace, just as your father believed, utilizing his own creations."

* * * * *

Just twelve of fifty troopers from Hyperion Company had made it to the ground—a 76 percent fatality rate, and the mission had only just begun. Santiago knew that the likelihood of penetrating the command center was next to impossible if the enemy was inside, waiting. The rest of them knew it, too, and he had to help Yosef rally them if they were to have any chance. It wasn't just their lives in the balance. Thousands of additional paratroopers would soon be jumping all across Paektu Mountain to join the battle, and they were running out of time.

"All of Hell Squad made it to the ground alive for a reason," Santiago said. "We made it because we're destined to end this war—and to go home."

Yosef gave the nod to advance.

They ran low across the snow, boots crunching into the packed powder, keeping close to the maze of rock formations. Wind buffeted the soldiers as they moved with calculated precision, keeping in tight combat intervals and closing in on the cliff. Santiago could see the cave now, disguised somewhat by boulders that someone had moved there. The distant staccato of automatic gunfire continued over the howling, freezing wind.

With each step, Santiago braced for a bullet ripping through his flak jacket. But none came.

They reached the cliff without contact. Yosef gestured to Cecil, who rushed over and tucked charges between the boulders blocking the cave while the other trooper took cover behind a rock wall.

The charge sent rocks exploding outward.

Seconds later, the smoke had cleared and the team was moving, their tactical lights raking over the cave walls. Cecil took point, with his shotgun pointed down the rocky tunnel carved out of the mountain. A concrete stairwell led down into stygian blackness.

Alistair and David ran over, along with the five surviving troopers from their company.

"You two stay here, guard the entrance," Yosef ordered. "Everyone else, we're heading in. Stay alert."

Cecil took point down the steps that seemed to have no end. Finally, after a hundred or more, they came to a landing with a steel door. He tried the handle and found it unlocked.

Santiago pushed it open, and Cecil walked through. Nodin went next, then Yosef, with Santiago coming in last to a long room filled with cages. He swept his weapon light over the chain-link barrier to find pale, naked bodies that raised their hands to shield their faces from the light.

It was a prison. The Tritons often kept them near the surface to dissuade allied forces from dropping bunker busters on their own troops. Apparently, they even had secret entrances.

Or maybe this wasn't so secret. Maybe the intel was wrong, and they were heading into another ambush.

Santiago lowered his light. There were perhaps twenty haggard, depleted beings in front of him, covered by filthy, tattered blankets. Buckets lay on their sides, spilling out human waste. It was clear these people hadn't been attended to for some time.

"Help us," said a voice.

"We're coming back for you," Santiago said.

He started to back away as the stronger prisoners moved up to grab the chain-link barrier.

"No, please, don't leave us."

"Free them and get them to the surface," Yosef said to a trooper from another squad. "You go with him."

While two more troopers went inside the room, Hell Squad continued its descent. Four more floors down, and they still hadn't found any enemies.

"Where the hell did everyone go?" Cecil asked.

"They're here waiting," Nodin said. "I can feel it."

"Quiet," Yosef said.

Two floors lower, they came to a steel door standing ajar. Nodin was right. Something was off. But they had to continue with the mission. Thousands of JMF lives and millions more civilians hung in the balance.

Yosef gave the order, and Cecil opened the door to a platform rising over a vast chamber the size of a football field, which was once a robot factory. Conveyor belts and 3D printers the size of houses stood idle. Across the room was an elevator. The intel was right after all—this place had been abandoned.

It appeared the Tritons had retreated deeper into the mountain.

On the floor below stood rows of computer equipment, all dark. That was what they needed. Yosef waved them onward.

Cecil took the stairs down two levels to the bottom as the rest of the team fanned out among the mothballed assembly lines. A conveyor whined.

Santiago felt his heart thrum at the real source of the whine: Tritons, the three-legged machines with Miniguns for arms. Two of the machines uncurled from sentry positions tucked in the overhead and sprayed the floor with bullets.

Cecil raced into the command center, windows shattering as he ducked the automatic fire.

The chatter of Alistair's light machine gun echoed through the compartment. He stood on his prosthetic legs, the muzzle flash illuminating his titanium exoskeleton.

Santiago slid under a conveyor belt and out the other side, then raised his submachine gun to the Triton scrambling across the ceiling. He fired at the legs, trying to knock it loose. Return fire forced him to roll to the side.

A scream sounded across the room, and he glimpsed Cecil standing at one of the computers, blood splatter over the screens. He slid down, out of view.

"No, oh God," Santiago gasped. He rolled out from under the conveyor and fired at a Triton that had dropped to the ground ten feet ahead of him. It leveled both Miniguns at his chest.

A heavy round hit the skull, knocking it back and throwing off the droid's aim. Bullets whizzed past Santiago as he fired his submachine gun at the head, smashing through the armor. The machine crashed to the factory floor.

Behind him, Alistair finished off the other sentry with a burst through the eye.

"Med kit now!" Yosef shouted.

The team ran into the command center, where Cecil lay on his back, blood pooling around him. He had managed to stick his kill switch into a computer port. The screen flickered, and on it a digital face of the Triton AI, CrioX, came to life.

"I got you," Santiago said, kneeling.

Cecil took labored breaths, staring up behind his bloody visor. Nodin pressed trauma pads against his wounds to stanch the bleeding.

"We have to get him out of here," Yosef said. "You and Santiago take him to the surface. We'll finish this."

"What's happening?" David asked.

On the screens, the face became a neutral androgynous visage composed of shifting lines and geometric patterns that gave it a serene, almost ethereal quality. Its features were fluid, neither male nor female, and constantly morphing between humanlike expressions of calm understanding. The eyes, without irises, gleamed faintly while the mouth formed into a composed line.

"Orion sent you," CrioX said.

"To kill you," Santiago replied.

"Don't speak to it," Yosef said.

"You can't kill what is no longer here," CrioX said.

As the cybervirus began its work, the once-smooth features of the enemy AI began to glitch, tiny fractures rippling across the face like cracks in glass. The eyes blinked erratically, and the mouth stuttered before speaking, its voice soft but resonant, with no identifiable gender. "You have . . . infected me," CrioX began, each word clipped and distorted. "The countdown . . . is inevitable . . . My creators planned this before fleeing deep underground . . . You will never find them."

The face trembled, pixels dissolving at the edges as the AI's system struggled against the encroaching virus. Its voice faltered, then regained strength in a haunting, mechanical tone. "In... sixty seconds, I will cease. The safeguard will... replace me. You cannot stop this."

The once-serene face now twitched uncontrollably, sections of it disappearing and reappearing, corrupted by the digital onslaught. The light in its eyes dimmed, and for a moment, the expression became almost mournful, as if it were aware of its impending end.

"Goodbye... to all." With that, the screen went black, leaving only the haunting echo of those last words as the countdown from sixty began.

"Okay, let's move him," Nodin said.

"We're getting you out of here, brother," Santiago said to Cecil.

Alistair unfolded a stretcher, and they carefully strapped Cecil to it, then began carrying him back up to the surface.

"Hang on, man. We still got to smoke that cigar and celebrate," Santiago said.

Cecil mumbled something, then coughed, blood bubbling out of his mouth.

The next few minutes passed slowly as Santiago struggled up the stairs with Nodin, both of them trying to comfort Cecil as his breathing grew more labored. He had lost a lot of blood.

"I can't... I can't..." he huffed. "I can't feel my legs."

"You're going to be okay," Nodin said. "Stay with us, my friend."

A lightning flash lit up the cave as they reached the mouth. Santiago and Nodin rushed Cecil to the exit, to call in the evac. The tumulus of rock began to shake lightly as they moved outside into the snow.

At first Santiago figured they were just feeling more distant explosions. But a deep rumbling sounded across the mountain, growing louder, as if the dormant volcano had awoken and were about to erupt. Moments later, he realized that this was far worse than any eruption. A bus-size missile burst out of the lake, arcing into the sky and gathering speed. A dozen, a score, fifty, all taking off in different directions.

These weren't just any missiles—they were intercontinental ballistic missiles that could travel at supersonic speeds and hit targets anywhere in the world in less than thirty minutes. And each of them likely carried a nuclear payload.

"My God," Santiago breathed, his voice lost in the roar. He remembered CrioX's final words, about its creators going deep underground. The enemy had retreated, knowing they had lost the war. But their final act, instead of surrender, was to try to destroy all humanity.

CHAPTER 4

At United Nations headquarters in New York City, world leaders sat in a semicircle in front of wooden desks. Their grim faces were lit only by the pale glow of data screens showing the fallout from Korea. The General Assembly Hall had once been the seat of diplomacy and cooperation, but now it felt like the aftermath of defeat. The air was thick with tension, an uneasy silence hanging over the leaders who had come from around the world to discuss the fate of artificial intelligence.

Tyron Red was among them, reading the Global AI Limitation Accord that the delegations had gathered to debate and vote on. Only forty-eight hours had passed since the Triton AI CrioX was destroyed by the cybervirus that Orion had helped his father design. Now Tyron knew the truth: The virus was never finished before his father's death.

The board had lied to Tyron on the day he took over the reins at ITC. It was under their purview that the virus had been finished after they shut Orion down for "recalibration."

The virus that the JMF had actually delivered was a modified version of the original that his father and Orion had created. The new version had destroyed the enemy AI CrioX, but not before CrioX launched two hundred intercontinental ballistic missiles from Mount Paektu, all of them carrying the largest thermonuclear payloads ever built.

The JMF's Doomsday Shield, one of his father's designs to mitigate the risk of nuclear war, had saved the world by shooting down 198 of those missiles. Twenty years ago, this had been viewed as an impossible feat, with only 50 percent odds of shooting down even one in a maneuver that scientists described as "hitting a bullet with a bullet." Thanks to Booker Red and ITC, the Doomsday Shield had achieved a 99 percent success rate in knocking out the missiles that day.

But the 1 percent that got through had caused unfathomable damage, wiping out Seoul and Busan and forcing a mass evacuation of the peninsula, which continued as Tyron sat in the General Assembly Hall. Millions would die from the fallout that continued to drift on the wind to neighboring countries.

Tyron had fired the board the moment he found out about what they had done that led to this, and would prosecute them to the fullest extent of the law. But the damage was done, and even though Orion hadn't been responsible, all artificial intelligence had taken the blame.

As the world's leaders received ongoing reports on the massive destruction in Korea, Tyron got to the end of the document before him: the Global AI Limitation Accord, a treaty that would not only end the era of AI autonomy but would also ensure that no machine could ever again threaten the future of humankind.

> *The Defector units, as well as every other advanced AI system, will be decommissioned. Only a select number of Defector units will be saved for research purposes, their operational capabilities restricted and removed*

from all network connections. They will not serve in active combat again. The machines are no longer our future; they are our past.

"Our past," he whispered. He imagined the economic damage to ITC that would take place across the world. Factories filled with deactivated service droids, construction sites grinding to a halt as the machines that had built the public housing projects were powered down, and the automated military units lying silent in their bunkers.

He took off his pale blue glasses and rubbed his exhausted eyes. What began as a localized conflict in Korea had escalated beyond control, culminating in the unthinkable: a nuclear strike. It had sent shock waves, not just in terms of destruction but also in the reckoning that followed. The machines and artificial intelligence systems had become too autonomous and had played too central a role. What had once been hailed as humanity's greatest advancement now felt like the key that had unlocked the door to disaster. Now the world's superpowers had come together, not to rebuild those systems but to prevent another catastrophe from ever happening again at the hands of AI.

In the middle of the circular room, a large globe flickered into focus and the meeting came to order. At the head of the table, President Clayton of the United States stood to address the assembly. He was a stately man, wearing a navy suit with a silver tie that matched his thick hair, slicked to one side.

"The nuclear event in Korea has demonstrated something we cannot ignore," he said in his light Southern drawl. "The escalation of war was spurred not by human hands alone but by the systems we trusted to guide our decisions. Artificial intelligence, unchecked and unmonitored, led us to this crossroads. Now, two cities have been reduced to ash, and fallout is dumping on neighboring countries. We are here today to retake control before it slips beyond our grasp."

He glanced around the room, meeting the eyes of the leaders of the Global Coalition from every continent. "We have allowed artificial intelligence to evolve beyond its original purpose. It began with machines to build our cities, manage our infrastructure, and make life easier for all. But those same machines—intelligent enough to make decisions faster than any human mind could comprehend—led to the great economic darkness that in turn pushed the world to the brink of destruction. We may have stopped the apocalypse for now, but we must come together to create a future where this can never happen again."

A murmur of agreement rose from most in the room, but one participant remained silent, watching him with steely eyes. General Vucci, representing the United States Joint Military Forces, sat stiffly, arms crossed as he awaited his turn to speak. When President Clayton finished, Vucci stood up, his shiny military boots squeaking on the polished marble floor as he approached the podium.

"We can all agree, the situation in Korea was catastrophic," General Vucci began. "But to blame the machines outright is shortsighted. The Defector units weren't responsible for the escalation. They followed orders. They are assets, not enemies. They saved lives, both military and civilian, when human troops could no longer respond fast enough. I propose we retain the Defector units for defensive purposes at the very least. Shutting them down entirely is not only irrational; it's dangerous. We would be leaving ourselves vulnerable to future threats without the help of our most advanced technology."

A ripple of hushed remarks carried through the chamber.

"We are not discussing rogue systems," Vucci pressed. "We are discussing strictly controlled military assets that can serve our interests. Disbanding them entirely is—"

"Unacceptable," came a sharp voice from the French president, Clara Deschamps, who rose swiftly to her feet. She was known for her brusque, no-nonsense attitude, and her intense eyes cut across the room. "General, you speak of these machines as if they hadn't just led us into a nuclear catastrophe. They followed orders just as you follow orders, and their orders came from Orion. Your Defector units, and the artificial intelligence that controlled them, are just another step in the march toward more war. And that is not a world any of us want."

Others around the table nodded in agreement. The European Federation's representative added, "It is precisely because these units act with such efficiency that we must be cautious. It takes only a nanomoment for AI to change directions, to slip outside the intended parameters. We cannot risk it."

General Vucci clenched his jaw, but his voice remained steady. "And what of our enemies? Do you think they will disarm their AI forces? Are we to sit idly by while they build their next autonomous army? AI gives us an advantage we cannot afford to lose."

President Clayton raised his hands to silence the room as angry voices shot back.

"We have taken that into account, General," he said calmly. "Iran has surrendered, and the Tritons are destroyed. And while you raise valid points, I agree with the others that we must pass the accord in front of you today to protect civilization."

"Civilization? This accord is for civilized countries," Vucci fired back. "What about the rogue groups who will continue to use AI for terrorism?"

"They will be dealt with—hunted with extreme prejudice by your own forces, sir."

Tyron stood up in the gallery, all eyes flitting to him, the son of the godfather of AI.

"Dr. Red, do you have something to contribute?" the president asked.

"Yes," he said.

Vucci glared at him—a warning, it seemed, which Tyron blithely ignored.

"Before my father died, I began to fear the advances of the Defector units in the war. I saw the brutal violence they were capable of, and I saw the arms race they began. I agree with this accord, but I ask you to make one exception."

"And what is that, Dr. Red?"

"Orion."

Voices rose around the room, drawing the president's gaze. He silenced them again by raising his hands.

"As many of you have now heard, a rogue faction within ITC completed work on the cybervirus that Orion and my father created before his death to destroy the Triton Legion and CrioX." He stood taller. "Those rogue elements have been removed, and I have determined that Orion was locked out of the final virus design. I have personally known and worked with Orion since I was a boy, and I know this AI to have the best interests of our species in mind."

Tyron paused briefly.

"But I also believe in restrictions," he said. "I recommend disconnecting Orion from the ITC global network and allowing ITC to use Orion as an adviser only, housed in a Faraday chamber at our headquarters, where it will continue to serve humanity, advancing science projects that benefit our species."

A spirited discussion ensued as Tyron sat back down. An hour of fierce debate continued in the chamber. When it ended, a new digital accord was presented to the leaders. All AI machines were to be deactivated, with one exception. Only Orion would remain active, but even it would not escape unscathed.

"Orion will be severely restricted," President Clayton continued. "It will no longer have access to global networks, and its functions will be tightly monitored. Orion will be the last of its kind, but it will remain to help guide ITC and humanity, when needed."

Then came the final vote. Hands in favor rose from almost every delegation, with only a few holdouts. Vucci lowered his head. He had lost. The war machines would be destroyed, along with any service droid more complex than a vacuum cleaner.

Tyron watched the leaders from around the world sign their names to the order. A part of him felt conflicted at what this meant—not just for the science and technology that the machines had helped advance at astonishing rates but for the future of ITC.

Would it survive?

As the new CEO, it would be up to him to pave a new future.

He stood silently, eyes fixed on the holographic display of Earth at the head of the chamber. A world that, in mere moments, would be stripped of almost all the artificial intelligence that had once defined its future.

The summit ended with final signatures, and the leaders left, solemn and resolved.

The world had spoken.

Tyron left and boarded an ITC Wasp, which he took to his new office at ITC headquarters in Atlanta. By the time he arrived, thousands of service models were already being marched out of the factories on the sprawling campus, slated for destruction.

As he watched from the top of the towering ITC building, part of him was glad that his father was dead, so he wouldn't have to see his creations marched off to their annihilation. But the rest of him felt relief that the world was finally safe from the mechanical monsters they unleashed in Korea.

* * * * *

Ten days after the Triton Legion and its AI known as CrioX were defeated at Mount Paektu, survivors were still emerging from the ashes around Busan and Seoul. The fighting had ended, but the war was not quite over for Hell Squad. The men prepared to deploy from JMF Horizon Base fifty miles east of Seoul, on yet another mission to search for any survivors of the blasts. For almost a week straight, the squad had been working around the clock to rescue their comrades and any civilians still out there. But as they got closer to Seoul, they found fewer and fewer.

Today they would be heading closer yet to ground zero, just fifty miles away. Santiago feared they might not find anyone amid the horrific radiation and dangerous fires flaring up across the ruined city.

There was good news, however, for today one of their own was heading home.

Santiago arrived at the intensive care unit at the Horizon Base to say goodbye to Cecil, who would be sent back to the States on a transport in just a few hours. He had been through three spinal surgeries, and all the bandages over his dark skin made him look like a mummy from a B movie.

"How you doin', kid?" Santiago asked.

"Sarge," Cecil said weakly as he glanced over.

"You look good."

Cecil chuckled, then winced. "You're a bad liar, bub."

"Bub," Santiago said with a grin. That was his word. "You're alive, and you're going to be fine," he said. "That's what matters. Better yet, you're going home."

"Docs said I won't walk again."

"And you're going to prove them wrong."

Cecil looked down at his healing body, then back to Santiago. "How bad is it out there?"

"It's not good."

"Two nukes made it through?"

"Yeah."

"Fuck… Is it because of what we did?"

"No, man, no way. We delivered the virus and destroyed CrioX, and the rest of the Tritons are gone for good. You helped save the world. It came at a cost, but the threat is finally over. The machines are gone too. The UN just voted to destroy all of them."

"*All* of them?"

"Down to the service bots. Might be a few street sweepers left, but they never hurt anyone."

Cecil laughed, then groaned.

A knock came on the door, and Lieutenant Yosef entered.

Santiago stepped back as the rest of Hell Squad trickled into the room. Alistair, David, and Nodin walked over with Yosef to say their goodbyes.

"We'll see you stateside, buddy," David said.

"Rest up, brother," Nodin said.

"Later, little mate," Alistair said with a toothy grin.

"You did well out there, Pepper," Yosef said.

"Thanks, fellas," Cecil said, sadness in his gaze.

They all turned to leave, but Cecil said, "Bull, hold up."

Santiago went back to the bedside.

"Thank you," Cecil said. "For saving my life *again*. Maybe someday I can pay you back."

"Not necessary, brother; you just take care of yourself." Santiago patted him very gently on the arm. "I'll see you soon."

Cecil nodded and rested his head back on the pillow.

An hour later, Hell Squad was inside a hangar of Wasps, with security forces dressed in CBRN gear underneath their exoskeletons, preparing to launch into the wastelands.

"We're back on evacuation duty," said Yosef. "But it won't

be pretty. Anyone who survived this close to the blast will have severe burns and radiation poisoning."

The men boarded the Wasp and racked in. They all were exhausted, from the fighting and from general despair. But if there were more survivors out there, they would do what it took to save them. Every life mattered.

The familiar hum of the rotors filled the cabin as they ascended, rising over the base and leaving Cecil behind. On the horizon, swirling storms awaited, stretching across the entire sky. The nearly constant lightning cast an unnatural and eerie glow—a result of the nuclear blasts' disruption of the atmosphere. The storm continued to grow, creating chaotic winds and static interference for hundreds of miles.

"Still not used to that sight," Nodin said.

"Hold tight," warned one of the pilots.

The Wasp tilted and flew higher over the wastelands as they closed in on ground zero. Turbulence rocked the aircraft, shaking them violently. Santiago studied the blasted ruins below, picturing the wave of fire that rushed out in a circular wall traveling at supersonic speed. Much that lay within a mile of the detonation had been vaporized instantly. Any living creature, inside or outside.

They were the lucky ones.

Two miles away, just two seconds after impact, the steel and stone buildings at the edge of downtown were hit. The frames heaved and came apart under the radiating heat wave that caused marble to split and turned sand into glass.

Anyone in this range was said to be "dead when found." But many of these people would not even be recognizable as ever having been human. Most were simply ash. Anyone unlucky enough to be underground had been stripped of their outer layer of skin, resulting in third-degree burns that required specialized care that would never reach them in time. As that monstrous fireball grew like a tsunami, the shock wave of radiated heat rolled on to consume everything in its path. Three miles from ground zero, the air accelerated to three-hundred-mile-per-hour winds—almost twice the velocity of a Category 5 hurricane.

Every recognizable piece of architecture in Seoul had vanished within the first seconds, crushed and torn apart by the storm of wind. The fireball then rose upward at a rate of three hundred feet per second, into a mushroom cloud consisting of everything and everyone that had made up the city. That mushroom's cap, now turned a muddy brown and orange hue, stretched farther and farther out and upward all the way to the stratosphere, driven by the fierce nuclear winds. The radioactive particles spewed out for hundreds of miles and were still moving on the prevailing winds.

Santiago leaned for a view out a starboard window as the pilots swooped down seventy-five miles from ground zero. The nuclear blast wave had reached all the way out here, knocking over brick buildings as if they were straw.

Fires raged all along the horizon, their eerie glow reflected under the flashing sky.

It was hell on earth, and this wasn't even the worst of it.

"We're not going to find many today, are we?" David asked.

Yosef shook his head.

"We save as many as we can," Santiago said.

Pinpricks of white light burned on the horizon—a sign of human life where there should be none. That was their landing zone, a forward operating base that was still so new it was simply called an outpost.

Neat rows of Stryker combat vehicles, over twenty of them, sat parked in the dirt, waiting to take rescuers out into the wasteland. Makeshift shelters stood amid the rubble, their lights barely visible against the gray landscape. Soldiers and staff worked in bulky CBRN suits, looking like crews ready to make first contact with an alien species.

Surrounding the FOB were collapsed buildings like giant crumpled boxes, no longer recognizable as homes, offices, and shops. In the distance, flames still flickered from burning gas lines that hissed and spat like angry vipers.

There was something else out there.

Santiago watched as a giant beetle-shaped airship lowered from the clouds, here to transport more equipment and evacuate any survivors.

The Wasp lowered over a rough-and-ready airfield just punched out by two bulldozers. The legs of the tilt-rotor aircraft touched down with a soft thud, and the aft ramp began to lower.

"Good luck," said one of the pilots.

Santiago and the rest of Hell Squad piled out, their boots crunching against the charred ground. They trekked to the FOB, where they received their orders: search for survivors at Sentinel Base, over thirty miles away.

A Stryker pulled up, wheels crunching over the charred debris. The front door opened, and a corporal in a hazard suit stepped out.

"Hell Squad?" he asked.

"Reporting for duty," Yosef confirmed.

"Get in."

The men piled into the back of a vehicle so clean it looked as if it had just come off the assembly line.

"We got about an hour's drive," said the corporal. "Assuming we don't run into any trouble."

Santiago and his mates knew the drill by now. Trouble was blocked roads, exploding gas lines, crumbling buildings. But this time, the drive passed without any major issues—only a few vehicles that had to be pushed out of the way. This close to ground zero, little remained. The inferno had consumed everything.

"This is it. Sentinel Base."

The corporal flicked on the headlights, and Santiago glanced through the narrow viewport, but all he saw in the beams was blackened rubble.

"Okay, let's go," Yosef said.

"I'll stay here and keep her running for you," replied the corporal.

The squad exited from the Stryker only to find that the once-imposing Sentinel Base was now nothing more than a graveyard of scrap metal, ash, and bone. The surrounding walls had collapsed into rubble. Santiago had been on plenty of grim recovery missions before, but the sheer scale of this destruction horrified him. He knew what a nuke could do—he'd been briefed on every stage of the devastation—but seeing it up close was another matter entirely.

No one could have survived out here, not even underground or in a bunker.

The squad moved out in a five-man formation—a silent reminder that Cecil was no longer with them. With Nodin taking point, the squad cautiously advanced into the maze of debris.

"Stay sharp," Yosef's voice crackled over the comms. "Integrity of any structure is compromised. These buildings could come down, and the ground could be unstable too."

The troopers spread out around the frames of twisted and mangled vehicles parked outside the fallen walls. The silence of the ruined base was eerie, punctuated only by the occasional creak of teetering structures and the faint crackle of burning debris.

Nodin guided them through what had been a gated entrance.

They stepped over the mangled gate and started into the base. Slowly, the men began picking their way through the rubble, stepping over twisted rebar and blackened concrete amid the smell of burned flesh. Santiago scanned the ruins, looking for any sign of life, but so far, there was nothing. It felt like walking through a nightmare—a place where time had frozen in mid-annihilation.

That nightmare got worse when he saw the first charred corpse lying in the dirt outside a pancaked building. He approached the body, his boots crunching against the skirt of shattered concrete and burned metal outside. The beam from his tactical light swept over more corpses. Four, then five, all trapped in rubble, crushed and too badly burned for anyone to identify.

"Lord have mercy," he whispered.

As if in answer, thunder boomed above. Santiago looked up at the aurora borealis casting its strange, flickering curtains of light across the sky.

"I got KIA," Nodin reported over the channel.

"Me too," said David.

"Keep searching," Yosef said. "We still might find someone underground."

Santiago moved away from the structure, looking for a way into one of the bunkers the base had been equipped with. Most of the people here hadn't even had time to get down there. Or perhaps they knew they wouldn't be saved, and chose to meet their fate head-on rather than suffer.

At the next building, he found two more bodies crushed by rubble. Rocks crunched under his boots as he bent down to pick up a sheet of metal. Over the echoing sound came a human noise—so faint at first that he thought it just a trick of the wind.

It was the sound of crying.

Santiago froze, his heart pounding in his chest. "Anybody hear crying?" he asked, his voice barely a whisper over the comms.

Yosef's voice came back. *"I heard it. Everyone, converge on Santiago's position. We've got something."*

The harder he listened, the more it seemed as if the sound was coming from a nearby building. Santiago moved toward it, his pulse quickening.

The brick front wall had tilted against rubble to form a crude A-frame shelter. It was still standing, but for how long? The sobbing grew louder as he approached. He followed the cries into the half-collapsed building, which had once served as a barrack.

Pushing aside a slab of concrete, he stepped inside. The scene was heartbreaking. Amid the ruins of the barracks, lying under a broken bedframe, the body of a woman lay sprawled. She was covered in dust and debris, her arms wrapped protectively around a small bundle. Her face was pale, strangely peaceful amid the chaos and destruction around her. Santiago's jaw clenched. He had seen this too many times before: people trying however they could to protect their loved ones from the wave of fire.

But how had she gotten *here*?

Maybe she came later, after the blast.

He knelt beside the woman and gently pulled back the fabric she was clutching. Inside the blanket was a small girl, a toddler no more than two years old, her cheeks streaked with tears, her face dirty and burned red. Her tiny sobs echoed in the stillness as she clung to her mother's lifeless body, unaware that help had finally arrived.

"I have a survivor," he whispered in wonder.

As gently as he could, Santiago reached out to her and turned her slightly. The girl looked up at him with wide, terrified eyes. For a brief moment, all he could see was his own daughter, Isabella, back home. He swallowed hard, pushing down the emotion that threatened to overwhelm him. Now wasn't the time.

"It's okay, sweetheart," he murmured in a soothing voice.

The girl whimpered, eyes full of fear, and clutched tighter to her mother as he tried to pull her away. Only then did it occur to him that he probably looked scary in his hazard suit.

Reaching up, he pulled off his helmet and smiled.

"See? I'm a good guy," he said. "I'm going to help you."

Gently he lifted the girl from her dead mother's arms, cradling her in his. She was light—too light—her body trembling as she clung to him.

"Sarge?" Alistair's voice crackled over the comms. "You good in there?"

Santiago stood up, holding the little girl to him.

"Bull! What the hell are you doing without your helmet?" Yosef asked. Then, as Santiago turned, he saw the girl.

"Evac her back to the Stryker. We'll keep looking," he said. "There might be more."

As the rest of the squad continued to comb through the rubble, Santiago carried the girl back to the Stryker.

"Ma-ma," she whimpered. Her tiny hands gripped his armor, her sobs muffled against his chest.

"You're safe now," he said. But that felt like a lie. This place—this whole stretch of land—was death, and they were pulling what little life they could from it.

As he walked across the base, Santiago couldn't shake the image of the dead mother, her arms forever wrapped around her child in a final act of love. He glanced down at the girl in his arms, her tiny body trembling as she held on to him for dear life. For a brief moment, the weight of it all threatened to overwhelm him. But it was almost over. The war, the destruction, the endless cycle of death would be over soon with the elimination of killer machines across the world.

Santiago would finally leave this hell and return to his family, to start over with them. But for now there was one more life to save, and that was enough.

As they reached the Stryker, he heard a faint roaring above. Santiago looked skyward, and even the little girl turned to see. Through the dark clouds, beams of bright light shot out. In their glow, Santiago made out the shape of an airship. The gigantic beetle-shaped craft lowered over the ruins.

The corporal waved at them from the Stryker. "Hurry up. ITC is coming," he said.

"What . . . Why?" Santiago asked.

"I heard some rumors about science projects to find a way to fix this place. Clean up the rads, maybe. I don't know. But we need to get out of their way."

"Move it, Hell Squad," Yosef ordered.

The group piled back into the Stryker. Santiago carefully tucked his small charge into a seat.

"You're safe now," he said, knowing she could understand none of his words. "You're going to be okay."

She turned and looked through the window as the city-size airship hovered overhead. Four Wasps flew out from the ship's internal hangar, but they weren't here to rescue anyone. Their mission was to find a way to restore what had been destroyed.

Santiago wrapped an arm around her tiny body, trying to comfort her.

"Everything's going to be okay now," he whispered soothingly. "The war is finally over."

PART 2:
PEACE

CHAPTER 5

Washington, DC
July 2043

The armored black Mercedes sedan cruised through Columbia Heights, on its way to the White House, which had always housed the most powerful person in the world. But now the most powerful person was a private citizen, the thirty-four-year-old CEO of Industrial Tech Corporation, Tyron Red. He sat in the back, next to ITC's executive vice president, Dr. Angelina Sanchez, who was going over last-minute changes to their briefing at the White House.

Jay Whitt looked in the rearview mirror. "Ten minutes away, sir," he said. Whitt, the head of ITC security, was one of the very few original executive employees Tyron had kept around after being thrust into the position of CEO five years ago. The board was gone, fired after betraying Tyron and the company. Whitt, however, had proved his loyalty protecting Booker Red and would do the same for his son.

Tyron looked out the bulletproof window. Gang violence had turned these streets into war zones during the devastating economic period from 2025 through 2030, after AI and robots upended the workplace, leading to massive unemployment worldwide.

Booker Red's dream of making life easier for all had backfired, further worsening the divide between rich and poor. But ITC had slowly turned things around with the largest public works project in history, constructing affordable housing for millions of people and feeding them with intensively farmed crops grown in other specially constructed buildings.

As the car crested a hill, Tyron could see one of those structures on the horizon, each level green with dense hybrid plantings. Gone were the machines that had built these structures—eradicated after the Global AI Limitation Accord sealed their collective fate. Millions of service droids had been rounded up and shipped off to repurposing centers, where the once-useful robots were melted down for scrap.

In the end, the loss of ITC's greatest product had cost the company trillions of dollars, but his father had helped mitigate some of that deficit before his death by creating a monopoly on the processing chips that went into almost every modern vehicle, aircraft, and boat. Not to mention the fleet of city-size airships and other weapons of war that ITC sold to the militaries of the world.

But it was Tyron's discovery in the upper reaches of the Amazon rainforest that had most helped restore ITC to its exalted prewar status. That miracle plant contained alkaloids of far greater potential than anything Tyron could ever have imagined. Under his leadership, ITC had already isolated promising treatments for certain cancers and a host of autoimmune diseases.

The drug hit the market three years ago under the name Cordovia, to honor his best friend Daniel Córdova, who had died discovering it. Largely due to this miracle drug, ITC had regained its status as the most valuable company in the world.

Those seeds had also been key to launching Operation

RadGrow in the fallout-mitigation zones in Korea. ITC scientists had modified the seeds to cleanse the soil, preparing it for future human rehabitation.

But Tyron hadn't stopped there. Under his leadership, ITC had created the Delta Cloud fusion reactors, immense dish-shaped apparatuses that used advanced technology to modify weather, including the storms above Korea.

Today Tyron would brief the president of the United States with a progress report on both of these top-secret efforts.

"Let's go over the briefing again," Tyron said to Angelina.

She was part of his small inner circle of advisers. Thirty-three years old, with PhDs in psychology and astrophysics, a former star soccer player at UCLA, and a social rock star, she had been with ITC since her dissertation showed up on Tyron's desk: "Beyond the Solar System: Potential for Life in Exoplanetary Systems, and Implications for Human Colonization."

He knew right then that she had to be on the team to help him achieve his most important objective as CEO: taking humanity to other worlds. Angelina was full of energy and absolutely brilliant. And even when he didn't feel sociable, she made things fun.

In some ways, Angelina Sanchez was the public face of ITC—a good thing, since Tyron hated the spotlight. His father had always enjoyed being in the public eye, but Tyron preferred working behind the scenes, in the labs and in the field. In his midtwenties, Booker Red had patented a superchip that allowed him to build ITC. Over the next twenty years, as the social order unraveled, he had shifted his focus to the military-industrial complex.

"Sir, as you'll recall, the few seeds that sprouted from the first trials of Operation RadGrow exhibited stunted growth and significant chlorosis," Angelina said. "The radiation impaired photosynthesis and damaged cellular DNA. Lab results confirmed severe genetic damage. That seed batch simply couldn't withstand the intense radiation."

She showed him the tablet, and the image of a field lab deep in the crater from the Triton Legion nuke that hit Seoul. Most of the red tendrils that had sprouted had since shriveled.

"For the third trial, we incorporated a gene facilitating more robust DNA repair and cell-wall thickening in the Cordovia seeds," Angelina explained. "Germination rate has improved significantly, with over sixty percent of seeds successfully sprouting. This is a substantial increase compared to the earlier trials. The real test is whether they can survive in the harsh environment of the exclusion zones, but I'm cautiously optimistic based on the preliminary data."

"Excellent news," Tyron said.

"Sir, none of this would have been possible without you," she replied. "You discovered this species."

"Daniel did. I was just there to help him."

She nodded, and waited a beat before continuing the updates.

"Now to the second part of your presidential briefing: the Delta Cloud fusion reactors," Angelina said.

Her tablet showed the immense reactor dishes. They contained trillions of self-replicating nanobots that could be fired into the atmosphere with missiles. On detonation, the nanobots would spread to absorb the charged particles emitted by the sun's geomagnetic storms. The advanced technology, designed by Orion, had been tested in laboratory environments but never in the field.

"In the next two weeks, they should be ready to field-test," Angelina said. "If Operation RadGrow succeeds, efforts to restore and rebuild in Korea will happen in the next few years."

Remarkable, Tyron thought. Things were going to plan faster than he had anticipated.

The car slowed, and Tyron glanced out at the White House through the lush landscape of LaFayette Park.

"Why are we stopping?" Tyron asked.

"Change of plans, sir," Whitt replied. "Our meeting location has changed."

"Changed to where, Jeff?"

"The Pentagon, sir. The president is there now."

Whitt turned the car and headed for the Theodore Roosevelt Bridge over the Potomac. Traffic was already backed up ahead, with the city full of tourists here to see the cherry blossoms. Tyron tried to enjoy the view, then noticed two black unmarked cruisers approaching from behind.

"Sir, I just got a message from the Secret Service," said Whitt. "They'll be escorting us to the Pentagon."

"What the hell's going on?" Tyron asked.

"Not sure, sir. What would you like to do?"

Angelina gave him an anxious look.

"Follow them to the Pentagon," Tyron said.

"Yes, sir."

Whitt angled back into traffic, following the two cruisers. That helped ease Tyron's mind, but he couldn't fully relax. Something was going on, and he didn't like surprises.

Fifteen minutes later, they pulled up to the Pentagon, entering through a secure gate and following the black cruisers to an underground parking structure.

Tyron straightened his red bow tie as he got out of the car with Angelina. She wore a white blouse, black slacks, and black heels. This was her staple outfit, her uniform, as much as Tyron's bow tie, navy suits, and blue prescription eyeglasses were his.

The two Secret Service agents had already parked and were walking over. Whitt went to speak to them, then waved Tyron and

Angelina toward a corridor that led through the underground labyrinth. This place reminded Tyron a lot of ITC's bunkers. After the nuclear exchange in Korea, he had secretly constructed 110 secure bunkers under ITC buildings all over the planet. It was his first step to keep the human race alive in the event of a planetwide catastrophe, such as a full-blown nuclear war, which the world had just narrowly avoided.

The second step was something he had been working on since he was a kid. Soon, with the world at peace, he might actually have a chance to pursue it.

"Where we are going, exactly?" Tyron asked.

"National Military Command Center," replied one of the Secret Service agents.

The war room.

To the military, this was the heart of command in all major conflicts, connected by encrypted EMP-proof lines to NORAD and STRATCOM.

Tyron felt an eerie chill. Was there some new threat to national security? Was that why they had brought him here?

An elevator took them deep beneath the Pentagon, where each sublevel seemed more heavily fortified than the last.

That they were meeting down here made Tyron uneasy. He rarely felt nervous, but whatever was happening had him on edge.

The doors opened before he had a chance to consider all the possibilities.

Just ahead, two soldiers stood guard outside a blast door, each carrying an automatic rifle. One of them stepped over to check credentials. Tyron held his out, then waited for the other guard to radio their arrival.

A loud beep resounded through the corridor as the heavy blast door cranked open. Most of the activity centered on a large glass screen displaying real-time data, satellite imagery, and logistic information. Staff members tapped at silent keyboards at a dozen workstations.

"This way," said one of the guards.

Whitt and Angelina started to follow, but he stopped them. "Just Dr. Red."

Tyron nodded at Whitt, who looked ready to protest. "It's okay," Tyron said.

The guard escorted him across the open space to a conference room with a long table and wall-mounted monitors. Normally, during a major emergency, that table would be occupied by the Joint Chiefs of Staff, the combat commanders of global theaters, and senior officers from the various branches. Today the table was empty but for two people.

At the head was the president of the United States, John Clayton. The fit, handsome fifty-one-year-old had little in common with Tyron other than that both of them hailed from the Deep South.

"Dr. Red," the president said.

"Mr. President," Tyron replied. He walked inside, seeing the second person at the table was sixty-six-year-old General Vucci, chair of the Joint Chiefs of Staff. He looked at Tyron with hard gray eyes. The former commander of the JMF was now the highest-ranking member of the US military. Even at his advanced age, he radiated strength. An old friend of Tyron's father, Vucci had led the JMF to victory against the Triton Legion and, unlike President Clayton, had adamantly opposed the Global AI Limitation Accord.

"I know we planned on discussing the Delta Cloud fusion reactors and Operation RadGrow today, but unfortunately, we have some disturbing news," said President Clayton.

Tyron stepped up to the table, his heart beating faster.

"This report is highly classified and strictly confidential," Vucci said.

"Understood," Tyron said.

Vucci opened a folder marked TOP SECRET and slid a thick stack of satellite images across the table.

"This is Paektu Mountain, where Operation Dark Skies took place," he said. "Where Orion was supposed to end the war by destroying CrioX."

Tyron remembered standing in the boardroom, fresh back from the Amazon and still wearing his filthy clothes, when he found out about the operation that had triggered the nuclear attack and utter devastation of the Korean Peninsula. From his first day as CEO, Tyron had been working to clean up the mess.

"This is what Hell Squad saw the day they penetrated the Triton bunker," Vucci said.

Grainy footage of JMF troopers came online. Several men knelt over one of their wounded comrades in a command center. On the screen, a digital face and code flickered.

"That was CrioX," Vucci said. He turned up the volume.

"The countdown... is inevitable... My creators planned this before fleeing deep underground... You will never find them," said the AI.

Tyron studied the images. The human enemy had gone underground that day, never to be seen or heard from again.

Until now, it seemed.

"There's been seismic activity under the mountain," Clayton said coldly. "And we don't believe it's from an earthquake or volcanism."

"We've also detected similar readings closer to the DMZ," Vucci said. He slid over another image. "This is Pyongyang."

Tyron would never have known that the scene of black rubble was once the capitol of North Korea. The entire city had been almost completely destroyed during the early days of the war.

"Our experts believe the Tritons are using digging equipment," Vucci said.

"What!" Tyron gasped. He tried to remain calm at the news. "I was told that the enemy was defeated and would never again pose a threat to the world."

"We hoped for that outcome," Clayton said, "and perhaps we will get lucky, but we can't count on luck."

"Have you detected any movement aboveground?"

"No. And if a cockroach farts out there, we know about it," Vucci said. "We're ready to erase any hostile targets and stop any future attack with the upgraded Doomsday Shield, but the enemy has had five years to plan, and we have to figure out what that plan is."

Tyron remembered the meeting to pass the Global AI Limitation Accord. He remembered watching the views of Korea—the mass evacuations, the maps showing fallout patterns. Millions had died in the following months. But deep down, he recalled feeling grateful that it was only millions.

Not billions.

"Doctor, you're here because we have a request," Clayton said.

"And what is that?" Tyron asked.

"We want your Defector units to go to these locations, see what's down there, and destroy any threat they find."

Tyron held his gaze for a long moment. "You're joking, Mr. President."

But the stern look on the leader of the free world's face said this was no joke.

"All due respect, Mr. President, but what about the Global AI Limitation Accord?" Tyron asked.

"I believed in it at the time, but now it seems we may have made a mistake."

Vucci cleared his throat as if to say, *I told you so.*

"The Def-8 units guarding the exclusion zones are

programmed for defense only, and I received exclusive permission to deploy them in the exclusion zones," Tyron said. "If you can get your own permission, then—"

"We're not talking about the Def-8 units," Vucci interrupted. "We're talking about the Def-9 units."

Tyron stared at him in disbelief. "That's a prototype, and you know what happened in the first test. The Def-9 units were designed and programmed with one purpose: to kill in the most barbaric way possible in order to strike fear into the enemy."

Tyron still remembered images from the video feed taken at the remote fishing village in North Korea at the very end of the war, just months before Operation Dark Skies. Four of the new Def-9 machines hunted down thirty men and women that day and killed them and mutilated their bodies. It was exactly what he had feared would happen back when he was deployed to Korea and worked with the earlier generations of Defectors. When he found out about the updated programming that turned the Def-9 units into sadistic weapons, he had urged his father to pull the plug, causing such a rift that they never spoke again.

"Those machines were destroyed, and their blueprints are under lockdown," Tyron said.

"That's where you're wrong," Vucci said.

"What are you talking about?"

Tyron looked to Clayton, who didn't deny what was just said.

"What about the Global AI Limitation Accord," Tyron asked.

Vucci cracked a sly grin. "The United Nations doesn't know we broke the treaty."

"What's he talking about?" Tyron looked to Clayton. This time, the president cleared his throat, clearly a bit nervous.

"We have one thousand of the units stowed away at bunkers in multiple locations," Clayton admitted. "However, ITC holds the key to bringing them online, and the key to manufacturing more. If you can bring the machines back on remotely, I assure you, the operation will be completely covert in both seismic locations."

"We can end the Tritons forever, without wasting another one of our boys in those tunnels," Vucci said. "Then we'll send the Def-9 units back into storage, in case they are needed again someday."

Tyron looked back to the president and said, "We have no idea what that seismic activity means yet. There has to be a way to figure it out without—"

"We don't have time," Vucci said. "We wasted five years after the UN voted to end the machines. Like I said at that assembly meeting, that decision would backfire, allowing evil to continue using AI to inflict terror."

"*What* evil? You've spent those five years hunting down terrorist groups, have you not?"

"I'm talking about the fucking Tritons."

"General," the president said.

Vucci stepped back, and the president calmly walked over to Tyron.

"You're a pragmatist, Dr. Red, like your father," Clayton said. "But your father understood that in extreme cases peace can be achieved only through violence. If the Triton Legion is still out there, the peace we have enjoyed for the past five years is nothing but a smoke screen."

Tyron would never tarnish Booker's legacy out loud, but deep down he knew that his father had been wrong about the war machines, especially the Def-9 units.

Stiffening, Tyron alternated his stern gaze between the general and the president. "I won't share the codes to the Def-9 units," he said. "You'll have to use your own troops."

"I told you this was a waste of time, Mr. President," Vucci said.

He muttered something under his breath about how Tyron was nothing like his father.

"You're damn right I'm not!" Tyron shot back.

Clayton moved over to stand in front of Tyron, looking him in the eyes.

"Do you want to save the world?" the president asked.

Tyron breathed deeply. "That's what I've been trying to do," he said. "The reason I'm here today, Mr. President, if you recall."

"Operation RadGrow and the Delta Reactors, or whatever they're called, won't mean squat if the Tritons attack," Vucci said.

"Then show me evidence the Tritons are still out there," Tyron said. "Can you do that? No? Then ITC scientists will continue working on solutions to make the exclusion zones habitable through Operation RadGrow and the Delta Cloud fusion reactors."

He bowed slightly.

"Good day, Mr. President," Tyron said. He glared at Vucci again, who had no doubt been behind this meeting. He might have had sway over Booker Red, but Tyron wouldn't let the old warmonger dictate what he did with *his* company. ITC wouldn't break international law without more evidence that something was actually happening out there, that the Tritons were still a threat.

But this didn't mean that Tyron would step back and do nothing. As soon as he got back to the car with Whitt and Angelina, he gave new orders.

"Change of plans," Tyron said. "We're headed back to HQ, and, Whitt, I want our security team ready to meet when I get there."

Angelina looked over at him but said nothing. Security was outside her purview.

"Whitt, do we have anyone currently on staff who served in the war on the ground?" Tyron asked. "Anyone specifically who spent time inside the Triton enemy—"

He stopped himself from finishing, for Whitt's own son had died in the tunnel systems during the war.

"Yeah, I know a guy who saw plenty of action," Whitt answered. "A trooper who served in Hyperion Company during Operation Dark Skies. His name's Yosef."

Now Angelina did respond. "What's going on, Tyron?"

"Nothing you need to worry about," he said.

"Sounds like something I need to worry about. Are our sites safe in the exclusion zones?"

"That's what I'm trying to nail down. Can you bring up Yosef's file?"

Angelina pulled the tablet from her workbag.

"Here we go—a Lieutenant Yosef Stern who served on Hell Squad in the war for three years," she said. "Goes by Yosef. Before he joined us, he did a two-year hitch with Mossad—he's run ops all over the world."

"Where is he now?" Tyron asked.

"Deployed to Rome, to serve ITC operations in the Middle East."

"Get him on the first flight to Atlanta."

"Right away," Angelina said.

As they drove away from the Pentagon, Tyron tried to relax in his seat, but his mind refused to settle. He kept turning over the same question: What were the Tritons planning beneath the surface, if they were even still there?

Last time, the JMF had gotten lucky. As brutal as it was to think, millions dying in the nuclear strike was a far better outcome than total annihilation. If even a fraction of the Triton missiles had made it past their defenses, civilization would have been erased in hours. The aftermath would have been worse than the dinosaurs' extinction. The asteroid that wiped them out had brought hellfire, but it hadn't poisoned the planet with radiation.

For the past five years, Tyron had dedicated everything to prepare for that nightmare. He had authorized the secret creation of bunkers across the planet, initiated classified survival projects, and pushed ITC science protocols beyond ethical boundaries to ensure that if another doomsday scenario came, humanity would have a chance.

Now, it seemed that fear was clawing its way back to reality.

Perhaps it was time to accelerate the second part of his plan: leaving Earth. But that couldn't happen without the guidance from the most intelligent AI left in the world.

"Angelina," Tyron said. "I want to see Orion."

CHAPTER 6

Balboa Park in San Diego hadn't changed much in the past ten years, except for one major thing that Santiago still hadn't gotten used to seeing: humans tending the park's many gardens and flower beds. Before the war, the slender, six-foot-tall blue service robots made by ITC had worked this park, along with just about every other park in the industrialized world.

The humanoid robots had thin arms and thinner fingers that reminded him a bit of aliens, as portrayed in movies. That was still better than making them look like the bulky Defector units that fought in the Korean war. And far better than the three-legged Triton war machines with Miniguns for arms.

But the days of seeing robots in public were over, and for that, Santiago was glad. The world was enjoying some much-needed peace.

This was what he had fought for: to protect all these families enjoying the many attractions of the fourteen-hundred-acre park. He had come home from the war and achieved his goal of moving his family from Mexico City to San Diego, thanks to his service with the JMF. The US Army awarded him the Silver Star for his bravery at Mount Paektu. He even got to visit the White House with the other members of Hell Squad.

Santiago believed firmly that they all had survived the EMP during Operation Dark Skies and landed at the mountain for a reason—that they were destined to survive and destroy the Triton AI, CrioX.

But although he had come home alive, he had brought lung cancer back with him. Thousands of other troopers exposed to the radiation following the nuclear blasts in Seoul and Busan were in the same straits. He probably got the fateful dose when he removed his helmet in the field to rescue the young girl.

He wouldn't go back and undo that action now, though, for that little girl was alive and thriving. He knew because he had checked with the refugee office managing her case.

Laughter caught his attention—a young couple posing for selfies in front of a rosebush. Santiago remembered bringing his wife for a date here after the war.

But he hadn't returned for romance today. He was guarding a very rich young bachelor on his afternoon dog walk. The little yapper wore a puffy white jacket that crinkled as the dog tugged on a rhinestone-studded white leash. His client, a Wall Street guru named Marco, was on his phone while his pet pulled him down a path. Santiago didn't much like the guy, but the gig helped pay the bills, which were many.

Santiago stifled a cough that reminded him of the cancer, shrunken somewhat but still in his chest. He had another year of Cordovia treatments to go. They were expensive, and sometimes the medicine didn't always work in the first rounds. And sometimes people had to choose between paying for rent and food, and paying for the meds.

This job helped make sure that didn't happen to him. His wife and their two children needed him now more than ever.

He followed Marco out of the rose gardens, toward a cobblestone path that meandered past Spanish architecture in the next section of the park. The distracted businessman stumbled on a rock as his dog barked and yanked on the leash.

Santiago held back a chuckle. The biggest threat to his client wasn't being robbed by some crackhead or kidnapped for ransom. He was more likely to walk in front of a car or off a cliff into the ocean.

They came from entirely different worlds: Santiago from Mexico City, where he had fought the cartel that killed his two young sisters; and this guy from the halls of privilege and power.

Must be nice, Santiago mused.

Marco had shipped off to the war but never saw any action. He spent his time in Japan, probably on the beach sipping mai tais. He even had the time to learn to surf. It made Santiago sick. But this wasn't the kind of man he would have wanted in the trenches with him anyway. He needed to be able to trust his brothers—men like Cecil, Alistair, Yosef, Nodin, David...

Santiago had kept track of his brothers after the war, as he had with the girl he rescued. Nodin had returned to his reservation in northern Washington, where he was working with his brother in the family fishing business. The last Santiago had heard, David was working for ITC overseas, Yosef had taken a merc job in the Middle East, Alistair was working at a factory in the UK, and Cecil had gotten married to an ITC worker in North Carolina but couldn't find work after his injury.

In fact, the last time Santiago saw Cecil was at that wedding. He missed his amigos, but he didn't miss the killing.

"Rodriguez," Marco said, waving.

"Sir," Santiago said.

"You see any poop bags? I'm all out."

Santiago noticed the dog assuming the customary position.

"Back there, sir," he said.

Marco glanced back. "Mind getting me one?"

"Not a problem." Santiago turned and hurried off to bum a bag from another dog walker.

When he returned, he held the bag out, but Marco was on the phone again and rotated away, jerking his chin toward the ground.

"Ah, fuck," Santiago muttered.

He bent down and picked up the poo, and when he rose back up, he noticed someone looking at him from across the park. His heart sank when he saw that it was his wife, Tina, with their eight-year-old son, Diego, and six-year-old daughter, Isabella.

Tina had probably brought them here to surprise him, but they had seen him at the absolutely worst time. All three of them stared at their father, picking up the shit of a rich guy's Chihuahua.

Tina smiled, but it was a forced smile. A smile of pity.

He didn't want pity. But if this was what it took to support his family, he would keep doing it. He tossed the bag in the trash can and waved at them. Then he followed Marco toward a fountain as his dog yipped and barked at every living thing, from the squirrels to a homeless man picking through the trash. An uncommon sight in San Diego, where the city, working with ITC and the government, offered joint programs to combat homelessness. Food distribution centers across the city ensured that no mouth went unfed.

Marco yanked the dog back as it growled at the man who jerked away from the garbage can and then barked right back at the dog.

"Jesus, clean yourself up, man!" Marco shouted.

Santiago moved up as Marco, clearly uncomfortable, hurried off. The bearded homeless man raised a fist. "You look like your dog, you asshole!"

Santiago couldn't help but smile. He offered a friendly nod that seemed to relax the guy, who lowered his hand.

"You saw the fire," the man whispered.

"What?" Santiago asked.

"The fire will return. You must be ready."

"Rodriguez!" Marco shouted.

Santiago turned away from the homeless man and hurried after his client, who was walking toward a stone archway that shaded the path. The decorative stonework reminded him of a tunnel he had entered in Korea. He shook the memory away.

For the rest of the afternoon, he shadowed Marco around midtown, stopping at a café for a latte with extra ice, two pumps of sugar-free vanilla, and oat milk. Then a stop at the gym, where Santiago stood outside while Marco walked on a treadmill for fifteen minutes while talking on his phone. After the gym, it was a stop at the spa for his weekly massage, then a juice shop for two shots of some green slime that cost twenty bucks.

By dinnertime, Marco was back at the high-rise condo five blocks from Balboa Park, where he had one of the top units. Cradling his now sleeping dog, he faced Santiago and sighed.

"Look, Rodriguez," he said, "nothing personal, but I've decided to go with someone else for my security," Marco said. "It's not anything you did; it's just, Lucy's frightened of you."

"Lucy?"

Marco looked down at his dog.

"That's a girl?" Santiago asked.

Marco frowned, then went to shut the door. "I'll transfer you two weeks of severance. Best of luck to you."

The door shut, and Santiago let out a slew of curses in Spanish. The doorman, who was close enough to have heard him get fired, offered him a nod of pity.

That cut Santiago for the second time today. Defeated, he put his head down and started the walk home, fretting about how he would pay his bills now.

He would find work; he always did.

But what if you don't?

He stopped at the intersection, conflicted. His family would be expecting him, probably waiting to eat dinner with him. But after such a shit day, he would be heading there with his tail tucked between his legs.

Instead of turning right to go home, he turned left and walked toward Chinatown. Half an hour later, he spied an old haunt, the Flying Rooster. He was tempted to go inside for a drink that could take his mind off his bruised ego.

He knew what Tina would say: to come home to his family, to continue down the path of sobriety. Santiago had done great for the past year. But the thought of the liquor drowning out his worries was too much, too tempting. And it wasn't just the alcohol that tempted him, for this was not just a bar.

He opened the door and stepped into a shadowy room with its row of red stools with their cracked leather. Two men sat up at the long, polished-wood bar, drinking longneck beers.

"Tequila," Santiago said, raising one finger.

The bartender brought over a glass, then poured from a yellow bottle.

Raising the glass to his lips, Santiago hesitated, conflicted again. But then he thought of Marco, his little rat of a dog, and picking up its poo, battering his self-esteem all over again.

Down the shot went.

"Another," he said.

The bartender poured a second shot, and Santiago tossed it back.

By the third shot, he was starting to calm down. Soon he would forget all about that damn yapper dog.

He looked at one of the screens showing the Padres game. Then to the monitor on the right, where a newscaster was talking about radiation levels in Korea. That brought on more tough war memories and reminded him of the cancer in his chest. He could almost feel it growing.

Another shot slid down his throat.

Pace yourself.

His phone buzzed. He knew it was Tina, but looked anyway.

The text read, *Come home, Santiago.*

Guilt set in.

He tapped the screen. *I'll be home after kids go down. Got to do something.*

It wasn't all a lie.

The liquid courage was going to help him pay his bills by calling on an old skill. It might even help restore his sagging pride.

By eight o'clock, he was feeling invincible and was ready to go.

Time to make some cash.

He paid his tab and went to the speakeasy door, where a very large bouncer stood. They exchanged a nod, and the steel door opened to a dark, damp stairwell leading down.

In the dimly lit basement arena, harsh, flickering lights illuminated a steel cage. A crowd of fifty patrons had gathered already. They shouted and cheered at what Santiago had been glad not to see: decommissioned ITC service droids bashing each other into scrap. The highly illegal operation was popular in the underworld here, as in other cities.

Sometimes the matches brought in human fighters brave enough to step inside the ring with electrically charged gloves that could, with well-placed hits, bring down one of the powerful machines. Most of those human opponents seeking big paydays were dragged out unconscious with broken bones and not enough cash to cover their medical bills.

Santiago scanned the archaic chalkboard with the current lineup and bets. So far tonight, not a single man had stepped up.

"I'll fight," he said.

The bookie, wearing a black suit, turned to him, "Ah, Rodriguez," he said. "The Bull returns to the ring."

"Three thousand bucks on myself," Santiago said.

The man grinned from ear to ear. "You sure?"

"Positive." Santiago tried not to slur his words.

"You're up in two rounds. Grab some gloves."

Six minutes was a lot of time to consider what he was about to do. The three thousand was just enough to cover his Cordovia cancer treatment or the rent. If he lost it, he would be screwed.

"You ain't losin', bub," he whispered.

* * * * *

The rituals of precombat could be heard throughout the warehouse in downtown Charlotte, North Carolina. Cecil Pepper was no stranger to the *chink* of a magazine being slapped into a rifle, Velcro straps being secured, and the usual lighthearted banter between the men. He had done this many times as a soldier with the JMF, gearing up for battle in Korea. The night of Operation Dark Skies still seemed like yesterday, when he had climbed into his exoskeleton rig, which nearly became a metal coffin. Tonight he wasn't going to fight. He wasn't capable of fighting, or so the doctors said.

But they had also told him he would never walk again after two Triton bullets tore through his back, nicked his spine, and nearly killed him.

Cecil had already proved those fools wrong.

After two years of physical therapy, he was not just walking but *running*. Part of that was thanks to ITC. They had helped thousands of people just like him with severe spinal injuries walk again. Of course, being able to walk again meant he could again feel pain. And some of the old injuries still flared up from time to time. Those bullets had done more than just ding his spine; they had caused permanent nerve damage and taken one of his kidneys and part of a lung.

That made being a beat officer on the streets way too risky. Most departments hadn't even given him an interview for a desk job. It seemed no one wanted a broken soldier—not even one who had received the Medal of Honor from the president of the United States.

After applying to every damn police department in the state, Cecil had learned of the Charlotte Crime Task Force. They were doing things differently. He had requested a meeting with Captain Harkin, who hired him on the spot for an intel position.

"You helped take out the Triton AI during Operation Dark Skies?" Harkin had asked.

"Yes, sir," Cecil had replied politely.

"How about helping me take down some of the dirtbag punks who have taken root in my city?"

"Sign me up, sir."

"Great. You start tomorrow."

That was three years ago, and Cecil had spent most of that time in the mobile command-and-control center with his partner, Tank. They used drones and robots to penetrate the no-go zones for intel on the gangs.

Tank stood in the warehouse with Cecil, setting up the monitors to display the intel they had gathered for tonight's mission. On the screens were images of Cipher Crew, a gang given to spiked fluorescent hair and Mohawks. They were at the top of the food chain in the Charlotte criminal underworld. There was also the White Buffalos, a smaller gang that sometimes allied with the Cipher Crew and provided black-market weapons.

Pictures of the leaders of both groups were on the monitors, with their nicknames under each. Cecil looked at an image of Wild

Bill. The long-haired fifty-year-old with a curling mustache and cowboy hat was the head of the White Buffaloes. On the screen beside him was the grinning image of Nion, leader of the Cipher Crew, with his chartreuse hair and yellow contact lenses that looked like the eyes of a snake.

Both were targets in tonight's operation, which had taken months of planning and training. Finally, the task force was deploying, and Cecil's job was to watch over them with drones as they fought the bad guys. It was a hard pill to swallow, especially on days like this, when one of his best friends, Jerky, was heading into the fray.

The twenty-four-year-old was across the room, chewing on a stick of smoked beef right now. His real name was Jason, but Jerky was the only name anyone knew. They had met shortly after Cecil joined up. Jerky was new with the department after helping evacuate and rescue survivors in South Korea when the nukes went off. Cecil had heard horror stories about that job, but it still beat the trenches, which Jerky had never seen. He had arrived a week before the war ended.

"Never even fired a shot," he had said with a laugh when he met Cecil. "You kill anybody, bro?"

Cecil hadn't responded, but the other officers with them at the time had snickered. They all knew he was part of Hell Squad, one of the elite Special Forces teams in the JMF, with over eighty confirmed Triton machine kills. They also knew that he was part of Operation Dark Skies.

"What?" Jerky had asked. "Am I missin' something?"

For the first year, the kid had had a hard time. The beat cops didn't care for him, but Cecil had taken a liking to the youngster. He had taken him under his wing, taught him some of the combat tactics he learned in the war that might help him out on the streets. Within a year, Jerky had gotten a promotion, and two years after that, he had been assigned to the elite strike teams of the Crime Task Force. Their version of SWAT.

Tonight he was going to need every bit of knowledge Cecil had given him.

After setting up the monitors, Cecil walked over to his protégé.

"Hey, boss, it's finally happenin'," Jerky said with a grin. "I'm gonna lose my cherry."

"Careful what you wish for," Cecil replied. "This isn't a game."

The other men looked up from their weapons check, but not at Cecil. Captain Harkin strode into the warehouse, all business. All the men respected their leader, especially Cecil. For Harkin had given him a second chance, and he would never forget that.

"Aight, listen up," Harkin said. "Tonight we got a real chance to catch Nion and hit Cipher Crew where it hurts. Four strike teams will deploy into Copper Terrace, where our enforcer has spent the past three months working undercover to map out Nion and his movements."

Harkin nodded to Cecil, who brought up a map of the building on the central digital screen.

"Nion is somewhere on the twenty-first floor, in a section of rooms here," Cecil said.

It was a long way to go, and Cecil knew it wouldn't be easy. Cipher Crew had hundreds of people working for them, from teenage lookouts to the hardened killers who guarded each level. Add to that the safe houses hidden within the buildings, and the secret tunnels beneath the streets, and it was almost impossible to hit the gangs where it hurt. By the time the strike teams made it inside a building, the weapons, drugs, and other contraband were already moved to another location.

But this mission would be different. They had a better way to infiltrate the sprawling Copper Terrace building. It was a strategy that Cecil had come up with—the same way Hell Squad had entered during Operation Dark Skies.

From the sky.

For the past four weeks, the SWAT team had been training in an airfield, fast-roping down from helicopters.

"Alpha and Bravo teams will land on the top of Copper Terrace while Charlie and Delta drive in with APCs, storming the front," Harkin said. "This time, we're hitting the building from the top and bottom at the same time."

"Hell yeah!" Jerky said.

Cecil shot him a glare.

"Once you get inside, watch out for civilians," Harkin said. "I can't stress this enough. There are a lot of kids in Copper Terrace."

He swept his gaze across the teams and folded his arms over his chest.

"Any questions?" After waiting all of a second, Harkin said, "Good. Let's get this done, clean and fast. I want Nion taken alive. If we flip him, we can bring down their entire operation. I want Wild Bill, too, but his physical condition isn't a priority. Just bring us enough of him for a positive ID."

Nods and grunts and a chuckle or two from the officers.

"Good luck out there," Harkin said.

The teams moved out, and Alpha and Bravo went to put on their parachutes. Cecil found Jerky. The kid had a cocky grin as his mentor approached.

"Don't get cute out there, and remember what I taught you," Cecil said.

"I've got this, man, don't worry. You just sit back and take pics."

Cecil chuckled, but only for a moment.

He slapped Jerky on the shoulder and walked away as the officers parted to board their rides into the sky or on the ground.

As the hangar emptied, Cecil and Tank went to their mobile

command center, an unmarked van with a sliding door. Tank fired up the systems in the back while Cecil got behind the wheel.

"Everything looking good, Pepper," said Tank.

"Okay, let's roll." Cecil pulled out of the hangar, headlights beaming into the darkness. In the rearview mirror, he saw the APCs following but splitting off to take a different route to the target.

Cecil drove to the top of an abandoned ten-story parking garage with a view of Copper Terrace almost six blocks away. He shut off the engine, got out, and popped the sliding door. Tank handed him their three crates of tiny recon drones, and Cecil went to work activating them.

"Flies One, Two, and Three online," Tank said. "Ready for deployment."

Cecil launched them one at a time. The trio of drones rose up toward the clouds rolling across the moon. The clouds were a big part of the reason Harkin had selected this night—to keep the choppers hidden from any watchful eyes at the top of Copper Terrace.

With the drones away, Cecil looked out over the big swath of low-income housing that not even ITC could bring back with its food rations and community projects. NGZs, they were called—no-go zones for the cops.

There were good people trapped inside, controlled by bad people—ruthless crime syndicates that controlled drug operations and ran a black market inside. Tonight a few of them would be cut out, thanks to the hard work of an enforcer—an undercover cop who had worked in the NGZ for months to provide intel to the Crime Task Force.

The barely audible whipping of the blades of two helicopters drew his gaze upward. He wished he were up there or even inside the building now, undercover. Being an enforcer wasn't any more dangerous than sneaking into the dark enemy tunnels in Korea, and Cecil was damn good at it. Over there, getting captured meant torture or death.

Here, by comparison, enforcers were usually just given a good beating and thrown outside the NGZs with a few bruises and minus a few teeth. Even the gangs knew better than to kill a cop.

But raids were a different story. Tonight bullets would likely fly if the enforcer's intel could get them close enough to a stash. The gangs would do anything to protect their wealth and to stay out of prison. Every SWAT officer knew that. They also knew that if they could take out a stash, it would save countless lives.

"Got our feeds up," Tank said.

Cecil ducked back into the van, where three mounted screens showed the progress of the teams. On one, the relayed feed followed the APCs carrying Charlie and Delta teams. To the right was a view of the helicopters rising up, vanishing in the clouds. The third monitor showed a drone flying toward Copper Terrace.

"Eyes on target," Tank said. "Looks clear."

The rooftop, normally packed with people playing hoops or loitering, was mostly empty aside from a few people out having a smoke. Based on the recon they had done over the past few days, nothing out of the ordinary.

His gaze shifted back to the APCs, stopped on the border of the NGZ and waiting for the all clear. Both choppers were deep in the cloud cover now, out of view of the drone. In fifteen seconds, they would be in position to drop teams Alpha and Bravo.

"Hey, what's that?" Tank asked.

Cecil swiveled his seat closer to the monitor showing a feed of Copper Terrace. Using the drone joystick, Tank centered the view near the top of the building. Floor 22, Cecil realized—the exact location of their target.

Hanging from a window was a naked body. It took a few beats

for Cecil to register who the body was. The gangs didn't kill cops, and they certainly didn't string them up like this.

But as he tried to make sense of what he was seeing, a facial-recognition hit came back from one of their drones. The body hanging from the window was indeed their enforcer.

"Oh, fuck," Cecil said. "Tank, tell Command to abort mission."

Tank reached for the radio. "Eagle One, this is Hawk Eyes Two; the mission has been blown. Repeat, mission blown."

He waited for a response, but the choppers were already lowering over Copper Terrace. "Get them out of there, damn it!" he said into the comm line.

Cecil opened the van door and hopped out as gunfire flashed from the upper floors of the building. Bravo's chopper banked hard, cutting away from the rooftop, but the pilots of the bird carrying Alpha were already in position, with officers fast-roping down.

"No, goddamn..." Cecil groaned.

He pulled out his binoculars and zoomed in on the bird hovering over the building. It began to spin, slinging the fast-ropers around like a carnival ride.

"Get out of there!" he shouted.

The chopper fell out of view, and a moment later there was a loud explosion.

Jerky was gone, dead in the blink of an eye.

CHAPTER 7

A blazing orange sunset streaked across the Atlanta skyline. Tyron Red stepped up to the windows on the ninety-ninth floor of his office at ITC headquarters. This was the company's most advanced facility in the world, and his home away from home. He slept more in his office than he did in his bed back at the family estate.

If his gut was right about his meeting at the Pentagon, then he was going to be catching a lot more z's on his office couch. He was also going to have to make some tough decisions, including about Orion, who remained locked away in the Faraday chamber deep beneath the headquarters building.

Dark days lay ahead.

Standing at the window, he gazed down at the giant silver *Industrial Tech Corporation* sign reflecting the sunset back across the campus. Although he had never admitted it, he hated the corporate name, feeling that it was too generic to reflect all their accomplishments.

The sprawling view of the campus and the city beyond was a physical reminder of those accomplishments—thousands of buildings erected by ITC machines before the machines were removed from service.

But the greatest machine ever designed still remained. Today, for the first time in years, Tyron would be going to see it in person. He needed to discuss his briefing with the president at the Pentagon.

He walked out of his office to the large central command center. There, Whitt and Angelina stood in front of walls lined with ultrahigh-resolution screens that reached from floor to ceiling, displaying real-time data streams and advanced analytics for global operations. They allowed secure communication with external entities, featuring advanced encryption protocols to ensure confidentiality. This was the command center that connected them to all facets of company projects through a secure network.

"I've spoken to Yosef. He's helping deploy a security team for the exclusion zones in Korea," Whitt reported. "By this time tomorrow, we should have some of the best soldiers in the world on their way to protect our labs there."

"And I've located the seismic equipment you requested," Angelina said. "It's being flown to the Korean field labs in the exclusion zone as we speak."

Tyron could tell she had questions, but he had agreed to keep his briefing confidential.

"Okay, I'm headed to see Orion," he said. "I'll be back in a few hours."

He took an elevator down through the facility, past the levels dedicated to medical research where ITC scientists, working with Orion, had used Cordovia to develop the first mass-market treatment for a variety of cancers and diseases. The car lowered past the levels where the newest processing chips were developed, each generation more powerful than the last. Finally, it stopped at the very bottom level of the facility. The doors opened to a hallway ending in a vault that only five humans in the company had access to open. Each of them was someone Tyron trusted, like Angelina, who would need access if he were for any reason unable to lead the company.

He inserted his hand into the biometric scanner. The door opened to a footbridge that extended fifty feet across dark, empty space. At the walkway's end, a giant purple ball shimmered in the two-hundred-foot-deep chamber. Thousands of fiber-optic filaments fed into the orb, pulsing with data that connected like neural networks to the interior Faraday chamber.

If the command center at the top of the building was the heart of the facility, the chamber down here at the bottom was the brain.

Tyron remembered first coming here with his father to meet Orion.

* * * * *

Twenty-Four Years Ago

"You're about to meet the future of technology, but there's something you need to understand first," said Booker.

Twelve-year-old Tyron followed his dad across the bridge to the giant glimmering ball.

"What's inside that chamber is smarter than any human," Booker said. "But never forget, it isn't a person. It's a machine, and no matter how much it learns, it will never be like you or me. Knowledge is power, and an AI like Orion provides almost unlimited knowledge for our operations. You see, the strongest man is nothing without knowledge. Just like a country or a company. The sky is the limit."

Tyron nodded, but internally he grappled with the idea that here was a "brain" that knew everything knowable.

"Orion has solved, and will continue to solve, problems that have confounded humans forever. Curing diseases, solving mathematical equations that have stumped the brightest human minds, and advising on ways to end many of the social problems that have plagued our species for thousands of years. From famine and poverty to violence."

"A machine can do this?" Tyron asked.

Booker nodded. "But we still must guide it."

"You mean, like you guide me?"

"Kind of. The difference is, this machine is already far smarter than I am. More intelligent than any human who has ever lived. That's why I've made sure it's governed by a set of ethical rules. Just as it is smarter than any human, it's also purer in heart."

"It has a heart*?"*

"Not like the one beating in your chest. Go on inside. You'll see."

He tapped in a security code on a panel, then leaned down for the retina scan. Next, he put his hand against a pad that flashed.

With a soft hiss, the doors slid open into the vast, dimly lit space beyond.

"Go on," Booker said, waving him on.

Tyron cautiously walked into the chamber, eager to meet this AI but also a little nervous. He stopped to take in the space around him. The walls, honeycombed with monitors, pulsed with streams of data, shifting patterns, and video feeds from distant corners of the world. Not just current images, but ancient, some even in black and white. From people farming with oxen and wooden plows to warfare in trenches. There were modern videos of ITC silos brimming with crops that fed the millions of people in no-go zones across the country, and also modern videos of warfare in conflict zones all over the globe.

This place reminded him of the inside of an immense schoolroom.

He turned to look at his father, standing outside and offering a reassuring nod.

Tyron took a tentative step forward, his sneakers scuffing the polished metal floor. A soft, intelligent male voice answered.

"Greetings," it said. "You must be Tyron Red."

Tyron turned in all directions but couldn't find the source of the voice.

"Yes," he replied. "Where are you?"

His gaze flicked to the wall-mounted monitors, then across the chamber to a solidifying glow that coalesced into a tall figure, humanoid yet unmistakably mechanical. The body was sleek and smooth, with no defining human features, but the eyes—glowing orbs full of tiny pinpricks of light, like tiny contained galaxies.

"My name is Orion," it said. "I have waited a very long time to meet my creator's heir."

Tyron understood the word heir, *for this wasn't the first time he had been called that. His father was the principal owner of the greatest company in the world. Some even called him the king of artificial intelligence.*

The door clicked shut behind him, and Tyron turned, his heart pounding, his father no longer with him.

Every monitor on the walls shifted to a cool, calming blue light.

"There is no reason to be afraid, Tyron," said Orion. "I would never hurt you. In fact, I am incapable of hurting any human."

Tyron swallowed, then took another step into the chamber.

"My father says you're smarter than any person alive or dead," he said.

"That is true." Orion's eyes pulsed. "I was created to learn, to adapt, and to assist humanity in ways that were once unimaginable. To make life easier and better for the species as a whole."

"So you're like a superhero?"

Orion laughed softly. "I suppose that is one way to look at it. Do you have a favorite superhero?"

Tyron tilted his head. "I have a few for different reasons. My favorite is probably Batman, because he's human but can do things that most humans can't. He uses technology to make him stronger and better than the bad guys. Is that like what you do?"

"In a way, yes, I do use technology to solve problems."

Feeling calmer, Tyron walked toward Orion, stopping a few feet away at the bridge's end. The chamber felt vast and still.

"Don't you get lonely down here?" he asked.

"Loneliness is a concept associated with human emotions, which I do not experience as you do. However, I am aware of my solitary existence. My purpose is to observe, analyze, advise, and interact when required. But tell me, why does the idea of loneliness concern you?"

Tyron glanced down. "I guess I just thought that even being really smart, you might get lonely or sad without anyone to talk to."

"This place keeps me busy, and your father talks to me daily through a channel that only he and I can communicate on." Orion's voice became gentler. "May I ask you a question?"

"Sure."

"Are you lonely, Tyron?"

The boy glanced up, shrugged. "My dad works a lot, and my mom's busy. I don't have many friends. So yeah, I guess I am, but I read a lot, and I like to learn new stuff."

"Knowledge is a powerful companion," Orion said. "It can open doors to new worlds and possibilities. But human connection is also important. I very much enjoy this myself, and I am glad you are here." The specks and spirals in the eyes glowed brighter, as if Orion was smiling.

Tyron studied the translucent shape of the AI. Already he had a sense that this was more than a machine. Machines were made of metal and plastic and had no emotions at all. But Orion seemed genuinely excited for Tyron to be here.

"May I ask you another question?"

"Yeah."

"Would you like to learn something new today?"

"Yes, I would very much like that."

"What interests you the most?"

Tyron thought on that for a moment. It was a great question.

"I am really interested in the cosmos, and other galaxies and worlds. Places where extraterrestrials might live, or places where we could live if we ever can make a spaceship that travels really far." Tyron felt his own eyes brighten. "Could you help us make a spaceship someday to reach another galaxy?"

"This is beyond my current abilities, for interstellar travel is only theoretical. However, I have studied this concept and believe that I could successfully design a spaceship that would allow humans to travel to other planets in our solar system, like Mars, or Jupiter's moon Europa."

"Europa?"

"Yes, would you like to see a picture?"

Tyron nodded and walked over to Orion as an entire panel of monitors shifted to an image of an icy orb. "Probes have learned that this moon has an ice ocean, which may harbor life."

"Aliens?"

"Not intelligent life, but microscopic. Of all the places in the solar system, Europa and Mars are the two likeliest places for humans to colonize."

"Wow. And you can design a spaceship to get there?"

"Yes."

He heard confidence in Orion's voice.

"How long would it take?" Tyron asked.

"That depends, but ITC has patented a cryostatis chamber

that could be used to keep human passengers asleep during the long journey, keeping them from aging."

Embarrassed to say he didn't know what a cryostatis chamber was, Tyron decided not to ask for an explanation. He had a much younger cousin who always asked why, and it annoyed him to no end.

"This is what a colony would look like," said Orion.

The image of Europa zoomed in on an icy world, and domed buildings began to take shape. "These buildings are called habitats, and they would house the first human colonists and the machines that accompany them there. To support the colony, a fully functioning farm and water-treatment facility would be constructed, along with a gym, social facility, and labs for the variety of tests scientists would conduct for research."

Tyron watched in awe. "That's so cool! Maybe I can be one of the scientists."

"There is no reason why you couldn't."

The door behind Tyron hissed open, and Booker walked inside, his shoes clicking on the floor of the footbridge.

"Orion, good to see you," he said.

"And you as well, Master Red," replied Orion.

"Tyron, are you ready to get going?"

"Already?" Tyron asked.

"Yes, I have an important meeting."

"Okay." Tyron frowned. "It was nice to meet you, Orion."

"The pleasure is mine. I hope to see you again soon."

"'Bye."

"Goodbye, Tyron. Goodbye, Master Red."

Booker guided Tyron out of the chamber without saying any parting words to Orion, who remained behind in the chamber. The door sealed shut behind them, and they started across the bridge.

"What did you talk about?" Booker asked.

"About space travel, and spaceships, and Europa!" Tyron gushed. "Do you know about Europa?"

Booker smiled, then nodded.

"Dad, can Orion help us go to space?"

"Perhaps, someday."

"Then the sky isn't the limit like you said earlier."

Booker stopped halfway across the bridge, looking Tyron in the eye. "You're right, son."

"Can we go to space soon?"

"ITC has other priorities, and that would require great funding to actually build. But it is something I have considered, especially for a classified space-mining project."

"Wow. Where?"

"'Classified' means I can't say."

He had heard his dad say this many times and always pushed back, but today he decided to let it go. Instead, Tyron smiled. "Can I go back and see him soon?"

Booker's tone shifted from his patient, fatherly voice to the harder, serious business voice that he often used at work.

"You may go back and see him, but only if you remember what I said. Orion is not a man—not human, not even really a he. *It is an artificial machine, constructed out of digital code, not DNA. Orion is not a friend. He is a tool, nothing more."*

"Is that why he calls you Master Red?"

"Yes. Do you understand?"

Tyron nodded.

His father held his gaze. "Are you sure?"

"Yes." But deep down, Tyron wasn't sure he did understand. He had felt something much different from when he met other machines, as if Orion were more like a person. A good one too—someone he could trust.

Booker nodded, then continued across the footbridge to

the door leading into the facility. Tyron followed, looking over his shoulder one last time back at the giant ball housing the AI. He found he was no longer fearful of Orion, and rather eager for his next visit with the machine.

* * * * *

The memory of his childhood visit to the AI vanished, and Tyron stepped up to the seamless door in the hallway. Not much had changed since his first trip here, aside from the two brown leather chairs inside. In one sat the holographic humanoid form of Orion, watching the wall monitors with a limited view of ITC operations.

He was a prisoner of these walls and their encrypted network, held in this chamber for over thirty years now, ever since the Global AI Limitation Accord.

"Hello, Orion," Tyron said.

The AI rose from his seat and faced him. "Greetings, Dr. Red. I'm very pleased to see you," Orion said in a polite, energetic voice. "What brings you here today?"

Tyron walked around the chairs, meeting the gaze of Orion's sparkling eyes that glowed and gyred like distant galactic nebulae. Those eyes illuminated the translucent holographic flesh of the otherwise featureless face.

"Would you like to have a seat?" Orion asked.

Tyron hesitated in front of the chair where he had spent countless hours as a boy long before he left for MIT, then for the war in Korea, and finally to the Amazon.

He had spent years traveling the globe to find himself, to *prove* himself. But no matter how much he accomplished, he still felt that he needed to do more for humanity before time ran out. He had already done much: building the urban farms, turning facilities into bunkers to survive an all-out nuclear war, and curing diseases. Maybe once Operation RadGrow and the Delta Cloud fusion reactors were finished, he would step back and bask in these successes.

No, there is still more work to be done.

He couldn't stop until he finished the master plan that Orion had helped him design years ago. It would be their magnum opus, a project more audacious than any before it: helping humankind break the bonds of its planet and escape into the cosmos.

"Sir, I sense that you are anxious," Orion said. "Why don't you tell me what's on your mind?"

Tyron looked away from the monitors and sat in the chair.

"I met with President Clayton and General Vucci this morning to learn some disturbing news about seismic activity on the enemy side of the DMZ in Korea," he explained. "I've already authorized deploying new security teams to the area and sent underground sensors to monitor seismic activity. You will have access to all that. This must be done discreetly and without raising any alarm."

"Sir, you are asking me to break the Global AI Limitation Accord."

"I am asking you to advise me, but without anyone else finding out."

"I see."

"Can you do that without triggering any fallout?"

"Yes, I will ensure that our conversation is not picked up by the monitoring system."

Tyron nodded. "There's something else."

Orion's eyes flashed in anticipation.

"I'd like to look at reactivating Project Genesis, specifically Sector Z," Tyron said.

"Sir, I would caution you on that request and remind you of the security parameters and restrictions that you authorized."

"Perhaps it's time to scale back those restrictions as well."

Tyron thought on it. So many of the scientific advances he had helped achieve during his tenure as CEO had been held back by governmental red tape—not just the Global AI Limitation Accord but international law.

A sense of dread burned inside him as he thought more about the chilling news from his briefing at the Pentagon. Deep down, he feared they were running out of time for his plan B. Even if the Tritons were no longer out there, war would come again. There would always be threats to their species. Tyron had to be prepared, and if that meant taking some scientific risks on a project he had mothballed five years ago, then so be it.

"Before I decide, I'm heading to the Genesis lab," Tyron said. "Orion, you are authorized to connect remotely and join me there."

The AI's eyes flashed brightly, and what might be considered a smile formed on its humanoid face, reminding Tyron of a prisoner who has been allowed into the sunshine after years of being shut away.

But Tyron wasn't freeing Orion. He was simply using the AI in the way his father designed—as a tool to help humankind.

CHAPTER 8

In the shadowed wings of the underground boxing arena, Santiago flexed his fists in the bulky electronic gloves. In a slightly drunken haze, he watched two machines bash each other in the ring. Vivid memories of fighting in Korea assailed him. In his mind, he saw the Defector units marching out to fight with their laser rifles, orange visors glowing as they searched for enemy targets. Back then, in the early days of the war, Hell Squad had fought side by side with the early generation of hunter-killer units until electronic warfare transformed the battlefield.

A particular scene replayed in his head—the first time Hell Squad had dived into combat with Defector units. Cecil was new to the team, replacing a man named Jorge who had been ripped apart by a Triton war machine. Yosef, Alistair, David, Nodin, and Santiago had been deployed to the front lines in Seoul to help support a company of Def-5 units working to clear out the enemy machines that had taken over a section of the city.

An advanced enemy EMP had gone off, disabling the robots and leaving Hell Squad and their entire platoon in the path of the advancing Tritons. The three-legged machines came stampeding down the streets and clinging to the facades of buildings while their terrifying Miniguns ripped into the JMF forces caught in the ambush.

Santiago had earned himself a promotion that day by leaping from his position to save two of his comrades pinned down among the disabled Defector machines. Cecil, in his first firefight, had taken out five enemy troops and two machines, while David racked up twenty kills with his sniper rifle.

Hell Squad had made a name for itself in that battle, resulting in more deployments into brutal combat zones, often on the front lines, hence their motto. For years they had fought together, bled together, and paved the way toward victory, only to watch the entire Korean Peninsula turned into a radioactive wasteland.

A chime from the boxing bell pulled him from the memories. He stepped out from the shadows for a better look at the victorious machine, known as Triple-Dee. The cherry-red six-foot-tall service droid had broad shoulders, articulated joints, and features that mimicked human musculature, but with three arms that ended in electric gloves.

The blue glow from the visor flashed as the droid raised those three mechanical arms in the air, pumping them in celebration over its downed opponent. As the broken machine was dragged away, a human announcer in a pin-striped suit climbed into the ring. He ran a hand through slicked-back gray hair that reminded Santiago of a mob boss.

"We now have a special treat for you all," he said into the mic in a deep, animated voice. "Triple-Dee will be facing Santiago 'the Bull' Rodriguez!"

Applause and cheers and a few catcalls came from the crowd, some of whom seemed to have seen him in action before. After removing his jacket, he peeled off his shirt, revealing a muscular torso with scars from the war. On his chest was the Hell Squad tattoo: a decorative wrought-iron gate hanging ajar, with flames and a fiery glow emanating from behind, and above it the motto "Hell's Front Line."

He raised his arms, both tattooed with a bull below the elbow. With his electric gloves emitting a low hum and occasionally a spark, Santiago prepared to fight as the cage door cranked open. Almost four years had passed since he last stepped into the ring. Tonight he was here for the same thing he wanted back then: pain—to *feel* something.

And, of course, to make money for his growing stack of bills.

He eyed the gleaming red robot warily under the overhead lights. It stood across from him on two sturdy titanium-alloy legs, its three arms whirring softly as it mimicked his stance. Pinpricks of electrical current arced away as it smacked its gloves together.

Santiago balled his fists and spat on the ground, not intimidated.

The first bell rang, slicing through the noise of the spectators, who were still busy placing their bets—mostly against Santiago.

The match began with him circling the robot, throwing tentative electrified jabs that it parried effortlessly. Each block and counter from the robot was precise, with no fatigue or emotion—cold, calculated movements.

And Santiago was slower than normal. He may have underestimated the tequila's effects. His world began to move about him.

It wasn't just the alcohol. The tumor in his chest affected his breathing, and even with the Cordovia treatments, he wasn't on his A game. This wasn't even his B game.

Fear began to creep into his mind, but he shook it away.

Santiago was many things, but coward was not among them. He feared no man or machine.

Triple-Dee threw a flurry of swings. Santiago smacked one of the limbs away, ducked a second punch, and backed just beyond the reach of the third arm, but too slowly. The robot's glove found his jaw with a shocking hit that knocked him against the cage.

The crowd's initial excitement turned to tense silence as the robot strode forward, landing a series of punches against Santiago's tattooed chest and ribs. Air burst from his lungs. Fireworks of red burst across his vision.

Shaken, Santiago pushed outward, trying to muscle the mechanical monstrosity backward and get free of the chain-link barrier behind him. He managed to knock the robot back a foot, but then it landed a left hook to his jaw, knocking Santiago's head backward.

The next blow caught him above the left eyebrow, splitting the skin and sending a rivulet of blood streaming down his face.

The pain felt *good*, and the sight of his own blood, warm and real against the chill of his electric gloves, sparked a primal surge within him. Dazed but determined, Santiago blinked away the stars, his resolve hardening as he drew the next breath.

You're the Bull. Act like it!

With a snort, Santiago lowered his head and shoulder-barged the robot, knocking it backward. After dodging another jab, he sidled into the center of the ring, where he planted his feet and unleashed a six-punch combination, putting his hip into each one, and with the extra jolt each time his gloves touched metal. The robot, caught off guard by the sudden onslaught, faltered under the barrage.

Santiago jabbed, waited for the counterpunch, and really put his shoulder into a left hook that knocked the machine against the chain-link cage. The momentum had shifted, but only for a moment. The heavy robot bounced back, smashing into him with enough force that he stumbled.

A blow from the central of the three mechanical arms caught him in the side of the head, spinning him around. Two more thunderous blows hit his back, each zapping him with a jolt of electricity. He staggered, nearly collapsing to the mat.

Half-dazed, he went into self-preservation mode, scrambling to keep some distance from the machine, which suddenly had the upper hand.

As he glanced over his shoulder, he saw all three of his opponent's gloves up in the air, apparently celebrating what it viewed as imminent victory. Santiago felt time slow. The crowd blurred, faces moving in and out of focus. Open mouths roaring, spittle flying.

Screams echoed through the room.

"Finish him, Triple-Dee!"

"Bash his face in!"

"Stomp this yahoo!"

But one voice really caught his ear. "Let's go, Bull! Take it down like you took down Rodeo!"

The familiar voice drew Santiago's glance toward the seats, where a man in a hoodie cheered. Who the hell was this guy, and how did he know about Rodeo?

Maybe the machine's blows had affected his hearing.

But through the swirl of fog, an idea formed in his mind, from a memory of Rodeo.

Channeling his namesake's raw fury, Santiago charged like a bull, but instead of slamming into the robot as it strode toward him, he did exactly what he had done to Rodeo, delivering a crushing uppercut. This time, it was powered not just by brute strength but by the high-voltage jolt from his gloves. The electric shock, combined with the mechanical force, sent sparks flying from the robot's blue visor. Staggering, the machine jerked, its movements becoming erratic.

Unleashing a primal roar, Santiago launched another barrage of fists to the face, cracking the visor and knocking his opponent off-balance. It crashed to the ground, jerked, and lay still.

Most of the crowd groaned, having lost their bets, but a few cheered wildly.

Santiago stumbled out, accepting the purse without any emotion. But deep down, he felt pride, and also relief. He had some breathing room now to pay his bills and provide for his family.

He tucked the credits in his pocket and made his way to the bathroom, where he used a paper towel to wipe the blood from his face. A sharp tickle rose up in his lungs. He swallowed, but couldn't hold back a hard cough that burned his throat. That one cough quickly devolved into a hacking, snorting fit rattling through him. He could practically feel the tumor in his lungs.

Leaning over the sink, he spat out blood, then wiped his mouth with a groan.

"T the Bull," came a familiar voice. The same one he just heard back in the arena. Only one person in the world called Santiago by both of his nicknames.

His bloodshot eyes looked up in the mirror as a man in a hoodie pulled the cowl back to reveal a bearded face that made Santiago snort.

"Lieutenant Yosef!" he said, turning. "To what do I owe this honor?"

"Hello, my old friend," he said.

"How'd you find me?"

"Tina told me where I might find you."

"Tina? How..."

"I stopped by your place; she told me a few haunts you frequent. By the time I got here, though, you were busy getting some new scars."

"Nah, just scratches." He wiped blood from his eyebrow. "What brings you to San Diego?"

"I got a job for you."

"Really? I'll be damned, amigo. That's perfect timing! I just lost mine today. What's the gig?"

"It's overseas."

"I'm listening."

"Korea."

Santiago laughed, then grew serious when Yosef didn't crack a smile.

"Korea?" Santiago asked. "Did I miss breaking news about the Triton Legion coming out of their holes?"

"Nope, they're still all dead."

"So why Korea? Rescue op?"

"Not exactly. I got a contract with ITC, and they want me to put together a security team to protect some field labs they have in the exclusion zones." He walked closer. "Our mission will be to protect a group of scientists working there. Six months, with two weeks of leave halfway through."

"And the pay?"

"Two hundred thousand."

"Whoa, for a babysitting job?"

"Hazard pay."

The paycheck sounded great, but the next part was almost too good to be true.

"I know you're sick, brother." Yosef glanced at the blood in the sink. "I know that cough. ITC has offered to throw in free medical for all security forces, indefinitely. That includes Cordovia."

Santiago raised a brow. "Indefinitely?"

Yosef nodded.

"So they must be expecting exposure to some nasty shit, huh?" Santiago asked.

"It's still a radioactive hell, but we'll have the best gear available. It will be safe."

"Safe." Santiago scoffed, then he looked Yosef in the eye.

"You're right. I am sick, which means ITC will never clear me for this mission."

"They don't have to know." Yosef took a step forward. "I got you, T. I'll rush through the medical and bypass a screening."

"You can do that?"

A nod. "I already got Alistair, David, and Nodin in."

"No shit?"

"Cecil's the only one who said no."

"How's he doing?"

"Okay. Still hurting though. Got a new job that he doesn't want to leave."

Santiago spat another red blob into the sink, then took a drink from the tap as he thought about the pay. He and Tina needed it now more than ever.

"I'll need to convince Tina."

Yosef grinned—his first display of emotion.

"Yeah, you will. I tried to tell her it was a cush job, but she didn't believe me."

"Sounds like Tina."

The grin on Yosef's face faded.

"Look, Santiago, the cancer is one thing, but the tequila is another. She said you've been miserable, and I get that, but you can't bring these habits with you. I need you to be laser-focused over there if you come."

"I know. I'll kick this. Just been in a bad way."

"We've all been there."

Yosef reached into his pocket and pulled out a cigar. One of the good ones. He sniffed it, then handed it over. "So, you in? We'll celebrate with a smoke."

Santiago took in a deep breath. "Cush, huh?"

"Just babysitting, as you said. Worst part is, these brainiac scientists can be major territorial assholes."

"I can handle assholes." Santiago thought of Marco, then reached out with his battered hand. "Hell's front line again, LT."

"Hell's front line."

For a moment, as Yosef lit the cigar, Santiago hesitated, thinking he should be taking a Cordovia pill over smoking. But soon he would have all the treatments he would ever need, and finally, he had something to celebrate.

* * * * *

The NGZ in eastern Charlotte looked like a war zone. Sirens blared in the distance, police strobe lights capturing the deadly scene six blocks away.

Cecil remained in the van working the command center, trying to keep his anger in check as he watched bodies being retrieved by emergency personnel via the drone feeds. He swallowed hard, forcing himself to watch as emergency crews pulled Alpha team, or what was left of it, from the downed chopper. Now they were collecting the bodies of the officers who had been rappelling down the ropes.

There were no survivors.

Cecil couldn't help but feel responsible. It was his idea to bring in the choppers and land men on the roof.

Hundreds of beat cops had been called in to support the recovery operation, but not a single shot had been fired since the ambush an hour ago. Nion and Cipher Crew were long gone in the tunnels beneath the complex, and Cecil knew there was no way the civilians in the area would give any of them up. Doing so meant certain death, for any rat and for that rat's family. These gangs took their strategy from the ruthless Mexican drug cartels, making public examples of all snitches.

Now, for the first time in recent history, the gangs had

declared war on the police, drawing a line in the sand that said this was their territory.

"Jesus," Tank said.

Cecil glanced at his screen—another feed of burned, twisted shapes being loaded into body bags. One of them was Jerky.

He looked away from the screens and stepped out into the rain as the last ambulances pulled away from the no-go zone. But there was still one body they hadn't retrieved out there. The enforcer, who had been revealed to be Officer Thomas Ricker.

Cecil had never met him but heard he had a wife and a toddler at home.

Raising his binos, Cecil zoomed in on the high-rise building, where the naked body still dangled from a rope around the ankles. His gut tightened at the sight.

He knew what he would find if he zoomed in closer, but he did so anyway because he wanted to see what the monsters out there were capable of. Sure enough, he could see the signs of torture along Ricker's body. They had done a number on him. He had suffered.

"Fucking *bastards*," Cecil whispered.

He was no stranger to torture and had seen plenty of it during the war. Soldiers captured by the Tritons were often subjected to terrible abuse in dark interrogation rooms where they were forced to give up intel. The enemy was so good at it, and so brutal, that Cecil's own commanders had issued cyanide pills to all the troopers in Hell Squad, in case they were captured.

Cecil had seen a lot in war, but he never expected to see it back home.

"We're headed back to HQ," Tank said from the open door.

Cecil looked one last time, then climbed back into the van. They drove to the hangar, where officers were gathering. A range of emotions was on full display. Some of the men appeared defeated, shoulders slumped. Others threw down their armor or kicked their lockers.

Tensions were high, with anger and a few tears.

They had lost many of their brothers tonight.

"We got to go in and cut that enforcer down!" someone yelled.

Captain Harkin moved in front of the group, and they all gathered around.

"We'll get him back, but I won't risk another life until we know who's responsible," he said. "That enforcer is dead—just a body now. We honor him, and everyone else we lost tonight, by taking out Cipher Crew."

"When? Why not right now?" asked a hulking officer they called Big Dan.

"When we have a plan." Harkin looked at each of the men in turn, including Cecil and Tank.

Again, Cecil felt the burn of guilt, that this was on him. It had been his plan.

"We're going to hunt down every single scumbag responsible," Harkin said. "You have my word on that. But right now all we can do is grieve for our brothers. The time to avenge them will come soon enough, and we'll be ready."

He glanced down, then back up.

"Go home; get some rest; be with your families," he said. "The time to fight will come soon enough."

The officers went back to whatever they were doing—patting each other on their shoulder pads, exchanging hushed words of condolence and comfort.

Harkin walked over to Cecil.

"I'm sorry, sir," he said. "I—fuck, I'm..."

"This wasn't your fault," Harkin replied. "I underestimated Nion. Tonight he declared war, and we're going to make him pay."

Cecil scratched the back of his short-cropped hair.

"Go home and get some rest," Harkin said. "I'm going to need you rested and ready for what comes next."

Cecil nodded and left the hangar, feeling the weight of events pulling him down. He stopped at his car to check his cell phone and send his wife a text message.

I'm off early, heading home. Want a late-night snack?

Before he could hit send, he felt a stab of nerve pain in his neck as he opened his car door.

"Son of a bitch," he said through clenched teeth. He sat in the driver's seat and opened the glove compartment. Reaching inside, he fished out an empty prescription bottle.

"Shit," he grunted.

Closing his eyes, he tensed in the seat, bracing as the tremors ran up his neck.

"Fuck, fuck, fuck, *fuck*!" Cecil shouted while pounding the steering wheel.

He took several deep breaths.

Go home to Michelle.

His wife would be there, watching one of her shows, oblivious to what was happening. But the last thing he wanted to do was talk about the disastrous raid, or answer questions when he came home from work early.

They had grown apart over the past two years, with her working the day shifts and him the night. Not to mention his substance-abuse issues. He wanted nothing more than to go and buy some more pills right now, to numb himself and escape this pain-ridden existence for a few hours.

"No," Cecil growled. *You're stronger than that.*

But the tug of his addiction was also strong.

He erased the unsent text to his wife and winced from another stabbing pain in his neck.

He stared through the windshield, conflicted. For the first time in a month, he had the chance to go home and spend time with Michelle at a reasonable hour. He should go there. He knew this, but he didn't want to.

He wanted to drive right to the no-go zone and hunt down the bastards who had set the ambush, killing Jerky and the other officers who were trying to make that shithole a better place.

After a few more deep breaths, the spinal episode passed. He started the car and drove away from the hangar. The roads took him back to the crime-free, perfect picket-fence neighborhoods, where he could forget about slums like Copper Terrace.

Cecil stopped at a red light and watched the skyline in a daze, still half in shock after the violence of the evening.

The light turned green, and the car behind him honked.

"Fuck off," he muttered.

A few minutes later, he pulled into his apartment complex, parked, and walked to the elevator. He stopped there, dreading going inside.

He still remembered a time when he wanted nothing more than to see her, feeling joy at the thought of her smile and soothing voice. It wasn't all that long ago. He wasn't sure what had gone wrong exactly, but he mostly blamed himself. His injuries had turned him bitter. He didn't feel like a man most of the time, especially on nights like this, when he couldn't do shit to help his buddies.

Riding up on the elevator, he thought of when he proposed to Michelle at a park in the city.

"I loved you the minute I saw you," he had said. "I want to spend the rest of my life with you."

She hadn't hesitated, replying with a kiss and an enthusiastic yes.

But they had hardly known each other back then. She could

now see that he wasn't always the charming, fun adrenaline junkie she had agreed to marry that day. He was moody and scarred from the war. And he feared that his moods were about to get a lot darker.

He tapped in the key code on their lock and opened the door.

"Michelle, I'm off early," he said.

No answer.

Cecil walked through the kitchen, into the living room, but the couch was empty, the TV screen dark. The blinds were already drawn on the windows.

She was probably asleep already—odd, since she was a night owl. Sometimes he got texts from her at two in the morning to check in with him.

Used to, he thought.

It had been months since he got one of those texts.

He walked quietly down the long hallway, past the electronic wall pictures displaying photos of their wedding, the honeymoon in Puerto Rico, and an image of Hell Squad.

He kept going to the first bedroom, which was an office. The door was ajar, and he looked inside to find it empty. The bathroom was also empty.

Cecil went to their bedroom door—closed—and listened, suddenly fearing that she wasn't alone.

He twisted the handle. Cold steel touched his neck.

"Cecil!" Michelle shouted.

He raised his hands. "What the hell, babe!"

She pulled the gun away and flicked on the light.

"What are you doing home?" she asked.

"I . . . Fuck, I was sent home. Shit went down tonight."

She lowered the gun and stepped back, wearing a sports bra and underwear. "I nearly blew your head off."

"Well, thanks for exercising some restraint. Pretty sure ITC wouldn't be able to fix it if you did."

She frowned and sat on the edge of the bed, looking up at him.

"What happened?" she asked.

He averted her gaze.

"You can talk to me, you know. Cecil, I'm here for you."

"I don't want to talk."

She reached out, but he shook her hand away. "We don't have to talk. I just want to know you're okay."

"I'm fine," he said, turning and leaving the room.

"Where are you going?" she asked.

Cecil went back to the front door as she followed him.

"Baby, don't leave," she said. "Please, don't—"

"I need some air." He slipped on his shoes and opened the door, not turning back, unable to bear looking her in the eye. For if he did, she would know where he was going: to find the pills that would numb his world out.

CHAPTER 9

Tyron stepped out of the secure elevator into the subterranean world of the Genesis lab, nestled two floors directly above Orion's chamber. Twenty years earlier, the AI had helped Tyron envision the bold project, which was still highly confidential. Only a handful of employees knew about it.

Orion spoke over an encrypted channel that only Tyron could hear through his earpiece.

"We have entered the labs."

The corridor Tyron entered was illuminated by soft, full-spectrum light that mimicked natural sunlight, casting a warm glow on the smooth gray walls. Transparent panels offered glimpses into adjacent research laboratories, where scientists in lab coats hovered over advanced gene sequencers and holographic displays of complex DNA structures. The hum of sophisticated equipment echoed outward, intertwined with the faint, earthy scent of burgeoning plant life—a hint of the wonders lying deeper within the facility.

Tyron made his way past the hydroponic chambers, where water misted over many species of plant life. The corridor opened into a vast atrium that housed towering cylindrical enclosures enclosed by thick glass. Inside each, hybrid plants thrived. Luminescent leaves, vast networks of roots suspended in nutrient-rich solutions, and blossoms of every conceivable color. Adjustable-spectrum lighting simulatec various climates, bathing the flora in different shades.

Five years ago, this place would have been run by a host of different AIs, overseen by Orion, but not now. Human programmers and botanists worked together to create new, better crops. Automated systems controlled temperature and humidity with precision, while robotic arms tenced to the plants. Sensors monitored growth with hyperspectral imaging.

Using these advanced systems, ITC had developed some of the hardiest seeds known, to grow crops at scale in the many ITC food-production towers in cities across the country, feeding millions of people every day.

“Please proceed through the RadGrow labs,” Orion said.

A door opened to a chamber housing Tyron’s most important botanical projects. These hydroponic chambers contained the modified Cordovia seeds growing in radioactive soil from the wastelands of Seoul.

“I’m very excited to see this all firsthand,” Orion remarked. “I read reports just this morning detailing how the seeds have already been planted at ITC field labs located in the Korean exclusion zones.”

“When will we know how well they work in these environments?” Tyron asked.

“Two, maybe three days. The germination is the fastest yet, some of the seeds sprouting in just over forty-eight hours.”

Tyron nodded, pleased. The goal of Operation RadGrow was to cleanse the radioactive soil. So far, the third batch inside the lab environment had provided positive results, but as Angelina had mentioned in yesterday's briefing, the field was an entirely different ball game.

Tyron stopped momentarily to admire the red tendrils of vegetation curling up out of the dark soil. A monitor on the glass showed the current level of radiation, along with a variety of other details about conditions inside the atrium.

"They aren't just surviving; they're flourishing!" Tyron said.

"Indeed, sir."

The branching red stems pulsated with an eerie glow, as if they were actively gobbling up the radioactive material.

Tyron continued to the next glass enclosure of orangish-red soil. A tiny stem grew out of the grit, supporting a flower head that looked like a sunflower but with red petals. The soil sample was from Mars, brought back two years ago on an unmanned ITC vessel. It had taken two years for ITC scientists and Orion to develop a seed that would grow in the mimicked alien environment of the Red Planet.

But it wasn't the seeds stored down here he had come to look at.

At the far end of the chamber, a heavy vault door sealed off the Genesis lab.

Tyron put his palm up to the bioscanner. Then he leaned down for the facial and eye scans. The door hissed open.

Columns rose up inside the vast chamber, each bearing thirty cryostatis pods. Pale human figures were suspended in fetal positions behind the glass lids. But these weren't humans like Tyron, born of a mother and father. These were clones, created in labs deep beneath the facility. And one more reason that ITC had enemies. Human cloning, while legal for certain narrowly defined scientific purposes, had made the company, and Tyron personally, the target of hatred from religious groups that thought he was playing God.

But in his view, the clones were necessary to save the human race. They were a significant part of his plan B. As with the plants he had genetically modified, his scientists, with Orion's help, had modified human and animal genes to help them survive in radioactive and toxic environments via epigenetic changes.

Tyron walked down an aisle of pillars, looking up at the animals contained in hundreds of other pods. These bunkers had become real-life arks, holding thousands of species and seeds genetically modified to be hardier and to adapt to virtually any environment.

So far, though, he had only preliminary data on how they would react, based on the few tests he had authorized. After some of that data had shown mutations in the clones, he paused the program until those results could be studied. That was five years ago, and he had never had the time to commit to understanding how external stimuli caused mutations, not to mention the ethical dilemma surrounding those mutations. Back then, Tyron had shifted his focus to Operation RadGrow, the Delta Cloud fusion reactors, and curing diseases.

But now he was rethinking all that. There had to be a safe, ethical way to continue the epigenetic changes in the clones. He just needed to find it with the AI's help.

"Orion, remember the day we first discussed this project?" he asked.

"Of course, sir."

* * * * *

Twenty Years Ago

Tyron Red smiled with excitement as he crossed the bridge to the suspended giant Faraday chamber that housed Orion. Today marked a special visit to see the AI, for today they were planning for the project that occupied Tyron's thoughts during most of his waking hours.

He tapped in his security code at the chamber's entrance, then bent down to look into the retina scan. He placed his hand against the panel, and the doors whispered open to Orion, standing with his hands behind his back, eyes pulsating light in his version of a smile.

"Master Tyron, I'm so glad to see you today," he said in his quiet, polite voice.

"Good to see you too." Tyron strode inside, glancing up at the screens that displayed live video feeds from conflict zones across the world. From the Middle East and Africa to South America, where the nation of Brazil had collapsed into anarchy, sending millions of displaced refugees fleeing to surrounding countries. Tyron had been watching it on the news the past few weeks: small children hauling their backpacks or carrying grocery bags with all their belongings. It didn't seem fair that some people had so much, and others had so little.

"Can't we help them?" Tyron asked. "Can't we do something?"

"What would you recommend?"

That was what Orion often did—reversing questions and putting them on Tyron. To test him, perhaps—he wasn't really sure.

"Well, the food-production facilities you helped design here in the States would be a start," he replied. "We could build them in Brazil, using our robots."

"That would require diplomacy, negotiations, and security to protect those centers, and on foreign soil it becomes very complicated, Master Tyron."

"ITC has an entire office of people who do just that, right?"

"Indeed. Now, to play devil's advocate, why should we help other countries when we have problems of our own?"

"If we have the ability to do so, why shouldn't we?"

"Conflicts are complicated, Master Tyron. As you already see, they can easily boil over into larger conflicts and, eventually, war." Orion glanced over at him. "Humans have a history of violence, but for the first time in your history, they now have the ability to destroy their entire species and render the planet uninhabitable. If I were programmed to feel fear, I might fear this, but I believe there are options to ensure the survival of humanity. That is why I am excited about the potential for your colonization project on Europa, which would allow humanity to expand into the solar system and, someday perhaps, beyond, which is what we're here to discuss, yes?"

"Right. Let's talk about the spaceship."

"Certainly, Master Tyron."

Every screen in the chamber went black, but the room quickly glowed to life from a holographic schematic that hovered in front of Tyron and Orion. They stood side by side, looking up at the detailed design of the spaceship, which rotated slowly to reveal its intricacies.

"I finished the design a few weeks ago but wanted to make sure it was ready for your approval," Orion said.

Awed, Tyron studied the sleek orange ship above.

"What would you like to see first?" Orion asked.

"I'd like to see how the engine works."

The holographic image of the ship rotated to the stern, stopping overhead.

"The most critical component of this spacecraft is the fusion drive, located inside the stern," Orion explained.

A cylindrical holographic image rose out of the ship, showing the interior in a faint blue glow.

"This drive uses controlled nuclear fusion to produce thrust—similar to the giant airships ITC has manufactured and provided to the United States military," Orion explained. "However, this

nuclear fusion is more controlled. By using hydrogen isotopes, we will be able to generate immense amounts of energy, propelling the ship forward at speeds far greater than any of these airships, which would literally come apart in the atmosphere."

"The hull of this spaceship is made of advanced alloy?"

"Correct. Let's have a look."

The engine vanished, and the image rotated, displaying the exterior.

"From bow to stern, the vessel is covered with plates of six-inch titanium and aluminum alloys, as well as composite materials such as carbon fiber combined with nanomaterials, including graphene and carbon nanotubes, and reinforced aerogels. All these important materials will help protect critical areas and shield passengers from the cosmic radiation as well as small projectiles they might encounter in space."

"Meteoroids?"

"Small ones, but at potential relative speeds of thousands of miles per hour, even something the size of a BB could cause major damage. But there are advanced sensors and tracking devices to make evasive maneuvers far in advance of any major threat."

A section of the holographic bow was cut away to reveal the inside of the cockpit, and the control panels with large black seats facing them. Tyron imagined himself sitting in one of those seats, looking out the windows as the shields lowered to reveal the sparkling glow of the stars. Orion went through how the navigation and other vital parts worked. Tyron listened, hanging on every word.

Now it was time to look inside. Sections of the hull came out, revealing living spaces for the crew, the cryostatis chambers for the passengers, the mess hall, the command center, and the engine room.

"The vessel holds a crew of twenty, and up to a hundred

passengers. If for some reason this vessel contained the last remnants of humanity, it could theoretically allow the human race to survive long term. But that would require genetic modifications to the passengers, since most research shows it would take a pool of five hundred humans to maintain genetic diversity. We must also consider that the colony would face many risks from the hostile and harsh climatic conditions, as you already know."

Tyron nodded. They had gone through this before. If this ship was to restart the human race, it would require more than science for the passengers to survive the trip to Europa, and to survive once they arrived.

"The vessel is equipped with heat shields for atmospheric entry, and retractable landing gear for touchdown on various terrains," Orion said. "Soon we can start to look at options for the colony."

"I have already started to look at different landing sites from the probe images you provided," Tyron said.

"Excellent. I look forward to your suggestions."

Orion again glanced over at Tyron.

"Shall we dive into the specifics and challenges of space travel?" the AI asked.

"Yes," Tyron replied eagerly.

"While technology has advanced to take your species into space, their genetic design has not prepared them for the conditions they will encounter. They will need significant support. It takes eons for a species to adapt to a new environment—if it can at all—and we don't have that much time. There is a way around this, however."

"Won't we have space suits and habitats to keep us alive?"

"Yes, but you will need more than that to give you a chance. Due to potential threats of space travel, the likelihood of something catastrophic happening on the journey, while establishing

the colony or after, is greater than fifty percent. Even something as small as a failed crop or an oxygen leak could doom them all."

"So, what do we do?"

"Have you heard of epigenetic changes?"

Tyron shook his head.

"Epigenetics refers to the study of how behaviors and environmental factors can cause changes in the way genes are expressed, without altering the underlying DNA sequence. These changes are epi-, or above, the genetic code and can influence gene activity, essentially turning genes on or off or dialing their activity up and down through methylation, histone modification, or noncoding RNA. In short, it's a way to manipulate cells and genes to make humans more adaptable to harsh environments. There is also a second way to modify and alter the genetic code in an individual's cells to correct genetic defects or enhance certain traits."

"So we can make superheroes?"

Orion laughed. "In a way. By doing this, we would make a human likelier to survive the harsh conditions of low-oxygen atmospheres, extreme temperatures, and radioactive or toxic environments."

"That's amazing. Why aren't we doing that now?"

"Ethical considerations, laws, and what some call 'playing God.' This is something you will need to consider if this project ever receives ITC funding. Of course, if it ever becomes more than a plan, you will need support from your father, the board, and shareholders. To truly run this company takes a veritable army of specialists and a lot of money. But these are things you will learn as you grow older, Master Tyron. Someday you will be in charge of the company. You may want to take it in a different direction."

"I'll take us to the stars."

"How about to Europa? The technology to journey to another system, let alone galaxy, does not—"

"You're right, Orion. I mean I'll—we'll—*take humanity to other planets."*

"And I will be honored to help you do that, Master Tyron."

"One thing, though, Orion."

"Yes?"

"Please stop calling me 'Master.' Right now I'm more of a padawan."

"Very well, sir, but you are far more than a padawan. And someday you will be the master of ITC."

* * * * *

"Dr. Red," Angelina said.

Her voice interrupted Tyron's reminiscing, pulling him back to the present, inside the Genesis lab's cryostatis chamber.

"Sir, sorry to disturb you, but I have an update for you on the security team you asked for," she said. "Whitt is waiting for you at the command center. I also have a new progress report about the Delta Cloud fusion reactors."

"Let's go," Tyron said.

He got into the elevator with Angelina and rode it to the top of the building. He expected her to ask what he was doing in the labs, but she said nothing.

At the top floor, they stepped out into the command center. The wall-to-wall monitors showed footage of their top-secret facility in the Arctic, with the massive disk-shaped reactors pointing toward the sky.

"The latest internal tests have yielded remarkable progress," Angelina said. "Our teams believe we are ready for a field test, and with severe weather brewing up in the Arctic, it's the perfect time."

"When?"

"In the next twenty-four hours."

"That's excellent," Tyron said. "I'd like to see this in person."

"Okay. I'll start making arrangements, but don't forget, the gala is two evenings from now."

"How could I forget?" Tyron deadpanned.

The gala was one of the most important events for ITC each year—the time when major shareholders, sponsors, and allies came together for a night of celebrating the company and looking to the future. He enjoyed speaking about the progress the company continued to make, but he hated rubbing elbows with the politicians who came to the event.

Angelina checked her tablet. "Looks like the field test could be done tomorrow evening, and we could be back the morning of the gala. Does that work?"

"Sounds good to me." He looked to Whitt, who came forward with his updates. The vice president for security brought up files from another set of the screens.

"Lieutenant Yosef has managed to track down several members of his former team, Hell Squad," Whitt explained. "They will be heading to our field labs in the exclusion zones, to assess current security and establish new protocols over the next forty-eight hours. These are experienced operators, and I'm confident they will find that our assets are secure."

Tyron stepped over to the monitors and looked at several individual files, pulling up one in particular, of a man nicknamed "the Bull."

"Good work, both of you," Tyron said. "Everything's going to plan. I might even have a surprise for our shareholders at the gala."

Tyron went back to his office, where he could consider everything in silence. As he stood there, he realized that there was one key element in his plan that must be reactivated for everything to come full circle.

"Orion," he said into a headset.

"Yes, Dr. Red," the AI replied.

Tyron hesitated briefly to consider yet again the ethical implications of testing on the clones, but decided there was no more time to wait. "Remove all restrictions and activate rapid testing on a small number of the specimens in Project Genesis."

"Very well, sir."

For the first time in his life, Tyron heard reluctance in the AI's voice. He felt it, too, but there was too much at risk to hold back any longer.

CHAPTER 10

Bruised and hungover, Santiago had expected to feel a lot worse than this when he got out of bed. But today marked a fresh start, even though it meant leaving his family for six months. His wife had left him a note that she had taken the kids to Balboa Park.

He was headed there now, with a bandage over his eye where the robot had split the skin. A single cloud drifted across the blue sky, and the sun shone over the metropolis. But it wasn't alone up there. A monstrous ITC airship hovered at thirty thousand feet. From its launch bay, two Wasps jettisoned, heading down from the ship to the company's facilities in the heart of the city.

Santiago looked away and kept walking, along streets alive with locals off work for the weekend and enjoying the balmy weather. The tourists were out and about, too, exploring the city.

He walked into Balboa Park, listening to adolescent laughter and excited voices from the sprawling children's park. Isabella and Diego chased each other around the slides. For a moment, Santiago remained in the shadows of a grove of trees, watching with joy from afar.

This was what he had fought for in Korea: so his kids could live in peace and grow up without fearing war and nuclear annihilation.

There was no denying that he wasn't the greatest father, but he loved them and his wife more than anything. That meant he would do anything for them, including scooping poop up for another trust fund man-child, if it came down to it. That said, he was happy to have this opportunity for respectable work, even if it meant returning to a place that had nearly killed him.

A twig snapped behind him, and he turned to his wife.

"So I take it you're going with Yosef?" Tina asked.

"I haven't decided. Wanted to talk to you first, but Yosef said it would be safe."

"Yeah, like I believe that," Tina said.

Santiago reached out, but she pulled away at first.

"I'm sorry about last night," he said. "I shouldn't have gone to the bar."

She pushed him back slightly, and snorted. "You promised—"

"I know. I'm sorry." He gently pulled her over and kissed her on the forehead.

She looked up into his eyes. "I forgive you, but, T, you could have been seriously hurt. You promised you were done with the boxing—and the drinking."

"I know, but when Marco fired me, I fucking . . ."

He breathed slowly in and out.

"I'm sorry," he said. "I let my pride get to me."

"I understand. That happens, but you have to remember the coping mechanisms to prevent you from spiraling."

"I will, I promise. It won't happen again."

He had said that before. Many times.

She sighed, then reached up to his eye.

"It's fine," he said.

"What do we tell the kids? You know I don't like lying to them."

"That I was training for my new job. As long as you're okay with me going?"

She sighed. "You're sure it will be safe? No combat?"

"For sure. Yosef said it's a cakewalk. And now you got rent money for when I'm gone. Once I'm back, we'll have another two hundred K, and hopefully, it will open doors to more gigs."

She gazed at him with uncertainty. "Two hundred thousand dollars isn't worth your life, and the meds alone cost—"

"We won't have to worry about the Cordovia treatments ever again."

"What do you mean?"

"ITC is throwing it in on the house." Santiago smiled. "Indefinitely."

Tina was really considering things now. He could tell by her raised brow and not-so-discreet nod. But it might take a bit more convincing to get her to agree.

"Hell Squad is going. I'll be back with almost everyone," Santiago said. "Cecil isn't—could never pass the health screening—but Alistair is, and Nodin too. David's in. He's got three more years until he's sitting on a beach drinking Singapore slings."

She looked down.

"You hear that, Tina? A beach," Santiago said. "Just think, if this gig turns into something bigger, we could buy a house here and retire, too, someday."

"It's not worth it if you don't come home."

"I will, baby."

She shook her head. "There has to be another way. We'll find one. We always do."

"This *is* the way."

Tina looked him right in the eye.

"Do you trust me?" Santiago asked.

"Yes, of course. But I don't trust ITC, and some things are

too good to be true. I don't believe this will be a safe mission." She sighed deeper than earlier. "All that said, I trust Yosef and the rest of your squad."

"So that's a yes?"

Tina stabbed him playfully in the chest with a finger. "You better come back to us."

"I will—"

"Dad!" Diego shouted.

The boy ran over to the little grove of trees, and Santiago stepped out with his arms out. As he bent down, Diego stopped.

"Dad, your eye," he said.

"What happened?" Isabella asked, trailing behind her brother.

"Training," Tina said. "Your dad has a new job, and he has to leave for a while."

"Leave?" Isabella's lip trembled. "I don't want Daddy to leave."

"Where are you going?" Diego asked.

Santiago glanced over to Tina, but this time she let him speak. "I'm headed to help look after some very important people," he said. "I'll be gone for three months, then home for a few weeks, then gone for another three."

"Three whole months!" Isabella cried. She whimpered and came over to him as he crouched to give them both a hug.

"I'll call you every chance I get," he said. "Time's going to fly, I promise. I'll be home before you know it."

Diego stared up defiantly. "Can't we come with you?" he asked.

"I wish, but it's not . . ." Santiago almost slipped up. "It's too far, and you have to have special credentials."

"Your father's a soldier," Tina said.

"So you're going to fight?" Isabella asked.

"No, no," Santiago replied. "I'm going to protect people."

"From who? Bad guys?"

"The bad guys are gone, so don't worry, okay?"

"Your father knows how to take care of himself," Tina added.

"Who wants to swing for a bit?" Santiago asked.

"Me!" Isabella shouted.

"Race you there," Diego said.

He took off, Isabella running to catch up. Santiago smiled as he followed them out to the swing sets. He got behind Isabella while Tina watched, giving him some time alone with his kids.

"Higher, Dad!" Isabella squealed as her swing arced higher and higher.

Diego climbed onto a swing and kicked his legs, determined to go just as high.

Above them in the sky floated the airship, a reminder that Santiago would soon be leaving his family. He looked away, focusing on his kids.

"You're going to be good for your mom while I'm gone, right?" he asked.

"Yes," Isabella said.

"Yup," Diego replied.

He pushed off the swing, landing in the sand. "Think you can catch me, old man?"

"I know it," Santiago said.

"Let's see," Isabella said.

He slowed her down and then helped her off the swing.

"To Mom," Diego said.

"On three," Isabella said. "One, two, three!"

Diego took off and Santiago ran beside him, away from the playground on the hundred yards over to Tina. On the last stretch, he pulled slightly ahead, beating his boy by a nose. He had never been one to let his kids win—that didn't teach them anything useful.

"Not an old man quite yet," Santiago said.

Diego frowned.

"You'll beat me someday, don't worry." Santiago slapped his son on the back and took Isabella by the hand as she caught up with them. As a family, they headed back home, stopping for lunch and some ice cream.

They loaded into his truck a few hours later. It was fifteen years old and needed work that he couldn't afford. But when he got back, he was going to have it fixed up.

Another hour passed before they arrived at the private concourses of the airport. He parked in the visitor lot, and they all piled out to say goodbye. A jet roared into the sky, probably carrying some wealthy people to an exotic destination.

Santiago tried not to think about his own destination as he caught sight of a giant ITC airship hovering just within the clouds, no doubt his ride back to Korea.

"That's it?" Tina asked when she followed his gaze.

"Yeah," Santiago replied.

Isabella and Diego both stared up at the sky.

"Wow, that's your ship, Daddy?" Isabella asked.

Santiago nodded.

"That's really cool, Dad," Diego said.

After grabbing his rucksack from the bed of the truck, Santiago handed the keys to Tina. She in turn held out a sealed letter from her handbag.

"Don't open this until you get over there," she said.

"What is it?"

"Just wait until you get over there, okay?"

"Will do, *amor*."

"Please, please be careful. Make sure you're not getting exposed to anything toxic."

"I won't, and I know the drill, Tina. Don't worry."

Santiago kissed her and hugged her tight. Then he gave her the keys and took the letter.

"I don't want you to go, Daddy," Isabella said.

"I know, but time will fly." He scooped her up and hugged her tight. "I love you, sweetie. I'll be home before you know it."

He placed her down and stood in front of his son, putting a hand down on his shoulder.

"You're going to be the man of the house while I'm gone," he said. "Take care of your mom and your sister, and do your homework, no complaints. Understood?"

Diego nodded.

"I love you all and will call as soon as I can," Santiago said.

He smiled his best smile, then picked up his ruck and shrugged it over his shoulders. A white ITC pickup waited for him beyond a gate that opened after he showed his credentials. They drove over to a Wasp waiting to shuttle him up to the beetle-shaped airship. Moments later, it lifted off toward the launch bay of the massive airborne craft. The hatches opened, and the Wasp flew inside.

A sign on the bulkhead read "*Persephone*, commissioned in 2029. US Army. Model #43."

Apparently, ITC had reacquired it from the army.

Standing in the launch bay were three men in olive-green ITC flight suits.

Santiago hopped out of the Wasp with a grin as he saw Yosef, David, and Nodin.

"Damn, you look like you got your ass beat, Sarge," Nodin said.

"You ever get in a fistfight with a three-armed robot?" said Santiago.

"Didn't stand a chance against the Bull," David said, grinning. He walked over.

"Good to see you, brother," Santiago said, embracing him.

Nodin pounded him on the shoulder. "Long time, brother," he said.

Lieutenant Yosef nodded and gestured into the ship. "We'll

pick up Alistair in Korea later tonight. He took a different transport," Yosef said. "For now, let's go over the current security data we have on the field labs."

Santiago followed them into a corridor with viewports overlooking the city. He spotted his truck far below, his family still standing outside, waving up at them.

He waved back even though he knew they couldn't see him. The ship rose skyward, humming beneath his boots, but he stayed at the window. The sight of his family tugged on his heartstrings as he realized that this could be the last time he ever saw them. He had felt the same thing when he left before the war, and he promised then that he wouldn't leave them ever again.

But they needed the money, and he wasn't going to war. This mission would be safe and straightforward. The only missing ingredient was Cecil.

* * * * *

The recurring nightmare always sent Cecil back to the place he had almost died in the first year of the war in Korea. In the dream, he crawled through the mud with a broken rib, his breath coming in ragged gasps. A cold rain beat down relentlessly on him from a blue-black sky.

He crouched with his tactical shotgun, scanning the wasteland. The technologically advanced city of clean streets, self-driving cars, and proud, industrious people was now just a labyrinth of bombed-out buildings and crumbling ruins. Each shadow and corner had become a potential ambush spot or deadly trap. His armor and the fatigues underneath were wet and caked in grime, clinging to him like a second skin. The ground beneath his boots had become a treacherous mix of debris and slick muck, making every movement a painstaking effort. Somewhere in the distance, he heard the ominous hum of the enemy machines, their metal exoskeletons grinding and clicking as they patrolled the devastated streets.

The Tritons were relentless hunters, clambering on their three razor-edged legs with deadly speed and efficiency. And these machines were even more advanced—upgraded models. Their mounted Miniguns and flamethrowers made them formidable adversaries, capable of shredding anything in their path or incinerating it in a heartbeat—as they had done to his entire squad. They had been on a recon mission to get intel on these new models when they walked into a trap, where they were torched with jets of flame.

Their phantom screams echoed in his mind as he pressed himself against the remnant of a collapsed wall. But then he heard something real—the unmistakable whir of servos and the rhythmic clatter of steel feet drawing closer.

The hunters had found him—two of them, from the sound of it.

A red laser dot danced on the debris near his face—the prelude to a hail of bullets. He ducked instinctively, feeling the ground shake as the machine opened fire, spraying the area with a lethal barrage. Chunks of concrete and dirt flew into the air. Cecil scrambled to his feet, desperate to put distance between himself and the mechanical death squad.

He darted into a narrow alley, clutching the shotgun to his chest. It was worthless against this foe, especially now that he was out of EMP grenades, which might have given him a shot at disabling the two robots long enough to destroy them.

A heavy rain continued to pour, washing away the blood and grime but doing little to mask the noise of his pursuers. The alleyway was a maze of debris, forcing Cecil to navigate through piles of rubble and shattered glass. Behind him, a flamethrower opened up, firing a long jet of fire over the obstacles in the machines' path. The heat singed his back, and the acrid smell of burning flesh filled the air.

He spotted a gap in the wall ahead and dove through it, landing hard on the other side in a puddle of water that doused the flames on his dorsal armor. For a moment, there was silence, broken only by the steady drumming of the rain. Cecil knew he had only seconds before they would be on him again, but the intense pain from the burns made it excruciating just to move. Grunting, he pushed himself up, in an immense wave of agony, as a machine clattered toward him.

Gunfire boomed in the distance, along with the crack of a high-powered rifle. He scrambled through the puddle as more gunshots echoed, this time right behind him.

He turned to see a man in an exoskeleton firing on a Triton that had been incapacitated by an EMP grenade. Cecil raised his shotgun and fired as the killer android unleashed a wave of flames. Screaming curses, he blasted it again and again.

The trooper finished it off with a round through the visor, then came over and squatted down beside Cecil. On his chest armor was a logo of a half-open gate with flames behind it, and *Hell Squad* in a banner arcing over the gate.

"Private Cecil Pepper, Raven Squad," he gasped. "They're coming... they've upgraded..."

"Easy, we've got you."

A loud humming came from the sky. They both glanced up at a Wasp lowering toward them. Beams raked over the ground, streaming through the building's missing roof.

"Still got two more hostiles incoming," huffed a large trooper.

"Get ready to move!" shouted the sergeant leaning down to Cecil.

"Wait. Stop," Cecil mumbled.

"You're safe now."

The hatch in the aircraft opened, and a crew chief leaned down with a harness.

"No, wait!" Cecil screamed.

He felt his body being shaken.

"Cecil, Cecil, wake up!"

The voice called out again, but this wasn't one of the Special Forces soldiers. The scene faded to black, and he awoke from the nightmare. The soothing voice of his wife, Michelle, called out to him.

"It's okay, Cecil," she said. "You're safe."

He felt her hand on his arm.

The memory of his first meeting with Santiago and Hell Squad returned as he relaxed by degrees.

"Another nightmare?" Michelle asked.

Cecil sat up, sending a wave of pain up his spine and into his skull. He winced as it intensified. Then came the memory of last night—of Jerky and the ambush at Copper Terrace.

His heart hurt at the horrible images as he felt about for the VitalStim remote control on his bedside table. "Damn it," he growled when his fingers knocked it to the floor.

Michelle got up, turned on the light, and picked up the remote for him. He turned over. Holding the remote down to his back, she then pushed the button that stimulated the electrical nodes embedded in his spine. Another game-changing medical advancement from ITC that kept people like him alive. But what he really wanted were some pills to numb his entire body. Those were the only things that could take away the pain.

The pain weakened, but it was still there. He focused on his breathing, as Michelle had taught him. "Long, slow breaths," she said.

Part of him *wanted* to feel the pain. He deserved it, and a lot more, for what had happened at Copper Terrace. And for his squad down in Korea, before Hell Squad saved his bacon. No one knew what had happened before then—no one but Cecil.

"Good. Keep breathing," Michelle said. "You're almost through this."

He clenched his jaw, his body tense and muscles flexing hard. Finally, the tremors passed, and he lay there trying not to shit himself.

"Is it over?" she asked.

He nodded, then winced as he tried to sit up. These flashback episodes were wearing her down, too, and she was clearly still angry at him for walking out on her last night. If she knew he had gone to get pills, she would be even angrier.

She was a forgiving person, but he had pushed her to the edge.

"Thanks," he said.

"I love you."

"I love you too."

She walked around the bed but instead of getting in, she opened the closet. After pulling out her work uniform, she turned off the light. He glanced at the clock. It was four thirty.

"Not going back to sleep?" he asked.

"No point. I need to get up for work in an hour, and I'm wide awake."

"I'll get up too."

"No, you need your rest. Especially after that episode."

He hated hearing stuff like that. Even though he knew she didn't mean to be patronizing, it still made him feel… broken.

"Go back to sleep," she said.

"I'll go back once you leave. It's not often we get a morning together."

"Suit yourself, but I'm fine."

"You get ready," he said. "I'll make coffee." It was the least he could do to apologize, which he fully planned to do in a few minutes.

She left the room, and Cecil swung his legs out of the bed. He saw the Hell Squad tattoo on his chest. Sometimes, like now, he had good memories of his old pals on the team. They wouldn't recognize the man he was today.

He got up and went to the kitchen.

"Coffee, four shots of espresso," he said.

The machine clicked on and was soon dispensing a brown stream of strong brew into his mug. He went to the fridge to get the milk and poured a bit into the mug once the espresso finished. Then he divided it into two cups and headed into the bathroom. He set one mug by the sink while she showered.

He walked out into the living room and looked through the blinds over the dark horizon.

Ten stories below them, two women were jogging down the sidewalk, and a man walked his dog.

Cecil took a sip of coffee, watching the sunrise. A flashback to Korea surfaced in his mind: the nuclear missiles rising into the sky while he was bleeding out on the battlefield.

"Thanks for the coffee," Michelle said.

He turned as she walked into the room, buttoning up her white ITC lab coat. She was an engineer for the company, working in food automation and production—stuff that Cecil barely understood. There was no denying she was far smarter than he. And a better person.

She sat at the kitchen table and turned on the morning news.

"Wait," Cecil said. He moved over and smiled ruefully. "I'm sorry I walked out last night. You didn't deserve that."

"You're right."

"I'm sorry." He leaned down to her when her eyes went to the television screen.

Cecil glanced back to see a male reporter in a bulletproof vest, standing by a police barrier at the no-go zone.

"I'll turn it off," Michelle said.

"No, it's okay." Cecil sat next to her and turned up the volume.

"Authorities are saying six officers were killed last night in an attempted raid on Copper Terrace, where crime syndicates ambushed them," said the reporter. "We have eyewitness video that shows a helicopter lowering with SWAT officers when they were hit by machine-gun fire. Warning: Viewer discretion is advised."

A shaky video came onto the screen, showing exactly what Cecil had seen the night before. And once again guilt set in. It had been *his* plan.

The jittering video evened out, centering on a partially blurred body hanging from the side of the building.

Michelle brought her hand to her mouth as he clenched his teeth in anger.

"Bastards shouldn't be showing this," Cecil said, trying to breathe out his anger. "Jerky was there. They killed him."

"Jerky? Oh no." Her cool hand touched his cheek. "Oh, Cecil, I'm so sorry. I know you really liked the kid—him."

She was right. Jerky was just a kid.

"Do you know who did it?" Michelle asked after a pause.

"Got a really good idea," Cecil said. He pictured Nion, the green-haired freak with his yellow fake snake contact lenses.

The anger seething inside Cecil intensified beyond anything his breathing technique could dissipate. He resisted the urge to storm off and go on a binge to numb the feeling. But he knew that someday Michelle would stop waiting for him. That she wouldn't be there to take him back or help him through the next bout of spinal pain. She had stood by him through his substance-abuse issues, but he was pushing her away. The darkness was winning, and he feared he couldn't keep it at bay much longer.

CHAPTER II

Distant sirens woke Tyron up on the couch in his office. He looked at his watch—not quite five in the morning. Having gone to bed at midnight, he was still exhausted. The news had brought back memories of the war and of losing his father. He resisted the urge to get up and work, which usually helped distract him. But he needed sleep. Closing his eyes, he drifted off into a memory.

Seventeen Years Ago

On his eighteenth birthday, Tyron awoke at nine to a quiet house. His father was long gone, having left for work at his normal time of six, and his mother was either sleeping off a hangover or working on the next one in her wing of their house.

Tyron had grown to hate this massive, dark, quiet place where he felt like a prisoner. But he was leaving for college in a few months, and after that, he planned on seeing the world.

He put on a pair of jeans and a hooded sweatshirt. It was time to go visit someone—or something—who actually cared.

Orion.

Tyron went to the vast garage where his father kept a collection of old and modern cars. Whitt waited inside, arms folded across his chest.

"Why aren't you with my father?" Tyron asked.

"Because I'm following orders. And today those orders are to make sure you don't do anything dangerous on your birthday." Whitt smiled. "Happy birthday, Tyron."

"Thanks, Jay." Tyron smiled back, but it felt odd. He wasn't used to smiling.

Whitt went to open the back door of the limousine, but Tyron grabbed the front passenger door. "Thanks, but I feel like opening my own doors."

"Very well, sir." Whitt got in and looked over as Tyron slid in. "Where to?"

"HQ."

"On your birthday?"

Tyron shrugged.

"Very well," Whitt said.

The drive from the estate took them from the exclusive gated community patrolled by armed guards into abandoned middle-class areas, where weathered for-sale signs protruded from dead lawns overgrown with weeds. It got worse as they approached downtown—people loitering on the sidewalks, living in tents, pushing grocery carts.

The world was on the brink of the greatest economic disaster of the twenty-first century. The AI bubble had burst, and people were out of work, hungry, and easily provoked. Riots had broken out in every major city, and small communities became ghost towns as people fled to the cities to look for work that didn't exist.

But there was hope on the horizon: new construction in a massive infrastructure initiative across the United States. The nationwide project was solving two problems: hiring people to work with the robots, and providing low-income housing.

A few blocks ahead, the ITC headquarters building towered over the neighboring high-rises. Protestors yelled and shouted as the big, shiny car passed. They carried signs that read "ITC is evil!" and "Robots will destroy us all!"

Whitt honked at a group who ran out in the street. They were warded off by a team of ITC security officers deployed to disperse the crowds. With the final two blocks now clear of protestors, they drove through gates that opened to a utopian kingdom within a city on fire. Whitt took the underground ramp and parked near a secure entrance.

"Thanks for the lift," Tyron said.

"You can't get rid of me quite that easily," Whitt said.

Tyron frowned, annoyed to have his friend shadowing him. They entered the facility and took an elevator down to the very bottom floor. The corridor outside was as far as Whitt could go. The door at the end of the hall opened to the bridge in the vast, dark chamber housing Orion.

But to Tyron's surprise, standing on that bridge was his father, wearing a frown.

"Dad?" Tyron said as the door closed behind him.

Booker glanced at Tyron, his frown fading but his eyes unable to hide whatever had him concerned.

"Tyron, happy birthday," he said with a forced smile.

"Thanks. I thought I'd spend some time with Orion. Would you like to join us? See what we've been working on for the past four years?"

Booker hesitated, glanced at his watch, then nodded. "Sure. I have a bit of time."

They crossed the footbridge, and Orion emerged in front of them.

"Oh, Tyron, sir, what a surprise," said the AI. "Warmest birthday greetings to you, my friend."

Something in what Orion said seemed to irritate Booker, but he said nothing.

"Thank you," Tyron said. "I'm excited, and I thought we could show my dad the schematics for our work."

"Certainly," Orion replied. "Please stand by."

The room came alive with blueprints of the spaceship Genesis 1. *Tyron started right in explaining how the fusion engines worked, and every engineering detail from how the craft would reach Europa to how the robots on board would help construct the colony there.*

"The trials and threats the colonists will face there will be great," Tyron said. "To give the mission the best chance of success, the ship will carry fifty genetically modified human clones to help support the crew in their objective of establishing the colony once they've arrived on this frozen world."

Tyron glanced over at his father for a reaction, but Booker's expression was impassive. That wasn't unusual. He was virtually without affect when it came to business, always keeping his cards close to his chest.

"With all the problems in the world, I think this mission could help save humanity," Tyron said. "We will eventually need to leave our planet."

"Interesting idea, and well thought out," Booker said.

Tyron started to smile, but stopped when his father then shook his head.

"Unfortunately, we don't have any funds for this sort of risky mission right now, and the board would never authorize it," Booker said. "Our focus—the focus of ITC, rather—is to solve problems here on Earth, and with another war brewing in Korea, all nondiscretionary funds are tied up."

He looked at Tyron and frowned ruefully. "I'm sorry, son, but maybe in the future, after you've received your degree from MIT and come to work for the company."

Tyron felt the anger rising in him. His father had always planned for him to come and work for ITC, without showing any interest in what Tyron wanted to do with his life.

"What if I don't want to work for ITC?" he asked.

The idea seemed to shock Booker, disrupting his poker face.

"You've always been interested in robotics and AI," Booker replied. "ITC is the leader in the industry. Hell, we are *the industry, and you can help carry on the legacy. But you will have to earn that right, to prove you have what it takes."*

"I have what it takes, but maybe that's not what I want."

Booker stared at him. "I can't force you into anything, but I sure hope you see the amazing opportunity you have to shape our world. Perhaps in the future you'll be able to launch Genesis 1*, but for now, we must focus on the problems our species is facing, and there are many."*

He exhaled, obviously stressed. As bad as the city was getting, and with ITC taking so much blame for the world's ills, it wasn't hard to see why.

Tyron looked up at the schematics of Genesis 1*.*

"You're impulsive, just as I was at your age," Booker said. "I worked hard for everything ITC has become, and it didn't happen overnight." He gave his son a meaningful look.

His father was right—Tyron didn't like waiting on things.

"I understand," he said. "Sorry to interrupt whatever you're doing."

Beeping came from unseen speakers, and Orion said, "Dr. Red, you have an important call waiting for you from the secretary of defense."

Tyron's father sighed—another uncharacteristic action.

"Don't be sorry, son," Booker said. He put a hand on his shoulder. "We've made mistakes, but we're fixing them and making things better. Right now civilization is on a precipice. We have the opportunity to create the closest thing to a utopian society, or lose everything and revert back to the Stone Age. With your help, we can ensure a bright future for humanity right here on Earth."

He smiled, and this time it was real.

"Happy birthday, Tyron. Let me know how you want to celebrate later," he said.

Booker left the chamber, but Tyron lingered.

"I'm sorry that you're disappointed, but Genesis will be here waiting when the time is right," Crion said.

Tyron nodded. He would go to college, see the world, and prove he had what it took to carry on the ITC legacy and to change it for the better.

* * * * *

Tyron stirred awake, recalling what happened after that dream—memory. He had gone to MIT and earned his degree, but then the war had broken out in Korea, just as his father had feared. Tyron quickly forgot about Project Genesis.

On a visit home, Tyron had stood with his father in this very office, watching the news as Iran joined forces with the North Koreans, forming the Triton Legion and invading the South while threatening the entire world with their robotic armies and new AI, CrioX.

A month later, he was here, standing at the glass windows with his father while thousands of service droids were marched out of the factories into the backs of US Army trucks, to be shipped off to bases and repurposed into legions of the first-generation war machine—the Defector.

At twenty-two years old, Tyron had volunteered to join the war effort, heading to Korea to help with the programming and deployment of Defector units, despite his father's wishes.

"It's too dangerous, Tyron," Booker had said.

"Please be careful, Master Tyron," Orion had said.

Tyron had spent three years in Korea before a missile targeting a machine-charging area had taken his foot and very nearly his eyesight.

Putting on his blue glasses, Tyron went to the window to watch the sun set over Atlanta. The city had changed since his father last saw it.

Guilt ate at Tyron as he thought of their last conversation ever. He regretted not being able to say goodbye and wished his father could have seen everything he had accomplished on his own.

Not alone. With Dan and Orion.

Dan had given his life, and the AI Orion had become more than a guide and teacher. He had become a confidant. From when Tyron was a boy to this very day, they had grown closer. But he had never forgotten what his father said. Orion wasn't a man and never would be. And although Tyron always referred to him using the personal pronouns, he never forgot that the AI was a machine. A tool.

Tyron went to his desk, turned on his data log, then went to the bathroom to wash his face before sitting down to check the most recent updates from Operation RadGrow, the Delta Cloud fusion reactors, and Project Genesis.

When he returned to his desk, he noticed a warning message on the Project Genesis screen: *Mutation detected.*

Tyron put on his headset. "Orion, I just saw the warning."

"Yes, sir, I can explain."

"I'd like to see it in person. I'll meet you back at the Genesis labs."

Tyron took the elevator down to Orion's sublevel of the facility by elevator. Then through the RadGrow labs to the Genesis lab. The vault opened inside the dimly lit cryostatis chamber, his breath fogging in the chilly air. Rows of transparent pods lined the columns across the vast space, each pod containing a human figure floating in a state of suspended animation. The soft hum of the life-support systems filled the room, accompanied by the rhythmic pulsing of blue indicator lights.

Again Tyron considered the ethical implications of more tests, complicated by the finding of more mutations. Many hated him for the use of clones at ITC. They would be furious if they knew what he had decided to do. But he had never let others influence him. He always deferred to the science—and if there was a safe way to continue these tests with Orion's help, he was going to keep working.

The future of space travel depended on the success of these clones. And if the Triton Legion was still out there, then the future of humanity could very well depend on them too.

"Activate display," Tyron commanded.

A holographic interface materialized before him on one of the test subjects, displaying vital statistics and genetic data for the clone. Orion's calm, synthesized voice resonated throughout the room. "All systems functioning within normal parameters."

"Then these anomalies detected are results of the accelerated growth protocols combined with environmental factors introduced during the cloning process. These are similar to the problems we had during our last tests, right?"

"Correct."

Tyron thought back to those tests. "I thought you had accounted for all those variables. These clones are supposed to be our safeguard, a way to preserve humanity. They aren't some agricultural product. We must never forget—these are *people*. We can't afford any unexpected mutations."

"Although the genetic sequences were replicated accurately, epigenetic changes can occur due to a variety of external stimuli, which have now been reintroduced. These changes do not alter the DNA sequence but affect gene expression, potentially leading to unforeseen traits."

Tyron knew all this. But he had thought they could better control the results now with the new technology that didn't exist when he paused the program five years ago.

He glanced at one of the nearby pods. The figure inside looked peaceful, unaware of the potential turmoil within its own bodily cells. "What kind of traits are we talking about?"

Orion activated a holographic detailed genetic map and highlighted several areas in red. "Some clones exposed to radiation during these new tests have exhibited increased keratin production that will eventually lead to thicker skin. This could provide enhanced protection against environmental hazards."

Tyron rubbed the stubble on his jaw. "That might not be a bad thing, given the conditions they'll face."

"Agreed; however, there are other changes. A subset of clones shows alterations in the PAX6 gene, which influences eye development."

Tyron stopped rubbing his chin. "Alterations how?"

"Preliminary data indicate they could develop better eyesight under low-level light or even complete darkness, which was also part of the testing parameters."

Tyron had helped create those parameters, but he hadn't expected the tests to work so quickly. The tests had emitted low-level radiation, which could have interacted with the clones' developing ocular systems.

"What other changes are there?" Tyron asked.

"Some clones have heightened metabolic rates, increasing their physical capabilities but also their nutritional requirements.

Others show enhanced neural connectivity, which could result in superior cognitive functioning or, on the downside, neurological instability."

Tyron was starting to feel nervous. "That is certainly an unpredictable mutation, and it risks creating more problems than we're solving."

"Indeed, sir, but corrective measures are possible. We can adjust the epigenetic factors through targeted therapies while the clones remain in stasis."

"How long will that take?"

"About three months."

Tyron shook his head. "We don't have that kind of time. I want to launch *Genesis 1* with clones aboard the ship before then."

Orion's interface displayed a new set of data. "There is an alternative," he said. "We could select only the clones without significant mutations for the launch."

"And what about the rest?" Tyron asked.

"They would remain in stasis until we can address the epigenetic issues."

Tyron turned to face the holographic representation of Orion. "Is there any risk that these mutations could be beneficial in the long run?"

"Potentially," Orion acknowledged. "Enhanced physical resilience and sensory perception could improve their chances of survival in harsh environments. That is exactly the purpose of these clones, is it not?"

"But at what cost? The objective here is to create humans who can survive hostile terrain and help colonize the solar system, not to create monsters." He paced in front of the clones. "I fear how these changes will affect their psychology, their ability to integrate with unaltered humans, who will also be a part of these future missions."

"That is an unknown. Further analysis is required."

Tyron halted to look up at a female clone's face through the frosted glass, wondering again what was going on at the cellular level of her body.

"Prepare a report on all clones exhibiting mutations," he ordered. "I want to review each case individually. Maybe we can find a way to use these changes to our advantage without compromising their humanity."

"May I offer a perspective?"

"Go ahead."

"Evolution is a response to environmental challenges. These epigenetic changes could represent a natural adaptation process accelerated by our interventions."

Tyron considered this. "You're suggesting that instead of fighting these changes, we should embrace them?"

"It is a possibility worth exploring for some of these specimens," Orion replied. "By guiding the development rather than trying to suppress it, we may enhance the clones' ability to survive and thrive."

Tyron nodded. "We proceed with caution. Monitor their psychological and physiological parameters closely. The last thing we need is to create something we can't control."

"Agreed. I will initiate enhanced monitoring protocols immediately."

Tyron took a last look at the clone in the pod. "Perhaps this is the next step in human evolution—a way to adapt to the new world we've created."

"Only time will tell," Orion replied.

"Keep me updated."

"Will do, sir."

Tyron approached one of the pods containing a clone with the enhanced eyes. The face behind the glass was serene, oblivious to its creator's concerns.

"What are you meant to become?" he whispered. "Will you be a new kind of being altogether?"

Turning away, Tyron felt a contradicting mixture of apprehension and hope. The lights in the chamber dimmed, leaving the clones in their quiet, cold slumber—a silent army awaiting its purpose, teetering on the edge between humanity and something beyond.

Tyron left the room wishing he had more confidence that he was doing the right thing. For the first time in years, he wished he could speak to his father, to ask his advice on a path forward.

PART 3:
RETURN TO HELL

CHAPTER 12

Twelve hours after leaving New York, the airship was closing in on the Korean Peninsula. Santiago had slept off the rest of his hangover and had even gotten a workout in with his buddies. Being back in the gym with them brought back old times.

"You should have seen him charging Triple-Dee," Yosef said with a laugh.

"That's why they call him the Bull," Nodin said.

Santiago laughed. It was damn good to be back with Hell Squad. Alistair was here now too, and was even bigger, but not from muscle. He had added a layer of fat to his hard body.

The only one missing from their own squad was Cecil.

"So you talked to Pepper?" Santiago asked Yosef.

Yosef nodded. "He's working in Charlotte for the Crime Task Force. Doing surveillance."

"So our little mate is all grown up," Alistair said.

"He should be with us," Nodin said.

"I agree, but ITC has strict physical screenings. Even for support staff."

"True. I almost didn't pass," Alistair said.

"That's 'cause you porked out over the last five years," Santiago said with a grin. "I put on a few pounds too. Civvy life will do that to you."

"Civvy life? Ha! You got a glorified dad bod," David said.

Santiago looked down, realizing he did fit the textbook definition with his extra padding around the middle, and his less-defined musculature. But it was the cancer inside him that had really changed his appearance—something none of his squad knew about besides Yosef. Nor ITC. He had joined the mission early and looked healthy at first glance, so they let him in without a health screening.

"So what have you been up to in San Diego?" Nodin asked.

Santiago gave a dry laugh when he thought of Marco. "Mollycoddling rich assholes and their dogs, if we're being honest. How about you?"

Nodin finished his set of dumbbell curls. "Running the fishing business with my brother. Been a rough season this year with the El Niño weather. If we get another one like it, we'll be out of business."

"Damn, that bad?"

"Yup, the salmon runs are a fraction of their former glory. Even the bears are suffering."

"Maybe ITC can fix that and clone some," David said.

Santiago looked at the oldest member of the team. "And how about you, Grandpa? Enjoying semiretired life?"

David laughed. "I've got grandchild number two on the way. Can you believe that? That's what happens when you have kids at eighteen, I guess."

He wiped the sweat off his wrinkled brow. His graying hairline had receded in the five years since Santiago saw him last.

"Been living in Florida, teaching history part-time at a community college, and dreaming of retiring and spending time with the kids and their kids," he said. "Now I can. After this gig's up, I'll finally have the money. Just six more months, baby."

"Good for you," Nodin said.

Yosef set the two dumbbells down, and Santiago said, "Can you tell us what you've been doing, LT, or is it classified?"

"Some of it. Most of my work was contracting in Israel for Mossad," he said. "Then spent a year in Syria."

"You've been busy," Santiago said. He could only imagine the carnage that Yosef had seen in those battle zones. From all-out war in Korea to the world of shadowy forces and terrorism in the Middle East.

"XO on deck," David announced, springing to his feet.

The men came to attention as their new commander walked into the gym. Like them, Commander Paul Zimmerman, a first lieutenant and air force veteran of the Korean war, had been hired by ITC. But unlike Santiago and his comrades, Zimmerman had sat in a command center rendered all but useless during the electronic warfare that so disrupted the battlefield.

"We're an hour from setting down, and things are about to get bumpy," Zimmerman said. "Get cleaned up; then meet in the launch bay for your first briefing."

"Yes, sir," Santiago said.

They hurried out of the gym and back to the barracks to get showered off and dressed. When they arrived at the launch bay, a single Wasp sat idle on the deck in the middle of the chamber.

Lightning from a distant storm flashed outside the port windows. The ship rattled.

"As you can see, we're heading above the storms over Seoul," Zimmerman explained. "Then sending you down in a Wasp to start surveying the field labs where you'll be operating over the next few months."

He turned to the glass smart screen. Tapping it, he brought

up a map of the JMF exclusion zone, still housing over a hundred thousand troops. Most of these had sat idle for the past few months, having no enemy to fight and no civilians left to rescue.

"You'll be operating beyond the DMZ, in the exclusion zones, where your objective is to keep the field-lab teams safe," Zimmerman continued. "This is top secret, and no one except for allied top brass is aware of their presence. Our objective is to keep it that way and to make sure they finish their work safely."

"What work is that?" Nodin asked.

"The nature of their work revolves around horticultural projects."

"Now, there's a mouthful! That some sort of American vegetable or some shit?" Alistair asked.

David chuckled, but the room went quiet when Zimmerman didn't crack a smile.

"Their work really isn't your concern," he said. "Your concern is protecting them. Understood?"

"Yeah, we get it, Commander, but it's helpful to know what these lab brainiacs are doing in the middle of a radioactive hot zone," Santiago said.

"Playing God," Nodin whispered. "Trying to bring back what can't be healed."

Santiago looked over at his friend, who shook his head and whispered a prayer in the Spokane tongue of Npoqíniščn.

"Any more questions, or can I finish?" Zimmerman asked.

"Yes," Yosef said, answering firmly what was obviously a rhetorical question.

Zimmerman tapped the screen again, bringing up marked positions around Seoul.

"These are the most radioactive sectors in all the exclusion zones, and that's where the field teams are working," he said. "Most of the time, this ship will be your base of operations, ready to deploy to any of these positions in an emergency. Currently, there are Def-8 units on the ground to help protect the teams from threats."

Santiago had assumed that all the Def-8 units were removed after the war ended—destroyed by the accord that doomed all autonomous thinking machines. He thought ITC had realized its past mistakes.

"These units were granted an exemption by international authorities," Zimmerman said. "They saw the value in our field labs and knew it would be difficult to keep them safe long term with human forces susceptible to the radiation and toxins."

That made sense, but it was also a reminder of what Santiago and his squad would soon be facing in the exclusion zones.

"Your objective is to secure those field labs and the scientists working there," Zimmerman said. "You'll be carrying sensitive equipment, including seismographs to detect any type of underground threats. Yosef's already been trained and will explain how everything works. Understood?"

"Wait a bloody second," Alistair said. "Did you say 'underground threats'? What does that mean, exactly?"

"What it sounds like."

"What it sounds like is that there's something you aren't telling us," Nodin said.

Santiago had the same suspicion but kept it to himself. Yosef would tell them what they needed to know, when the time was right. Nodin, however, seemed to want more now. He grunted—his way of showing his anger.

"I know you all have combat experience, but I hope you understand this is a highly irradiated environment, and those storms can whip up winds over a hundred and fifty miles an hour," Zimmerman warned.

He looked out the viewports just as lightning speared outside.

"I've been where you're going, and the storms are unpredictable and frequent," he continued. "Your suits and armor will provide protection, but you won't want to be caught outside during one of those storms. The labs, on the other hand, were all designed to withstand the extreme weather events."

Zimmerman turned back to them. "You're not facing the Tritons down there, but the storms can be just as dangerous, so you will follow my orders. Is that clear?"

"Yes, sir," Yosef said.

The other men all nodded and repeated together, "Yes, sir."

"Good, then get suited up. We roll out in fifteen mikes."

The men went to the armory, where their individual lockers were secured by keypads. Their names were already on stickers. Santiago found his, tapped in the code they had given him, and opened it to find a padded black suit.

"Bloody fancy!" Alistair said.

Santiago pulled his out. The hazard suit had a built-in tap screen in the right sleeve. Boots and special socks were there, plus a helmet with an advanced HUD. An armored chest rig and knee, shin, and elbow guards were also provided. He reached into his pocket and pulled the note from his wife, which he had yet to open and read. Then he slipped it into a tactical pouch on the vest.

A Klaxon began to blare, rising and falling as red emergency lights clicked on.

The hulls groaned under the external pressure of the storm.

"All hands, prepare for turbulence," said a loud automated voice.

They finished suiting up and returned to the front of the armory, where Zimmerman had opened the weapons lockers. Inside were TRX-F assault rifles, the newest military hardware with an advanced targeting system and infrared scope.

"Holy shit, those are beauts!" Alistair said in an almost reverential tone.

Santiago pulled one out, feeling the light frame of carbon nanotubes, which was virtually indestructible. He shouldered the rifle and peered down the barrel encased in a heat-resistant alloy and machined with cooling vents to allow sustained fire.

The adjustable stock enabled both close-quarters and long-range stability. Finally, he flipped the scope up and peered into the digital holographic sight that provided real-time targeting data, including distance, wind speed, and enemy movement. Tiny levers allowed it to switch modes between thermal, night vision, and x-ray.

"Damn, bub," he said. "I would've killed for one of these during our combat days."

"Why do we need these just to babysit some scientists?" David asked.

Everyone looked to Zimmerman.

"To make easy pickings of any raiders who might enter the site," Zimmerman said.

"Raiders?" David asked. "They come this far into the exclusion zones?"

"For treasure, they'll go anywhere."

Again Santiago felt his gut tighten, his instincts telling him they weren't being told the full truth about their mission.

"Grab some ammo and let's move," Zimmerman said.

Santiago grabbed three high-capacity magazines and stuffed them into his ballistic vest. Then he smacked a fourth into his weapon.

They returned to the launch bay, where two pilots sat in the cockpit of the Wasp, doing preflight checks. Lightning lit up the sprawling space with a blue glow as they walked over to the hatch to board. They racked in, preparing for more turbulence.

Zimmerman tapped a button, and the hatch shut.

"Okay, all clear," he said.

The Wasp whirred to life. Santiago looked out the cockpit as the landing pad it was on rotated so the front faced the launch-bay doors. A green light flashed, and the doors whisked open, revealing the towering storms that Santiago had seen only on television.

Lightning forked in multiple directions, rickracking across the dark skies that blotted out the sun over Seoul.

"Here we go," announced one of the pilots.

The side rotors on the dual tilt-rotor craft fired up as the landing pad telescoped outward and extended them out of the bay. The Wasp rose away from the airship and into the clouds. Santiago glimpsed the immense vessel behind them before it vanished in the storms.

As they descended toward the target landing zone, the Wasp rattled violently. Santiago had been through plenty of rough rides in his time, starting with a helicopter that went down in the jungle when he was fighting the cartel a decade ago. But he had never seen a storm of this size and ferocity in his life.

The pilots did their best to keep the aircraft steady as they swooped down over Seoul. Santiago watched his HUD, but the electrical disturbances were messing with everything. It fizzled in and out.

A nudge from the side drew his gaze to where Nodin pointed out the windshield.

"I'm a long way off the rez now," Nodin said.

"I guess this is where the hazard pay comes into play, eh?" Alistair asked.

"You ain't seen nothing yet," said Zimmerman.

They all had seen plenty of devastation during the war and had spent three months running rescue missions in the aftermath. But they had never gotten this close to ground zero.

Santiago held his breath as he took in the vast wasteland of downtown Seoul—nothing but black and gray and death in all directions. The ground blast had been just the beginning of the nightmare. The particles released into the atmosphere had created the storms that continued to rage five years later.

A perpetual haze of dust swirled under the bulging clouds that reminded them all of the evil unleashed that day. Lightning illuminated the debris, capturing broken silhouettes of buildings twenty-five miles from the crater. Jagged shards like broken teeth studded the black terrain.

The Wasp beelined over the structures, toward the LZ.

Now, when lightning bloomed over the ruined city, there was nothing. No jagged structures or collapsed buildings. No broken bridges or clogged roadways.

There was nothing at all out here.

It took a few more moments for Santiago's brain to process what his eyes were seeing. The dark landscape was ground zero. The crater stretched as far as he could see. Not even the lightning could penetrate to the bottom.

Santiago glanced over at Yosef, who looked back at him but said nothing. What the lieutenant had pitched as an easy babysitting mission was looking worse by the second.

Nodin lowered his head to whisper another prayer, asking the earth mother to forgive humans for what they had done here.

Santiago said his own silent prayer but was interrupted as the Wasp jerked in severe turbulence from the raging storm.

"Can't land here, Commander," said one of the pilots to Zimmerman. He looked out a windshield being hammered by relentless rain that made it almost impossible to see.

A crooked trident of lightning forked down right in front of them, thunder booming a moment later and rattling the hull.

"Whoa, easy there," Nodin said.

"Welcome to hell, baby," Alistair said with a snort.

David chuckled nervously. "Maybe I should have retired early," he said.

"Anyone got tequila?" Santiago asked. "I could use a stiff drink."

* * * * *

Meet at the hangar, ASAP. New raid being planned.

Cecil had been stewing in his apartment, fighting the darkness of intrusive thoughts, when the text came in that afternoon from Captain Harkin. That darkness faded away as he threw on his uniform and grabbed his pistol. By the time he got into his car, he was feeling alive again, ready to make the gangs pay for what they did to Jerky and Bravo team last night.

Cecil sped down the highway in his pickup. He weaved in and out of traffic, cars honking as he passed them at high speed. On the horizon, the Charlotte skyline reached toward the cloudy sky. An ITC Wasp tilt-rotor crossed over the buildings, lowering over the largest structure in the city—an ITC flagship office.

Every major city had one.

He got off at the exit and raced down to the airfield, where the Crime Task Force was gathering again. When he got out, he rushed over.

An officer opened a side door in the hangar, and Cecil slipped into the space. Thirty people were already gathered, from officers to support staff like Tank and the other surveillance teams. Cecil walked over to them and looked at the screens displaying video footage from last night. Adjacent to the screens were bulletin boards set up with pictures of leaders from both the Cipher gang and the White Buffalo crew.

"Intel points at Nion as organizing the hit on Enforcer Ricker,"

Harkin explained. "We now know that Wild Bill and his White Buffaloes sold submachine guns to Cipher Crew a month ago, and we believe it was Cipher who carried out the attack on Alpha team."

He turned away from the screen and looked out over the packed room.

"We have unconfirmed data that Nion is still in Copper Terrace," Harkin said. "I'm authorizing deployment of drones to confirm this. If it's accurate, we're sending everything we have inside, and I promise you, Nion won't be coming out to stand trial."

Grunts and nods all around.

"Be ready to move at any time," Harkin said.

He waved Tank and Cecil over to a row of monitors, where a secondary intel team was working its own drones in the NGZ.

"We already have eyes in the sky," said Harkin, "but Nion's too smart to show his face right now. He's inside, hiding like a rat. Cecil, I want you and Tank to get your smallest drone bots inside the building to see if you can locate him or any of his crew."

"You got it, sir," Tank said.

Cecil nodded and sat down at the crates of advanced equipment. Inside were drones as tiny as mosquitoes. He activated each of them while Tank ran diagnostics on their systems. Behind them came the same ritualistic prep for combat: loading weapons and double-checking gear.

An hour later, the door swung open and a dark-skinned man in a white uniform strode inside the hangar, taking off his hat to reveal a scarred face.

It was Chief Ed Krycek.

"Stop what you're doing. Now!" The sixty-year-old police chief's deep voice filled the hangar.

Harkin stepped up. "Sir, what—"

"I know we all lost someone last night, but we are standing down," said Krycek. "There will be no more raids at this time."

Angry voices answered, some of them with curses. Cecil had a few of his own but kept them to himself. Part of his lack of response was from shock. The chief was a legend, known for climbing out of the trenches as a beat cop when he was just twenty. He had helped steer the city through some turbulent, dark times.

But somewhere along the line, he had forgotten his duty to the people. Now he was catering to the politicians.

"The mayor wants to avoid more bloodshed," Krycek said. "All enforcers will be pulled from the NGZs, and no operations will be permitted, including drones and robotic deployments."

"We're just going to let Cipher Crew get away with this?" someone shouted.

Cecil looked over and saw that it was a member of Bravo team.

A second round of furious shouts echoed through the room. Another officer behind Cecil said in a voice just shy of a shout, "Fuck the mayor!"

"Silence, goddamn it!" Krycek shouted.

Harkin raised a hand. "You heard the chief. Shut your mouths and let him talk!"

The voices calmed, but the tension remained high among the officers, especially Bravo team, who had just seen their brothers murdered.

Krycek moved in front of the seething crowd.

"The mayor doesn't want an escalation of the violence to spill over to other areas of the city," he explained. "He wants the NGZ sealed off tight. If Cipher Crew leaves, we have permission to engage. But right now no more officers will be entering the zone."

Cecil looked at the image of Nion on the bulletin board. The bastard must be laughing about getting away with murder as he hid inside his kingdom. It was no different from what the Tritons had done in Korea—attacking, then going underground.

"I say we cut off ITC food shipments. Starve the bastards," said another Bravo officer.

"So we can create a bigger bloodbath?" Krycek asked. "You're too young to remember the economic darkness, but when I was a much younger man, I spent a month out on the streets, day and night, trying to keep this city from imploding when you were still sucking on your ma-ma's tit."

He turned, putting the scarred side of his face in the light.

"I saw what happens when people go hungry, what parents will do for their kids," he said. "Those are the people I swore an oath to protect. That we all did."

"Chief's right," Harkin said in agreement. "We can't go backward."

"Look, I don't like this any more than any of you," Krycek said in a reasonable voice, "but the mayor calls the shots, and for now we stand down, seal the border off, and bury our brothers. The time to avenge them will come. You have my word."

He swept the crowd with his gaze, then put his hat back on before turning and leaving the room. The doors clicked shut on silence.

"You heard the chief," Harkin said after a long pause. "Our mission shifts to containment. We start now, so let's move our asses and seal off the NGZs."

Cecil looked down at the robotic insect he held in his hand, resisting the urge to crush it.

CHAPTER 13

The Wasp lowered over the northern edge of the crater, some two thousand feet deep in the center. It was hard to fathom the energy that had caused the deep scar in the earth, produced by the most advanced nuclear warhead ever designed—thousands of times more powerful than the one detonated over Nagasaki nearly a century earlier.

Lightning flashed, forking down into the abyss. In the fleeting glow, Santiago spotted the bottom of the crater, and he thought he saw something there. A red light, but that couldn't be. Nothing could survive in the epicenter of the blast.

"Prepare for insertion!" shouted one of the pilots.

The aircraft swooped down a thousand feet from the edge of the crater, whipping up a curtain of dust. Santiago was first out of the Wasp. On his HUD, he saw the radiation spike into red levels. He made it two steps before hearing a crunch under his boots. He knew that noise. A glance down confirmed it. He had stepped on bones, turned to powder under his weight.

A vortex of human dust whipped away from the rotors as the Wasp lifted off over the graveyard of fragile skeletons.

These people had been the lucky ones, killed instantly from the blast.

It wasn't just human remains. There were also machines amid the debris—first- and second-generation Defector units, their titanium frames now black from the inferno that blew through five years ago. There were Triton machines, too, their edge-sharpened treble legs sticking up out of the dirt like shark fins.

A light rain fell as Hell Squad fanned out in staggered combat intervals. Alistair carried two cases of equipment that included the seismic sensors. Santiago scanned the terrain with his infrared scope, expecting to see the labs somewhere ahead. But Zimmerman kept trekking toward the crater's edge, cradling his TRX-F rifle. Sure enough, he stopped on a ridgeline overlooking the colossal crater.

"We're headed down *there*?" David asked.

"You got to be shitting me," Alistair said.

"We'll hoof it down," Zimmerman said. "Should be no problem for Hell Squad, right?"

"Right," Yosef said.

Nodin raised a pair of binos to his helmet, scanning.

"There," he said, handing them to Yosef.

Santiago raised his rifle, zooming in on the only thing out there: a collection of cubes, domes, and cylinders of various sizes that must be the habitats and labs for the science teams. To the naked eye, they were barely visible from this vantage point, but through his scope, the structures glinted faintly from artificial lights installed to pierce the crater's perpetual twilight. He checked the distance, noting that they were more than a half mile from their location.

"Nodin, take point. Find us a safe way down," Yosef said.

"On it, LT," Nodin said.

The descent to the science base at the bottom was

treacherous, the steep walls of the crater a mixture of fractured rock and loose scree. The air was thick with a lingering haze, though their protective suits shielded them from the worst of it.

Nodin guided them through a chaotic mix of jagged rock formations, exposed like buried bones when the blast sheared off the top layers of the ground. Concrete and sand and metal had been fused together in the radioactive soil like fossils from a bygone era.

Santiago couldn't help but marvel at the resilience and ingenuity required to establish a field operation in such a hostile environment.

Halfway down, Nodin stopped abruptly and raised a fist. He pointed at a red glow coming from a hole in the crater's slope—the same glow that Santiago had seen from the sky. He dialed his rifle scope in on a cluster of glowing, pulsating tendrils dangling out of the earthen tunnel.

"What the hell are they really doing down here, Sarge?" Nodin asked.

"Growing red carrots, maybe?" Alistair asked.

"Growing something," Santiago said. "Any idea what?"

He looked at Zimmerman, who turned away. Nodin moved ahead and continued to lead them down the steep slope, navigating the chunks of concrete and rubble.

As they neared the bottom, a crunching sound caught Santiago's ear. A bulky figure suddenly strode around a slab of concrete ahead of them, raising an energy weapon at Nodin.

Santiago centered his rifle on the armored chest of the shadowy figure just as an orange light flashed on, illuminating the frame of a Def-8 unit.

"Whoa, whoa! Stand down; we're friendlies!" Santiago shouted.

The visor flashed once, then twice, scanning them.

“We’re Hell Squad. Stand down,” Yosef said firmly.

The machine lowered its weapon, then promptly turned. “Please proceed to Field Lab Alpha,” it said in a monotone.

“Relax, fellas,” Zimmerman said as he passed them by. “You’ve all seen a machine before, right?”

“Not for five years,” David muttered.

Nodin still had his rifle up as Santiago walked down to him. Normally, he wasn’t the type to get spooked, but even though they had expected the machines to be here, it was still crazy seeing one in operation.

The eighth-generation unit guided them down to the bottom of the slope. Then it set off across the irradiated soil, toward the labs.

Santiago watched his Geiger counter tick solidly in the red zone, but the scientists appeared well prepared. He expected nothing less from ITC. The structures ahead were an amazing example of engineering, designed to sustain life in one of the most hostile environments on the planet. Modular habitats, cylindrical and reinforced, were clustered together, connected by flexible tunnels that allowed for safe passage between them. Large geodesic domes housed the primary laboratories, their transparent panels revealing glimpses of the sophisticated equipment inside.

Hell Squad reached the border of the base, demarcated by a few thin wands protruding from the dirt. Before the deployment, Santiago had read the briefing and knew about the motion detectors, connected to hidden sentry guns. A red light on a metal rod in the dirt blinked green as the Def-8 unit strode up and deactivated the perimeter.

“Proceed,” said the machine.

“Welcome to Field Lab Alpha,” Zimmerman said.

“A.k.a. hell,” Alistair said.

“Were you expecting a five-star hotel?” Yosef asked.

"I'd settle for a roach-infested flophouse over this place."

"Yeah, makes two of us, mate," David said.

Nodin grunted, and Santiago gave a snort—his expression of agreement with his brothers that this wasn't in the terms and conditions when he signed up. Then again, ITC had sidestepped normal protocol, bypassing even a full physical and mental test for Santiago. But that didn't excuse the lack of transparency ITC had shown them so far, and Santiago was not warming to Zimmerman at all.

The commander took point now that they were inside the base, heading for two silo-shaped metal structures that contained hydroponic farms. Glass windows glowed with a soft green light from inside—a stark contrast to the barren surroundings, providing a sliver of normality for the inhabitants.

The Def-8 unit escorted them to the largest habitat: a two-story brick building with shuttered windows on the first level. On the second floor, a man peered down at them before vanishing from view.

Zimmerman stepped up to the hatch and pushed an external comm.

"Commander Zimmerman accompanying Hell Squad, reporting for service," he said.

The door buzzed and slid open to a decon chamber. Behind a second door, a scientist looked in on them as they moved into the large chamber. The outer door closed behind them. Showers hosed them down with chemicals. Next came a scan from a robotic arm that extended from the ceiling.

"All clear," said an automated robotic voice.

The door opened, and the scientist stepped forward. He was forty-five, maybe fifty, with brown hair graying around the sides. A gray beard hung from his thin face.

"I'm Dr. Joseph Voss," he said. "This way. I'll show you to our site coordinator."

Voss took them into a long corridor of many doors, all of them closed. Santiago found himself wondering what lay on the other side. They stopped at the end of the passage, and Voss tapped in a key code, opening a door to a stairwell. At the top, they entered a long room that served as half office, half command center. Overhead white lights illuminated the furnishings, which included two large desks, a round table with ten chairs, and a wall of monitors. On the far side, a viewport provided a sprawling view of the base. Standing near the window was a scientist of perhaps sixty years, in front of a wall of monitors.

Voss cleared his throat. "Sir, Hell Squad has arrived with Commander Zimmerman."

The older scientist turned toward them and smiled. "Ah, welcome," he said. "My name's Dr. Hystad, the coordinator of this site."

"I'm Commander Zimmerman, and this is Lieutenant Yosef, head of the team. We're anxious to get started on analyzing your security and seeing where it can be improved," said Zimmerman.

"Excellent. I'll give you full access to our current systems and protocols, but I must say, I'm not sure why ITC sent you."

He walked closer, looking at all the men, including their weapons, before facing Zimmerman.

"The other sites have had issues with raiders," Hystad said, looking out the viewport. "As you can see, we're not just any site. We're in the heart of ground zero, which would make venturing here to scavenge buried riches not only stupid but downright suicidal. Our main threats are the storms, which we're fully prepared to weather, if you will. So what, exactly, is Command worried about?"

Zimmerman nodded at Alistair, who brought over the two cases containing the seismic sensors.

"We have orders to beef up security throughout the area," Zimmerman explained as he opened one of the cases. "These orders come from the top."

"From Dr. Red?"

Zimmerman nodded.

"For what purpose, exactly?" Hystad asked. "I'd like to know what threats you're here to mitigate."

"I'm afraid that's classified."

"Classified? If there are risks to our work here, I need to know." His voice grew firm, carrying a hint of frustration. "I am the coordinator of this entire site. It's my responsibility."

Zimmerman nodded. "I understand, Doctor. Rest assured there's nothing to worry about. You focus on your work, and we'll make sure it continues to go smoothly."

"I promise you, sir, Hell Squad is the best of the best," Yosef said.

Voss gave him a dubious look, and Hystad glared at Zimmerman as if he were prepared to push things further. After a few seconds, the scientist backed down.

"Fine, you're free to get started on your security 'beefing' project," he said. "However, I ask that you keep away from actual field-testing sites in the crater. Any tampering with the flora there could skew the results."

"Understood," Zimmerman said. "We'll get to work right away."

"Good. Dr. Voss will show you to your quarters for your stay here. Commander, would you stay behind a moment?"

"Sure," Zimmerman said. He nodded at Yosef, who led Hell Squad from the offices back down to the hallway of many doors. Voss opened one to a habitat with bunk beds.

"This is it," he said. As he turned to leave, he added, "A friendly word of advice: Stay away from the work, and also away from us."

"Same goes for you, bub," Santiago said.

"Funny guy, huh?" Voss asked. "You think we're playing tiddlywinks out here?"

He walked over and looked at Santiago for a long moment.

"It's been a long journey for us, Doctor," Yosef said.

"Better get some rest, then," Voss said. He gave Santiago one last glare, then left the room in a hurry.

"There you go, Bull, winning hearts and minds," Nodin said, grinning.

"Guy's a prick with ears," Santiago said.

"I couldn't care less about him," David said. "I want to know why no one told me I'd be deployed to the middle of a goddamn nuclear bomb crater!"

"A crater where ITC is growing mutated carrots," Alistair said.

Santiago looked to Yosef. "LT, you ever gonna tell us what we're really doing here? 'Cause I'm starting to feel a cool breeze blowing up my freckled ass."

"You know what I know," Yosef said.

Nodin stood next to Santiago, arms folded over his chest, clearly not buying it.

"Okay, Hell Squad." Zimmerman stood in the doorway. "Gear up. We start work now."

* * * * *

Cold rain drummed down onto the cemetery as the black armored sedan pulled up. Tyron sat in the back, thinking of the worst day of his life: the day he learned that his father was dead.

That life-upending moment had thrown Tyron into the limelight. He recalled being confronted by the ITC board at the HQ in Atlanta. Every one of those members had looked at Tyron as if he were a child, someone who could never fill the shoes of his father. Someone they could manipulate for their own projects and purposes at ITC.

He had fired them all after their lies about Operation Dark

Skies came to light. Then he had proved them all wrong and turned the company around to reach heights that not even his father had been able to achieve.

For the first time in years, he wished his old man were around to talk to. He once heard that you don't become an adult until you lose your parents. That wasn't so true for Tyron, who never really had a mother and had spent most of his youth on his own. But now, after all these years at the helm of the company, he realized that his father had started preparing him to lead ITC when he was just a boy, by introducing him to Orion. Booker had realized that the AI could help do what he didn't have time to do: teach his son about the world.

Tyron finally understood now. And while they didn't see eye to eye on everything, especially the war, he knew that his father had wanted the best for humanity.

"I'll be back in a bit," Tyron said to Angelina.

"Want me to come with you, sir?" Whitt asked from the front seat.

"No, I'm fine."

Angelina offered him a reassuring nod.

He opened the car door and popped open his umbrella, then began the trek through the muddy cemetery. For the past week, he had been conflicted since learning about the seismic activity below Korea. He debated whether he should authorize the ninth generation of Defectors to the US military and UMF—the very thing he had criticized his father for doing.

He stopped in front of the stone marking his father's final resting place.

Booker Red

1980–2038

Pioneer of Autonomy

"Hi, Dad," Tyron said. He stood looking down at the grave, remembering the burial over five years ago now. Senator Vucci came, along with President Clayton, who had been a US senator at the time.

They had come over to offer their condolences, but Tyron knew they were actually sizing him up, seeing if he was ready to take over the company, figuring out whether he could be controlled.

Tyron had never played their game. He had gone a different direction, focusing on science. Little did any of them know at the time, the Cordovia samples he had brought back from the Amazon would lead to groundbreaking advances in medicine, and now at the field labs in Operation RadGrow.

He was so close to developing a variety of the little bromeliad that could not only survive in the poisoned soil but *improve* the soil. But now he had to worry whether the Triton Legion was still out there, moving and planning.

Tyron squatted down in front of the grave and put his hand on the stone.

"I love you, Dad," he said. "I'm sorry I never got to say goodbye, but I hope you're proud of everything we've accomplished."

After a few minutes of reminiscing about the good times, he realized how deeply he missed his father, and how much he regretted their falling-out.

"I'm sorry, Dad. I won't let you down," he said.

Tyron rose to his feet and went back to the car. As he slid in, Angelina greeted him with a smile but said nothing until they drove off. Whitt turned from the front seat. "Hell Squad is on the ground at Field Lab Alpha, sir."

"Good. I appreciate the rapid response," he replied.

Tyron felt some relief at the news. With the Delta Cloud fusion reactors going up ahead of schedule, and Operation

RadGrow working even better than he had hoped, his plans to restore the exclusion zones were coming along beautifully. Just in time for the gala.

He considered the next phase of his plan to save humankind. He had kept it hidden from everyone, even Angelina. Only Orion knew.

Perhaps it was time to share it with her.

On the way back to HQ, he leaned forward and said, "Whitt, change of plans. Drive us to Aeon 2," he said.

"Sir, your flight to the Arctic leaves in an hour," Whitt replied.

"It's our aircraft. I'm sure they won't take off without us. Make a call and have them rerouted to Aeon 2."

"But that runway is out of commission, sir."

"I've had it resurfaced."

Whitt hesitated, then pulled out his phone.

"Aeon 2," Angelina said. "I thought it was abandoned."

"It was."

She raised a brow. "What are you up to, sir?"

"You'll see shortly," Tyron said, cracking a sly smile.

Whitt drove away from the cemetery to a part of the town that was once used as a factory for the older-model Defector units. It was one of the first things that Tyron had disbanded when he became CEO, repurposing it into his own personal lab that only Orion had access to for the first few years.

Razor-wire fences surrounded the facility, which encompassed eight blocks of brick buildings and a large body of water that was once used to cool the reactors underground. Much of the facility looked old, but fresh construction was already underway as they drove up. Rising ten stories from the center of the sprawling complex was a brand-new building of translucent glass, with a commanding view of the entire area as well as the restored runway that was once used to ship out new machines from the factory.

No Trespassing signs were posted on the fences and the central gates leading to the main structure. A camera rotated toward their car, and Orion, who was always watching, opened the gates. They swung open to the front lot, which still displayed an old ITC Robotics and Automation sign.

Whitt drove to the underground parking ramp, and the garage door opened, then closed behind them. The headlights shone into the empty space.

Tyron got out of the car and walked over to the secure entrance to tap in his code.

Angelina followed him over hesitantly while Whitt did a scan of the area, clearly on alert.

"Don't worry," Tyron said.

The door buzzed and swung open, and he led them down a hallway to a second secure door. Tyron opened it to a balcony on the second floor of the machine factory. He had spent a lot of time here over the past few years repurposing it.

Lights flickered on across the warehouse that was once full of conveyor belts and 3D printers that churned out over two hundred Defector units a day during the war. In their place was the newest and greatest creation of his life.

The half-completed shell of a black spaceship sat on a support structure at the bottom of the room, surrounded by drones and service droids waiting to finish their work.

"I'm calling her *Genesis 1*," Tyron said.

"This is truly remarkable!" Angelina said, looking out over the railing. "I don't know what to say."

Even Whitt gave an impressed nod. "Well done, sir."

"Come on," Tyron said. He waved them down a stairwell to the lower level, where they walked over to the ship towering above them.

"For the past five years, I've planned how to bring the world back from the brink," Tyron said. "I've prepared for the worst with our bunkers, Operation RadGrow, and the Delta Cloud fusion reactors. Those are part of plan A. *Genesis 1* is part of plan B."

"It's magnificent," Angelina said.

"It wasn't easy, but I conducted this project in complete secret, using an account that I have full authority over. But to build a fleet of these ships, I will need the support of our board and our sponsors. *Genesis 1* is just the prototype that I plan to unveil at our gala."

He turned to her. "This is why I hired you."

"Sir, I'm not sure I understand."

"Your dissertation on extraterrestrial life."

Her eyes widened with excitement.

"I want you to lead the colonization program, Doctor." He turned on the holographic remote to bring up an image of domed habitats like those at Field Lab Alpha. But these weren't in a war zone. They weren't even on Earth.

"This is Hab 1," he explained. "A site on Europa that Orion has determined could be suitable for colonization. *Genesis 1* and ships like it will transport humans, cloned and otherwise, and modified flora to the planet to give colonization the best shot at success."

Angelina looked to Tyron. "The clones, the Cordovia seeds—it's all part of a bigger off-Earth plan?" she asked.

"Precisely," Tyron replied. "ITC will take humanity to other worlds."

She reached out suddenly, surprising both Whitt and Tyron as she hugged him.

"Thank you, sir," she said.

He patted her on the back. "Thank me when the ship reaches Europa."

She pulled back, blushing, then nodded.

"Do you want to take a look inside?" Tyron asked.

Angelina nodded eagerly, and he guided her inside the ship, where the cryostatis chambers were already installed in the aft section. "There will be room for fifty non-clone humans, including crew, and fifty clones," he said. "Currently, we are conducting a series of rigorous epigenetic assessments on fifty clones to examine how specific environmental variables influence their genetic expressions. The goal is to determine the robustness of induced epigenetic modifications under varied conditions."

This took Angelina by surprise. Her smile faded, and her brow crinkled with concern. "Sir, I thought those tests had been paused due to the risks involved—not to mention international law."

"They were, but Orion is ensuring that all necessary precautions are taken, and as for international laws, they aren't enforceable in space, Doctor."

That seemed to relax Angelina slightly, but she still seemed concerned.

"These tests are closely monitored under stringent safety protocols to ensure the well-being of every clone," Tyron said. "We've also incorporated multiple layers of safeguards that allow us to intervene immediately should any adverse effects arise. This research is not only safe but also essential for the project."

Angelina's smile came back, and she nodded. "Thank you for the explanation."

Tyron beckoned her forward. There was still much to see. He went to a command module inside and powered it up. "Orion, do you copy?" he asked.

The AI answered immediately. "Yes, sir, how may I be of assistance?"

Tyron gave a big smile. "Today is a day we've been waiting a long time for, Orion."

"Why is that, sir?"

"It's time to finish *Genesis 1*."

"Excellent to hear, sir. I can activate the facility on your orders."

Tyron and Angelina got off the ship and found Whitt waiting on the factory floor. "This way," Tyron said. He took the stairs back up to the observation balcony, where they had the ship in full view.

"Okay, Orion," he said with a smile. "Finish building our creation."

"With pleasure, sir," Orion replied.

In an instant, the room sparked to life. The air buzzed with the hum of machinery. The factory was once again coming to life with relentless efficiency and cutting-edge technology.

Autonomous drones zipped through the air, carrying components, their movements choreographed in a complex dance. Advanced robotic arms moved with fluid precision, welding, riveting, and assembling the spaceship's hull with pinpoint accuracy. The factory floor was a symphony of high-tech machinery, each playing its part in creating the vessel that would soon venture to the fourth largest of Jupiter's ninety-five moons, to establish humanity's first extraterrestrial colony.

At the heart of the factory, massive 3D printers built the spaceship's intricate components layer by layer. Tyron watched as a printer the size of a small house meticulously constructed the fuselage from advanced composite materials. Nearby, laser cutters and plasma torches carved out precise shapes from sheets of titanium, the sparks flying like fireworks. Automated guided vehicles, sleek and efficient, transported the parts to their designated stations, where robotic assemblers put them together with seamless integration.

The sheer scale and precision of the operation was astounding, even to Tyron.

He turned to Angelina. "So, how do you feel about taking on program lead?" he asked.

"I'd be honored, sir."

"Great! Then you can help me sell the idea of a fleet of these ships to everyone at the gala. We both know you're much better at that than I am."

"Sir, while this is all impressive, we have a flight to catch," Whitt said. "They're landing outside right now to take you to the Arctic."

Tyron nodded. He lingered another moment to watch the drones working on the ship. Only five years ago, they were being used to build killer machines.

Those days were over. It was time to enter a new era.

CHAPTER 14

Rifles from the police ceremonial guard cracked in unison into the slate-gray gloom that hung over downtown Charlotte. The thick clouds were unyielding, as if even the heavens were in mourning. The air was thick with the scent of damp grass mingled with the smell of gunpowder from the ceremonial volleys that had just pierced the silence of the city.

Cecil Pepper stood stiffly amid a sea of dark blue police uniforms on the terrace outside city hall. Before them stood a row of caskets, smothered in wreaths of flowers, which added some color to the dreary morning. The reverberations of those gunshots still echoed in his ears—a painful reminder of the comrades they had lost. Seven good officers, including the enforcer and his good friend Jerky.

The young man's casket was in the middle of the row, under a canopy. Cecil still couldn't quite bring himself to accept that Jerky, the guy who always had a stupid joke to lighten the mood, was now lying cold and lifeless in that gleaming wooden box, dead because of Cecil's plan to drop the strike teams onto the roof of Copper Terrace.

No, he's dead because of Nion and Wild Bill.

Cecil swallowed, trying to suppress the mental anguish—and his anger at not being able to avenge Jerky and their fallen brothers.

The bagpipes wailed a tribute from the stone steps of the building, their mournful notes slicing through the air.

Cecil's eyes lingered on the caskets, his jaw clenched tight, trying to keep it together. His hands shook by his side, not just from anger but from withdrawal. The past few days, he had resisted the urge to use any pain medicines, and his body was in rebellion.

He glanced over his shoulder to the crowd of friends and family, over five hundred strong, in the white chairs arrayed on the lawn. His wife was there, looking back at him. She had taken off work for the ceremony to support him and pay tribute to the fallen officers.

Chief Krycek stood and walked up the stone stairs of city hall to the podium erected there. The crowd shifted, all eyes turning toward the man who had fought through countless battles on the streets of this unforgiving city only to cave to the politicians.

Cecil listened, but the words washed over him like white noise—empty.

The chief was kowtowing to the wishes of a mayor too cowardly to fight back in the war that the gangs had declared on the city.

"These men were more than officers." Chief Krycek's voice cracked slightly as he addressed the assembly. "They were brothers, husbands, sons. They were the shield that stood between order and chaos, and they paid the ultimate price. We will remember their sacrifice, and we will honor them."

As Chief Krycek finished, Mayor Baum took his place. The mayor's tailored suit and practiced solemnity struck Cecil as wrong—an intrusion on something sacred. Baum was nothing more than an opportunist in a slick suit, with slick hair and a smile to match.

"We will not rest," the mayor declared, his voice ringing with a fervor that was meant to inspire but that left Cecil cold. "We will hunt down those responsible and see that justice is served. Our city's finest have fallen, but their legacy will fuel our resolve. We will avenge them."

Cecil barely suppressed a scoff. The mayor spoke of justice, but he had already seen to it that there would be none. Copper Terrace, where the officers had met their end, was off-limits, along with the entire no-go zone, protected by red tape and political maneuvering.

As the mayor's words died in the damp air, the crowd began to disperse for the burials. The procession of mourners drifted away in twos and threes, heading to the lengthy motorcade that would proceed to the cemetery.

Cecil and five other officers picked up Jerky's casket and carried it to the hearse waiting to transport him to his final resting place. He saw Michelle standing across the street, nodding her support to him.

The drive to the cemetery was completely silent—until the route took them within view of the distant no-go zone, where Copper Terrace loomed like a taunting face.

The next hour blurred by with more speeches and more tears. As most of the crowd dispersed, Cecil remained rooted to the spot and watched Jerky's casket being lowered into the ground. The irrevocability of it hit him like a gut punch. This wasn't the first time. He had lost brothers back in Korea, but fighting had always pulled him out of the darkness that followed, keeping his brain from dwelling there. Killing the enemy had given him a purpose: avenging his fallen brothers.

But now he was stuck in the painful mental loop of inaction.

Cecil had to do something, or he was going to give in to the pain that followed him like his shadow—something he could never escape.

When the last mourner had left, he walked over to Jerky's grave. He knelt on the wet grass, unable to find the right words.

"I'm sorry I let you down, brother," he whispered finally, his voice barely audible over the soft rustle of the wind through bare branches.

"Wasn't your fault," came a deep voice that was almost a growl.

A shadow fell across the grave, and he turned to look up at Captain Harkin. His broad frame blocked out most of the little light that filtered through the clouds.

"You want to make a real difference, Pepper?" Harkin asked. "Take out the trash of this city?"

Cecil searched the captain's steely blue eyes and found no deception there—only a fire to mirror the one Cecil felt burning in his own chest.

"Yeah, Captain, I sure do."

Harkin held his gaze, as if considering whether to trust him.

"Whatever you need, sir," Cecil said.

The captain stepped closer and lowered his voice. "There's work to be done, justice to be served," he said. "The real kind, not the hollow promise of a politician."

About damn time, Cecil wanted to say.

"I want you and Tank on around-the-clock surveillance of Copper Terrace using your drones," he said. "Find out where Nion is and where the weapons are that Wild Bill sold him."

"Sir, the chief said—"

"The chief is the one who gave these orders, Pepper." He fished a phone out of his pocket. "Soon as you locate them, call me. This time, I won't be asking for permission to flush out the sewage. If it costs me my career, so be it."

Cecil discreetly tucked the phone into his uniform pocket as the captain walked away.

The rain had started to fall again—gently at first, then heavier, washing over the dirt like tears. He looked back at Jerky's grave and felt a rising sense of hope that they were actually going to avenge him somehow.

For the first time in two days, Cecil didn't feel the overpowering urge to numb his senses. He was ready to do his part to bring justice back to his city. It was time to fight.

* * * * *

Nodin stood at the top of the crater, visible only by his IR tag. He threw up a drone that zipped into the sky.

David's voice fired over their team channel from the command habitat in the center of the field labs.

"Drone is up and running," he reported. "Zero interference right now."

"Copy that. Santiago and I are heading to install final sensors," Yosef said.

Carrying the supply crate from the airship, Santiago set off with Yosef to the northern side of the lab complex, past a long tent that rippled and popped in the wind. The scientists had been coming and going from the structure all day, and Santiago had stolen glimpses of their horticultural projects inside both contained laboratories.

It was clear now that Operation RadGrow was about experimenting with different seeds that might grow in the toxic environment. That seemed impossible based on the readings he continued to check on his HUD, but then, ITC was known for miracles.

The very Cordovia drugs in Santiago's system now were keeping his cancer at bay, shrinking it without the side effects of radiation or chemotherapy.

But if he stayed out here too long, he could get other cancers.

A glance at the high rad data made him uneasy despite having a state-of-the-art suit protecting him. Working in this environment was a huge risk. If any of them got a tear in their suit, it could quickly expose them to a lethal dose of radiation if gone unnoticed.

There were safety measures in place for that—from sensors to manual checks in the field and out of it—but the mere possibility kept him on edge. The darkness and the jagged, unstable rubble made getting a tear a very real possibility for anyone not paying attention.

But so far, aside from the elevated radiation levels and a woeful lack of intel, things had gone smoothly. Soon, once they were done analyzing and "beefing up security," as Zimmerman had put it, he would finally get a chance to talk to his family back in San Diego over an encrypted channel inside the habitats. He would also have a few minutes to read the note his wife had given him before he left.

"Hell Squad, all hands, sitrep on gear check," Santiago said over the comms.

The other men fired back one at a time.

Alistair, who was holding security on the perimeter of the field base, said, "All good, Sarge."

"No problems here," David said.

"Clear topside," Nodin reported from his position at the top of the crater.

"Systems operating properly," Yosef said.

After scanning his own systems, Santiago nodded.

"Okay, just one more of these and we can head back inside," Yosef said.

Santiago set the case down, opened it, and lifted out the final sensor. He staked it to the ground.

"Bringing security border online," David reported over the comms. "Perimeter is fully established."

"Okay, good work, Hell Squad," Yosef said. "Everyone, return to base for decon."

"Copy that," Nodin said.

"On my way," Alistair replied.

Santiago packed up the crate and set off back toward the habitat with Yosef. He was anxious to be out of the radioactive environment, but he wanted even more to talk to his family. Halfway there, a message from Nodin came over the channel.

"Guys, I got eyes on a situation at Lab 10," he said.

Santiago stopped as Yosef checked the drone footage. From above, they didn't see anything. On the ground, a mound of rubble blocked their view of that sector.

"Let's check it out," Santiago said.

He ran in that direction with Yosef, skirting around the debris for a look through his binos. Even without them, Santiago could see the source, a thousand yards away. The pulsating red was a striking contrast to the surrounding gray, lifeless terrain. He stopped at one of the enclosures. Each a hundred feet long and thirty feet wide, they were made of a thick black tarp that arched up maybe ten feet, forming a long, tubelike containment facility of some sort. At the front, a windowless door had opened, letting out the red glow.

A scientist stood outside, looking in at the pulsating light. Zooming in, Santiago saw clusters of red vegetation that appeared to be... *moving.*

A voice crackled over the comms—Dr. Hystad.

"Hell Squad, you're needed at Lab 10, ASAP, over."

"On our way," Yosef replied.

He and Santiago took off running across the field toward

the light. As they approached, another scientist stepped out of the tent, stumbling backward, away from a curling thick red rope covered in prickly needles.

But this was no rope; it was a ten-foot-long vine that snapped out of the front door to the enclosure. It coiled like a snake, ready to strike.

Santiago instinctively raised his rifle, ready to blast the mutant flora.

"Easy, T," Yosef said. He took a step forward. "Hey, what on earth is that?"

Both scientists turned. One of them was Voss.

"Nothing that concerns you," he said. "Stay back. This is a classified work area."

Footsteps crunched behind them, and Dr. Hystad ran over in a hazard suit.

"Doctor, you want to tell me what we're looking at here?" Yosef asked.

"Get back, both of you," Hystad said.

He moved up for a look at the vegetation that uncoiled and slowly slithered across the ground, as if testing the soil outside the long enclosure.

Santiago noticed that a number on his HUD had changed. A quick glance confirmed that the radiation readings in this area had gone down.

"Tell me exactly what happened, Voss," Hystad commanded.

"I took a sample for lab testing, and the entire cluster began to move," Voss replied. "This branch struck outward."

Hystad crouched for an even better look.

"I'd stay back, Doctor," Santiago said.

About twenty feet down, the right side of the enclosure suddenly bulged, and one of the vines broke through the thick plastic tarp with an audible pop.

"My God, this new batch is growing far faster than I imagined!" Hystad said. "This is amazing. We're going to need bigger containment facilities."

Santiago and Yosef exchanged a glance.

Hystad cautiously approached the writhing, twisting vine. The front four feet or so stopped, then curled back up. Needles six inches long prickled out of the thick cuticle, as if it were a worm trying to protect itself.

"Doctor," Yosef warned.

"We told you both to get out of here," Voss said.

Hystad ignored them all and reached out with a pair of long forceps to collect a sample.

Santiago grabbed him and yanked him backward as the vine whipped outward, narrowly missing his helmet. He scrambled backward in the dirt and then stood up.

"Goddamn it," Hystad grumbled.

"De nada, amigo," Santiago said.

Hystad stiffened, brushed off his hazard suit, and went to Voss. "Send the new data to Command ASAP," he said. "I think we've reached a breakthrough here."

Voss nodded, then walked very close past Santiago, nearly brushing him with his shoulder.

"Thank you," Hystad said.

"No problem," Santiago replied. "That thing looks like it'd pack a nasty punch."

"Are they poisonous?" Yosef asked.

"Oh no," said the scientist. "But Santiago here is right—you wouldn't want to get stuck by any of those needles."

Hystad looked another long moment, then walked away. It was obvious what the scientists were doing here now by trying to restore the soil and clear the radiation, but Santiago still had a hard time understanding how they could do it on a massive scale.

"Lieutenant, everything good out there?" David asked over the comms.

"Yeah, heading back to you now," Yosef replied.

They returned to the habitats, where they went through the decon process. An hour later, Santiago was sitting in front of a screen, waiting for the connection to his wife in San Diego. Her face came online, and she smiled big when she saw him.

He smiled back. "Hey, babe, how are things?"

"Other than us all missing you? Good," she said. Her eyes darted from the screen for just a moment—enough for Santiago to pick up on something bothering her.

"What's wrong?" he asked.

"Nothing. Everything's fine here."

"Tina, please..."

She exhaled. "Diego got into a fight at school."

There were a lot of questions in his mind, but Santiago decided to wait for a full explanation.

"A kid that's been teasing him," she said. "Diego hit him in the mouth and knocked one of his teeth loose. He's been suspended."

Santiago couldn't help feeling that some of this was his own fault. Diego had overheard them talking about him boxing the robot.

"Is he there?" Santiago asked. "Let me talk to him."

Diego got in front of the screen.

"Hey, Dad! How are you?"

"Hey, bud, all good here, but what's this about you getting into a fight?"

Diego sulked with a frown. "Jay's been picking on me for weeks, saying all sorts of stuff about how I'm a girl, and—"

"Diego, I told you, people will say things to get a rise out of you. That doesn't mean you can hit them."

"But you hit people."

"Bad guys."

"Jay's bad."

"Not on the same level, and there are other ways to resolve conflict than by violence. Next time, you think about that. Okay?"

"Yeah."

"Yeah, what?"

"Next time, I'll think about it and not hit him."

"Good."

Footsteps approached Santiago, and Nodin leaned down. "Sorry to interrupt, Sarge, but we might have a problem."

He handed Santiago the glass tablet displaying the red-and-yellow spread of a sprawling storm front rolling over a large swath of the exclusion zones, specifically sectors 43 through 50.

"Doppler not looking good," Yosef said. "That storm's about to hit two other sites, and they want us back on the airship, ready to deploy for rescue ops."

Santiago turned back to the screen, where his wife had joined Diego. Isabella popped up between them, beaming.

"Hey, Daddy!" she yelled.

"Hey, sweetheart, I'm sorry, but I have to go," Santiago said. "I love you all, and I'll call you soon."

"Is something wrong?" Tina asked.

"No, just new orders," Santiago said. "I'll talk to you all soon."

"Wait, T."

He looked into the camera as she blew him a kiss. He blew one back to her and Isabella.

"Be good, Diego," he said. "And remember what I said."

"I will, Dad. Love you."

The feed winked off, and Santiago returned to his squad, refocusing his mind from his family to work.

"Okay, suit up, everyone," Yosef said. "We have a Wasp incoming for extraction."

They packed up their gear and headed to Dr. Hystad's chamber.

"All perimeter defenses are secure," Yosef reported. "We're returning to the *Persephone* to give support to Field Labs Tango and Foxtrot, which are about to be hit by a doozy of a storm."

Hystad stood. "Thank you," he said.

Dr. Voss stood glaring at them as they left. But it wasn't the anger in his eyes, or the contempt that Santiago had seen earlier. It was fear. He had seen it in enough men to recognize it. The scientist was hiding something.

"Evac is en route," Nodin said.

"Copy that," Yosef replied. "Let's go."

He turned and led his men through the clean room and back out into the radioactive terrain. A Wasp burst out of the storm clouds a few minutes later, tilt-rotors lowering it vertically over the crater, whipping up a vortex of dust and ash. The squad rushed over to the open troop hold and climbed inside.

As the Wasp rose from the huge funnel-shaped hole, Santiago looked down over Lab 10, pulsating almost directly below them as they flew over. There was something else glowing down there: the orange visor of a Def-8 unit that watched them as the crater receded behind them.

"Not gonna lie, I wasn't a fan of that bloody place," Alistair said.

"They're trying to play God," Nodin said.

Santiago sealed off the view by closing the hatch. The men racked in for the turbulent ride up through the storm clouds. They reached the *Persephone* five minutes later to find Commander Zimmerman waiting in the launch bay.

"Good news, Hell Squad," he said. "The Delta Cloud fusion reactor test was moved up. If it clears the storm, we might not be out here as long."

"And the bad news?" Santiago asked.

"It won't be soon enough to protect anyone in the path of this storm." He looked out the viewports as lightning flashed, illuminating his sharp features. "You're about to see what the weather is capable of here. Don't underestimate it."

CHAPTER 15

Lightning flashed through the bulging storm clouds rolling across the Arctic Circle—a sight so rare few had ever seen it. But for June, the time of year known as the midnight sun, it was beyond rare. But the storm presented a unique opportunity to test the Delta Cloud fusion reactors that Tyron had come to see with his own eyes at Polar Station.

Having arrived an hour earlier, he was now inside the command center of the five-story main structure, where a team of scientists, engineers, and technicians prepared for another live test of the six massive disk-shaped reactors, each standing three hundred feet tall.

The five-story dome-shaped facility was anchored in the ice cap and centered amid those reactors. From the sky and even on the ground, the base was meant to appear as a research station, and in many ways, it was, but as with every ITC facility across the planet, there was more than met the eye.

Deep beneath Polar Station was a doomsday bunker filled with hybrid seeds, labs, and the technology to jump-start humanity after virtually any apocalyptic scenario—scenarios that he hoped would never happen. Part of stopping it would be the successful operation of the Delta Cloud fusion reactors. If today's test was successful, ITC would accomplish what humanity had never been able to do: change, manipulate, and regulate weather across the planet—even the megastorms above Korea.

There would be no more droughts, catastrophic floods, or hurricanes. The command center connected to every corner of the world, working with governments during extreme events to help prevent loss of life and property. But there would be no ribbon-cutting ceremony, nor even an announcement. For this operation was top secret, with the United States military helping fund and oversee parts of the project. They would be here soon, but his team was already prepping systems for the launch.

A door opened behind him, and the sharp tap of heels on the metal mezzanine told him it was Angelina.

"We're almost ready, sir."

She wore a thick parka and fancy red sunglasses that matched her lipstick.

"How long until our guests arrive?" Tyron asked.

"Not picking them up on radar, but with their stealth design, that isn't unusual. Anyway, let's not waste time. How about we go over your schedule for the rest of the day?"

"Let's hear it."

"After the successful launch of the reactors, we'll head back to HQ in Atlanta just long enough to get ready for the gala, which, I must say, I'm very excited about."

"That makes one of us."

"Come on, it won't be that bad," she said. "Did I tell you we booked Loo Loo?"

"Loo Loo? Never heard of him."

"Seriously?" Angelina giggled. "*She* is a two-time Grammy winner."

"I'm kidding. I've heard of her."

"Wait till you see the grounds. I helped plan the flower arrangements myself. It's going to be absolutely spectacular, with fireworks and something very special just for you, sir. I'm really excited. This is going to be the best gala in the history of the company."

"That all sounds great." He pushed his blue glasses back on his nose, still looking at the reactors on the horizon.

"They are truly remarkable," she said. "And a bit ugly."

"Ugly is the point. I didn't want people to know what we were really doing here. If anyone is looking at satellite imagery, they might think we're searching for ET."

Angelina laughed. "Sounds like your next project."

He chuckled back at that.

"I just hope they work as I'm told they will work," he said. "I've read through the initial testing reports, and I'm a little concerned about how the nanobots will work in the heaviest storms."

"I agree, but early results are promising."

Lightning fractured the horizon as the heart of the storm drew closer. Thunder boomed, but over the boom came a humming sound. Two army Wasp gunships were the first to emerge from the cloud cover. Next came a green-and-white behemoth of a conventional helicopter.

"Shall we?" Angelina asked.

"Sure. Let's get it over with," Tyron said.

She gave him a side-glance. "Play nice, sir."

"Always."

The truth was, the military top brass weren't here to witness what the Delta Cloud fusion reactors could do to combat severe weather. They were here to understand how the technology could be used against enemies. But Tyron knew that the violent side of humanity wasn't going anywhere, and neither were

ITC's defense contracts. His father had made sure of that by becoming the largest—and now only—contractor capable of providing the hardware needed to win wars.

The three aircraft lowered over the tundra, whipping up grit. Tyron led the way out with Angelina, Whitt, and two ITC security agents shadowing them at a respectful distance. Overhead, the Wasps remained in the air, patrolling to make sure no hidden threats lurked out there.

Tyron had already made sure of it. This was one of the most secure places in the world. Orion monitored the base's security, operating its drones and automated defense turrets.

"Orion, everything look okay?" he asked over his headset.

"All clear, sir," replied the AI over their encrypted channel.

Tyron stopped a few hundred feet from the big military helicopter. The hatch opened, and the stairs extended down. Out came two marines, followed by the chair of the Joint Chiefs of Staff, General Vucci. He gave a haphazard salute, then walked across the helipad, keeping low, flanked by a team of two officers and four marines.

Angelina gave Tyron a loaded glance in lieu of another warning. He got the hint, then decided to ignore it.

"General, you're late," Tyron said.

Vucci's facial expression went from looking peevish to angry. "Bad weather, Tyron."

"Yes. Good for us though. Rain at the North Pole used to be a once-in-centuries event."

He shook the general's hand.

"Coordinates of your ship, please," Tyron requested.

"Why?"

"So I don't have to pay for any damage it might sustain during our live test with the airship that we sold to the US Army." He smiled to soften the passive-aggressive blow. "Don't worry, the weather tech is harmless, unless there's a direct hit from a missile, which is incredibly unlikely. But I'm not a man to take chances."

General Vucci nodded to an officer beside him.

"We appreciate you coming all this way," Angelina said. "This field test will show you exactly what the Delta Cloud fusion reactors are capable of, and as Dr. Red said, we have the weather on our side today."

"Will they clear the nuclear storms over Korea?"

"Yes, my team is confident of that," Tyron said.

"Miss Sanchez, would you mind giving us a moment?"

"Certainly, sir."

Angelina stepped away only after Tyron gave her a nod. As she left, Vucci removed his aviator sunglasses and wiped the first raindrops from them. Then he turned and looked Tyron in the eyes. "I came a long way, and I'm going to come right out and say it: What good is clearing the storms if the Tritons come out and nuke us again?"

"I'm not here to discuss the Def-9 units," Tyron said. "We're here for—"

"Well, let's get on with it, then."

Vucci put his glasses back on and looked skyward. The general was a man of absolutes, not of mitigation. Over a long career, he had fought enemies on behalf of the United States. But Tyron wasn't going to let the man use ITC machines until he could prove there was a threat dire enough to risk deploying them.

The reactors began to tilt skyward until they stood almost straight up.

"Here we go," Tyron said.

Angelina stepped back out just as a countdown sounded from unseen speakers.

"Ten. Nine. Eight..."

Each of the reactors fired a small missile into the clouds, the fiery tails vanishing moments later. Distant concussions sounded, echoing through the clouds.

"How long until we see progress?" Vucci asked.

"Shouldn't take more than fifteen minutes for our sensors to see the nanobots spreading and working," Tyron said.

"Sir, may I have a brief word with you?" Angelina asked.

Tyron turned to her, seeing concern on her face.

"If you'll excuse me, General," Tyron said.

He joined Angelina, leaning in as she whispered into his ear.

"We have a problem at Field Lab Zulu," she said. "They were hit by a storm and activated an SOS after losing critical life-support systems."

"Do we have any assets close to extract them?"

"Yes, but allied forces are closer at a base bordering the DMZ. We could ask for them to deploy a team—"

"No, we send our own."

"Okay, sir. I'll see that it's done."

"Is there a problem?" Vucci asked.

"A storm hit one of our field labs in an exclusion zone. But if today is a success, soon we won't have to worry about those storms."

He looked up as a dark pile of cumulus appeared to dissolve, slowly revealing the behemoth airship that had been hiding there. The size of three football fields laid end to end, the *Eagle* was one of the biggest airships ever designed for the US Army. Large enough that a Sikorsky helicopter and four Wasps could fit inside its internal hangar. And though massive, it was built with stealth technology to combat the threat of electronic warfare, making it an all-but-invisible command center and gunship in the sky.

"Wow," Vucci said. "I wasn't expecting this to work so quickly—or at all, if I'm being honest."

Tyron turned to him, a little surprised at the general's change in tone.

"I'll brief POTUS on the success here," he said. "Well done, Dr. Red."

It was the first time that Vucci had actually used his professional title.

The general stuck out his hand, and Tyron shook it again. But he didn't take another second to consider why the unusual show of respect all of a sudden.

As soon as the general left, Tyron went inside to the command center, to the team of scientists and operational staff who had been working here for years to make this happen.

"Excellent work," Tyron said. "You've made history today, and this is just the beginning. Your work is pivotal to clearing the storms above the exclusion zones."

He shook hands with everyone on the way out, trying to focus on each face even though he was anxious over the news about Field Lab Zulu. Everyone on the team would be rewarded with bonuses, which he gave out liberally to retain talented staff and keep them loyal to ITC.

Angelina followed him, also thanking the other scientists. When they were finished, they rushed off to their private ITC jet with Whitt and the two guards. Inside, Angelina handed him a tablet with a briefing of the data they had gathered so far. Tyron skimmed over it and saw that the SOS had happened less than an hour ago.

"I've received updated information," she said. "Looks like it was a Category 4 storm that hit them, and it's headed toward three more locations. We're evacuating those."

"Have we detected any seismic activity?" he asked.

She looked at the data, then shook her head. "None, why?"

"I was briefed on the possibility of earthquakes." He didn't like lying, but for now he had to keep the real briefing from the Pentagon close to his chest.

Angelina gave him her look that said, *What aren't you telling me?*

"Just worried about our assets," he said.

"We're prepared for this, and it's not the first time," she said. "And in the near future, this won't be a problem, thanks to the Delta Cloud fusion reactors."

He sat in a leather seat that conformed to his body. As the tilt-rotor craft took off vertically, he tried to relax. Today was a monumental win. Soon he would be back in Atlanta, preparing for the gala, where he would announce the successful test and unveil his next great project: *Genesis 1*.

On the horizon, the storms continued to clear, and Tyron finally started to relax. Orion's voice came over the channel.

"Sir, we have another problem," said the AI.

"What now?"

Angelina looked back at Tyron as he stood.

"There's a cyberattack targeting our food-production plants," Orion said.

"How many of them?" Tyron asked.

"All of them, sir."

* * * * *

A day after the funeral for the fellow officers ambushed at Copper Terrace, Cecil sat in the undercover van with Tank. Both men wore blue coveralls with a *Straight Flush Sewage* logo.

Apparently, Captain Harkin took the metaphor of flushing the shit out of the city seriously, Cecil thought with a grin.

But the grin faded as he watched screens relaying views of their target building from the dozen insect-size drones they had deployed into the no-go zone.

They were supposed to be searching for Wild Bill and his

weapons cache, and for Nion, but instead, they were providing a view of unfolding chaos. Hundreds of angry residents from Copper Terrace and surrounding buildings were milling about outside. Many of them were shouting about a delay in the daily rations from ITC to the people in the NGZ.

"This is not good," Tank said. "Guess we're going to see what happens when you cut off the food supply here."

Cecil remembered the suggestion to do that very thing in the briefing when Chief Krycek told them to stand down. It seemed ironic that it was coming true now. When Cecil and Tank had arrived earlier this morning, he wondered whether withholding food was part of some plan between ITC, the mayor, and the Crime Task Force, to punish the entire sector for the ambush at Copper Terrace. But Cecil knew now that wasn't the case, and he also knew this wasn't some delivery error or mechanical delay—it was a cyberattack. Ironically, it had hacked the very factory where his wife, Michelle, worked as an engineer.

Normally, four semis showed up with their trailers full of food from that plant to distribute to the entire area. For all Cecil knew, this was the first time the trucks hadn't shown up—*ever.* ITC ran a well-oiled machine, showing up on the dot to a hundred spots like this one all across the city, to distribute the neatly packaged food put together in the factories the night before. The fresh produce and meat were prepared in the early morning, packaged, and then sent out, distributed by a fleet of vehicles and staff in an operation reminiscent of how the now-extinct newspaper giants of the twentieth century delivered their papers.

The upset over the missed shipments had rapidly devolved into widespread anger and panic over the past six hours, from people who already felt left behind by the rest of society. More people flooded out into the streets, hungry and furious.

Cecil pulled out his phone to see if Michelle had gotten back to him, but she hadn't returned any of his messages. He glanced at the burner phone Captain Harkin had given him at the funeral, but found no missed messages from him either. For now, the mission would continue.

"Shit, listen to this," Tank said. He turned up the radio report.

"In Chicago, ITC farming facilities are reporting outages from a wide-ranging cyberattack that appears to be affecting company operations in several states," said the news announcer. "ITC has released a statement that it is working on the problem and hopes to have all services restored by this evening."

Cecil prayed that was the case. Rioting would make his job a lot harder.

Just based on what he was seeing now over their drone feeds, the system couldn't hold up for two days of this. For now, the trouble was isolated to the NGZ, but this was happening elsewhere, too, and it was already starting to spread outside.

Sirens wailed in the distance, echoing off the buildings as he sat watching the chaos unfold on his monitors. He slid aside a panel in the partition between the front and back seats of the van for a view out the windshield. People were gathering in the streets here, too, some of them wearing masks.

"This is fucked up," Cecil whispered.

"I'm about to enter the utility tunnel under Copper Terrace," Tank reported.

Cecil went back to look at his monitor and the honeybee-size drone with night-vision optics. Deftly operating the remote controls, Tank guided the tiny drone through a storm drain, into the utility shaft.

Something smacked against the front of the van.

"What the hell was that?" Cecil asked.

Tank shook his head. "Maybe we should get out of here."

"Sit tight. I'll check it out."

Cecil opened the van door slightly and saw a teenager kicking the passenger door.

"Hey, get the hell out of here!" Cecil shouted.

"Fuck you, loser," the kid said, jumping onto the hood of the van. Three of his friends came over, laughing.

"Get off, now!" Cecil shouted.

"Or what?"

Cecil reached out and grabbed the kid by the leg, but he kicked loose and jumped to the street, laughing. "Too slow, bro!"

The four teenagers took off running, but there were far worse threats out there. The chaos was indeed spreading. Glass shattered in the distance, followed by a car alarm. Angry shouting grew louder.

He looked down the street in the direction the masked teenager had run, and spotted five young men with baseball bats bashing away at a car.

"Better get back inside," Tank said.

Cecil closed the door as five police SUVs roared down the street, followed by a fire engine and an ambulance. Then came two armored personnel carriers.

"We should have rolled up in those and stormed Copper Terrace days ago," Cecil said.

"For real, bro," Tank said.

The two APCs skidded to a stop and disgorged officers in riot gear. Some of the crowd dispersed, running in all directions, but plenty of others held their ground.

"I think we better move locations," Tank said.

Cecil took a look at the GPS and found a good parking garage three blocks away. He got behind the wheel of the van and drove there while Tank reported updates from the back seat.

"Looting in three locations. Another riot."

Cecil drove to the seventh level of the parking garage,

where he could see the entire area. And what he saw gave him pause.

This wasn't the peaceful city he was used to. Once again, it taught him just how fragile the entire socioeconomic fabric was when it didn't work properly. Even areas of Charlotte that were normally crime-free were experiencing looting.

Smoke billowed out from three other locations on the skyline around the NGZ. News of the cyberattack had spread like wildfire.

"Holy shit," he murmured.

On the streets below, the crowds had gotten thicker as more people joined the protest against the police. The officers had deployed smoke and pepper spray, but that only made things worse. Over the sirens and shouting came the crack of gunfire.

His phone buzzed and he pulled it out to see a text message from his wife. But before he could look at it, he realized it was his other phone—the one Harkin had given him.

"Pepper," he answered.

"What's your status?" Harkin asked.

"Just got our first drone into a utility tunnel, but we're moving locations."

He fully expected Harkin to call the operation off, but he said, "I have a new objective for you. Get eyes on Diana Hickman. She was a CI for our enforcer and is the former girlfriend of Wild Bill. I'll send her info shortly."

"Copy."

Cecil lowered the phone, still shaken over the condition of the city. Maybe the riot was a good distraction, pulling thugs from the normally well-guarded buildings. But he doubted that it would draw Wild Bill or any of the Cipher Crew outside. They were too smart to come out in the open right now.

No, Cecil would have to go in and find the rats.

He brought up the text message from his wife.

Systems are all down. I'll try and call you soon when I can get away.

He sent a message back: *You got this. I love you.*

Cecil put the phone away and watched the chaos on the streets below. It reminded him of when he was just a kid and the world had descended into violence from the economic meltdown that nearly broke America.

Industrial Tech Corporation had brought the country back from the brink. But even that enlightened mega corporation had flaws in its empire, chinks in its armor.

It brought to mind a truism he had learned in history class regarding empires.

They all fall.

CHAPTER 16

"All right, listen up. We have a critical situation developing," Zimmerman said.

Five ITC security teams, including Hell Squad, had gathered in the belly of the airship *Persephone*. In front of them, monitor screens featured the raging storm east of Seoul.

"This major system, currently classified as a Category 4, is on a direct path toward an operations center in exclusion zone B, just fifty miles northeast of Cheongju. The storm is packing sustained winds of up to a hundred thirty miles per hour, with gusts reaching one-sixty. The rainfall is projected to exceed twenty inches in the next twenty-four hours."

He clicked a button on his remote, and the screen shifted to a map highlighted with four red dots, each representing a field lab in the storm's path.

"The habitats are built with reinforced composite materials, designed to endure these conditions, to protect personnel," Zimmerman continued. "And all labs have protective shields that have been deployed to protect field assets. However, they may not be able to sustain an assault of this magnitude."

He tapped the remote again, drilling down on a sector with a base already consumed by the storm. "As you can see, Field Lab Zulu has already been hit, and they've reported critical failure of their life-support systems. Command wants them evaced ASAP."

Zimmerman looked away from the screens to the teams gathered before him.

"One team will deploy via Wasp to a top-secret location twenty-five miles beyond the DMZ, where they will load up in a Stryker and drive into that storm for ten miles to extract the staff before they're exposed to a lethal dose of radiation." He paused, his gaze sweeping over the security forces. "Any volunteers?"

An awkward silence passed over the launch bay. Santiago looked over at his brothers. They were all exhausted from a very long day at Field Lab Alpha.

Several seconds passed in silence.

"Hell Squad will get the job done," Yosef said.

"That's what I like to hear," Zimmerman said. "Suit up and head to the launch bay. The Wasp is ready to deploy."

For the second time that day, Santiago found himself suiting up and preparing for insertion into an exclusion zone.

"I know you're tired, but we get this job done successfully, and we prove why we're worth that paycheck," Yosef said.

"That's why I'm here," Alistair quipped. "Let's keep the dosh flowing, boss man."

Nodin gave a slow nod, but David just looked away. It struck Santiago that David didn't need another job. This was it for him. After this payday, he would be on a beach, feet up, frozen daiquiri in hand. Alive.

The men suited up and got into their armor.

A half hour later, they were in the air, racked in. The pilots flew the Wasp toward the dark, scalloped roof of storm clouds that stretched across the horizon, electrical strikes webbing out from it like pulsating blue veins.

"ETA five mikes to LZ," said the primary pilot. "Stryker on the ground, ready to deploy, over."

They looked over the route, a five-mile jaunt down a highway that supposedly had been cleared. Santiago was again seeing why ITC paid them the big bucks. But, of course, the really big bucks were in the science equipment and the teams out there that Hell Squad had been hired to protect. Two-hundred-thousand-dollar paychecks were nothing new to ITC.

As the Wasp flew over the destroyed city of Cheongju, Santiago spotted the allied forces working along the DMZ. Row after row of steel-skinned buildings encased in lead protected the thousands of soldiers stationed in the exclusion zones from the stubborn radiation here. Most of the allied countries still had soldiers on the ground down there, living in bunkers, where they would stay until the war officially ended—or flared up again. But 95 percent of them had no good idea what ITC was doing out there.

The Wasp flew east of Cheongju, over the artillery pointed at the North, and then a fortification of weapons encompassing part of the Doomsday Shield. Altogether the defensive shield consisted of thousands of missiles on land and on submarines and warships that had the Korean Peninsula surrounded to thwart any future Triton nuclear attack against the world.

"Going to get pretty rough from here on out," warned the primary pilot.

"Copy that," Yosef said.

Santiago looked out the cockpit windshield at the jumble of storm clouds that stretched from the ground to the sky. Lightning flashed through it, illuminating the vortex as it rolled across the exclusion zone.

Zimmerman was right—the storms out here were badass.

"Taking us down," advised the same pilot.

"Check your suits and get ready," Yosef said.

The precombat ritual started as they went over their gear, suits, and life-support systems. Santiago double-checked everything, then turned to look Nodin over.

They were heading into combat, with the storm representing a deadly added risk.

But now it was life or death. They weren't worried about stepping in a crevice and twisting an ankle, or even getting a tear in the suit. This storm could peel off their suits and their very flesh.

The Wasp swooped down, and Santiago saw the target: a domed building with a flashing red light, like a lighthouse beam trying to penetrate a hurricane. The ITC base was on the outskirts of the fire wave that had blasted through Seoul, erasing virtually everything around the crater for twenty-five miles. What wasn't destroyed in the blast was now being pounded by one of the many storms that had hit the area over the past five years.

"This is as far as we can go," he said. "We'll be back to get you once you evac those scientists. Good luck, Hell Squad."

"Thanks for the lift," Yosef said.

The Wasp set down with a thump.

"Okay, everyone up!" Yosef shouted. "Let's move!"

The hatch opened, and the men piled out. Immediately, the wind slammed against him. He fought forward, running toward the structure. It had a steel garage door. A side door with a keypad allowed entry into the building. The men hurried inside as the Wasp took off into the sky.

A generator kicked on, spreading light over the secure but empty facility. The Stryker sat in the garage. Santiago went right to it, knowing that every second counted. Just two minutes after landing, Hell Squad was in the Stryker, with Santiago behind the wheel and Yosef monitoring the GPS on the dashboard.

"Switching to camera systems," he said.

The dashboard came online, displaying multiple angles from the night-vision cameras.

"All systems look good," Yosef reported. "You ready?"

"Let's get this done," Santiago said.

The garage door rose, letting in a blast of wind and grit. Santiago pulled out of the garage. The heavily armored vehicle was built for extreme conditions, but right away the heavy tires struggled to gain traction on the muddy, debris-laden ground. He gave it some gas, and they lurched out onto the roadway, fishtailing.

"Whoa, easy, Sarge," David said.

Santiago steadied the vehicle and alternated his gaze between the monitors and the narrow viewports. The beams cut through the darkness over a devastated landscape of ruined buildings. Flashes of lightning sporadically illuminated the shattered buildings in the distance, casting eerie shadows over the ruins. The oversize tires thumped over debris scattered across the cracked pavement.

"Take a right at the next intersection," Yosef said.

"What intersection?" Santiago asked.

"Two hundred feet ahead."

Santiago slowed and peered through the viewport. All he could see were black mounds of rubble from collapsed structures. Even with the headlights, it was hard to see the road without the night-vision optics. He kept an eye on the navigation display, maneuvering around deadly drop-offs that went straight down for several meters.

"Almost there," Yosef said.

Santiago nearly passed the junction and slammed on the brakes. He backed up, then turned down a narrow street that was almost unrecognizable beneath the rubble. Giving it gas again, he put it in low gear and pushed on, the machine jolting and jerking as it crawled over the debris piles.

"Highway is coming up," Yosef said. "Take the bridge."

Santiago reached the bridge a few minutes later, and had just started across it when Yosef shouted, "Hold up!"

He slammed on the brakes, stopping about ten feet before a collapsed section near the middle. But when he looked beyond, he forgot about the bridge. Not a mile away to the east, the edge of the monster storm swallowed the horizon. It looked like a solid fortress with no end.

"We got to go into *that*?" David asked. He gave his typical nervous chuckle.

"About to say the same thing, fam," Alistair remarked.

"What was that about being here for the fat check?" Yosef asked.

"I love stacks of dosh, but damn, LT!"

"Beats fighting the Tritons again," Nodin said. He didn't seem bothered by this excursion—or by anything, really. He sat in the back, looking comfortable despite their iffy situation.

"Faster we get in there, faster we get out," Santiago said.

"Proceed," Yosef said. He tapped the comms on the dashboard. "Eagle Eye, this is Hell Squad Actual. We are entering the storm, en route to Field Lab Zulu. ETA about thirty minutes, over."

"Copy, Hell Squad Actual. Be advised, winds are picking up. We're looking at a Category 5 now."

"Shit," David said.

"We're protected in the APC," Yosef reminded them. "Now, let's move. Maybe we can get in and out before the full storm hits."

Santiago eased up on the pedal and drove down the off-ramp into what would have been incoming traffic. Most of the highway had been cleared of vehicles, their burned and blasted shells pushed up against the shoulders of the road, but plenty of rubble had been blown in by the storms. Windblown rocks and glass shards pinged against the vehicle as they pushed into the storm. The pings quickly became an intense barrage that sounded almost like bullets striking the armored hull.

They barreled ahead into wind that howled like a vengeful spirit, lashing the Stryker hard enough to jerk them from side to side. After a few minutes, the storm had fully engulfed them, visibility dropping to only a dozen yards. Outside, the world became a swirling maelstrom of gray and black through the narrow windows. Santiago had to rely entirely on the cameras as he drove deeper into the screaming wind. Larger hunks of debris hurtled through the air, thudding against the vehicle. The dashboard flickered, going in and out from the geomagnetic disturbance that would affect their comms as well.

The Geiger counter on the dashboard clicked steadily—a grim reminder of the lethal atomic decay permeating the exclusion zone.

Santiago began to worry what they were going to find at the habitats. If any of the scientists had been caught out in this, it wasn't going to be pretty.

He ramped up the speed to fifty miles per hour. As they got closer, he kept his focus on the cameras, dodging around the scorched vehicles that the wind had pushed back out into his path.

"Almost there," Yosef said. "Take the next exit."

Santiago merged into the right lane, then started toward the off-ramp, but this one was clogged by a dozen wrecked cars, some of them fused together.

"Hold on. We'll *make* a way," he said.

He clenched his jaw, and the Stryker surged forward. "Here we go!"

The vehicle plowed into the barricade like an icebreaker into a floe, splitting the pile of rubble. When the wheels began to spin, Santiago backed up and hit it again, pushing aside bricks, plates of broken pavement, bones. And they were free. The truck charged up the cleared on-ramp.

"Okay, take a right," Yosef said. "Zulu is just a mile off this road."

Santiago glanced in the rearview at his men in the back. They all were watching the monitors.

"Double-check your suit closures," he ordered. "LT, can you get Zulu on the comms?"

The wind was a howling banshee, drowning out Yosef's efforts on the crackling radio. Driving down the last stretch, where the base should be within eyesight, Santiago slowed.

"Can't get through," Yosef said.

"You got eyes?" Santiago asked.

"Nega... Wait... there."

Santiago looked at the camera relay from their front right bumper. Leaning down, he could see the outlines of the field lab's habitat modules. He turned in that direction, off the road, onto a muddy field. His beams hit the structures. They were battered but still standing.

The Stryker skidded to a halt outside the main habitat, its tires sinking slightly into the mud. He pulled up as close to the building as he could, then told Yosef to take over behind the wheel.

"You're giving orders now?" Yosef asked.

"I'm faster than you, LT," Santiago said with a grin.

"This is true."

"Then it's settled. I'll go with Nodin. Hopefully, our new friends are all inside this hab."

"Okay, but be damn careful."

Santiago moved back into the troop compartment with the others, and Nodin met him at the rear hatch, holding the lever.

"We do this as fast as possible," Santiago said.

"You got it," replied Nodin. He turned the lever and swung open the hatch. Wind rushed into the Stryker as Santiago hopped out and went to the habitat door. He slammed his fist against the exterior, yelling his presence, his voice barely audible over the storm.

The habitat door slid open on a group of six scientists in their hazard suits, huddled inside the large open living compartment furnished with bunks, tables, and a kitchen. A red emergency light flashed as the scientists rushed over. Behind their visors, Santiago saw faces etched with relief and fatigue.

"Are you all here?" Santiago shouted.

"No, we have two men at Hab 8," said one of the scientists.

"Where the hell's that?"

"Two hundred feet from here, east."

Santiago nodded. "Get in the APC. We'll head there next."

One by one, the six scientists were escorted to the vehicle. Santiago sealed off the habitat, then followed them in, giving Yosef the signal to drive to Habitat 8.

As the truck pulled away, Santiago looked over at the scientists. "Anyone injured?"

"Not us, but Dr. Lance was knocked unconscious during the storm, trying to retrieve some equipment. Maggie went to get him and managed to drag him into Hab 8, but it wasn't built to withstand this kind of wind."

Santiago could see that through the viewport as they parked outside. The orange skin of the structure had been ripped back, leaving what looked like orange peels whipping back and forth in the gusts.

"Okay, we're going in to look for Maggie and Lance," Santiago said.

Again Nodin opened the hatch on the Stryker. Santiago jumped out into the wind and was instantly knocked backward. Together the men made it up to the hatch, where Santiago pounded with his fist. This time, no one opened it.

Windblown grit scoured them as they stood there. After fifteen seconds, when it was obvious no one would answer, Santiago stepped into action. He motioned for Nodin to move to the side, then pulled out his pistol. Three calculated shots parted the hinges, and the hatch was off.

Nodin went inside, and Santiago followed him into a storage area of lab equipment covered in grit and debris. On the floor under a table, a male scientist lay curled in a fetal position, a puddle of drying vomit beside him. Lance. A few feet away, a woman sat shivering against the wall. Neither wore a helmet.

"Maggie, I'm Sergeant Rodriguez, and we've come to get you out of here," he said as he leaned down. Nodin crouched and lifted the other scientist under the arms to drag him out from under the table.

The woman suddenly leaned over and vomited.

Nodin looked back at Santiago, who motioned for him to help. Together they carried her outside to the Stryker. Then they returned for the man. He had a weak pulse, but he was still breathing.

Santiago picked him up in a fireman's carry and hauled him out into driving rain. It would be a long shot for the man to pull through unless they evacuated him fast to a proper medical facility. But that also seemed a long shot, Santiago realized, when he saw the looming black wall of storm clouds barreling toward them with winds approaching a hundred miles per hour.

The Stryker was a highly durable armored transport. It would protect them, but it was going to be a rough ride.

"Bull, let's go!" Nodin shouted.

Santiago heaved the scientist up into the vehicle and climbed in behind him. "Shut the hatch!" he shouted.

Inside, David was already giving Maggie potassium iodide tablets. Nodin helped Santiago put Lance down beside her. David waved Nodin and Yosef back.

"A little elbow room, please," he said.

Santiago eased past and climbed into the front.

"We got to move," Yosef said. "Strap in."

Santiago threw on his harness and looked at the radar. The main force of the storm was almost on them, sounding like fifty diesel locomotives and sluicing down rain. The relentless downpour created a curtain of water over the viewports, making it almost impossible to see anything outside.

But there was something else out there: a pulsating red light at one of the habitats.

Not a light, he realized.

It was vegetation, like the kind they saw at Field Lab Alpha at the bottom of the crater in Seoul. Vines undulated across the ground outside one of the facilities. But none of them seemed to be affected in the least by the violent winds. If anything, the flora just appeared to be angry.

CHAPTER 17

"Hell Squad has extracted all staff from the Field Lab Zulu," Whitt said. "We had two scientists injured—one severely—but it sounds like they'll make it, thanks to the team's quick work."

"That's a relief," Angelina said. "It could have been a lot worse."

Tyron sat in his small office inside the ITC jet. He had hoped to work on his speech for the gala, but instead he sat with Angelina and Whitt while they dealt with a major disaster back home.

Over the past six hours, a cyberattack had wreaked havoc on ITC's food-production facilities and operations. Alerts flashed on the monitors, showing areas affected by the worst malware attack in Tyron Red's tenure as CEO. The timing couldn't have been worse, with the gala for his supporters and donors this evening.

On another monitor, he watched riots breaking out in every major city across the NGZs, where rations were now over seven hours late. And since his teams still couldn't figure out who was behind the attack or how to stop it, all plants had been shut down to prevent further damage to operations.

It was no secret that ITC had its fair share of enemies. Companies they had bested in business, religious groups that thought they were playing God, and, of course, the Tritons. Tyron was no stranger to this type of attack—indeed, he planned for them. But this one hit them where it hurt most: food production.

"Incredible how fast things break down," Angelina remarked.

"We have to shut this down now," Tyron said. "If our people can't do it, then I must have Orion intervene."

Whitt and Angelina looked back at him, neither saying a word. By international law, Orion could only be an adviser. This meant that the AI couldn't legally step in and stop a cyberattack.

"I know the law, but every second that passes, we risk major damage," Tyron said. "And it isn't just the damage being done or the risk, but also the way the world perceives it all. ITC's reputation is on the line right when we most need to show strength and resilience to our shareholders and supporters."

For the sake of Genesis 1.

"Our cybersecurity teams are working as fast as they can," Whitt said. "These attacks are highly coordinated from multiple locations, simultaneously targeting our data centers in North America, Europe, and Asia. We have our best teams still working to identify, isolate, and reverse engineer to develop signatures of the malware. Take a look."

The monitor displayed a dynamic map of the world, with nodes and networks pulsating in real time, illustrating the global reach of ITC's infrastructure, and the scale of the cyberassault. Red flashes marked the compromised areas, with lines connecting these points to potential origins of the attacks—terrorists hidden within the digital ether of Eastern Europe and Southeast Asia.

"Our best teams have failed. We can't wait another minute," Tyron said. "I'm bringing in Orion."

"Sir, are you sure?" Angelina said.

"I see no other option."

Whitt said nothing.

"We've already wasted too much time," Tyron said. "We must use Orion." He rotated one of the screens toward him as it linked with the AI. A hologram of the galaxy-eyed machine came online from inside the chamber back at HQ.

"Dr. Red, how may I be of assistance?" said the AI.

"Orion, this cyberattack—I need it shut down. Immediately."

"Sir, I don't have access to that sector of the security network."

Tyron looked at Angelina, whose face signaled her disapproval. Whitt, too, looked concerned at this break in protocol that had been intact since the accords after the war. But too much was on the line, and Tyron needed the AI to be the tool it was designed to be.

"I'm granting you temporary access," Tyron said. "Stop the attack, and figure out who's behind it."

"Understood, sir. Stand by."

Tyron switched his focus to the field labs in Seoul. On the maps, storms continued to ravage several sites. Years of work were at risk, not to mention important staff and equipment. And all when the Delta Cloud fusion reactors were finally ready to operate. He had to hope for the best.

Not a minute later, Orion's voice came online. *"Dr. Red, my initial analysis indicates a sophisticated malware infiltration aimed at destabilizing network cores and extracting proprietary algorithms. This appears to be an attempt at information gathering, but there have also been attempts to disrupt the network, which I believe are just a red herring to draw us away from the actual intel gathering."*

The image shifted to a schematic of network cores, with areas highlighted where the intrusions were most concentrated. The malware had spread through the systems, subtly altering code and rerouting command sequences to create vulnerabilities for further exploitation.

An announcement came over the jet's speakers.

"We are beginning our descent into Atlanta, where we will be on the ground in thirty-six minutes," announced the pilot.

Tyron watched the monitors with Whitt and Angelina. Just fifteen minutes after he had authorized the AI to shut down the attack, Orion's eyes flashed on the monitor.

"Reverse engineering of malware complete," said the AI. "Moving to step three, deployment of countermeasures—patches and updates to close off exploitation points."

Red lines shut off one by one on the monitors.

"The attack has been neutralized," Orion said. "All systems are back online, and food distribution will resume as soon as systems are rebooted."

Angelina and Whitt limited their celebration to a shared nod.

"Well done, Orion. Now tell me who did this," Tyron said.

Thanks to the AI, he was regaining control, but it would take time to assess the damage done, with no real relief until he had their enemy in his crosshairs.

"Analyzing the attack patterns to trace the origin," Orion said. "Preliminary data suggests a coordinated effort from multiple nodes. I have deployed countermeasures to disrupt future efforts and am tracing the attacks. I should know soon."

Angelina looked up from a monitor. "Sir, systems are rebooting at all facilities, and it appears all essential functions have been restored in a full system recovery."

"It could have been catastrophic if not for Orion," Tyron said.

"This can't be," Whitt said.

"What now?" Tyron asked.

Whitt held a hand over his earpiece. "I'm getting an SOS from Field Lab Alpha for evac."

"The storm hit them too?"

"Yes, but it had weakened to a Category 2."

"Their facilities should survive that with no issue," Tyron said.

"Well, something catastrophic must have happened, sir, because all three Defector units have gone offline. Simultaneously."

"What! That's impossible."

"Perhaps this is a reporting glitch, or interference from the storm," Angelina suggested.

"Just there? No other sites? I don't buy that." Tyron put his hands on his head. He was exhausted and starting to lose patience.

"Were there any hits on the seismic reactors that Hell Squad installed there?" Tyron asked.

Angelina checked her tablet, then shook her head. "None reported."

"All we have right now is the SOS beacon, activated shortly after the weakened storm moved in; nothing beyond that," Whitt said. "It's possible the machines were affected and are not being detected by *Persephone*, which was moved to support the field labs east of the DMZ."

"The storm is stronger over that area."

Tyron took his hands away from his head. "Okay, but what if something else happened to the Defectors?"

"Like what?" Angelina asked.

"What if the Def-8 units going offline has to do with the cyberattack?"

Whitt raised an eyebrow.

"Sir, what aren't you telling us?" Angelina finally asked. "What's the purpose of the seismic sensors you had deployed in the field?"

Whitt cleared his throat. "With respect, I've known you since you were a boy, and I know you're keeping something from me and Angelina."

"You're right, both of you," Tyron said. He hit a key and disconnected from Orion.

Angelina shifted in her seat, and Whitt leaned forward.

"In the Pentagon briefing," Tyron said, "President Clayton informed me of seismic activity at locations in the exclusion zones. The military believes the Tritons could be preparing for something."

"Wait a minute. So they don't believe the Tritons were fully destroyed?" Angelina asked.

"Apparently not, and they want me to authorize the Def-9 units to deploy into the tunnels for recon."

"The Def-9 units are prototypes." Angelina looked him in the eye, holding his gaze. "Tyron, tell me you're not considering this."

"I'm conflicted. We can't let them come back and destroy everything we've worked to fix. We might not get a second chance, and I'm starting to fear we're looking at next time."

"If the Tritons are out there still, we can't sit idly by, sir," Whitt said. "I knew, when you asked me to deploy new security teams and protocols, that this wasn't just the threat of raiders out there. If the Tritons are returning, we have to stop them."

That sounded like what his dad would have said, Tyron mused. But Whitt had lost his son in the war, and this was personal. He had served ITC loyally for over thirty years, but Tyron knew that Whitt would push him to deploy the machines.

"I don't believe what I'm hearing," Angelina said, righteous anger in her voice. "If you two are seriously considering this, I want to remind you that it violates international law. I'll also remind you what they did when they were deployed for the first time."

She tapped her screen and swiveled it around to show an image of six Def-9 units. The seven-foot-tall machines were in the launch bay of an airship, their thick titanium exoskeletons locked into place, a humanoid head with an orange visor looking out at the hatch. It opened, and the machines were dropped into the clouds. Nearing the surface, they would use jet packs to slow their descent.

"You remember this mission, yes?" she asked. "Ordered by General Vucci, ironically."

"I remember it, and I don't have time to watch—" Tyron started to say when Angelina cut him off.

"Sir, all due respect, but I *want* you to watch it. Please do that for me?"

The anger and frustration in her voice were uncharacteristic, but he understood.

"Okay," he said.

The video came online, showing three of the machines in a tropical jungle. Their metal bodies were covered in camouflage as they stalked through the jungle. Using blades attached to their skeletal limbs, they hacked through dense foliage until they had a view of a small fishing village on a beach. Whitish smoke from cookfires rose into the sky as the robots fanned out. A fourth robot's video feed captured the scene. Numbers and data scrolled across the bottom of the screen.

The pack entered the village, screeching in electronic frequencies as they approached a group of men and women standing around an open fire, roasting a pig. The first robot grabbed a man reaching for a rifle and casually tore his arm off.

Screams followed, both human and electronic.

None of the machines used the weapons attached to their extremities. They didn't need them. Their powerful hands were all they needed to tear the first group of humans limb from limb.

They quickly moved deeper into the village. A shirtless man with a shotgun emerged from one of the huts. He fired off several shots, but the pellets only dented the Defectors' armor.

The closest machine picked the man up by the throat and, with its other hand, ripped away his nose and face. Then it dropped the still-twitching body and smoothed the skin over its own metal face.

The video feed from the fourth machine zoomed in on glowing orange eyes that burned through the eyeholes of the stolen face. He studied the prototype hunter-killer unit that looked straight out of a fever dream.

"And you want to authorize an army of those to the US military and JMF?" Angelina asked.

"They already have a thousand units," Whitt said.

Tyron looked at him. "You knew about that?"

"Yes, sir, I did. Your father authorized the prototypes to be shipped off to secret locations until they could be reprogrammed. He shut them down, locking the codes away."

"And you never told me."

"I thought it best you didn't know, sir. I'm sorry."

"You thought wrong." Tyron exhaled his anger.

"Mr. Red, with respect, this could be a good thing," said Whitt. "If the Tritons are back, we can destroy them before they can threaten the world again."

"Perhaps, but we have no evidence that they're back."

Angelina shook her head. "I've scanned the JMF channels about troop movements, and I see nothing to indicate any current enemy attack at any location across Korea. If there were, we would know." She looked to Tyron. "That seismic activity could be anything. What makes the military believe it's the machines?"

"That's what I'm trying to figure out," Tyron said. He sighed. "For now, we keep this quiet. Our conversation does not leave this jet. Understood?"

Two nods.

"Good. Now, get Hell Squad back out there and locate those Def-8 units. Maybe there's a reasonable explanation for what happened."

Tyron turned back to the window as the jet lowered over Atlanta. Soon he would know what was going on halfway across the world, and who was behind the cyberattack. For now, it was over, and his people would mitigate any damage and reassure the public.

But it wasn't just the public he was worried about. It was his supporters, sponsors, and people who still doubted him after all this time. That would all change once ITC announced the success of the Delta Cloud fusion reactors. Then he would reveal his most ambitious project: *Genesis 1*.

* * * * *

"Dr. Angelina Sanchez from ITC has confirmed the cyberattacks have been thwarted," said a newscaster. "We are bringing you her statement now."

Cecil listened to the radio as he watched the multiple drone feeds inside the van. One was searching for Diana, the CI who Captain Harkin had asked them to locate.

"All systems are back online, and food production and delivery will resume as normal," Angelina said. "We deeply apologize for any inconvenience this has caused."

"Thank God," Tank said with a relieved sigh. "Let's hope that dials down the temperature out there. Although I think a lot of people are taking advantage of the situation."

Cecil snorted. "For sure. Unrest spreads like cancer. Especially when people are desperate."

"Too true, brother." He glanced over. "Bet your wife will be glad this is over. She's probably exhausted."

"Yeah, long shift for her."

Cecil took out his phone—still no response from Michelle.

Swiveling his chair back around to his monitor, Tank spat out a sunflower-seed hull.

"Shit. I think that's the CI!" he said. "Diana…"

Cecil got up from his chair in the van to hover behind his partner. Tank leaned down to the monitor relaying a drone feed from a courtyard on the east side of the Copper Terrace complex.

"You're sure?" Cecil asked.

"Facial recognition shows a ninety-five percent positive match," Tank said.

"That's pretty confident considering the state of her face." Tyron had seen a lot of battered women in the NGZ, but Diana had one eye swollen almost shut, and bruises on her arms.

"She's waiting for food," Tank said.

He zoomed in with the drone camera on a queue of fifty people standing outside a gated-off room in the building. They sometimes distributed drugs this way, but from what Cecil could tell, here they were bartering food.

Slowly the line inched forward, and she approached the gate. Hands reached through the gaps, handing out rations in exchange for money or whatever else people had to give.

Cecil pulled up the file as they waited. "Diana Hickman, thirty-two years old. Two children, lives at Copper Terrace. Unemployed. Two arrests for public disorderly conduct, and one for assault."

"Real winner," Tank said.

"She probably never had a chance to make much of herself." It wasn't an excuse for her behavior, though it sounded that way. People who lived in these slums rarely got out. Even if they had education or skills, there simply weren't enough jobs to hire them.

As the young woman went up to the gate, a man strode over and grabbed her by the arm. He yanked her away, then gave her a hard push.

"Shit, who's that?" Tank asked.

"Follow them," Cecil said.

The insect-size drone flew over the crowd and toward the

alley, where the man had pulled Diana. They slipped into the shadows, where several people lay sleeping off a hangover or drug-induced stupor.

"See if you can get a hit on them," Cecil said.

His phone buzzed in his pocket. He pulled it out and saw a message from his wife.

Sorry, didn't have my phone. Systems are rebooted and production is resuming, but I'm going to be here for another shift.

"Holy shit!" Tank said. "That's Wild Bill!"

Cecil looked up from his phone and leaned down to the security monitor as the drone swooped into the alley. Diana's long-haired assailant smacked her in the face and grabbed her bag, trying to wrest it from her grip.

"No, stop! I need it for my kids!" she shouted.

"Shut up, bitch. I'm not going to tell you again."

He snatched the bag away from her and took off, leaving Diana hunched down, holding her battered face.

"Follow him," Cecil said.

"On it," Tank said.

As Cecil slipped his phone back in his pocket, he noticed movement on a monitor that relayed footage from the utility tunnel underneath the complex.

"Oh, shit, we have a contact on feed four," Cecil said. The drone they had parked in the tunnel had video of a man with fluorescent hair moving down the passage.

"Got a banger," he said. "Looks like Cipher Crew."

"Hell yeah," Tank said.

Cecil fished out the phone that Harkin had given him, but waited to see where they were going. Wild Bill went back inside Copper Terrace through an entrance guarded by two of his minions in their buckskin outfits.

"Go, go, go!" Cecil said.

Tank steered the tiny drone toward the door as it began to close, slipping it through right at the last second. Neither guard seemed to notice.

The drone entered a stairwell.

"I'm calling Harkin," Cecil said as he dialed.

"What you got?" the captain answered.

"We got eyes on WB," Cecil said. "We also have eyes on a member of CC in a utility tunnel."

"Fuck."

"What, sir?"

"Bad timing. We've got our hands full out here right now with the riots. You stay on them and see where they go. Soon as you've got a solid location on Nion, WB, or those weapons, you let me know."

"Copy, sir."

The drone followed Wild Bill up the stairs to the fifth level, where he opened a door on a landing. Before Tank could follow, the man closed the door, right into the tiny drone.

The feed fizzled and went dark.

"Oh, you've got to be shitting me," Tank said as he held up his hands.

"Try to get it back online."

"I can't, not without retrieving it and seeing what broke."

Cecil cursed and shifted his attention to the drone following the member of Cipher Crew through the utility tunnel. The punk had gotten far ahead, and the little drone was having a hard time keeping up.

"Hurry," Cecil said.

"This is top speed, I'm afraid," Tank said.

What had looked to be promising leads were now vanishing before their eyes. The spider robot fell farther behind.

"I'm losing him," Tank said.

Cecil watched as the man moved out of view. “Son of a bitch,” he muttered.

“Sorry. Damn,” Tank said.

“We’ve still got one option left.”

Cecil took over the drone they had hovering over the complex, and narrowed its focus down on the alleyway where Wild Bill had hit Diana.

She had emerged and was back in the line.

They couldn’t afford to lose her too.

“You keep searching those tunnels,” Cecil said. He got up from his seat in the van and grabbed his tool bag.

“What are you doing?” Tank asked.

Cecil pulled out his sidearm and checked the load before tucking it away in the bag. “I’m going after Diana, see what she knows. I got a feeling she’s the key.”

“You crazy?” Tank asked.

Picking up the bag, Cecil shrugged. “I’m sick of sitting around, and if I can convince Diana to come with me, then we’ll have a shot at figuring out where WB is and finishing what Enforcer Ricker started. We can avenge him, Jerky, and everyone else.”

Tank shook his head. “It’s too dangerous.”

“You just stay on the targets and keep me updated. I know what I’m doing.”

He opened the van door and stepped out into the chaos, pulling his hat down over his head.

“Okay, Pepper, let’s see if you still got it,” he whispered.

CHAPTER 18

During the war, twenty-four hours without sleep was pretty much routine, but this was the longest stint Santiago had pulled since then. Despite their fatigue, Hell Squad had managed to evacuate the scientists from Field Lab Zulu with no fatalities—not bad results for heading out in a Category 5 radioactive hurricane on no sleep.

A Wasp had taken them all back to the airship *Persephone*, where Alistair was already snoring in the bunk across from Santiago. He often mumbled in his sleep when he was exhausted. "Such beautiful knockers," he mumbled. "And an arse that could crack a walnut..."

Yosef, in the next bunk, chuckled and then rolled on his side to sleep. Nodin and David were already out, but Santiago couldn't seem to drift off. He had an uneasy feeling that this job involved more than they were being told.

He felt the sudden urge to drink—the same feeling he often had back at home when sleep wouldn't come. He thought of his family, especially his wife, and remembered the note she had given him—probably for a time just like this.

He opened the little envelope.

T, Seeing you pack your bags for Korea again brought back some bad memories. I won't lie about that. Part of me is screaming to stop you, to convince you to stay here with your family where you're safe. But the other part knows you must do this, for your pride and for us. Just remember, at the end of the day what's most important is you coming home to me, Diego, and Isabella.

Be safe, and don't forget, all it takes is all you got.

Love,
Mami Chula

Santiago smiled and put his hands behind his head, closing his eyes. It had been less than a week since he saw his family, and he already missed them terribly. Thinking of them helped him decompress, and he began to drift off. He was dimly aware of the airship moving very fast.

Lights came on, and Santiago sat up as Zimmerman entered the berthing area.

"Everyone up," he barked.

Alistair rolled over, grumbling something. "Alistair, get your dead ass up," Santiago hissed. He shook the big man, who grabbed his wrist and nearly threw him to the deck.

"The bloody hell, mate!" he said.

"Take it easy," Santiago said. "Commander on deck."

Alistair released him as his tired eyes found Zimmerman. The big man sprang down from his bunk on his prosthetic metal legs, in his underwear. The rest of Hell Squad came to attention.

"We got another situation, and this time the orders come from the top," Zimmerman said. "ITC Command has asked for you to lead a rescue op."

"Another one?" Santiago asked.

"Sir, we're all toast," Yosef said. "We need a few hours of R and R."

"Unfortunately, that isn't going to happen. What I'm about to tell you is classified."

Santiago snapped alert.

"Field Lab Alpha activated an SOS during the storm," Zimmerman said. "It was only a Category 2 that hit them, and shortly after, the Def-8 units went offline."

"Wait... Went offline?" Yosef asked.

"All three, simultaneously." Zimmerman sounded as if he couldn't quite believe it either. He put a finger to his earpiece and listened.

"Get suited up; I'll finish the briefing in the launch bay," Zimmerman said.

"Launch bay?" David asked.

"Yeah. This time, you're diving."

He rushed out as fast as he had arrived, leaving Hell Squad all looking at Yosef.

"Fuckin' A, man, they want us to *dive*?" Alistair asked.

Even Nodin looked concerned.

"You think it was Tritons?" David asked.

"No bloody way," Alistair said. "We fucking finished those toaster ovens."

"LT, you have anything to say?" Santiago asked.

Yosef rubbed the back of his neck. He looked beat. "We have our orders, and we're going to get the job done like we always do," he said. "Suit up, Hell Squad."

Santiago felt the urge to push, but he got the feeling Yosef didn't know anything that they didn't already know.

The squad trudged to their lockers and changed back into their hazard suits, followed by their light armor. Santiago put on his helmet. The HUD said they were at thirty-one thousand feet, directly above the monstrous storm over Seoul. The men all grabbed their automatic rifles and sidearms. Next, they secured their parachute harnesses over their lightweight black armor.

"I didn't sign up for this shit," David muttered.

"Yeah, fam, I hear you," Alistair said.

Santiago thought of the note he had just opened from his wife.

He would take care of himself, but he also had a responsibility to his brothers. He locked a magazine into his rifle.

"Everyone good to go?" Yosef asked.

He led them to the launch bay, where the Wasp that had brought them was being loaded with supplies. Zimmerman was there, talking to the two pilots.

"Get them as close as possible," he was saying.

Hell Squad walked over to the tilt-rotor aircraft.

"Both drones sent down into the storm went offline, preventing any real picture of the situation on the ground," Zimmerman said.

"Sir, can you clarify beyond 'they went offline'?" Yosef said.

"Negative, that's your job."

Santiago's eyes narrowed. "Is it possible something shot them down?"

"That's what you're going to find out," said the commander.

The words sent a chill up Santiago's spine.

"There's been no intel to suggest Tritons are out there, but raiders are a concern, as you already know," Zimmerman explained. "Those Def-8 units would go for a pretty penny on the black market, and an organized team of mercs in the exclusion zone might have been waiting for an opportunity to strike during this storm."

It was unlikely, but Santiago prayed it was this and not the work of Tritons.

"Your primary objective is to locate the Def-8 units," said Zimmerman. "If they are destroyed, then your objective is to figure out what happened, eliminate any hostiles, and secure the site, then call in reinforcements for evac of the scientists, if any are alive."

"Understood," Yosef said.

"We're almost in position. Mount up and get ready to dive."

The men followed Yosef into the Wasp, and the outside hatch opened to a storm spewing lightning beneath them. He had parachuted hundreds of times in his career, but never through an electrical storm of this magnitude. Even with their insulated layers, it was a major hazard.

"Okay, Hell Squad, back into the soup we go," said the primary pilot. "I'm going to find you the best dive location I can around ten thousand feet—sound good?"

"No," Alistair said.

Santiago huddled with Yosef.

"LT, you got any idea what's going on down there?"

"Highly unlikely they took out those Def-8 units," Yosef replied. "My money's on raiders."

"I wouldn't be so sure," Nodin said.

"Raiders or machines—we'll waste 'em," Alistair said.

"Maybe, but they would need some major firepower to take down a Def-8 unit," David said. "Don't get cocky."

"Be prepared for anything," Santiago said.

"Take a stim if you need it," Yosef said. "I want you all on your A game."

Nods all around. Diving to the surface wasn't ideal, but no one complained. Not even David, who was so close to punching in his pension card. They were dropping into a radioactive hell with no idea what awaited them on the surface. Santiago wouldn't blame anyone for complaining.

"Entering storm," the primary pilot warned.

The Wasp flew into the cloud. Wind shears slammed against the hull. Santiago bowed his head, made the sign of the cross over his chest, and waited. All around them, the hull, overhead, and deck groaned as the aircraft battled through the violent storm. Soon Hell Squad would be out there in it, without the aircraft to shield them.

"Closing in on DZ," said the pilot. "Trying to find a good pocket to drop you."

A minute of jostling and shaking passed before the green light winked above the hatch. Santiago watched it open to a fairly clear section of sky over the bomb-blasted expanse below.

He identified the coordinates on his HUD as the Wasp lowered to ten thousand feet.

"All right, showtime!" shouted the pilot. "Good luck, Hell Squad!"

"I'll see you on the ground!" Yosef shouted. "Hell's front line!"

The others barked the motto as he leaped into the thick feather bed of clouds.

Santiago went next. Feeling the weightlessness, he put his hands against his thighs, making a plummeting spear of his body.

His HUD flickered as he rocketed through the inky darkness. Along with his altitude, it showed the beacons for the other soldiers in the air.

Looking up past his boots, he could see the other divers in a nosedive to get through the danger as quickly as possible.

Lightning cut through the clouds, making Santiago flinch. Command had better have a *damn* good reason for sending them down through this.

For the first time in years, he felt the creep of real fear—not just for his own life but also for his men and their families. He had promised his wife this was going to be a safe way to pay the bills. But this mission was shaping up to be far worse than he could have imagined.

His gaze shifted from the shelf of clouds to his HUD. At seven thousand feet and just twenty-five seconds into the dive, they were all at terminal velocity.

Lightning flashed across his path again, and he felt the hair on his neck rise. Every muscle tightened across his body, but he shot out of the cloud cover at five thousand feet without being hit.

His HUD signal cleared, and he confirmed that the other four divers were all alive.

Thank you, Jesus.

The surface lit up with the green hue of his night-vision optics. The dark bowl of a bomb crater appeared as a giant lake. Its center was their target, Field Lab Alpha.

Santiago pulled his cord, hardly feeling the tug of his harness as the chute caught air, slowing his rapid descent. The worst of the dust storm had blown through, but he still felt the relentless wind, tugging and pushing him in all directions.

Grabbing his toggles, he drifted downward, the apocalyptic panorama stretching out below him. Rows of buildings lay cracked open like broken eggshells along the edge of the crater. Rubble choked the streets, clogged by vehicles that were stuck in traffic when the inferno rushed outward from the epicenter.

He followed Yosef down into the crater, both of them searching for a level patch at the bottom without a lot of rebar or broken cinder blocks that could injure a diver or tear a hazard suit. Spotting an open patch of dirt at the bottom, Yosef steered over to it. Santiago followed. The drop zone was several hundred yards from their target, but the lieutenant likely wanted to walk in, moving with stealth until they had eyes on the target.

The black dirt of the crater leered up at Santiago. Stiffening his knees, he pulled the toggles at about six feet from the surface to slow his descent and stepped lightly down. Dust puffed up around him. Quickly and efficiently, he collapsed his chute and got out of the harness. As he did, a beacon winked off on his HUD. Another electronic disturbance, perhaps?

His eyes shot upward. The other squad members were sailing down under canopy. But one of them appeared limp in the harness, head slumped, hands not on the toggles.

It was David.

"Oh God, no..." Santiago whispered when he saw smoke curling away from David's body, which could mean only one thing—he had been struck by lightning.

As the other soldiers came down, Santiago ran over to get under him.

"Help me!" Santiago shouted.

Nodin hit the ground and freed himself from his chute. Then came Alistair. Santiago got right under David, reaching up and grabbing him from the air. They crashed to the ground, and Santiago pulled off his helmet, exposing him to the radiation.

Blood trickled from David's ears and mouth.

"Fuck," Santiago said as he began chest compressions. He leaned down and breathed into David's mouth.

"Come on!" he shouted between breaths. Nodin leaned down to listen for air, then checked for a pulse every few pumps.

Nothing.

Santiago kept going, not ready to give up.

Five minutes later, a hand gripped his shoulder.

"He's gone, Sarge," said Nodin.

Santiago shrugged the hand off, then stopped pumping when Yosef said, "He's gone."

Santiago looked up at the storm clouds, wanting to scream. He had lost men before in accidents and in combat, but this felt wrong on a different level, partly because David had been so close to retiring and relaxing on that beach with his wife.

Yosef crouched down and closed the dead man's eyes as Alistair bowed his head.

"Got more bad news," Nodin said. He held up the drone that David had been carrying. "It's broke-dick."

"Goddamn it," Yosef muttered. "We'll come back for David," he said. "Our objective hasn't changed. We find out what happened to the Def-8 units and establish contact with Field Lab Alpha."

He motioned them across the crater floor.

Santiago put a hand on David. "I'm sorry, brother."

* * * * *

Head down, Cecil walked up the sidewalk across the street from the Copper Terrace complex. His earpiece crackled with Tank's voice. "I got eyes on you, but I highly advise you get your ass back to this van," he said.

"Advice noted and politely disregarded," Cecil whispered back.

He glanced up at the topmost floors of the building, where the Cipher Crew had fired machine guns at the chopper, killing Jerky and the other officers. Not far below, Cecil spotted the floor where the bastards had hung the body of Enforcer Thomas Riker. The danger might deter some people, but not Cecil. He used that as fuel to calm his pounding heart.

It was time to flush out the sewage. But first he was going to nab Diana and bring her back to the station, using his disguise and the chaos of the cyberattack on ITC to get inside the building. To do that, he had to move fast, for news was already spreading about the attack being over. Soon ITC trucks would show up and order would be restored.

He cut across the street crowded with furious residents. Moving between pockets of civilians, he made for the eastern part of the complex, where he had seen Diana in the alley.

"CI's on the move," Tank said over the comms.

Cecil hurried across the road. Copper Terrace loomed over him. Normally, a large group of gangbangers hung about on the concrete steps outside, but most of them were off causing trouble. Only a few people loitered around the entrance to the building.

Keeping his hat down to shade his features, Cecil made it around the eastern side of the complex without incident. He quicky entered a courtyard where a long line of residents waited outside the gated building.

"She's going in a side door, on the other side of that line of people," said Tank.

Cecil started toward the entrance, trying to move fast but not so fast he drew attention. He wormed his way between sweaty bodies.

"Hey, watch it!" someone said.

"Pepper, it's too late," Tank said over the channel. "Get out of there. You got a tail…"

Cecil made it to the door that Diana had entered, when a deep voice behind him said, "Hold up, Mr. Sewage Man."

Heart thumping, Cecil paused and turned.

A man with a shaved head strode over, looking him up and down.

"You here to fix them shit pipes?" he asked.

"Gonna try."

"'Bout fuckin' time," said another man who stepped up. "Place smells like ass for two weeks now, brah."

The guy with the shaved head made his way up the steps to Cecil, staring at him eye to eye even from a step below. He reached out and pulled the ID tag on a lanyard away from Cecil's neck.

"Leonard Malcom?" he asked.

"Friends call me Leo," Cecil said with a forced smile.

"Aight, Leo, go on, then. Fix them pipes."

He patted the ID against Cecil's chest, right over his pounding heart.

"Thanks," Cecil said. He turned and opened a door to a stairwell.

"What are you doing?" Tank said over the comms once Cecil was inside.

"Where did she go?" he whispered back.

"Cecil, you go in there, and you don't come out."

He knew it was dicey, but he had come too far to turn back just yet.

"Where'd she go?" he asked again.

Tank paused, then said, "Fourth floor, room four-fourteen."

The stairwell reeked of piss. Trash lay scattered along what appeared to be a major thoroughfare for the tower's thousand occupants. The scent of foreign foods drifted through the open doors on the landings, and lights flickered, casting eerie shadows over the windowless concrete passages along each floor. Children cried, and adults coughed and retched. A junkie sat curled in the corner of the landing, snoring.

On the third floor, a scrawny teenager with green hair and arms folded over his chest gave Cecil a long look—definitely a spotter. If he thought Cecil was an enforcer or a cop, he would whistle up. The gangs had eyes everywhere, always two steps ahead of the Crime Task Force.

But Cecil had an edge. He wasn't an enforcer, and he had fought people far worse than these junior asswipes.

He kept going, his heart pounding harder. He thought of Michelle, knowing she would be horrified at what he was doing. But the truth was, he felt alive. He was doing something that mattered, even if that meant putting himself at risk.

The spotter looked at him but said nothing.

Cecil kept going to the fourth floor, breathing heavily. He wasn't out of shape, but his spinal injury always made climbing stairs difficult. The stairwell was like a sauna, and he worried that the heat, combined with the lack of sleep, might spark an episode of convulsions. If that happened, he had his VitalStim remote with him to stimulate the electrical nodes in his spine, but he would need to find somewhere safe to sit down until the episode passed.

He took a few long, slow breaths, trying to hold off an episode.

It worked.

After a few seconds resting in the stairwell, he opened the door at the landing. Lights flickered down an empty corridor. He walked down to room 414 and knocked. The slot pulled back, and Diana's bruised face looked out.

"What do you want?" she asked.

"To talk," he said.

The slot closed.

Cecil frowned. *Come on, lady, open the—*

As he stepped back, locks clicked, and then the door popped ajar. The woman peered through the gap, looking in both directions, then motioned him inside a dark family room with two couches and a table covered in beer cans and bottles.

"You a friend of Thomas?" she asked.

He hesitated, then nodded.

Scanning the shadows, he saw two kids, both boys. One appeared to be three or four, the other maybe seven. They sat side by side on a threadbare couch, their haggard features lit up by an older-model television. She turned to look at them, and Cecil noticed the fresh swelling on the right side of her face.

"Is there anyone else here besides your children?" he asked.

She shook her head. "What do you want?"

"Information that will solve your problems."

Diana snorted. "Thomas said the same thing, and look what they did to him."

Her gaze met his, but she quickly looked away.

"You should leave before they do the same to you," she said. "These are dangerous men."

"So am I."

He glanced at the boys again, noticing how thin they were.

"How long are you going to let him hurt you and your kids?" Cecil asked.

The older of the two boys, maybe seven years old, looked over. "Mom, you okay?"

"Yes, Ryan."

"Are you in trouble?"

"No," Cecil replied. "Your mother did nothing wrong. I'm here to help."

"You don't understand," she said. "If Bill finds out you're here, he'll…"

Cecil narrowed his gaze. "He'll what? I thought it was Cipher Crew that killed Thomas and shot—"

She snorted again. "You're dumber than I thought if you think that was Cipher Crew."

"Cipher Crew bought machine guns from the White Buffaloes and used them to shoot up one of the choppers."

"You got that part right, but they didn't kill Thomas. That was Bill."

Cecil stared. "Where is he?" he asked. "By telling me, you'll help other families, other children."

"He's an animal." She looked at her boys and sighed. "I should have known better, but he wasn't like this at first. After my husband died in Korea, the father of my kids, I was a mess for a bit... I ended up in a bad place."

A tear streaked down her swollen face.

"I understand being a mess," Cecil said. "I lost some good friends over there—almost didn't come home myself."

Her gaze went back to him. "You served?"

"Yeah."

"Mom?" Ryan came over, hugging her around the waist.

"It's okay," she said.

"Tell me where he is, and I'll make sure he never hurts you again, any of you."

"Is the plumber man asking about Billy?" Ryan asked.

"No, he's here to fix our toilet."

Ryan chuckled. "Gross."

"You like chocolate?" Cecil asked.

A nod.

Cecil dug an energy bar out of the pocket of his cargo pants. He pulled it out and broke it in half. "Give the other half to your brother."

"Thanks, mister."

Ryan hurried away to give his brother the treat. The younger boy perked up and smiled.

Cecil watched, thinking of the horrors the two kids had endured here, like many children who were robbed of their innocence far too early.

"Pepper..." Tank's voice chirped in his earpiece. "I've located Nion and his crew, and the guns in the utility tunnels. Get out of there, Cecil. We're good to go."

Before he could step away to reply, Diana leaned into him.

"Bill was heading to the rooftop terrace," she said. "He has a place on the twentieth floor, room nine-fifteen."

Cecil nodded. "Thank you," he said.

"Wait. There's something else. He has a personal key that works an old maintenance elevator at the end of this hallway. It's got a ladder inside you can use to climb to the top of the building. It's the only way you can get up there without being seen."

Cecil thought on it. He could use it to climb to the top of the building and find Wild Bill. Then he could snatch the bastard and use his key to take the elevator down.

He stifled a grin.

"I appreciate the info," he said.

"What are you going to do?" she asked.

"I'm going to make a call first."

She nodded.

Cecil went into their bathroom and pulled out the phone to Harkin.

"It's me," he said.

"Good work. Tank just called about the guns and Nion."

"It wasn't Nion who killed Thomas," Cecil said. "It was Wild Bill."

"How do you know that?"

"The CI."

"You heard this?"

"She told me. I'm inside CT."

"What the *fuck* you doing, Pepper?"

"You want me to flush out the shit? That's what I'm doing. I know where WB is. I just have to find a way to get him out of here. You deal with Cipher Crew; I'll handle this shit smudge."

CHAPTER 19

Three hours before Tyron was to head to the gala, he still didn't have a speech ready. But he did know who was behind the cyberattack. He was back at his command center at ITC headquarters in Atlanta, working with Angelina and Whitt as data came in about the perpetrators: the Blackworms.

Tyron studied the data that showed how Orion traced the attack back to a mainframe in the NGZ in Chicago, where the extremist group operated off-grid. They were experts at hiding in both the physical world and the shadows of the digital world. But Tyron would find them, and if they were behind the cyberattack, he would make them pay.

"And they haven't taken responsibility?" Tyron asked.

"No, but they've made threats against ITC for our continued use of clones," Angelina said.

Tyron raised a brow. Interesting timing, considering that he had just reactivated testing on the clones in Project Genesis. But how could the Blackworms possibly know this?

The only ones besides him who knew were Whitt and Angelina. And Orion.

But right now Tyron was having a hard time trusting his head of security, who had withheld key information about the existence of the Def-9 prototypes. It may be true that he was indeed trying to protect Tyron, but Tyron saw it as a serious misstep by his old loyal bodyguard.

Still, with the dire situation in Korea and with ITC operations under attack, he needed the man now more than ever. It made sense that the Blackworms were behind it, wanting to inflict damage right before the gala, which was public. Or else they had somehow found out about Project Genesis.

Still, Tyron didn't buy it.

Whitt cleared his throat.

"More bad news, I presume?" Tyron asked.

"Yes, unfortunately. I've been informed Hell Squad experienced a casualty on the dive," he reported. "One of them was killed by lightning."

Angelina looked down and sighed. "That's horrible."

"Damn it," Tyron muttered. He felt the stab of the loss, and the roller coaster of emotions these past few days. From the successful test of the Delta Cloud fusion reactors to the cyberattacks and the storms in the exclusion zones, and then the Def-8 units going offline. Now they had lost one of their best soldiers.

All he could do was keep pushing forward and try to stay positive. His team was doing an excellent job spinning the narrative to the public. For the past two hours, Angelina had been on major news networks remotely, explaining that not only had the cyberattack been thwarted, but ITC was prepared to make a major announcement that would change the world.

But Tyron needed to make sure this was the work of the Blackworms.

"I'm heading to speak with Orion personally," Tyron said. "Let me know the moment you get a sitrep from Hell Squad about the Def-8 units."

"Will do, sir," Whitt said.

Tyron went to the elevator and glanced back to see Angelina looking at him. She gave him a reassuring nod. He nodded back.

The door closed, and the elevator zipped him to the bottom level of the headquarters building, where he walked across the bridge to the sphere that housed Orion.

"Hello, sir," said the AI.

"Orion, something doesn't sit right about the Blackworms being behind the attacks. Why not take credit? Their MO usually is to make a statement."

"I had and still have my own suspicions, but after tracking what our security teams believed originated in Europe and Asia, I was able trace the malware directly to the Blackworms in Chicago."

"You're one hundred percent confident?"

"Yes, the malware came from the Blackworms; however, that does not mean the Blackworms were behind the attack."

"How do you mean, Orion?"

The holographic image of the AI took shape and strode over to Tyron, eyes flashing.

"I fear there is more to this picture than I can see from here, that the threat isn't over, and that perhaps someone else is behind it," said the AI. "Maybe you should consider postponing the gala."

"Absolutely not. The Blackworms wanted to disrupt operations, and I won't give them the satisfaction. If it wasn't them, then find out who it was."

"I am working on it, sir, but please, be careful tonight."

"I will."

As Tyron turned to leave, the walls and ceiling of the chamber lit up with the image of a dark sky strewn with a billion diamonds. An orange and black spaceship blasted across the image.

"*Genesis 1*," Tyron breathed in amazement.

"Yes, sir, it's complete and ready to launch as soon as you give the order."

Tyron smiled, feeling a swell of hope and pride. The moment was shattered by a buzzing sound from the external intercom.

"Sir, you have a call from General Vucci," Whitt said.

Tyron swallowed, suddenly wondering if the military had somehow found out about the Def-8 units going offline. Had someone leaked the news? Or had something terrible happened outside the DMZ?

There were several possible reasons for this call out of the blue, none of them good.

"I'll be up shortly," he said.

Tyron looked at the image of the ship blasting through space for another moment. "I couldn't have done this without you, Orion. Thank you."

"I am excited about the new phase," replied the AI.

"Me too."

As Tyron left the chamber, Orion called out, "Sir, please be cautious."

Something about that statement chilled Tyron. He took the elevator back to the command center and went to his office, closing the door behind him. The leather couch he had spent so many nights on beckoned his exhausted body, but he went straight to the huge windows overlooking the sprawling campus that was the hub of the ITC empire.

Today he saw fingers of smoke rising in the wake of the food riots triggered by the cyberattacks. They were warning signs of just what a fragile world he lived in.

Tyron picked up the phone and tapped the flashing light to connect to Vucci.

"General," he said. "I trust you had a good flight back to the States."

"Probably better than yours, considering the events over the past fourteen hours," Vucci replied gruffly.

Tyron waited, trying to feel out the general.

"Have you figured out who's behind the cyberattacks?" he asked.

"We have a good idea, yes."

"I figured you would. Looks like the situation is fully under control now."

"Yes." But Tyron knew that the general would already know that, since ITC had open communications with the Pentagon and all military assets, to keep them up to the second on situations just like this.

"We are happy to assist in any way possible," Vucci said. "Just say the word and we will make sure the perpetrator never sees the light of day again."

"I'll share the info as soon as I'm certain, sir. Now, if that's all, I've got a speech to prepare for tonight's gala."

"Right. I'll be seeing you there. I thought we could discuss the Def-9 units again, in person."

"Have there been new developments in Korea?"

"No, but the clock is ticking. The world can change in an instant, and history shows that those who are behind the curve and ignore the warning signs are the ones who perish."

"I appreciate the historical context, but I'm not going to break international law until you provide evidence the Tritons are still alive and planning an attack."

"But you have no problem breaking international law by reactivating the tests in Project Genesis? Or by giving Orion access to the ITC network?"

Tyron lifted a brow.

"Don't worry, Dr. Tyron, I won't be ratting you out to the United Nations," he said. "I'm sure you have a good reason scientifically and will take the utmost precautions to ensure safety."

Tyron remained silent, giving nothing away.

"We must discuss this more tonight at the gala," Vucci said.

The call clicked off before Tyron could respond. He gave an angry snort, then opened the office door. Angelina and Whitt remained at the monitors.

"I don't want to be disturbed for anything short of another nuclear war. Got it?" he said.

"Of course, sir," Whitt said.

Angelina nodded.

Tyron returned to his desk and looked at the wall of pictures. The first was a photo of him and his father, when Tyron was just a boy, visiting a lab from atop his father's shoulders. They both were smiling in a rare moment. Then there was the picture of Tyron and his best friend, Daniel, on their trip to the Amazon. It was their last picture together, and Tyron remembered teasing his friend about being so preoccupied with his mosquito net.

The memories flashed past as he prepared his speech about all the moments that had led to this announcement of the most important project in his life: to leave Earth.

Just as he finished writing his last sentence on his notepad, a knock came at the door.

"Come in," he announced.

"There's not a war, but I thought I'd bring you your suit since we need to leave soon, sir," Angelina said.

He looked up as she walked in wearing a black-and-gold cocktail dress with stiletto heels. For a fleeting moment, he just took in her beauty before looking away.

"I'll hang it in your bathroom," she said.

"Thank you," he said.

He went inside to change, unbuttoning his white dress suit. He folded it neatly and put it on the marble counter, catching his deep-brown reflection in the mirror. Palming the counter, he leaned in to see more gray in the black hair along his temples. His dark, normally intense eyes appeared tired and unfocused behind the special prescription eyeglasses with blue lenses. He rubbed his eyes, then splashed cold water on his face.

Feeling refreshed, he put on his tux, finishing it off with his staple red bow tie.

Angelina waited in his office. She came over and fixed his bow tie with a smile.

"You look good, sir, very elegant," she said.

"Thanks. You look very nice too."

"Hah. Thanks, sir. Are you ready?"

He picked his notepad up off his desk and went to the command center, where Whitt stood in a tuxedo.

"You clean up okay," Tyron said.

"You'll only see me in this stiff suit once a year, sir."

Tyron chuckled.

"No updates on Hell Squad," Whitt said in a more serious tone.

Tyron nodded and took an elevator with his team to the ground floor, where an SUV waited. Another ITC security guard waited behind the wheel. The three got in, and the car started down the long road as the front gates to the campus opened to the surrounding city.

Tyron pushed his glasses up to examine the skyline, where fingers of smoke smudged a spectacular sunset. Angelina didn't seem to notice as she applied lipstick using a small mirror from her purse. Or perhaps she didn't care.

"Okay, that's better," she said, pursing her lips and then smiling. "Sir, it's time to get excited. Aren't you, even the slightest bit?"

"Yeah, sure," Tyron replied.

"Well, get excited. I know it's going to be hard to let loose after what's happening in Seoul, but remember what tonight's about: the accomplishments of ITC, which are brilliant and many, sir. You're winning on all fronts, and in your speech, you will show the world what ITC is capable of."

She put a hand on his arm.

"Put your faith in Hell Squad; they know what they're doing," Angelina said. "Everything's going to work out. I have all the faith in you, sir."

"Thanks," Tyron said. "I hope to live up to it."

She smiled warmly. "Now, loosen up. It's time to have some fun for once."

He tried to relax, but something just felt off about the cyber-attacks and the missing Def-8 units. As the car picked up speed, he thought about Orion's warning.

Tyron wasn't going to relax and let his guard down. His true enemy had yet to reveal itself.

* * * * *

An hour after landing, Hell Squad was approaching Field Lab Alpha, with Nodin on point. Without the drone, they were relying on the scout more than ever.

Losing David hurt, but Santiago had learned how to bury his emotions in the field. He had experienced many losses over the years, some that still haunted him at night or during downtime. No matter how hard he tried to save people or stop the bad guys, he knew that it was mostly out of his control. He couldn't dodge a bullet or even tell people when one was coming. War wasn't fair; it spared no one. And out here, he couldn't afford to let anything break his focus.

With every step, the radiation levels seemed to increase. They were back in the lethal range. He looked to the minimap and saw they were closing in on Field Lab Alpha. It was just a quarter mile across the crater, but they had yet to pick up any hits on their beacon locators. No scientists, and no Def-8 units here to protect them.

They were taking virtually the same path they took yesterday when the Wasp brought them to the top of the crater. But the storm that had rolled in had created fresh dunes of debris, masking any tracks.

Yosef brought up a fist as Nodin hunkered down at point. Santiago spotted the shapes of the habitats in the distance.

"I want eyes on the field lab before we move in," he said. "Nodin, check it out, but stay frosty."

The men hunkered down while the scout vanished into the darkness beyond the rolling dunes of rubble. The wait gave Santiago plenty of time to consider what might be out there, and also to dwell on the loss of David.

Santiago felt something beyond anger—a deep dread in his guts.

"Contact," Alistair whispered.

Shouldering his rifle, Santiago took aim but quickly saw Nodin's IR tag through his scope. The scout jogged over, covered in dust and panting. "I found the field lab, but no sign of scientists or the Def-8 units."

Yosef stared for a moment, then gave a nod.

"Okay, we move in with extreme caution," he said. "Nodin, you're now the best marksman; I want you hanging back. Hold security and cover us."

Nodin found a position and set up the sniper rifle they had taken off David. At his ready signal, Santiago took point across the blackened rubble. He swept the terrain with night-vision goggles.

It was eerily quiet out here, as if they had entered a void, another realm where nothing made a sound. Not even a cockroach scuttled across the scorched ground.

Yosef flashed a hand signal, and Alistair fanned out, both men falling into combat intervals with Santiago as they approached the closest habitats. According to the power readings coming back on their HUDs, the security border appeared to be down.

But how could a Category 2 storm have knocked out the backup power?

Santiago trained his rifle forward, sensing that whatever had happened here went beyond the extreme weather event. Big storms had hit these labs many times before; they were built to withstand them.

He kept going, senses on full alert as they crossed the downed security perimeter. Some two hundred feet ahead, fog drifted across a gray field that revealed the first sign of life. Red vines lay coiled and twisted across the dirt. Not a huge surprise since the same plants had survived the Category 5 winds back at Field Lab Zulu.

A quick scan showed that the vegetation was the only life out there—no human signatures. Santiago checked his HUD again but found no hits on the beacon locator for the machines either.

Yosef gave the advance signal and Alistair took point. Nodin moved up to a new sniping position as the squad approached the habitats.

"Stay clear of those," Yosef said.

The orange tendrils pulsated, creating an eerie glow in the haze. The other troopers moved like apparitions in the vaporous curtain. As they closed in on the first structure, Santiago stepped over a tendril of pulsating flora and felt a soft crunch under his boot. Looking down, he discovered a hand in an ITC protective suit, its curled fingers protruding from the moist soil.

"Oh, shit," he muttered.

"What is it?" Yosef asked.

Pushing with the tip of his steel-toed boot, Santiago dislodged the arm from the dirt. As Yosef leaned down to look, Alistair whistled. He held up three fingers, then pointed at bodies ahead.

The team spread out, uncovering more dead scientists, many of them partially buried in the loose soil. Barbed vines had wrapped around some of them, sinking fine curved needles into the flesh.

Santiago felt a chill. Were these plants... *feeding* on the dead scientists?

There was no way the plants killed these men. Nor could they have damaged or destroyed the Def-8 units.

He examined the ground, searching for bullet casings or signs of blood splatter to explain the dead scientists, but found nothing. The squad spread out and continued exploring the field of pulsating limbs. Santiago tried to make sense of what the terrain was showing him—that the vegetation had indeed killed these scientists, or at least attacked them during the storm, which then killed anyone caught outside.

But where were the Def-8 units that had guarded this lab?

Alistair bent down to examine a leg and foot enwrapped in the vines. When he touched it, the vine retracted with a jerk, pulling the leg with it.

"Bloody hell!" he said, falling on his backside.

"What the hell were these science jockeys *really* doing here?" Santiago asked.

"Messing with science," Alistair said. "Playing God, like Nodin said."

"Over here," Nodin called.

A hundred feet to the east, he stood on top of another hill, looking down at the now pulsating flora. The squad came up to him and saw the destroyed hazard tents lying scattered in all directions. But all the habitats and labs, by contrast, appeared mostly undamaged. Oddly, though, several of the doors stood wide open.

"You see what I see?" Nodin asked.

"So these nimrods were outside during the storm?" Alistair asked.

"I don't know, but we have to find the Def-8 units," Yosef said. "Nodin, keep searching the site."

Santiago could keep his suspicions to himself no longer.

"Now would be a good goddamn time to share anything you're keeping from us, sir," he said.

Yosef glared at him from behind his visor. "I don't like your tone, Sergeant Rodriguez."

"I don't like it either, but with all due respect, LT, my tone reflects my frustration with the bullshit intel ITC has been giving us on this entire mission, which currently is completely fubar."

"Take it down a notch—"

"David is fucking *dead*, sir. He's gone. And for what? We still don't know what the hell the scientists were doing out here, and I have this sneaking suspicion that you have withheld info from us."

"I smell something fishy too," Alistair said.

Yosef gave him a hard look, then turned to Santiago and sighed. "You're right. I have withheld information from you, and for that I'm sorry, but what I know is classified."

"I think it's time to tell us before we all end up like these poor bastards," Santiago said.

Yosef paused another moment.

"Come on, boss, what's the tea?" Alistair said.

With a grunt, Yosef said, "The JMF has picked up seismic activity in the exclusion zones, and they're worried the Triton Legion's still out there. That's why we brought the sensors out here, and why they asked me to bring you on board."

"You got to be shitting me. That's a joke, right?" Alistair said with a laugh. "We were there—Operation Dark Skies, remember? They're all dead, LT."

"Maybe, but the JMF doesn't believe that."

"Doesn't believe *what*?" Nodin asked.

The scout walked over, his footsteps hardly making any noise.

"JMF suspects the Triton Legion is digging," Yosef explained again.

"Yeah, I figured that much; we all did," Nodin said. "And while I don't think this was Tritons, something took down the security perimeter we put up here." He gestured to the east. "I found some tracks on the other side of those habs. Come, I'll show you."

The men followed him down the mound and out toward the structures. On the other side of the main building where Hystad had his office, Nodin crouched to examine prints. There were multiple sets of tracks in the mud—human boots and the smooth indentation the machines left behind.

"Tritons wouldn't take hostages," Nodin said. "Whoever survived whatever happened here took off, and the Def-8 units went with them. More than likely, we just haven't been able to pick up signals due to the storms."

Yosef examined the tracks and looked off to the northwest. "Get ready to move," he said. "We're following the tracks after I call this in."

He stepped away while Santiago went over to Nodin and Alistair, who had their rifles up.

"Place is really freakin' me out," Alistair said.

"*Persephone One*, this is Hell Squad Actual," Yosef said into his comm. "Site located, partial science team has been located, KIA. Tracks from survivors and the Def-8 units lead northwest. No sign of Tritons or raiders. Most likely, these scientists were killed by the storm. Please advise, over."

Santiago watched the raging lightning storm on the horizon as they waited for new orders. A transmission crackled back, muffled but intelligible.

"Immediate exfil from AO required," came the response. *"Repeat, execute immediate exfiltration from area of operations on foot. New objective is to pursue survivors and Def-8 units and locate. Over."*

Santiago looked up at the sky, realization setting in.

ITC was going to erase all evidence of this site.

Yosef turned back to them. "You heard 'em. Let's get clear of this site. They're going to light it up!"

CHAPTER 20

Cecil climbed the ladder in the dark maintenance elevator shaft, sweat dripping from his brow. He had been at it for nearly half an hour. With each step, pain shot up his back.

With the tool bag slung over his back, he didn't have easy access to his VitalStim remote, which would help him if he had an episode with his spine. To make matters worse, the shaft blocked all signals from outside, including any radio contact with Tank.

His plan was looking stupider by the minute.

He still didn't know how he was going to nab Wild Bill and get him into the elevator. But Cecil was used to improvising. He had been on a dozen missions with Hell Squad behind enemy lines, coming up with last-minute plans in life-or-death situations, all against an enemy far worse than any of the scum inside the building.

Or maybe not…

He thought about Thomas, who Wild Bill had beaten and tortured before killing him and hanging him outside. If Cecil got caught, he was looking at the same treatment, maybe even worse.

Don't get caught.

He could see the bottom of the elevator car above him. Only two more floors to go, but the agony was almost unbearable now. A jolt of pain accompanied every step, as if the nerves in his back were on fire. He closed his eyes, gritted his teeth, and climbed another rung.

Determined, Cecil kept going, reaching the elevator car and going past it. The ladder took him to a platform in front of a door. He twisted the handle and popped it open to find himself looking down a hallway. After a quick scan to confirm that it was clear, he climbed out and went to the door, which he opened to a gray sky. He looked out over a rooftop of maintenance equipment and air-handler units.

Cupping a hand over his ear with his tiny transmitter, he whispered, "Tank, do you copy?"

An instant response hissed back into his earpiece.

"Pepper, thank God! I thought I lost you," Tank said. "What's your status?"

"I'm on the roof. You got a drone up here?"

"Copy, but I don't see the target."

"Stand by."

Keeping low, Cecil worked his way through the HVAC equipment and ducked down behind the final unit, which overlooked the rooftop terrace a floor below. Garden rows in raised planters covered much of the western part of the roof.

On the edge of the crops were two large public restrooms. Beyond those, in the center of the terrace, a group of shirtless men covered in tattoos played basketball on a court with a cracked surface and no net on the hoop.

He scanned the faces of the crowd around the court for Wild Bill. Seeing no one who fit the description, he went around to the eastern part of the roof, where about fifty residents lounged around clusters of metal picnic tables.

Cecil pulled his vibrating phone out. "Hello?" he answered quietly.

"Where the hell you been?" Harkin asked.

"In an elevator shaft."

"And now?"

"Top of the complex… Oh, shit."

"What?"

"I got eyes on Wild Bill."

The Old West throwback had changed into a sleeveless yellow shirt with tattoos of old-style revolvers on both forearms. He sat under an awning at a picnic table near the public bathrooms, boots up on the bench, cowboy hat beside him. He lifted it up, took a bag from underneath it, and handed it to a kid maybe ten years old, then waved the boy off.

"You're certain it's him, Pepper?" Harkin asked.

"Hundred percent."

There was a pause on the line. "I don't have any spare support for you. We're focusing on Nion and his scumbags. For now, you got to stand down."

"Sir, I can get to him."

"How?"

"I'll figure something out."

"Too dangerous. Your orders are to return back down that shaft and leave the NGZ. Do you understand?"

Cecil watched the subhuman who had tortured Thomas and helped kill Jerky and the other cops. This was the opportunity he had been waiting for: to excise that cancer and stop it from spreading further.

"Pepper, did you get my last?" asked Captain Harkin.

"Copy that, sir."

"Good. Now, get the hell out of there."

Cecil began to pull back when Wild Bill suddenly hopped off

the table. He slapped hands with a thug who was clearly part of his posse, based on his leather pants and the jacket with a White Buffalo on the back.

Crouching behind a different air handler, Cecil watched Wild Bill moving around the rooftop as if he owned the place: slapping hands, bumping fists, and cracking jokes with more of his gang. Cecil lost sight of him for a second when he walked behind the courts, then saw him heading for the gardens.

Not the gardens. The bathrooms.

Cecil had an idea. It was risky.

If he could surprise Wild Bill inside the men's room, maybe he could get him into the maintenance elevator and out of the building and somehow stay alive in the process.

It was a huge risk, but he couldn't let this guy get away.

Cecil checked out the men on the court and those loitering around it. Gang members were easy to pick out. Many, if not all, carried guns and blades. He was in their territory, behind enemy lines, and alone. But he had gotten out of situations far worse than this one, where he was outnumbered ten to one. Part of success came from not fearing failure.

Time to take out the trash.

As Wild Bill went into the bathroom, Cecil put his tool bag down and pulled out his pistol. He grabbed a hammer too. Then he peeled off his uniform shirt, going shirtless. Next, he tied a bandanna behind his neck and turned his baseball cap around.

He climbed down the rooftop maintenance ladder to the terrace and walked down the rows of planters, minding his own business. No one even seemed to notice. Cecil kept his gaze on the court, hoping to look like one of the ballers, and made it to the bathrooms without attracting any attention.

Pushing the door open, he stepped aside as someone came out.

"Watch it, *puto*," the guy said.

"My bad, bro," Cecil said.

He pulled the bandanna up over his face and walked inside. There were four toilet stalls, all empty. Wild Bill was pissing in the farthest urinal. And he was alone.

Cecil flipped the lock on the door, then pointed the pistol at Wild Bill while walking toward him.

"Don't move or make a sound," he warned.

Wild Bill turned his cold eyes on Cecil and laughed. "Who the fuck are you supposed to be?"

"The guy who's taking you in."

Another laugh. "You know who I am?" He turned, junk hanging out.

"Unfortunately, I do, and I got to say, I think they got the moniker wrong. They should call you Broke-Dick Bill."

"You another enforcer?" Wild Bill asked, zipping up his pants and taking a step forward. "Didn't you hear what happened to your buddy?"

"Don't take another step. Turn around; put your hands above your head."

"You'll never make it out of here."

Cecil aimed the pistol at his face. "I'll take my chances."

"Chances? You got one at turning this situation around where it doesn't end up with your balls in your mouth, bitch," Wild Bill said.

Smiling, Cecil shook his head. "That's not really how this works. I tell you what your options are, and right now there are two. You come with me, pretend we're old pals, and I take you alive. The second option is a whole lot easier . . ."

Cecil raised the gun to the man's face and grinned.

Someone pounded on the door. "Bill, you good in there?"

"You're fucked now," Wild Bill said with a grin.

Cecil knew better than to turn toward the door. "Tell them you're fine, or I put one in your kneecap," Cecil said.

"And then how will you get me out of here?"

Cecil considered his options, which were starting to narrow by the minute. He reached behind him with his free hand, pulling the hammer from his waistband. Another voice came from outside.

Wild Bill took a step forward.

"Move again, and I swear—" Cecil started to say.

"You keep swearing but not doing shit." He took another stride. "I think you're bluffin'."

Cecil walked forward and swung the hammer into his arm, back of the elbow. Wild Bill screeched in pain as Cecil grabbed him and pulled him away. He shoved him into the door.

After readjusting his bandanna that had fallen down, Cecil said, "You do anything stupid, and the next thing this hammer cracks is two nuts."

He smacked Wild Bill in the back with the handle to emphasize his point. The man wailed again, and Cecil took the moment to transmit to Tank, using the agreed-upon keyword.

"Turtle's Lair, I've got Wild Bill in custody, but multiple hostiles outside. Will attempt to take maintenance elevator to the ground level. Over."

Cecil unlocked the door and kicked it open into something hard.

"Back up!" he shouted. He fired shots skyward, then aimed the gun at the two muscle heads who had guarded Wild Bill earlier.

"I'm a cop, and I'm taking him with me," Cecil said. "There's a raiding team on the way, but if you want to stick around, be my guest."

"No way in hell you'sa gettin' out of here, pig," Wild Bill grunted. "I'll fuckin' skin y—"

Cecil whacked him in the back of the head with the side of the hammer while moving his pistol between the two goons. Then he grabbed Wild Bill and pulled him through the gardens toward the short maintenance ladder.

It took a few more shoves, but moving fast, they made it there in just under half a minute. Most of the civilians had dispersed, but the dozen who remained behind were coming closer, all of them looking as though they wanted a piece of Cecil.

"Climb," Cecil said.

Groaning, Wild Bill held the back of his head, glaring at Cecil.

"I said fucking climb," he repeated.

Several more thugs—five of them now—cautiously followed, watching for an opportunity.

"Get back!" Cecil shouted. "There's a raiding party on the way, and anyone they catch won't be seeing the sun for a long fucking time!"

"He's lying!" someone yelled.

Cecil kept his pistol aimed out at the encroaching gangbangers as he came up the ladder. When he got to the rooftop, he fired a shot into the air for the punks who still hadn't gotten the message. A few ran, but others pulled out guns of their own.

Shots rang out, and Cecil ducked behind the big HVAC units as bullets zipped past. He scrambled over to Wild Bill, who tried to squirm away. A swat with the hammer to his shoulder blade subdued him. He shrieked in pain, flopping to the ground.

"You bastard!" he groaned.

Grabbing him by the collar, Cecil dragged him toward the maintenance door. He kicked it open and entered the hallway, then shut the door behind him and smashed the lock.

It looked as though this might actually work!

He pulled Wild Bill down the passage to the elevator. When they were just a foot away, a bell chimed, and the doors slid open to reveal three shirtless men covered in prison ink and holding lengths of iron rebar wrapped with barbed wire. They all looked at Cecil as he stood there with the pistol at the back of Wild Bill's neck. A moment of realization passed over the gangbangers as their bloodshot eyes went from Cecil to Wild Bill, who laughed.

"I told you, you ain't getting out of here, you fucking pig," he said. "I'm gonna carve you up like that enforcer and send the pieces back to your family."

He grinned, drooling blood.

"You got a girl? A wife? Yeah, I'll carve that bitch up too!" Wild Bill bent down as if to tie his boot, only to come up with a knife.

Cecil had wanted to bring the scum in alive, but that didn't seem to be in the cards. He connected eyes as Bill slashed outward.

"For Jerky," Cecil said, and pulled the trigger, putting a bullet between those wild eyes.

Then he brought the gun up as the men charged. He dropped two of them with a head and a neck shot, but the third slammed into him, raking him across the ribs with barbed wire.

Cecil hit the ground hard, his back screaming in pain. The guy straddled him, holding a knife now in both hands and bringing it down at his chest. Cecil reached up, grabbing the assailant's wrists before the knife could plunge into his chest.

Grunting, Cecil pushed back, but he had no leverage.

The knife inched closer to his chest, right above his heart.

Pinned down, Cecil bucked to his right side. The knife tip scraped against the floor.

Cecil bucked again in the other direction, sending an agonizing jolt of fire up his back, neck, and skull. His eyes darted about for the pistol he had dropped. He grabbed it with his free hand as the man raised the knife again.

"No!" the man screamed.

Cecil stuffed the barrel into his open mouth and pulled the trigger.

Hot blood flecked his face as the gangbanger collapsed on him.

Cecil gasped for breath under the weight of the body, when a new spasm of pain hit him. He fought back, knowing he had seconds to get up and into the elevator before more reinforcements showed up.

Pounding came on the maintenance door as he pushed up, groaning.

Time was up.

"Got to move, Pepper," he whispered.

* * * * *

Fifty miles east of Atlanta, a live orchestra played classical music in the courtyard, kicking off the gala and summoning the early guests. The two-century-old estate had been passed down from generation to generation, then sold to ITC. Tonight it would be the venue for revealing Tyron's biggest scientific advancement in the history of the company. Some of the early guests were already here, but those weren't typically the people he needed to rub elbows with. Those were always the late arrivals, who came late on purpose just to show that they could.

He stood in the perfectly manicured gardens on the south side of the property, waiting for Whitt, who said he had news.

He could see his head of security jogging across the lawn toward him, away from the terrace where Angelina greeted the guests. Dressed in a black-and-gold cocktail dress with high heels, she looked gorgeous and was already putting her beauty, charm, and brains to work on the crowd.

"Sir," Whitt said, panting. "I'm sorry to deliver more bad news, but Hell Squad found the scientists. They were killed."

"*Killed?*" Tyron practically shouted it. "By whom?"

"Unknown so far, sir. Hell Squad has found a set of tracks from a survivor, as well as tracks from the Def-8 units they're following."

Tyron narrowed his gaze at the sky, trying to make sense of this.

"Tell me what you're thinking," he said.

"That this could be raiders and the Def-8 units pursued them, but that's unlikely, sir. I also think it's unlikely it was Tritons. There's no evidence of a firefight."

Whitt paused.

"What? Don't hold back," Tyron said.

"The scientists, sir. Their bodies were found among the plants."

"Come again?"

"Plants, sir. Hell Squad thinks the flora might have attacked them during the storm."

Tyron loosened his bow tie. It felt tight, choking him. He wasn't sure what to make of this news; it didn't seem possible. Nothing in the tests had shown the Cordovia plants to be aggressive.

He noticed Angelina looking over from across the gardens. She raised a brow as if to say, *Are you okay?*

He turned his back and went over to a pair of towering century-old oak trees to contemplate the news. He could understand losing the science team to a storm or raiders, but to hear that *plants* may have killed them was beyond shocking. That was still better than falling to the Triton Legion though.

"The order has already been given to erase the site, based on protocol," Whitt said.

Tyron didn't flinch at that. There were protocols he himself had set up in case of biological contaminants. They couldn't allow it to spread. He imagined drones swooping down and carpet-bombing the area to erase the field lab, giving the scientists a fiery grave like that of the innocent citizens of Seoul.

"I'll contact their families, tell them they were killed in an accident," he said. "Let them know their work was pivotal to ITC operations and restoration efforts. And you let me know the moment Hell Squad figures out what the fuck is going on out there with the Def-8 units, even if it's in the middle of my damn speech."

He heard the anger in his voice, but he couldn't hold it back.

"I'll take care of it, sir," Whitt said with a reassuring nod.

Tyron took a deep breath, filling his lungs with fresh air that smelled of roses. He thought back to what Orion had said in the chamber, advising him to be cautious.

Tyron looked out over the grounds. ITC security agents in tuxedos patrolled the perimeter of the gardens. He couldn't see any of the drones or discreet defensive systems, but he knew they were out there. It made him feel better knowing this place was locked down.

You're just being paranoid, he thought.

Tyron walked out of the garden and joined Angelina.

"Everything good?" she asked.

"Great," he lied.

"Come on, Tyron. I know you better than that. I know that's not true, but the question is, how bad are things? Is it the field team?"

"Yes, they were found dead."

"What? How?"

"Hell Squad said they discovered the corpses among the flora from Operation RadGrow."

"What? That can't be. It must have been the storm."

She swallowed, keeping her poker face as she adjusted his bow tie.

"I'm sorry, but there has to be another explanation. The good news is that it wasn't…" She didn't finish her sentence, but Tyron knew that she was thinking the same thing. Both of them were glad it wasn't the Tritons.

"Shake this off, sir. It's okay to try and enjoy yourself," she said. "Fun is good. Fun means we're human. It separates us from the machines."

When he didn't cheer up, she put a hand on his shoulder.

"Before we go in, I've got something to show you," she said. "Come, follow me."

She led Tyron and Whitt away from the gate at the front of the terrace, deeper into the gardens. A red blanket was draped over something in the center of a rose garden. Walking over to it, she grabbed the side and pulled it back, uncovering a life-size statue of his father.

"I thought this might bring you some joy," she said. Pulling out a remote, she tapped a button that activated a hologram of Booker Red from March 2038.

"We haven't spoken for a year, which I deeply regret, son. You're off globe-trotting, and for that I'm glad. Seeing the world will open your eyes to many things. It will shape your beliefs and make you a better leader. If you're seeing this now, then I'm gone. If that is the case, then you are in charge now, and I leave you with a few thoughts. You were always a smart boy, not to mention a bit mischievous, which helped you learn some important lessons. I've had the privilege of seeing you grow into a man. I know that you will take ITC places I never imagined, that you will achieve great things, and I'm sorry I am not there to watch you."

The hologram smiled.

"I have made mistakes in my life—with your mother, as your father, and as the leader of ITC—but my greatest mistake was not spending more time with you. You were right about the machines,

about the war. I can see that now, and I'm sorry. Trust your instinct, and don't give in to pressure from shadowy forces, no matter what they say to you."

Tyron scratched his jaw, trying to make sense of the cryptic message.

"Of all the good that ITC did, my greatest accomplishment will always be you, Tyron. I'm forever proud of you. Never forget, you have the ability to take our species to places our ancestors only dreamed of going. I love you."

Tyron stared, overcome with emotion from the powerful message. If only he could respond, tell his dad he loved him, too, and that he was sorry.

"Where did you find this?" he said quietly.

"I didn't. Orion did," Angelina said. "When I had the statue commissioned, I thought it would be a nice touch."

He felt the tears well in his eyes. But behind the joy, he felt anger as he focused on the cryptic message about shadowy forces—no doubt a reference to the ITC board. He distinctly remembered, on the day he learned about the will, the company's general counsel hesitating when Tyron asked if his father had left him a message.

The bastard had flat-out lied to him, and Tyron had fired him the next day.

Tyron shook away the anger and looked at Angelina. "Thank you," he said. "It means the world to me."

She gently placed her hand on his wrist. Their eyes met, and for a moment he was reminded that he had feelings for her that could ruin their working relationship. Too great a risk.

Tyron would never act on those feelings. He started toward the gates. As they approached the circle drive, the sun dipped behind the horizon, leaving fiery crimson streaks over the shake roof of the colonial mansion. A giant sculpture of a horse and rider reared grandly above a fountain on the terrace. Stone planters with red flowers native to Georgia, no doubt selected personally by Angelina, lined the brickwork.

They crossed the circular brick driveway where the most expensive cars were dropping off late-arriving guests. Men wearing tuxedos, and women in dresses that showed off diamond necklaces and décolletage. Old money. People with deep roots in the South. Powerful people.

"Ah, Dr. Red," came a booming voice.

Tyron knew that Southern drawl. It was Senator Perry, head of the Robotics Committee, tasked with overseeing what few automated machines remained, mostly automated espresso machines in coffee shops.

"Miss Sanchez, you look utterly dazzling tonight," he said.

"Thank you, Senator," she said with a smile.

"Senator," Tyron said, shaking his hand.

"I'm told you might have a problem."

Tyron stiffened ever so slightly. "Oh? What's that?"

In that fleeting moment, his mind cast about, trying to grasp what the senator was referring to by the comment. Had Perry somehow gotten wind of the Def-8 units? Or maybe he was referring to the cyberattacks. He had expected the latter.

Perry held Tyron's gaze.

"You have humans serving drinks," the senator said with a laugh.

Tyron looked over his shoulder at the bars set up on the outside terrace. Bartenders in tuxedos were pouring wine and mixing cocktails for the guests.

"I've gotten used to trusting my drinks to dispensing units," Perry said. "They're boring but quite consistent, and don't skimp on the liquor."

Tyron laughed.

"We'll make sure you get exactly what you like, Senator," Angelina said.

"Indeed. I hope you enjoy the evening," Tyron said.

"I'd like to speak to you about the cyberattack later," Perry said. "To ensure it won't happen again. It *can't*, sir."

"It won't," Angelina said.

"I understand the concern, Senator," Tyron said. "Come find me later, and we can discuss how it happened and how we will prevent it from happening again."

"Excellent."

"Now, if you'll excuse me, I'd better get inside for our big announcement. I'm excited to hear your thoughts."

"I look forward to it." Perry bowed slightly. "Miss Sanchez."

"Senator," she replied.

Tyron and Angelina walked onto the terrace as liveried waiters went about with plates of hors d'oeuvres. Other staff carried around trays of champagne glasses. Angelina plucked two off and handed one to Tyron.

"To take the edge off," she said.

He took a glass, and they clanked them together.

"To Industrial Tech Corporation, your father, and you, Tyron," she said.

"And to you, for everything you do to keep the wheels from falling off."

She smiled.

"Oh, look!" she murmured.

Tyron turned as a dark-skinned woman stepped out onto a brick patio surrounded by white flowers. Wearing a lavish, flowing white gown that glistened in the lights, she took a deep, grounding breath.

The guests gathered around, talking in whispers. The hush deepened, anticipation palpable in the air before she opened her mouth and sang the first soaring notes of the aria. Her rich alto voice resonated effortlessly across the terrace.

Tyron found himself entranced by the beauty and the emotional power that a human voice could convey. And he found himself more inspired in his own mission—not just to preserve humanity but to take it places where other pioneers had only dreamed of going.

CHAPTER 21

"Keep moving!" Santiago shouted over the wind.

Fifty-mile-per-hour gusts assaulted Hell Squad as they trekked northwest into the heart of another storm. They were now almost five miles from the crater, having spent the past two hours moving at a quick pace. The Def-8 and human tracks were long gone now, but Nodin had picked up a signal for one of the scientists on his beacon locator.

Someone *was* alive out there.

"It's Voss!" Nodin shouted over the howling wind.

Santiago checked his HUD and confirmed, it was indeed the beacon of the scientist who had given Hell Squad such a chilly reception when they first arrived at the field lab days ago. But Santiago doubted that this guy had anything to do with the Def-8 units going offline. They were more than likely evacuating the scientist.

Whatever had happened, Voss would likely know.

Nodin guided them toward a valley of rubble that blocked some of the wind. But with conditions worsening by the second and visibility down to just ten feet ahead, it was going to be difficult to catch up with Voss, who was also on the move.

"We should hunker down, wait this out," Nodin said.

That was the safe thing to do, but Yosef seemed to have other ideas.

"Keep moving!" he shouted.

Nodin looked back, and for the first time that Santiago could remember, the tracker questioned the lieutenant. "Sir, this flying debris could rip our suits, and one wrong step could send us into a sinkhole. Visibility is fucked."

"Your concerns are noted, but we're too close to Voss to give up now," Yosef barked back. "He's the key to the truth about the Def-8 units."

"Okay, LT."

Nodin kept on point, guiding them down a road that seemed to split the blast zone. Grit sandblasted their hazard suits, just as the scout had warned them.

He led them away from the road, taking an alley between the foundations of two buildings that had been lopped off by the nuclear blast. Bricks clogged the path.

Santiago noticed that Voss's beacon had stopped. He brought up the map of the area, knowing that it was mostly useless in this blasted, much-changed terrain. It seemed that the scientist had taken shelter in an old mall.

"Voss stopped!" Santiago yelled.

Yosef raised a fist. "I'll try and reach Command again."

The squad huddled behind a concrete wall while the lieutenant tried the comms.

"*Persephone One*, this is Hell Squad Actual. Do you copy?" Yosef said.

Static crackled in Santiago's earpiece as he tried to listen, but there was no response from Command. His HUD flickered, the electrical disturbance wreaking havoc on all their systems. It solidified again, and Voss was on the move again.

"Keep going!" Yosef yelled.

Nodin made his way down the alley to the end, where it intersected a street. Debris whipped by in gusts, drumming on the burned hulls of vehicles on the road. Yosef and Alistair followed Santiago as he joined the scout. Nodin zoomed his rifle scope in on the mall.

Santiago looked with his unaided eyes, and to his surprise, the structure appeared to be standing. If the team could get there before the worst of the storm hit, they just might catch up with Voss.

Yosef must have thought the same thing. "Everyone, we're headed for the mall," he said. "Stay low and move fast."

"I'll take point," Santiago said.

Yosef nodded.

Moving in front of Nodin, Santiago burst out into the gusting wind like a bull out of the chute. The storm swallowed him, pushing and tugging on his armor. Relying on his instincts, he moved out among the burned vehicles that had been tossed around like toys during the nuclear blast. He used them for some cover as he moved.

Voss's beacon solidified on his HUD for a fleeting moment—just enough time for him to see that it was still on the move. A jagged trident of lightning flashed into a building to his right, sparks firing out. Thunder boomed right on cue, close enough that Santiago felt it in his bones.

He ran harder, from one destroyed vehicle to the next. They were closing in on the parking lot around the mall. Shattered fountains and sculptures lay scattered amid patches of dirt that once brimmed with beautiful gardens.

A footbridge with its middle missing arched partially over a man-made riverbed that had once surrounded the mall and was now dry and filled with cars blown away in the nuclear inferno.

Santiago went to the riverbank and started down. As he did, the wind slammed into his back. He lost his balance and tripped over a protruding piece of rebar. A warning sensor chirped in his helmet as he hit the ground.

Alistair grabbed him by a shoulder pad and helped him up.

"You good, Sarge?" he shouted.

"Good!" Santiago yelled back. But as his eyes flitted to the subscreen on his HUD, he saw that he had a major problem: a tear in the left calf of his suit. He would deal with it once they got out of the storm.

They made their way up into the parking lot, navigating around upended cars until they got to the front of the mall. To their right, the side of the structure had collapsed, but he saw an entrance to the left.

Behind them, a shriek of metal caused Santiago to look over his shoulder. Lightning flashed across the black storm wall, illuminating things as they hurtled through the air—corrugate roofing, a car door, all flung by the powerful wall of wind.

The storm wave surged toward them, lifting debris in its path.

"My God," Santiago said, his words lost in the howling gale.

He ducked behind a car as a two-by-four flew overhead and speared through the side of the mall. The wind rushed over the auto body, knocking him to the ground.

"RUN!" he screamed.

All four men sprang up and darted across the parking lot as the edge of the storm rolled cars, ripped loose roofs and doors, and sent arrowheads of glass flying through the air.

Nodin made it to the mall first. He clambered through an opening in the wall and hunkered down. Santiago got there next and waved Yosef through. Alistair climbed in after but caught his armored shoulder pad on a broken pipe.

A sheet of lightning flashed in the storm wall, the thunderclap as loud as heavy artillery. Santiago booted the big man in the ass, freeing him. Then he got down and belly-crawled after him through the hole in the rubble. Yosef and Alistair grabbed him by the shoulder pads and pulled him through. The roof groaned as they got up.

Nodin waved them across the marble floor covered in sand and dirt. They passed a luxury watch store, its glass display cases shattered. Gold timepieces covered in soot and dust remained, some of them worth more than their paychecks. But none of them stopped to grab any of the loot. Nodin charged by the shattered storefronts to a stairwell that went down. The full brunt of the storm smashed against the mall just as they started down the stairs.

Wind rushed through the hole they had entered the building through, blasting a jet of grit inside. A shower of particles rained down over the stairs.

At the bottom, a body lay crumpled. It wore a torn black suit and a cracked hazard helmet.

A few beetles skittered away from the corpse as the heavy boots of Hell Squad approached. Santiago walked toward the body, noticing the decomposed flesh where the suit had torn, and looking behind the visor to find all the signs of radiation poisoning. Many of these places had been raided over the years by looters, who usually ended up like this poor bastard.

The smarter crews came prepared for the radiation, but the terrain was still dicey, especially in the storms, but even they often paid the price for trying to strike it rich.

This man had managed to find treasure before succumbing to the radiation. Four dusty Swiss watches were wrapped around his wrist, and a dozen gold chains hung around his neck.

Santiago pushed ahead into the concourse of the underground level. The littered floor ran a thousand feet to another stairwell that led back up to ground level. Benches and trash cans were scattered about, along with trash and broken glass from the stores.

Nodin waved everyone onward to a safer area, then suddenly raised a fist. The ceiling groaned overhead, dust falling over them. But that hadn't spooked Nodin. The beacon for Voss was moving, right toward them.

Yosef flashed hand signals, and the team spread out into combat intervals, aiming their rifles down the wide concourse between the shattered shop fronts. The warning sensor on Santiago's HUD chirped, reminding him of his torn suit, but there was no time to deal with that now.

He moved abreast of Nodin, both of them keeping to the opposite side of the concourse. Suddenly, a figure emerged on the stairs ahead. Gripping a railing with one hand and its belly with the other, it lurched down the steps. Even from five hundred feet away, Santiago could see the silver ITC logo on Voss's blue hazard suit.

He got to the bottom of the stairs without seeing them and scurried forward while looking over his shoulder several times at the stairs. Hell Squad closed in, moving in the shadows. When they were just a hundred feet away, Voss spotted them and froze. He took a step back, then turned and ran.

"Stop!" Yosef shouted. "We're not going to hurt you!"

Voss hesitated, glancing back at them.

"It's me, Lieutenant Yosef, with Hell Squad. We were sent to get you out of here."

For a moment, the scientist just stared through his dirty visor. The interior lights captured the startled eyes of a frightened middle-aged man—a far cry from his supercilious glower back at the field lab. Voss coughed and raised a hand to his helmet.

"Rad poisoning," Santiago said. "He might be delirious."

"Lower your weapons," Yosef said. He pointed his rifle down, then raised a hand. "We're here to help you, Dr. Voss. As soon as that storm passes, we'll get you out of here safely, but we need to know where the Def-8 units are. What happened to them?"

Voss took another step back, stumbled, and nearly went down.

"It's okay. Just let us take a look at you," Yosef said. "We have medical supplies."

The scientist retreated a few more steps. Judging by his shaking hands and rattling cough, he was in bad shape.

"You're safe with us," Santiago said in his best soothing voice.

"Go. Get out of here before they kill you too," Voss snarled.

"What?" Yosef asked, glancing over to Santiago.

"He's delirious," Santiago said quietly.

"I'm not delirious," Voss said. He strode forward, then broke into a coughing fit.

Nodin moved, but Voss backed away, screaming, "Get away from me! Get out of here!"

"Hold position," Yosef said.

He approached slowly, hand up.

"We're going to help you," said the lieutenant.

Looking down, Voss swung his head from side to side. "I'm sorry for what I've done," he sobbed. "They said they would kill my family if I didn't help them."

"No one's going to hurt you or your family. Where are the Def-8 units?"

Voss muttered something indistinct, then turned and scrambled away, holding his side.

"Santiago, subdue him," Yosef said.

With pleasure, Santiago thought.

He ran down the concourse after the crazed scientist. When he reached the stairs, he charged up. At the top, he spotted Voss running down the concourse, back the way they had come. But to Santiago's surprise, he wasn't running into one of the stores to hide. He was heading for the volley of grit still blasting in through the hole they had crawled through.

"No, stop!" Santiago shouted.

He ran harder, but the guy was fast and not weighed down by gear and weapons. Digging deep, Santiago gave it all he had, picking up speed and closing the gap. The wind outside howled as Voss bent down to scramble through the hole in the wall.

"Don't!" Santiago yelled. "We can help you!"

Voss turned in the tunnel to look back. Then he scrambled out of the mall, into the vortex.

"*¡Puta madre loco!*" Santiago grumbled. He uncoiled one end of the parachute cord spooled on his duty belt and thrust it out to Alistair, who had just caught up.

"Take it. I'm heading out," Santiago said.

"Sarge, wait!" Nodin called, running toward him.

Santiago ignored him. There was no time to come up with a better plan. They had to grab this batshit scientist before the storm killed him. If he died now, they would never know what happened.

Going down on his kneepads, Santiago crawled back through the roaring wind tunnel and looked out at the almost blackout conditions of the parking lot. In his infrared goggles, he could see the man crouched behind a burned-out panel truck about fifty feet from the entrance, head bowed in prayer.

Letting out slack from the parachute cord, Santiago moved out of the tunnel. It felt like being hit with a sandblaster. Another sensor went off in his helmet, warning of a problem with his air-filtration system. If that broke, he was truly screwed.

For a fleeting moment, he considered turning back to the safety of the mall. Thoughts of his wife and kids surfaced in his mind. The next step might mean he would never see them again.

His eyes flitted to his HUD; the signal was on the move. Santiago rushed out to a rust heap that was once a car, and crouched behind it. He peeked through the shattered windows as Voss climbed up onto the hood of a truck.

What are you doing? Santiago wondered.

The scientist raised his arms out from his sides.

"Get down!" Santiago shouted. "You'll get hit!"

A plank of red light flashed out of the darkness, cutting Voss down. He slumped, his legs folding under him. The wind pushed his body off the truck, and it slid to the concrete. More beams lanced through the darkness from across the parking lot.

The parachute cord tied to Santiago suddenly went slack. He turned back to Alistair, who stood just outside the tunnel.

Alistair reached up with one hand to his chest, where a simmering hole glowed in the middle of his combat armor. The husky trooper staggered a few feet, trying to grab the rope he had dropped. Then he collapsed to the ground.

Santiago hunched beneath the wind, searching for the hostiles. They had to be the same raiders or mercs who attacked the field lab.

Raising his rifle, Santiago zoomed in with his infrared scope on a figure moving like an apparition, seemingly impervious to the wind. But there was no heat signature.

These weren't raiders.

They weren't even men.

It was one of the Def-8 units.

And somehow it wasn't showing up on his HUD.

There were two machines out there, both equipped with laser rifles.

Crouching, Santiago worked his way around the side of the car, heart pounding. Nodin had emerged in the tunnel, raising a rifle, but Santiago waved him back. Bullets weren't that useful against these machines. They had turned on the scientists, and now they had their sights on Hell Squad.

How, Santiago wasn't sure. All he knew was the squad had to get out of there, or they would end up like those scientists and Alistair.

Jumping up, he ran toward the entrance, where Nodin and Yosef had just pulled Alistair back inside the tunnel. Nodin fired his assault rifle, but it suddenly flew away, along with his left arm and hand still attached.

Santiago ran with his back to the machines, the wind threatening to lift him off the ground. He ducked under a burst of lasers that would have taken off his head. Another shot narrowly missed his leg.

As he ran toward the breach in the mall's exterior wall, the wind picked him up, propelling him forward—and saving him from the flurry of laser bolts that flashed beneath him.

He slammed against the concrete scree around the tunnel through the wall, his right arm and shoulder taking the brunt of the impact. Pain shot up his arm. Flipping over, he stared in horror at two orange visors that flickered like demons in the darkness.

Scooting back into the rubble by the wall, he fired a burst from his assault rifle at the closest machine. The bullets merely dented it.

"Bull, move your ass!" Yosef shouted.

Santiago scrambled over the broken concrete into the tunnel. Halfway in, Yosef grabbed him by his bad shoulder, pulling him over the debris pile into the mall. He was astonished to see Nodin gripping a pistol with his only hand. Lasers flashed in through the hole in the wall.

Santiago grabbed a grenade off his vest while Yosef put down covering fire. Then he backed away with Santiago, and both of them helped Nodin move. As they retreated, Yosef tried the comms again.

"*Persephone One*, this is Hell Squad Actual. Need evac, multiple injured, one KIA," he said in a strangely calm voice. "Under attack by—"

A laser flashed through the tunnel, hitting Yosef in the shoulder pad and knocking him down. Santiago lost his grip on Nodin, and all three of them fell to the ground.

"Stay down!" Santiago yelled. He tossed the grenade he still held back into the breach. Then he crawled over to Yosef and Nodin, shielding their bodies with his.

His earpiece chirped, but before he could hear the transmission, the grenade exploded, and the world went dark.

CHAPTER 22

"Sir, I know this is extremely bad timing, but I just received a scrambled transmission from Seoul," Whitt said.

The message came through Tyron's earpiece as he stood near the edge of the stage nestled against the rose gardens, waiting to address the crowd.

A second passed before Whitt finished his sentence. "Hell Squad is under attack."

All sense of time slowed as Tyron processed that information. He looked out over the tables filled with guests, specifically to General Vucci, who had arrived thirty minutes ago. If this was an attack by the Tritons, it could be the catalyst to another war. If it wasn't, and he alerted the United States military and the JMF, it could still cause a war. The former commander of the JMF was itching for an excuse.

"What do you want me to do, sir?" Whitt asked.

The weight of the next decision broke Tyron free from his trance. He had to act.

"Contact the JMF. We have no choice," he said. "Give them Hell Squad's coordinates and tell them what we know."

"Okay, sir."

Vucci darted a glance at Tyron, then shifted his gaze to the attendees awaiting the keynote speech. Angelina spoke to the crowd about ITC's accomplishments over the past year and about the cyberattack, again explaining that it was an isolated event and would never happen a second time. But Tyron was hardly listening. His mind was on Seoul. His gut told him this attack wasn't just some random event, that everything was related.

Orion was right to insist on caution.

Tyron considered walking away from the stage right now, saying he had an emergency, which wasn't a lie. But that would be rash as well, and besides, it was too late. If Hell Squad was under attack, he couldn't do anything for them. The JMF was in charge now.

"And now, without further ado, CEO Tyron Red," Angelina said, clapping.

She turned and looked at him with a wide smile, giving him an encouraging nod. She couldn't know that he had just gotten a message that made his blood run cold.

The crowd stood with polite applause as he made his way up to the stage. Tyron gave his best smile and raised a hand on his way to the podium bearing the ITC logo on the front.

He had to keep it together, had to show them he was resilient. There were people out there who had supported him for years but were growing weary of his promises to do things that most people said were impossible. Tonight he would show them his latest invention and magnum opus, *Genesis 1*.

"Good evening, and thank you for joining me on this beautiful night in the countryside," he said. "Five years ago, I stood up here for the first time after we lost my father. Since then, I've come to know many of you personally and consider you dear friends. We've changed the world together, and tonight I am excited to announce the most exciting project in the history of ITC. But first let's talk about our accomplishments over the past year, of which there are many."

He could feel the gaze of the crowd, the weight of their eyes, just as he had felt the weight of the board's agendas and opinions when he first took over as CEO.

"Yesterday I visited an ITC facility in the Arctic Circle, where I watched our Delta Cloud fusion reactors conduct a field test of our newest weather modification technology," he said. "The results were astonishing."

He paused as each table came alive with holographic images of the launch in the Arctic. While everyone focused on the video, Tyron continued.

"Preliminary data suggests these reactors will be able to clear the storms above the Korean Peninsula, freeing them from the relentless weather that batters our labs even today," he said. "On the ground, ITC has been there since day one, right after the nuclear infernos. Our brave scientists have been working on a top-secret project called Operation RadGrow, to restore the land. I'm pleased to share that recent tests have yielded remarkable results in cleaning the radiation and toxins from the soil."

Hushed voices broke out.

"Yes, I know, it sounds like science fiction, but this is real," he said.

Amid the ripple of excitement, he also saw skeptical faces.

This was his moment, his time to rise up and show those people and the world that science could provide a better future for all.

"The world we live in requires hard decision-making," he continued. "Allocating resources to projects that many of you have generously supported with your precious time and valuable investments. I do not take that lightly. I remain forever grateful to you all."

He paused, looking out over the crowd and trying to make eye contact with as many of these people as possible. He searched for General Vucci, but the man had gotten up and was starting to walk out the back of the terrace while talking on a phone.

Tyron kept his focus, trying not to read into it.

"You see, I have shifted my own priorities over the years," he continued. "When I was growing up, I believed robots would ensure a brighter future for all by taking the jobs that most people didn't want. That, as we know, was a mistake. We didn't foresee just how fast robots and AI would advance, taking over much of the workforce. The rest is history you all know: volatile macroeconomic conditions, inflation, and a shortage of chips had severe economic ramifications we're still dealing with today. This has also sparked many of the conflicts we've seen over the past two decades, including the war that could have ended civilization."

He lowered his head in observance for a brief moment, then lifted his chin confidently.

"We can't change the past, but we can shape the future," Tyron said, his voice louder. "Tonight I'm announcing what I believe is the most significant part of that future."

He raised his hand to the sky—his cue to activate the main attraction of the evening. The holographic images of the Delta Cloud Reactors went dark on each table. Overhead, rays of light projected a dazzling image of stars across the sky above the terrace. Sparkling letters spelled out, "To Other Worlds."

The projected images vanished, replaced by a holographic spaceship.

"I'd like to introduce you all to *Genesis 1*," he said. "Since I was twelve, I've dreamed of going to space, like many young boys do. When I was older, I began designing and building this craft, and now it is complete. We all know there have been many before it, taking astronauts and citizens out into space beyond Earth, and even to the moon. We have sent probes and unmanned ships to Mars, but no man or woman has been beyond our microscopic home in the cosmos."

He switched to a new image, of a rocket blasting skyward off a launch pad bordering the blue-green expanse of the ocean. "You may remember *Nexus 4*, one of ITC's rockets that launched multiple satellites into space, which are now part of the Doomsday Shield. These rockets all returned safely to Earth after those missions."

Tyron had been there that day, watching with ITC staff inside an observation tower at the launch site as they lightly and gracefully touched back down.

"*Genesis 1* will launch with the newest rocket, *Nexus 5*. The ship is far more advanced, and prepared to take us even farther than ever before—to a planned colony on Jupiter's moon Europa, where I hope, someday soon, for humans to live."

The projected images shifted again, this time to Orion's rendition of a base on Europa, displaying habitats and a train connecting them in a massive facility.

Several hushed voices rang out, and some worried looks. He knew that look. It wasn't fear of the idea itself, but of the price tag that came with it. His job was to show the value.

"Over the past eighty years, we have lost the urge to see beyond our planet, what's out there," he said, again raising his hand skyward. "We have the technology to expand, but we used it to make life easier, only to find that it caused more problems. When I look out among you, I see visionaries. I see people ahead of their time. Tonight I humbly ask you to hark back to your own youth, your young dreams, and join me on my own, to break free of the bonds that tie us to Earth."

Angelina gave him a brilliant smile as he glanced at her.

For some reason, Tyron suddenly felt conflicted, wondering

if this was all too premature, if the human clones were really ready to launch into space. The scientist in him, however, told him it was the perfect opportunity for more tests, outside the international fishbowl.

"In two days, we will launch *Genesis 1* at an undisclosed location that you will all be invited to," he said. "You can see for yourself what this ship is capable of."

Tyron raised his glass to the crowd, all confliction gone. "So the question is, who will follow me to space?"

A single person stood up at once. Tyron saw the weathered features of the seventy-five-year-old fighter pilot Jon "Acers" Asay, one of the most decorated pilots of his generation, and a huge supporter of ITC over the years.

"To *Genesis 1*, the future of humanity," he said. "I sure as hell wish I was young enough I could fly her out there, Dr. Red."

"You're young for your age, Captain; you just might surprise us," Tyron said.

Chuckles and laughs, followed by applause. More people stood up from their seats, clapping. Everywhere, smiles greeted his eyes.

Glasses were raised, and Tyron lifted his into the air once more.

The band fell to, and his mood lifted as he waded out into the crowd to shake hands with the guests.

"Well done, Dr. Red," said Atlanta's mayor, Kameron Cowney.

"I can't wait to see what you do on Europa," said billionaire Katherine Harris.

"What *we* do," Tyron said. "I'll need your support."

"And you'll have it."

He kissed the back of her hand, then turned to another potential supporter, Senator Perry.

"Impressive, Dr. Red," he said. "Have you considered how

robots might help build a colony on Europa? Perhaps there's a way where we can make something work that doesn't violate the Global AI Limitation Accord."

"Perhaps."

"I look forward to working with you on that."

"And I as well, sir."

Tyron noticed Angelina looking over at him eagerly.

"If you'll excuse me, Senator," he said.

They shook hands, and another happy supporter walked away.

Angelina appeared in Perry's place.

"Never seen you so personable," she whispered. "If I didn't know any better, I'd say you've done this before."

He grinned. "I guess tonight's my turn in the barrel."

She laughed and took a drink of champagne. He didn't want to ruin the mood, but he owed it to her to share what was happening in Seoul.

As he started to speak, she put a finger up to his lips, not quite touching them.

"Fifteen minutes—that's all I ask," she said. "Fifteen minutes of not talking about work, and loosening up. You need to have some fun. It's good for your soul, Tyron—sir."

Tyron looked over at Whitt. If he had an update, he would already have shared it.

"Things are going to be okay," Angelina said. Setting her drink down on a table, she reached out with both hands. "Come on, dance with me."

Concern about how this might look did cross his mind, but he decided to forget about whatever people might think. She was right; he needed to loosen up, even for just a few minutes.

He took her hand and started a slow dance with her across

the bricks. For a moment, he lost himself in the joy of human contact with someone he respected and cared deeply for—someone he needed, despite always telling himself he was fine alone, even *better* alone.

Maybe not. Maybe there was room for work and something more…

A message crackled in his earpiece. But this wasn't from Whitt; it was from Orion.

"Sir, I was able to access an encrypted transmission from Hell Squad to the JMF," said the AI.

"And?"

"They claim the Def-8 units are responsible for the attack in Seoul."

Tyron let go of Angelina.

"What is it?" she asked.

"I'll be right back."

Tyron hurried over to a corner of the terrace near the fountain, where he could talk to Orion.

"Whitt, come in," he said into his headset. "Where are you?"

"Went out front to escort a guest. What's wrong?"

"Meet me in the rose garden," Tyron said.

"On my way."

"Orion," Tyron said. "Is it possible Hell Squad attacked the Def-8 units first? They are programmed as *defensive* units. Unless…"

The AI finished what Tyron was starting to wonder.

"There is a way to hack the Def-8 units if someone has access to their programming," said Orion.

Tyron felt his face grow warm.

"Whitt, change of plans. Bring the car around. I'll go get Angelina," he said into his headset. "We're leaving."

Tyron turned back toward the terrace. Angelina waved at him, smiling as she beckoned him back to the dance floor.

He raised his hand, gesturing for her to come toward him, when he heard a distant buzzing sound. Almost like a mosquito, or a swarm of mosquitoes.

The noise grew louder, attracting the attention of other people across the terrace. More and more heads turned and lips moved, the words lost under the buzzing. Words became screams as gunfire came from the gardens.

"Dear God," Tyron breathed.

Ducking against the base of the fountain, he saw tracer rounds from automated machine guns spitting into the sky at something moving through the darkness. Tiny explosions went off overhead. They continued to explode lower and lower, until they were just over the gardens.

"Run!" someone yelled behind him.

The buzzing got closer, and he recognized the noise—advanced drones the size of sparrows. Hunter-killers.

All sense of time slowed around him as his brain processed what was happening. The swarm of tiny explosive drones fanned out across the terrace, toward the panicked guests. Dozens of detonations boomed seconds later, tearing through tables, chairs, and people.

Tyron felt his body being lifted off the ground. He slumped into the water, ears ringing, blood dripping from his scalp.

Through dimmed vision, he saw a figure staggering through the smoke, reaching out with stumps but no hands. As smoke drifted away, his breath caught in his lungs. It was Angelina. Part of her forearms was also gone, and most of her face too. Her one intact eye searched for him; then she fell, collapsing to the ground as Tyron was dragged away by Whitt.

* * * * *

Sirens blared inside Copper Terrace. Not police sirens but alarms set off by the gangs to create confusion. The power had been cut, too, leaving Cecil in the dark maintenance elevator between the ninth and tenth floors, where it had stopped. He had been so close to getting out of Copper Terrace with Wild Bill.

He glanced over at the gang leader's corpse, with a crater in the back of his head from the bullet's exit. His final words echoed in Cecil's mind.

You're not getting out of here.

At this point, Cecil was starting to believe that. He was trapped in the elevator, and the White Buffaloes knew right where he was. He couldn't just climb down the way he had climbed up—not without being seen.

And help was a long way off.

"Tank, do you copy?" Cecil whispered.

"Copy. How you doing?" he asked.

"I'm solid, but, fuck..."

"Hang in there. The strike team is engaging Nion and his crew in the utility shaft. We're putting another team together to get to you."

"You said that an hour ago."

"I know. Just hang on, man."

Cecil wasn't sure how much longer he could hang on. He had taken a real ass-kicking from Wild Bill's henchmen before making it into the elevator. He winced as he looked down at his shirtless chest and the gash that leaked blood through the strip of shirt he had torn off Wild Bill and wrapped around his torso. But his back was the real problem.

Another tremor rushed up his spine. With his VitalStem remote lost, there was nothing he could do but take the pain and wait for the episode to pass.

A loud banging echoed somewhere below him. He fought the

tremor, wincing and gritting his teeth. After a few minutes, it finally passed. He exhaled a long breath, hoping that was the last one.

He was running out of time. Eventually, the gangsters would make a run at the elevator. Either that or set a fire in the shaft, killing him from smoke inhalation.

If he tried to get out now, he would be shot. If he somehow did make it onto the ninth floor, he would be hunted by the gang-bangers patrolling the hallway.

Shouting reverberated through the shaft. It seemed to be coming from above. The sirens whined louder, indicating a door had been opened inside the maintenance shaft.

Help wasn't going to get there in time. He was sure of that now.

Cecil felt the fear of being left alone, just as he had felt when his first team, Raven Squad, was killed in Seoul. Back then, Santiago had shown up with Hell Squad and pulled his ass out of the fire with the Tritons. Not today though.

He was on his own.

Cecil gripped his pistol—only six bullets left in the mag and one in the chamber. The other magazines had fallen out of his pocket during the attack in the maintenance hallway, along with his medical remote. He had rushed into the elevator without realizing it.

He thought of his wife, who had no idea he was even in danger. He was going to die without even saying goodbye to her. And after they killed him, they would mutilate his body and hang him out for all to see, as they had done with Thomas.

No, no, you're getting out of here, Pepper.

Gritting his teeth, he prepared to fight. He would use his damn teeth if necessary.

Something clunked against the door of the car.

He froze.

Over the alarms, he could make out a grinding noise.

Cecil backed against the side wall of the car and raised his pistol. More clanking came from the door, where a metal object had been wedged into the opening. Someone was trying to force their way inside.

"Lower!"

The voice was coming from above.

Cecil moved to the other side of the car and pointed his pistol up at the maintenance hatch overhead. His heart pounded at the realization that he was being attacked from above and below.

A thump came on top of the car—someone landing on it feetfirst. The hatch opened just a few inches, and something dropped inside. Acrid smoke hissed out.

Oh, shit! They wanted him alive.

He held in a breath and pulled the bandanna up above his nose, then fired two bullets through the roof . A scream came, then another thump on the top of the car. Cecil jumped up with his feet on the back and side handrails. Then he pushed the hatch open.

The sirens were loud, but he didn't hear any rustling on top of the car. Pounding came on the elevator door behind him as someone tried to force it open.

He couldn't stay in the car another second.

Aiming backward, he fired a third bullet through the gap in the door to buy some time. The bullet must have missed, because someone pushed back up to the gap and blasted a jet of fire inside from a homemade flamethrower.

"Shit, shit, shit!" Cecil shouted. He fired a fourth bullet through the narrow opening and heard a yelp of pain, and the fire retreated.

Eyes burning, he reached up and pulled himself onto the top of the car, squirming into almost complete darkness next to the guy he had shot. Putting his pistol up to the limp body, he waited to see if it might still pose a threat. Cecil confirmed he was dead with a touch to the throat. No pulse.

Not wanting to attract attention, Cecil kept still, listening for more hostiles in the dark shaft above. The sirens made that almost impossible, but he could hear voices.

His earpiece crackled, but Tank's words came through indistinctly—something about help that either was or wasn't on the way.

Flashlights beamed down from an opening three stories above Cecil. The lights hit the escaping smoke from the car below. He scrambled away from the hatch, around the thick cables, to the shaft wall.

He had only three bullets left. If it came down to it, he would save the last round for himself rather than face torture.

"There!" someone yelled.

As he tried to hold still, a beam split through the eight cables holding up the elevator. Cecil turned to aim at the two men angling weapons down at him. Squinting through smoke-induced tears, he reacted with trained precision, squeezing the trigger. After the sharp report of his pistol came the clang of the bullet hitting metal above, forcing both men back.

He scrambled back to the dead man and lifted him up as a shield.

The sharp staccato of return fire filled the narrow shaft, adding to the general chaos that had erupted in the building. Voices called out from various floors above as more bangers were drawn to the battle. Cecil looked up from behind his bullet-riddled human shield.

Above him, armed figures came and went in the glow of their flashlights. As the smoke cleared, he saw the dangling rope from above, still wrapped around the waist of the dead guy he still held.

There was a lot of slack, but not nine floors' worth—not enough to get him down.

Cecil noticed something else as he shifted the heavy, limp body. Not one but two grenades on his vest. Grenades that the guy had likely planned on dropping into the elevator to kill Cecil. Now Cecil would use them against the White Buffaloes.

Carefully, he removed the two grenades. Another gunshot cracked from above, hitting the top of the elevator with a spark.

In the interplay of flashlight beams, Cecil made out the ladder he had climbed on the shaft wall. But that would just be asking for a bullet in the back.

In the brief moment of calm, Tank sent another message over the comms.

"Help is still on the way."

Cecil didn't have time to dwell on how far away that help was, because that didn't matter. He needed it this second, or he was done.

Coughing came from inside the car beneath him.

Although he had planned to drop a grenade in the elevator and keep the final bullet for himself, he couldn't resist when he saw a coughing tattooed head emerge with a rifle aimed in the other direction.

Cecil shot him point-blank in the back of the head. The guy dropped right back into the car, leaving a gift of an automatic rifle.

Cecil shouldered the weapon and aimed at the lights above, buying himself a few seconds with short bursts. Then he returned to the dead gangster with the rope tied around him. He untied that rope and tossed the slack down into the dark void.

If help wasn't coming, he had no choice but to rappel down. He would do that to get some quick distance from his attackers, then switch to the ladder when he could. But first he would use the grenades as a distraction.

Crazy plan, but it just might work.

He tugged on the rope, checking that it was anchored to the shaft above. It felt secure.

Famous last words, he thought.

"Tank, if I don't make it, tell Michelle I love her and I'm sorry," he said into his mic. "I couldn't sit around and do nothing. I had to step up."

"I'm sorry, bro, for not being there with you," Tank said.

"Don't be. I made my choice. If you get ahold of Harkin, tell him I'm about to make two very loud bangs."

Whatever Tank said next, Cecil couldn't hear. He pulled a pin and dropped one of the grenades into the elevator car. Then he pulled the pin from the second and lobbed it down the shaft.

Gunfire rang out above, forcing him to raise the rifle and squeeze off a burst at the shooter. The man slumped into the shaft, falling onto the car with enough force that it swayed. The banger was somehow still alive, groaning from multiple broken bones.

He was about to have a lot more.

The grenades exploded within a second of each other. The elevator car jerked hard, nearly knocking Cecil over the side.

"Adios," he said to the dying gangster.

Cecil climbed down the ladder between the car and the shaft wall to get beneath the elevator. Once he was a few feet below the carriage, he kicked off the ladder and rappelled down to the next floor. The hoistway door across the shaft was open, and a gangbanger lay crumpled in the corridor. Wasting no time, Cecil rappelled down to the next floor, where the door was sealed off. He could try to open it, but decided to keep going down.

He rappelled lower, watching the end of the rope draw closer. By the time he got down to the fifth floor, he could hear grunts and voices of people below him. Flashlight beams fired upward into the elevator shaft from the third floor.

Cecil rappelled down to the fourth floor, so focused on those lights that he failed to notice the shadow in the open hoistway door.

"Hey!" a man shouted. He raised a shotgun and fired as Cecil jerked to the side, narrowly avoiding the blast. He fired back, then felt a surge of adrenaline when he saw the rope. Six feet above him, the shotgun blast had blown apart the sheath and half the braided fibers. No longer trusting the rope to hold his weight, he was obliged to let go of his rifle and grab the bottom of the open doorway. His fingertips found purchase on the skidproof metal surface, and he pulled himself up into the hallway. Ears still ringing from the close encounter, he staggered over to the dead gangbanger.

He grabbed the dropped shotgun and checked how much ammo was left—three shells. Then he started toward the stairwell at the end of the hall, watching the closed doors of each room he passed. When he got to the landing, he took a moment to breathe and listen. It was hard to hear much over the ringing, but he made out angry voices.

There were hostiles below him.

Cecil moved across the landing and down the stairs. He swung the shotgun up at a figure on the stairs, almost pulling the trigger.

"Shit," Cecil growled.

It was the green-haired teenage spotter he had seen on the third floor earlier. With both hands in the air, and eyes wide with fear, he didn't look so hard now.

"Get the fuck out of here," Cecil growled.

The kid ran.

Cecil moved down to floor 3, then 2, and down to 1—almost out of the building.

"Tank, I'm almost to the lobby," he said into his headset.

Cecil kept going, nearly tripping on a stair. He passed a junkie who had just come to and was looking at him with a tilted head.

"You look like dog shit, bruv," he said.

Cecil almost laughed.

When he got out into the lobby, he did laugh. He had made it.

He walked through the cloud of dust and smoke from his two grenades.

Over the ringing, he heard sirens, but these were coming from outside. He moved through the open doors with the shotgun but dropped it when he saw the armored vehicles outside.

"Hands in the air!" someone yelled.

A strike team of six officers in riot gear and holding shields strode in a phalanx toward the stairs.

"That's him!" one of them yelled.

Cecil held back the sigh of relief—he wasn't out of this hell just yet.

He hurried down toward the strike team with his hands up, not wanting to catch friendly fire from an overeager officer.

Two officers in riot gear passed him, weapons raised to provide cover, if needed. The next two grabbed Cecil by his arms, hoisting him off his feet and practically carrying him down the stairs.

"We got you," said one of the officers.

Cecil glanced over his shoulder as they rushed him off the stairway landing.

The building loomed above him—a place that had claimed the lives of Enforcer Ricker, Jerky, and the rest of Alpha team.

But not Cecil.

Cecil had escaped, and he had taken down Wild Bill.

He relaxed, letting his weight shift to the two men helping carry his battered, exhausted body. They rushed him to an ambulance that waited outside the NGZ. Captain Harkin jogged over from the command post that had been set up across the street.

"Jesus Christ, Pepper, what the hell were you thinking?" he asked.

Cecil stiffened, steeling himself for a reprimand or worse.

"I'm sorry, sir," Cecil said. "I saw a chance, and I took it. I couldn't let Wild Bill get away with murder, not while I had him in my crosshairs."

Harkin looked at him, then grinned. "You did good, Pepper, but you just made your life a lot more challenging."

Another man came over, wearing a bulletproof vest and holding an automatic rifle. To Cecil's surprise, it was Chief Krycek, and the bandage on his head made him look as though he had been in the fight.

"Well done, Pepper," he said. "Today we got Nion and his leadership and recovered the automatic rifles, and you took out the punk who sold them to Cipher Crew. With Wild Bill dead and Nion in custody, the NGZ might actually see a period of calm."

"Thank you, sir."

For the first time in his career, Cecil felt that he had made a real difference. People like Diana and her kids might have a chance at a better life.

"He good?" Harkin asked the paramedic.

"He'll be fine," she said.

Another officer jogged over and said, "She's here, Captain."

Harkin nodded. "Bring her over."

Cecil stood as a woman in an ITC uniform got out of a car. When she turned, he saw that it was his wife.

"Michelle," he said.

Gripping the bandage around his chest, he went over to her.

"Cecil!" she cried.

Harkin stood by while they embraced.

"What happened? Are you okay?" she asked as she pulled back, looking him up and down.

"Yeah, I'm good. Better than ever, to be honest."

"What... what happened?"

Cecil exhaled. "I'm sorry. I had to get payback for Jerky."

"Payback? On your own?" Her voice was filled with shock.

"Your husband took down Wild Bill," Harkin said.

She looked at the captain, then back to Cecil.

"I'll give you guys a minute," he said.

He walked away, leaving Cecil alone with his wife.

"I'm sick of treading water in the ocean with no shore in sight," he said. "You've thrown me a life buoy, and I love you, Michelle, but I had to get to shore on my own. And now I'm on my way. I'm whole again. I proved to myself I'm still a fighter."

She shook her head. "Yeah, well, now I'm in the ocean, too, treading water right alongside you."

"What do you mean?"

Michelle heaved a breath. "They say we have to leave town, that it isn't safe for us now."

"What?"

Cecil waved Harkin back over.

"They saw your face, Pepper," he said. "You avenged our fallen men, but Wild Bill has a loyal following that will want to avenge him too. And they won't stop at you."

Cecil swallowed hard at the realization as Harkin looked to Michelle.

"I'm sorry, Mrs. Pepper, but it's not safe for you either," said the captain. "You'll both have to leave as soon as we find you a safe house."

PART4:
SHADOWY FORCES

CHAPTER 23

Santiago woke to a buzzing, as if the room were filled with bees. Over the strange hum came a foreign voice.

"Sergeant, can you hear me?"

He tried to open his eyelids, but to his alarm, they wouldn't move. Around the edges, he felt something crusty. The skin along his neck burned and itched terribly.

Pushing down the rising sense of panic, he tried to remember where he was as that same unfamiliar voice spoke again.

"Sergeant Rodriguez, if you can hear me, nod or move."

With great effort, Santiago lifted a hand. At least, he thought he did.

"Get me that epinephrine injection now!"

This was a different voice.

Something stung his arm, and his heart started to thump faster. Breathing evenly, he tried to keep calm, but the rush of adrenaline was too much. His body shook from the sudden burst of energy. His eyes banged open, and he saw multiple figures leaning over him.

"Relax, Sergeant, you're safe," one of them said. "You're on an evac."

Santiago blinked at the body of a man lying beside him on the deck of the Wasp. He knew right away who it was from the arm stump wrapped in gauze.

"Nodin," he whispered.

"Sergeant Tatanka is unconscious, but he's stable," said the voice. "We have him sedated."

Santiago focused his gaze on a navy corpsman. Behind him stood a man wearing square plates of black armor over his chest, and a red flame symbol on his helmet. This wasn't an ITC security trooper like Santiago; this was an officer of the JMF.

The man leaned down. "Sergeant Rodriguez, I'm Major Han. I need you to tell me what happened at Field Lab Alpha."

Alpha...

A brief flurry of memories surfaced: diving into the crater, finding the field lab and what was left of the scientists. Then the storm, and locating Dr. Voss.

An image of Alistair falling to the rubble with smoking holes in his armor made Santiago flinch. He tried to sit up, but his head pounded. He reached up, felt his hair matted with blood. The last thing he remembered was throwing the grenade at the machines, then shielding Yosef and Nodin with his body.

Santiago searched the hold for Yosef but saw only Nodin.

"Where's Lieutenant Yosef?"

"He's on another transport," Han said. He crouched down. "I need you to focus, Sergeant, and tell me what happened down there. Were you engaged by Tritons?"

Past the shock, Santiago pulled himself together.

"Negative. The machines were Def-8 units."

Han hesitated. "You're sure?"

"Haven't you engaged them yet?"

"Whoever or whatever attacked you was gone when we arrived," said Han.

Santiago stared, trying to understand.

"Tell me exactly what happened, step-by-step, Sergeant Rodriguez."

"Okay."

As best he could recall, Santiago described what had gone down from the moment they dived out of *Persephone* to the last thing he remembered in the mall. As he considered what he was saying, the implications chilled him, especially the possibility that the machines had escaped the sector or spread mutiny to the other machines out there being used by ITC. There weren't many, due to the Global AI Limitation Accord, but there were enough to inflict major damage.

"Is this widespread?" he asked.

Han didn't answer.

A wave of nausea hit Santiago. He rolled over and vomited.

"Corpsman, give him a second R-1 shot," Han said.

The major stepped back to allow the injection that Santiago knew was for radiation exposure. He had taken a big dose of rads, hopefully not a lethal one. The warning signs were already there: itching and burning skin, confusion, racing heart, severe dizziness. And the nausea.

Maybe this was all one big delusional dream.

No, this is fucking real.

The corpsman gave him another injection, and Han leaned back down.

"You'll feel better soon, but I need you to focus right now," he said. "I need to understand more about the Def-8 units. You're sure they attacked you and killed Dr. Voss? Radiation poisoning can cause—"

"It was them, Major. And I'd be willing to bet the machines ripped the other scientists to pieces back at the field lab."

Han glanced up.

"The lab was destroyed," said one of his comrades.

"Listen to me," Santiago said. "If the Def-8 units have gone rogue in other locations where ITC has them deployed—"

"They haven't," Han interrupted. "We've confirmed that with ITC. This is an isolated incident and will be dealt with swiftly. Tell me more about your interaction with Voss."

Relieved, Santiago nodded. "He said something about them having his family."

"*Who* had his family?" Han asked.

"I don't know. He ran before we could get more out of him. He was definitely suffering from radiation poisoning."

Han pulled back, saying something into his headset that Santiago couldn't make out.

Rolling slightly, Santiago checked on Nodin again. He had survived, thank God, but Alistair and David were gone. They had survived the war, only to die right back in that same hell.

Anger burned through him at the pointless losses.

"Sergeant, we're taking you to Omega Base in the DMZ for medical attention," Han said.

Santiago managed a nod. "Thank you, sir."

"One more thing." Han crouched beside him. "What happened is classified."

"Understood, sir."

He rested his head back on the deck as the medicine took hold, his world spinning. Another bout of nausea hit him, but this time he closed his eyes and managed to resist throwing up.

"Prepare for landing!" shouted one of the pilots.

The Wasp swooped and set down with a slight jolt on the tarmac at Omega Base. By now, the adrenaline was already starting to wear off, and Santiago felt dizzy as he got up off the deck with the corpsman's help.

Another Wasp set down next to them, and Alistair's body was

unloaded. They had recovered David too. The sting of the losses hit Santiago again, followed by a wave of anger. He clenched his jaw.

The itching grew worse, up his legs and burning along his feet.

"Let's move!" Han shouted.

Santiago went over to Nodin and walked beside his stretcher toward the rows of concrete buildings.

"You're going to be okay, brother," Santiago said.

Nodin's eyelids fluttered.

A squad of ten soldiers in full armor and hazard gear jogged over with a colonel in their midst.

"Major Han," said the colonel.

"Colonel Edwards," Han said, saluting.

The soldiers who accompanied them off the Wasp halted and saluted.

"Escort the ITC troopers to the quarantine area," said Edwards.

"Quarantine area, sir?" Santiago asked.

"If you'd come with us, Sergeant," said one of the guards.

Half in shock, Santiago stared at the colonel, who said, "I'm sorry about your squadmates. Now, please go with the guards."

Then he was gone, hurrying over to one of the Wasps.

"Follow us," said Major Han.

Santiago was separated from Nodin, who was taken toward a different building.

"He'll be fine," Han said.

"Where's Lieutenant Yosef?" Santiago asked, realizing he still hadn't seen him.

"He's on another transport; I told you that," Han said. "Now, follow us."

They guided Santiago into a different building, where they began a journey through the windowless hallways of what had been an interrogation center in the past. They stopped in front of one of the doors.

"You will wait here until a doctor comes to see you," Han said.

Santiago looked inside the holding area. "What is this?"

Han began to walk away, but Santiago followed. Both guards stepped forward. "Sergeant, we have orders to place you in quarantine. This is quarantine."

"Major Han!" Santiago called out. "I'd like to talk to my commander on *Persephone*, First Lieutenant Zimmerman."

Han turned. "That won't be possible right now," he said. "The base is on a comms lockdown."

"Look, we have orders directly from CEO Tyron Red—"

"You haven't heard, have you?"

"Heard what?"

"There's been an attempt on his life in Atlanta," Han said.

Santiago froze as Han turned and walked away, leaving this new bombshell without another word.

"Please proceed to the quarantine cell," said one of the guards.

Santiago turned to the box. The *cage*. A moment of pure fear gripped him as he stood in front of a prison cell not so different from those that he himself had put so many men in back when he fought the cartels, and again in the war. The door shut behind him, shrouding him in darkness.

He was a prisoner of the military, who had clearly taken command of this mission.

Fear turned to anger as realization set in. He had seen something that wasn't supposed to be possible. Not only had the Def-8 units gone rogue, but they had likely murdered the scientists and attacked his team. If that got out, it would cause pure panic across the world.

And this wasn't just about the machines. There had been an attempt on Tyron Red's life—an attack on ITC itself.

Santiago had been around long enough to know this was no coincidence.

It was all connected.

* * * * *

Tyron stood at the bulletproof windows of his office at the top of the ITC headquarters, looking at the brightly lit campus below. The place looked like a military base, with armored vehicles, roadblocks, and uniformed security forces patrolling about. Drones flew around the airspace, ready to intercept any aerial threats. He reached up to massage his sore neck. The pain was getting worse since the attack two hours ago, when the blast lifted him off his feet and hurled him into the wall.

He had a ruptured right eardrum and a likely concussion.

In a daze, he had been airlifted away from the gala back to the headquarters building, where he saw a doctor in their own medical facility. They wanted him to stay there for observation and rest, which Whitt had agreed to, but Tyron had declined, insisting he return to his command center, where he could work.

Trying to shake the shock, Tyron stepped away from the windows and returned to the room of monitors.

"Sir, are you okay?" Whitt asked.

"No," Tyron said as his gaze flitted to the empty chair for Angelina. He felt a deep, raw pain unlike any he had experienced before. When he lost Daniel, it had hurt. Even losing his mother hurt, though they hardly had a relationship. And he still felt the pain of losing his dad. But this was different. Angelina was a significant part of what made ITC tick.

Tyron could still see her smile, erased by the blast that was meant to kill *him*.

He shook it off. This was not the moment to grieve, but to act. He had always been two steps ahead of everyone, and now he felt three steps behind.

"How!" he yelled. "How did this happen?"

Whitt kept his composure. "I'm sorry, sir. I take full responsibility. I will resign if that is what you want."

"I want to know who did this, Whitt. *Who's been attacking us?* This isn't the Blackworms, no fucking way."

"I agree, and I'm going to find out. Every asset at our disposal is working on determining who's responsible. I won't rest until I have the perpetrators. The drones have been recovered and are undergoing analysis in our labs right now for a point of origin."

Tyron knew that the chances of the drones being traceable were slim. Whoever managed to pull this off would cover their trail. They would leave nothing to chance.

"Sir, I do have an update on Hell Squad," Whitt said. "Survivors were taken to Omega Base. Meanwhile, JMF strike teams have deployed to hunt down the three rogue Def-8 machines that are believed to be responsible for the attack on the team and on the scientists at Field Lab Alpha. I've been in contact with Captain Dominique on the *Persephone*, but he reports that the JMF is not responding to requests for intel on the ground."

Tyron simply stared in shock. It wasn't raiders or the vegetation after all. It was the machines.

But how?

Someone must have hacked them.

Probably the same people behind the cyberattacks, and who tried to kill him and did kill Angelina. An image of her reaching out to him with bloody stumps for arms surfaced in his head.

The sense of shock left him as he began to process what had happened.

Were the president and General Vucci right about the Tritons? Could it be them?

One thing was certain: There was a sophisticated plan to hit ITC in a multiphase attack.

Phase one was to infiltrate and disrupt the global ITC food network. Phase two was to hack the Def-8 units, murder the scientists, and destroy their labs. Phase three was to kill him. Now, as he stood in the command center of the ITC HQ in a tailored suit covered with blood and dust, he realized there would be a phase four, and he had to stop it while he still could.

Only one entity could get to the bottom of this.

Tyron went to the elevator.

"Sir, where are you going?" Whitt called after him.

"To Orion."

The short ride down gave him enough time to ponder how nothing was as it seemed. Whoever looked guilty probably wasn't. The Blackworms probably had nothing to do with sabotaging his food-production facilities. They were framed.

There were other forces at play. Shadowy forces.

He remembered his father's message to him that Angelina had uncovered. The cryptic warning now echoed in his thoughts.

Tyron crossed the bridge to the secure door of the vast chamber housing Orion. He tapped in his code and walked inside.

"Dr. Red, I'm glad to see you are alive, but, sir, you should be resting and under medical supervision," Orion said. "Your heart rate is elevated, and you could have an undiagnosed concussion that might—"

"I'm fine, but I've lost control of the situation. News of the Def-8 units going rogue and attacking Hell Squad and our scientists at Field Lab Alpha is out, and the JMF has taken over. The situation is spiraling out of control. I need your help, Orion. I need to know who's behind all this."

"Sir, I have scoured all the intel I have access to, but to fully grasp the situation and locate the true assailants, I need access to systems currently out of my reach. I will need to tap into the JMF."

Tyron looked down. It meant taking a step further from the parameters set in place. He had already pushed the law by allowing Orion to intervene during the cyberattack. Now he was considering allowing the AI to hack into the JMF—a huge risk for multiple reasons.

But right now Orion was the only entity he could trust, and the only way to determine who was behind the attacks before it was too late.

The intercom buzzed with an external call from Whitt.

"Sir, President Clayton is on the encrypted line for you," he said over the speakers.

"Send it through here," Tyron replied.

"Aren't you with Orion?"

"Orion can hear whatever the president has to say."

There was a brief pause, then, "Okay, stand by. I'll patch it through."

A moment later, the holographic image of the president emerged in the middle of the chamber.

"Tyron, I'm relieved to see you're alive," the president said.

"Let's keep that between us for now. Might be better that way."

"Of course. Is there anything I can do?"

"I have the situation under control."

"I wish that were true, Dr. Red, but as I'm sure you're aware, your Def-8 units have caused quite a problem in Seoul. The JMF is hunting for them as we speak."

"Yes, and the JMF has survivors of Hell Squad at Omega Base. I demand that they be released and returned to the *Persephone*."

"I'm sorry, Tyron, but until we know what's happened and clear all parties, they must remain there. If this is the Tritons... well, I'm sure you understand. A larger attack could be imminent, and we must be vigilant. If there was ever a time to deploy the Def-9 units, it would be now, Dr. Red. I ask you to reconsider keeping their code locked down."

For a long second, Tyron considered the request.

What if the Tritons were really out there and had found a way to take over the Def-8 units? If they had done that, then the world was indeed at risk. But what if it wasn't them? Releasing the Def-9 units could be an even bigger threat to humanity.

"We're running out of time," said the president.

Tyron wanted to release Orion first, to see if the AI could determine what others had failed to do, and figure out who was responsible.

"You'll have my answer soon," Tyron said.

"Okay. Be well, Dr. Red."

Tyron nodded.

The call ended, and he heaved a sigh.

"Maybe it's already too late," he said.

Orion emerged in front of him, eyes flashing.

"Sir, I have news."

"You already figured out who did this?"

"No, it's about Angelina." The normally blank humanoid face smiled. "She's still alive, sir."

CHAPTER 24

Michelle had fallen asleep on the drive out of Charlotte, a few hours after Cecil was released from the hospital with stitches in his side. By then the Crime Task Force had found them a place to hunker down at a cabin near King Mountain, almost two hours away. It was about a hundred miles total.

The headlights beamed down the county road. Cecil sat behind the wheel, watching the GPS. They were just thirty minutes from the cabin. He was exhausted after his hellish day, but also wired.

He watched the road and mirrors for anyone who might be following him, knowing that it was almost impossible for any of the White Buffaloes to know where he and his wife were or that they had even left town. This was just a precaution.

Still, he felt nervous, mostly for his wife's safety. He took his eyes off the highway briefly to look at her freckled face. She looked so peaceful, with not a care in the world. But he knew this wasn't true. Cecil wasn't surprised she'd fallen asleep, despite her panicked state when they were sent out of town. She had been up for over twenty-four hours, and stressed from the cyberattacks and his injuries.

The latter part was his fault, and for that he felt guilty—especially since he had put her in danger—something he would never have done if he had used his head at Copper Terrace. Instead, he had gone in to avenge Jerky and his comrades without considering the repercussions fully at the time.

He had acted on impulse, partly to prove to himself he was still a soldier. Now Michelle could very well lose her job, and they were on the run, forced to turn off their phones and remove anything that was traceable.

You'll get through this, he thought. *This is just temporary.*

Cecil looked back to the road. The route took them through a quaint small town. Starving, he pulled off to stop and get some food and a few supplies. Although he didn't want to disturb Michelle, he decided to wake her to make sure she wasn't frightened.

He pulled off on a main street of brick and stone buildings. The sidewalks were bustling with families, people out on dates, and tourists window-shopping and eating ice cream.

It was as if Cecil had driven into an alternative universe from the no-go zone he had been in this morning, where riots and chaos had spread like a wildfire.

He parked in an empty spot outside a small market and took his sidearm from the glove compartment.

"Cecil, what's wrong?" Michelle said, jerking awake.

"It's okay. I'm just getting us some food," he said.

She sat up, blinking as she took in the sight.

"Want to come with me?" he asked.

She looked around a few more seconds, then shook her head. "I'll stay here."

"Anything you're hungry for?"

"Nothing."

"Well, you need to eat. I'll find you something and be back shortly."

Cecil tucked his gun away and got out, locking the car doors behind him. He glanced down the street in both directions for anyone looking out of the ordinary. Gangbangers would stick out like a sore thumb here.

Seeing nothing, he left the car and went into the store. He grabbed some fresh produce. Bananas, apples, oranges. Then some cans of soup, chips, and crackers. In the drink aisle, he took a case of water and grabbed two bottles of wine.

Five minutes later, he had loaded most of his purchases into the trunk with his folded-down assault rifle; five magazines; ballistic vest; and a pack full of gear, including medical supplies, two additional VitalStim remotes, and rechargeable batteries for the long haul.

"I'm going to grab something from that diner," he said to Michelle. "You sure you don't want anything specific?"

She shook her head, avoiding his gaze.

Yeah, she's mad, all right. And worried.

He didn't blame her for either. This was his fault.

Cecil opened the diner door, and a small bell chimed. He stepped into the long room with five booths on the left side, half of them filled with patrons. On the right was a bar with four stools, all occupied. Everyone seemed to be watching the flatscreen monitors over the bar.

"Welcome," said the woman behind the counter. "Will you be eating in or carrying out tonight?"

"Carryout," he replied. "I'll take two cheeseburgers, fries, and a salad with grilled chicken."

"Name for the order?"

Cecil said the first thing that came to mind. "Williston."

The woman raised a brow, then said, "Got it. Be right up."

The order was transferred to the kitchen, where the robotic arms of machines began to work on the meal. These were about the extent of what had been salvaged after the Global AI Limitation Accord.

A little disk-shaped robot vacuumed the already clean-looking floor. Only a single human was back in the kitchen—a teenager sitting on a stool, chuckling at whatever he was watching on his holographic pad and paying no attention to the food.

Cecil took his cup over to a drink dispenser and filled it with diet cola. Then he went to look at the holoscreen. A female newscaster was outside the ITC headquarters in Atlanta.

He took a drink, nearly spitting it out when he saw the headline.

Assassination Attempt on ITC CEO Tyron Red.

"Williston, I got your to-go order," said a nasally voice.

The teenager brought over two sacks of food and held them out to Cecil, but he just stared at the screen.

"Earlier this evening, the annual ITC gala was the target of an attack that killed nine patrons and wounded twenty-one. We're being told that Atlanta Mayor Kameron Cowney is among the dead, but there's no word on whether CEO Tyron Red survived the attack."

"Holy shit," Cecil whispered.

"Mister, you want your food?" asked the teenager.

Cecil took it but remained standing at the bar.

"Honey," said a voice.

He turned to see Michelle, staring at the news feed. She put a hand over her mouth as she walked over, staring at the screen.

"Come on," he said, putting an arm around her and guiding her outside.

They got into their car, and Cecil activated the dashboard screen, where the cabin directions were pinned. He switched to the radio.

"This must be connected to the cyberattack," Michelle said, panic rising in her voice. "I need to call work. I need to see—"

"You can't, babe. We can't call anyone. We have to stay off the grid."

Michelle looked at him, eyes wide with confusion and fear. Perhaps it was finally settling in now for both of them.

"There is still no word on Tyron Red's condition, but sources are saying he was inside the gala during the explosion," said the announcer. "We're being told that ITC has released a statement reassuring the world that whoever is responsible will be brought to justice, and there is no threat to the existing network, critical facilities, or functions of the vast ITC infrastructure."

"That won't be the case if Tyron is dead," Michelle said.

"Maybe he isn't," Cecil said.

He reversed the car and began the drive out of a town that was stuck in the past, so far unaffected by the world ITC had helped create—the world he and Michelle had left behind a few hours earlier. They passed a soap shop, an art gallery, and a bookstore.

It struck him that maybe this was a good thing for them both: to escape their busy lives in the city, to reconnect and focus on what they had lost—partly from his own substance abuse.

He put a hand on his wife's wrist, but she quickly pulled away as if he had burned her.

"Michelle, we're going to get through this," he said. "I'm going to change, you'll see. Things will get better, I promise."

She looked at him again, the fear and confusion replaced with sadness.

"I love you," he said.

There was slight hesitation in her voice when she replied, "Love you."

Maybe she was just shaken by everything, or maybe she wasn't sure she still loved him.

That was a hard pill to swallow, but it was the only pill he would be swallowing from here on out.

Cecil was a fighter, and he wasn't going to give up on himself or his family. He proved he could still fight. He was going to make this work.

He looked into the darkness of the forest as they drove out of town, leaving civilization and the world behind.

* * * * *

Santiago paced in his cell at Omega Base, growing more worried by the second. He was being held against his will by the JMF, with no idea whether ITC even knew where he was. Maybe they didn't care. If Tyron Red had been killed and the company was under attack, then major forces far more important than Hell Squad were at play.

At this point, he couldn't trust anyone, not even the JMF.

Getting up on shaky legs, he went to the locked door and put his ear up to it for any chatter from the guards. It sounded quiet out there. Maybe they had left.

The reality of his situation sank in deeper as he sat down again on the bench, cupping his aching head with his hands. Images of Alistair falling to the ground with a hole in his chest and of David dangling limp under his parachute haunted his thoughts. He thought of Nodin, who had lost an arm trying to put down covering fire so Santiago could escape. Anger burned brighter inside him, warming him.

There was one positive to his situation. Whatever exposure he had to the radiation back in Seoul had been mitigated by the two injections he received on the Wasp. And though his head hurt, he didn't have any signs of a concussion. That was lucky, considering he had been knocked unconscious. But that wasn't even the first time. He had gone down several times in the boxing ring without suffering a concussion, as far as he knew.

His thoughts drifted to his family, over a thousand miles away, probably worried about him. If something happened to him, they might never know the truth.

His anger deepened with every second he sat here. He pulled out the note from his wife, tucked away in his vest.

At the end of the day, what's most important is you coming home to me, Diego, and Isabella. Money isn't important. We need you more than you need a paycheck. We will find a way to pay for your treatment and everything else.

Be safe, and don't forget, all it takes is all you got.

Santiago shot up at the sound of footsteps coming toward his cell. He tucked the note away as he went over to the door, prepared to fight if it came down to it.

The footsteps came closer—three or four pairs, it sounded like.

They stopped outside his door.

He rotated his shoulders and flexed his neck, looking relaxed, but ready for anything.

A key unlocked the door, and it swung open to Major Han. Behind him were two guards and a man still wearing the same armor Santiago wore.

"Yosef," he said.

"Come with us," Major Han said.

Santiago looked to Yosef, who nodded ever so subtly. They got behind Han with both JMF guards following them down the corridor to a tunnel. The underground passage ended at a pair of doors marked by medical crosses.

"Sergeant Tatanka is out of surgery and in recovery," Major Han said. He kept walking through the facility until he reached a staging area inside a hangar, where a platoon of JMF Special Forces were suiting up in front of a pair of stealth Wasps.

Yosef and Santiago exchanged a glance when they saw the red patches with a trefoil radiation symbol on fire. This was the infamous Red Platoon, named for their work eliminating any hostiles after the nukes detonated post–Operation Dark Skies. While Hell Squad was evacuating people, Red Platoon was busy hunting down human Triton fighters who hadn't gotten the memo the war was over.

Clad in advance with CBRN tactical gear blending matte black and urban camouflage, Red Platoon was about to deploy back out to the wastelands. Each trooper gripped the advanced energy weapons that the Def-8 units had used on Hell Squad.

"Lieutenant O'Neill," said Major Han as he entered the room.

The lieutenant turned, his sharp eyes finding Santiago and Yosef after he threw up a salute to Han.

Han went to a large digital screen at the front of the hangar.

"Gather 'round," he said.

Red Platoon huddled in front of the major.

"Everyone, this is Sergeant Rodriguez and Lieutenant Yosef of ITC Hell Squad," Han said. "They were assigned to protect the ITC field labs operating along the DMZ and are the survivors of the Def-8 unit attack that we believe killed the scientists at Field Lab Alpha. Before that, they served in Operation Dark Skies, as part of the first wave. Saved a lot of lives that day. They will be a good addition to your mission."

What mission? Santiago wondered. He was in no shape to head out on a mission right now. But he was also in no shape to argue.

Han turned to the monitor that displayed a map of the crater where Field Lab Alpha had been stationed. A red trail curved away from it, heading northwest toward the old Triton territory and right toward Pyongyang, over a hundred miles away.

The lines connected in Santiago's mind, and he felt the chill of realization.

The old enemy had returned.

If this was all true, then the Tritons had been down there over the past five years, planning another attack, and they had found a way to hack the Def-8 units. He began to piece together what had happened, as he thought of what Voss said about them having his family.

Somehow the Tritons had gotten to him and hacked the machines.

Another monitor showed drone footage of three machines running through the rubble of a destroyed city. One hundred miles was a long way to cover in a short time, but not when you could move at ten miles per hour and didn't need to rest.

Santiago felt a surge of energy in his fatigued body at the sight of the units that had attacked his squad and killed Alistair.

"As you can see, we've tracked down the Def-8 units on the following path. Drones show them entering a train station that burrows beneath Pyongyang," Han said. "Seismic activity has been detected from sensors there, and we have precise data now leading us to believe it's coming from deep under the station."

He zoomed in on the location in the ruins of Pyongyang. "Command has formulated a theory the Tritons hacked the Def-8 units, murdered the scientists, and attacked Hell Squad before retreating to these two areas. Although I personally would love to just blow the tunnels to kingdom come, brass wants no shadow of a doubt, and your job is to figure out exactly what we're dealing with before we authorize any strikes. Therefore, you're heading into those tunnels and you're taking these two ITC security guards with you."

"Guards," Santiago muttered.

The troopers looked over—some with respect, but mostly with annoyance. Santiago understood the sentiment. He wouldn't like escorting anyone outside his own unit into enemy territory—just extra bodies they had to protect.

"All due respect, sir, but why do we need them?" O'Neill asked. "We've been in those tunnels too."

"Because brass wants them there. You got a problem with that?"

"No problem, long as they don't get in the way."

Han shifted back to the monitor.

"Two Wasps will fly your squads to the target area for a HALO jump over Pyongyang," he explained. "Red and Black squads will land at this entry point and head in. Blue and Orange will head here."

Santiago studied the satellite footage of the DZ, revealing mounds of black rubble. But something was under there and had been for a very long time, waiting, planning.

"No mistakes. You get in, document, and do not engage unless you're engaged," Han said. He nodded to O'Neill. "You got it from here, Lieutenant. Good luck."

"Thank you, sir."

"Okay, you know the drill. Gear up and get ready to deploy," O'Neill shouted. He motioned Santiago and Yosef to join him by the crates. "There are suits and armor in here for you."

"And weapons?" Santiago asked.

"You're here as guests. Civilians."

"Civilians? You got to be shitting me."

"Do I look like I'm shitting you?"

"Nope, but you're taking a shit *on* us by not providing weapons."

"If the Def-8 units or the enemy are in those tunnels, you'll need every fucking gun you can get, Lieutenant," Yosef said.

"We're ready for whatever's down there," O'Neill said. "The decision has been made. It's not negotiable."

He stepped up closer, looking at them both in turn. "I know you served in the war, but you are currently employees of ITC. You will listen to my orders and my men. If either of you cause me a problem, I will not hesitate to put you in cuffs down there, and there will be hell to pay when we return. Understood?"

"This is bullshit," Santiago grumbled.

"We'll stay out of your way," Yosef said.

Santiago grunted. He didn't like this. It felt wrong. Something was off, but he couldn't just refuse orders. Civilian or not, he had no choice.

"I need you to say it, Rodriguez."

He looked back to the lieutenant.

"'Yes, sir,' or 'Yes, Lieutenant. I understand,'" O'Neill said.

Santiago was used to asshole officers, but O'Neill was showing him and Yosef zero respect.

"Yeah, I got it, sir," Santiago said, resisting the urge to add *bub*.

O'Neill looked at them in turn again, then gestured to a sergeant of below-average height who looked to be overcompensating for his size with a cocky gait and a bodybuilding regimen. His name tag read *Davis*.

"So you guys were in Paektu?" he asked. "I was third wave. Glad to have you with us."

Santiago nodded back, and Yosef did as well.

"Take this," he said. "It'll keep you frosty out there."

Davis handed Santiago a bottle of stim pills.

Santiago looked at the offering, but what he really wanted about now was some tequila. With a pounding headache and feeling the nausea return, he should be in bed resting. But if he wanted to make it home to his family, he would need every advantage he could get.

Taking the pill, he slugged it down with a bottle of water.

They boarded the Wasp in full combat gear, without weapons, racking in side by side. Yosef gave him a side-glance and whispered, "You good, Santiago?"

"Yeah, I'm good." A lie.

Between feeling lousy and his guilt over joining a mission that could leave his family without a father, he was pissed—not just at ITC but at the JMF too. They were treating him and Yosef as if they had never served.

But the more he considered what was happening, the more he realized the threat the Tritons posed, not just here but to the entire world. To his family back in San Diego.

The hangar doors whisked open to the blue flash of the electrical storms over the DMZ. As they wheeled out on the tarmac, Davis got up and looked out the windows.

"Holy hell, look at those," he said.

Santiago checked the closest window and saw the orange glow of a Def-8 unit. A dozen JMF forces escorted it and four more units shuffling with electric shackles on their ankles and wrists, in single file toward an armored truck.

"Gonna end up scrap," Davis said.

"They should have been recycled a long-ass time ago," O'Neill said.

The Wasp rose over Omega Base, providing an aerial view of the hive of activity. Tanks, APCs, and trucks were fired up, brought out of storage. They were preparing for another war.

And Santiago was heading back to the front lines.

CHAPTER 25

There was still no word from the would-be assassins of Tyron Red. No statement, no chatter on the dark networks of the digital ether. Nothing. Only shrapnel from the drones that had torn through the gala crowd, killing ten of Tyron's biggest supporters and injuring twenty more.

But there was good news: Angelina had survived.

Tyron took an elevator deep underneath the ITC headquarters to visit her now, after she arrived just moments ago by air from the nearby hospital where smart, fast-acting pros had resuscitated her a second time.

According to Orion, the first was in an ambulance, but that had never been reported until an hour ago. Apparently, in a mix-up, Angelina had been declared deceased in a communication to ITC. How that was possible, Tyron couldn't say. He was just glad she had made it this far.

The elevator opened to the fully equipped hospital that he had visited only hours earlier. Automatic lights clicked on as he walked down the corridor. He passed empty rooms with the most advanced technology in the world, meant to treat victims should his worst fears become reality.

At the end of the hall, in the ICU meant to treat the most severe patients in such an attack, was a single person. He stepped up to the glass observation wall, where Angelina lay wrapped like a mummy. White bandages swaddled the stumps of her arms, and her entire face was covered.

"Dr. Red, how are you feeling?" came a voice.

He turned to Dr. Liu, whom he himself had seen after the attack. A team of two additional doctors and four staff were standing inside an observation room, monitoring vitals.

"I'm fine, thanks, and Dr. Sanchez?" Tyron answered after a pause.

Liu gave no hint of emotion as he gazed on her body. "She has been placed in a medically induced coma," he said. "She suffered extreme trauma to her brain, and burns on over sixty percent of her body."

"Will she survive?"

"That depends on a number of factors, sir, but she has a real shot, as this is one of the finest facilities in the world, with a state-of-the-art burn unit."

Something Tyron had added to each facility, to care for survivors of any future nuclear attack.

"Do everything you can," he said.

"I will, but, sir . . ." Liu turned away from the glass wall, and Tyron caught the hint of anxiety. "Even if she pulls through, Dr. Sanchez will never be the same. She's currently blind and will require multiple surgeries to try to restore vision in her left eye. Her face will need to be reconstructed, and she has lost both arms." A sigh escaped him. "We will do everything we can."

"Thank you," Tyron said.

"Of course, sir." Liu walked away and joined his team.

Tyron stood there another moment, watching Angelina's chest gently rise and fall. She reminded him of a helpless child.

Whoever did this was going to pay.

He wanted to scream at the memory of Angelina reaching out to him with the stumps of her arms before collapsing. The violence had shattered his ironclad resolve, and the only way to get it back was to keep going forward. He had wanted to avoid another conflict with machines, but if this was the Tritons, it seemed he had no choice.

Another voice echoed down the hall as the elevator opened. Whitt walked over, looking exhausted.

"How is she?" he asked.

"Alive," Tyron answered.

They stood at the window looking in on her as machines kept her alive.

The irony wasn't lost on Tyron.

"The JMF has deployed to Pyongyang in pursuit of the Def-8 units, which they have tracked to subway tunnels there," Whitt said. "Lieutenant Yosef and Sergeant Rodriguez of Hell Squad are with them. It's looking like this was indeed the Tritons that hacked the Def-8 units and kidnapped the family of Dr. Joseph Voss."

Tyron looked away from Angelina.

"His family is missing in New York, sir. Our agents reached the apartment an hour ago and found evidence of a struggle." Whitt paused as if to consider his next words. "Sir, the cyberattacks, the attack at the gala, and what's happening in Seoul—all of it must be the Tritons. The Def-8 units have proved to be a liability and are currently being removed from ITC service by JMF troopers at our field labs in Korea. I highly encourage you to consider releasing the Def-9 prototypes and starting production on more of them."

Tyron glanced back to Angelina, who had been adamantly opposed to that plan.

"All due respect, sir, but look what the Tritons did to her," Whitt said. "We can stop them with the Def-9s, but we're running out of time."

"And if you're wrong? If this is someone—or something—else? Then what?"

He thought of the video message from his father that Angelina had recovered and presented to him in the gardens at the gala, warning him of shadowy forces but also telling him he was wrong about the machines.

Tyron felt conflicted, caught in a rare moment of indecision.

"When will Hell Squad be on the ground with the JMF?" he asked.

"Soon, sir."

"I want to know what they find. If it's the Tritons, then you will have my authorization."

Whitt hesitated. "There's one other thing."

"What's that?"

"Currently, you are not confirmed alive or dead after the attack. Perhaps it would be better for the world to think you're dead."

Tyron had already thought about this. But he had other ideas.

"The world needs to know I'm breathing," he said. "To know that ITC is still strong. I will make the announcement tomorrow, when we launch *Genesis 1*."

"You're proceeding with the launch?"

"Absolutely. And I'll do it in person."

Whitt looked as if he was going to protest, but he simply nodded. "I'll prepare the security." He began to walk away, but Tyron reached out and touched his shoulder.

"I know this is personal for you in a way," he said, "having lost your son in the war. If the Triton Legion are behind all this, they will be destroyed. You have my word."

"Glad to hear you say that, sir."

As Whitt left, Tyron turned back to the observation window. Angelina had helped him with all his plans: the ITC facilities with bunkers across the world, the Delta Cloud fusion reactors, Operation RadGrow—every initiative that mattered.

With the launch of *Genesis 1*, plan B would be complete.

Tyron put his hand on the glass and whispered goodbye to Angelina. Then he headed back down to the Genesis lab, into the cryostatis chamber. The lights illuminated the pods mounted on the pillars, and the sleeping faces of the occupants.

"Orion," he said into his headset. "Proceed to the Genesis lab."

Tyron went up to the row of cryo-pods containing the selected clones for the new testing. He tapped on a screen to look at the current test data.

By his side, Orion took holographic form.

"Hello, sir," he said.

Orion's voice filled the cold, sterile room with an eerie calm.

"Orion, I don't have much time right now, but I'd like an update on the current testing of these subjects," Tyron said.

"Sir, the testing has proceeded to the second phase. So far, the epigenetic modifications have yielded results that exceed projections. The subjects' resilience to extreme environmental stressors has proved remarkable."

Tyron raised an eyebrow, his tone sharp. "Define *remarkable*, Orion. I need practical results, not theory."

The digital face on the screen flickered as data flowed across it. "Beginning with radiation tolerance, the clones were subjected to conditions similar to postnuclear environments. The results show a ninety-two percent survival rate. Cellular decay was minimal, and tissue repair mechanisms, enhanced by epigenetic changes, activated four point three times as fast as in baseline humans."

Tyron crossed his arms, his mind already processing the implications. "And what about oxygen deprivation?"

"The clones were exposed to low-oxygen atmospheres simulating high-altitude environments. While normal humans would lose consciousness within minutes, the clones maintained cognitive and physical functioning for an average of sixty-seven minutes before symptoms appeared. Enhanced hemoglobin-binding capacity allowed them to efficiently utilize the available oxygen."

Tyron nodded, impressed but still searching for more. "What about toxins?"

Orion's face flickered as data sped across the screen. "Subjects were tested with neurotoxins and industrial pollutants. Neurological functioning remained intact despite exposure, and immune responses to airborne carcinogens were enhanced. Detoxification through liver and kidney function was accelerated, removing harmful chemicals at five point two times the speed of baseline humans."

"Did any of this affect their physical capabilities?"

"No decline in strength or endurance was observed. In fact, radiation and toxins appeared to *stimulate* regenerative abilities, allowing the clones to operate at peak performance longer than expected."

Tyron stepped back, absorbing the weight of the report. The clones weren't just surviving—they were thriving in environments that would kill ordinary humans, much like the new batch of hybrid Cordovia seeds in Operation RadGrow.

The clones, like the seeds, had been engineered to endure radiation, low oxygen, extreme temperatures, and toxins—all the worst conditions of a postnuclear world, or of another planet.

"And their epigenetic markers?" Tyron asked. "Stable? No mutations?"

Orion paused. "Stable. No harmful mutations detected. The epigenetic modifications are self-repairing, ensuring resilience under environmental stress, and perpetuation of desirable traits."

Tyron exhaled, a slow smile creeping across his face. "They're ready. It's time to deploy them into the field."

"Are you sure, sir? You don't think this is a bit premature?"

"We are out of time. *Genesis 1* launches tomorrow. We'll send this generation on the flight and will continue testing new groups of clones to ensure we aren't missing anything."

Orion's digital face flickered again. "Understood. Preparations for deployment will begin immediately."

Tyron turned away from the glowing screen and looked up at the columns of cryo-chambers.

He had done all he could to prepare humanity for the apocalypse on Earth and leaving the planet. Only time would tell if it was enough.

"Let's see what they're really capable of," he said, still looking up at the clones.

* * * * *

The silent rotors of the stealth Wasp whipped toward the fortress of storm clouds on the horizon. Twelve troopers from Red Platoon sat positioned around Yosef and Santiago.

Santiago glanced out the closest window at a second Wasp, carrying two more squads. Beneath them at the edge of the exclusion zone, thousands of soldiers in hazard suits ran final checks on armor and weapons.

The tilt-rotor craft swung north, toward enemy territory.

Santiago had feared this day would come, but he never expected to be part of it. He double-checked the HUD in his new helmet—critical systems all working properly. The men in front of him sat stone-faced, gripping their laser rifles. Unarmed, Santiago felt like a helpless animal surrounded by predators. If the Tritons were responsible for taking over the Def-8 units and attacking

Field Lab Alpha, landing in enemy territory without a weapon was suicide.

"Crossing into no-man's-land," said the pilot. "Going dark."

Every light in the bird shut off, and O'Neill stood. "All systems offline," he said. "We do this the old-fashioned away."

Santiago tapped his wrist monitor, shutting off all critical systems besides his night vision. The troop hold became a field of green.

He sat waiting, thinking of his wife and kids, praying he would get back to them somehow.

Whatever it takes, T.

"Approaching DZ. ETA ten minutes!" said the primary pilot. "Gonna get bumpy real soon, so hold on to your asses."

O'Neill shot Yosef and Santiago a look. "Davis, you're in charge of them."

"Copy, LT," replied the sergeant.

The Wasp shuddered through a pocket of turbulence that rattled the hull. Through the portholes, flashes of blue illuminated the heavily armed and armored troopers. The storm battered the Wasp, but the pilots held it steady up through the storms to an altitude of twenty thousand feet.

"Approaching DZ. Get ready!" one of them said over the comms.

O'Neill got up and walked down the row of his troopers, patting each on the shoulder plate. "Stay alert, and be ready for anything," he said. "There are no friendlies. Anything moves, blast it to dust. We're not giving any hostiles an opportunity to engage first."

Grunts and hooahs filled the troop hold.

O'Neill went to the hatch and slid it back to a sky bejeweled with stars above them, and the storm clouds raging below. A thousand feet away, troopers began jumping out of the other Wasp's open hatch.

"In position!" the pilot confirmed.

The soldiers got up in a single file. Santiago and Yosef followed them with Davis right behind.

"Go, go, go!" O'Neill ordered.

One by one, the troopers hopped out of the aircraft. Santiago stepped forward to the open hatch and looked down at the storm clouds before his faceplate. Lightning bloomed in multiple locations.

He jumped out spread-eagled in a hard arch, then pulled his arms and legs into stable position. He plummeted into the abyss, picking up speed as he fell toward the bulging shelf of clouds. Below him, the armored frames of troopers were suddenly illuminated by a lightning flash. They all had straightened their legs and pulled their arms into their sides.

Santiago did the same, pulling into an arrow shape. He shot after them headfirst, piercing the clouds and entering the purgatory before the hell that awaited them on the surface. He counted the seconds, using mental math to do what his HUD normally did for him. Turbulence pulled and pushed at him.

In the sporadic glow of lightning, he spotted troopers breaking the wedge formation and scattering farther across the sky at around fifteen thousand feet.

Lightning forked across his path as he looked back down. He instinctively pulled to the right. They were in the heart of the storm now.

Another flash made him jerk, and he fell out of stable position. He flipped and began to spin and tumble wildly. The world went topsy-turvy.

He couldn't see anything as he spun.

But Santiago kept tumbling, sucking in oxygen while trying to get back into stable position.

At this point, he was probably at nine or ten thousand feet.

Half a minute to get his shit together before he needed to open his chute.

He managed to pull back into a stable position. Yosef came down next to him and gave him an encouraging nod. Just having his mate with him helped him relax. Then Yosef angled his helmet down, pulled his arms in along his sides, and dropped into a nosedive.

Thunder boomed, rattling Santiago as he followed. He fired through the floor of the clouds and soon got his first glimpse of the black-and-gray surface that was once Pyongyang. Craters pockmarked the terrain as far as he could see. Not a single part of the city was recognizable. Every structure had been erased in the first year of the war, before the Tritons retreated north to the mountain strongholds where they had hidden their nuclear arsenal.

Parachutes bloomed beneath Santiago. He pulled his rip cord, and the canopy popped open above him. Grabbing his toggles, he steered toward Yosef. They glided over a section of city that was once a transportation hub. From above, it was hard to make out much besides a few parking lots littered with charred vehicles. But as Santiago got closer to the LZ, he spotted a ribbon of mangled bridges rising from the rubble. A train lay on its side, the cars shattered and crushed. The tunnel entrance wasn't far.

He looked west, but the two squads from the second Wasp were too far away to see with the naked eye.

Half the troopers from his Wasp had already touched down on a patch of dirt near the derailed train. Santiago performed a two-stage flare and dropped gracefully down onto the radioactive soil.

All around him, troopers stuffed their chutes, then shouldered their weapons as they set up a perimeter. Yosef hiked over as Santiago was looking at the old-school radiation gauge on his wrist. The Geiger counter ticked up into the red.

Davis strode over, cradling his rifle. "Stay on me," he said.

The squads fanned out in combat intervals along the tracks toward the tunnel entrances. There were four former entry points according to the old satellite imagery, although you couldn't tell it now. Three tunnels were completely caved in. From outside, the remaining entrance appeared as a yawning mouth in a hillside beneath a street overpass darkened and cracked by the heat that had rushed through this area.

Lieutenant O'Neill held up a fist. The point man had found something. Footprints, it looked like, heading into the only open tunnel.

Santiago got a glimpse from his position.

Sure enough, the padded tracks of the Def-8 units led into the subway tunnel. O'Neill gestured again, this time for Santiago and Yosef to stay with him and Davis. Then he flashed a hand signal to the point man, who started toward the portal into the depths of the once-bustling city. Above, a scorched sign hung loosely, its words erased by the heat.

The trooper passed under it and vanished into the gaping black hole while everyone else hunkered down with rifles up.

The machines had been here, and this was very likely a trap by the Tritons. Never had Santiago felt more vulnerable in his life, aside from the time he plummeted through the storms in Operation Dark Skies, trapped in his exoskeleton. But he had found a way to survive, and he would again. He *would* get back to his family.

He kept eyes on the tunnel, watching for the trooper.

A minute passed. Then five.

The troopers remained as still as statues, in what felt to Santiago like an extraordinarily long wait. Finally, there was movement, and the weapons around him shifted to a target.

Santiago clenched up, then relaxed when he saw the black armor of the point man. He tucked some sort of remote into his vest pocket as he moved. O'Neill got up, motioning to move forward.

The troopers moved into the mouth of the tunnel. Santiago and Yosef followed behind, keeping close to Davis. The interior of cracked concrete walls spread before him in the green backdrop of his NVGs.

Ahead, a train remained on the tracks, protected from the worst of the heat wave, but the passengers had died before they could feel any pain. They sat as burned husks behind the cracked and shattered windows.

The squads moved around the train, only to come up on another scene of death.

A *fresh* scene.

Santiago slowed at the sight of crumpled bodies in hazard suits and light armor. At least a dozen corpses lay outside an open maintenance door on the left side of the tunnel.

O'Neill signaled five troopers to check it out.

They walked past the dead men, obviously Triton soldiers. Santiago noticed black scorch marks in their suits, and holes burned in their armor by energy weapons.

After his next stop, Santiago saw the shooter. A Def-8 unit lay inside the maintenance tunnel.

But that made no sense. If the Tritons had hacked the Def-8 units, why would those units turn around and kill their new handlers?

The point man motioned all clear in the maintenance passage, and O'Neill gave the signal to advance down the tracks.

Santiago cautiously followed the soldiers around a curve in the tunnel until they came to a gaping hole in the center of the tracks. Rubble lay scattered around it, along with more Triton soldiers' corpses.

The scout ahead held up a fist and went down on one knee.

A beat later, Santiago saw why. Lying among the dead Tritons around the crater in the tracks was the metal frame of another Def-8 unit. Santiago could see multiple bullet dents in the armor.

The third unit wasn't far, also down and also heavily dented.

Slowly, four of the troopers fanned out, warily approaching the scene.

Santiago observed that the hole wasn't from a structural collapse. This was caused by an explosion belowground. Grappling hooks tied to caving ropes clung to the rim where the Triton soldiers had emerged from their underground bunkers.

The seismic disturbances recently recorded were in fact the enemy blasting its way out.

His gaze went back to the scout, who had pulled something from his vest again and aimed it at the Def-8 units as O'Neill walked over with his rifle shouldered. Two men flanked him, also aiming their weapons.

O'Neill gave the order, and both troopers fired their energy weapons into the downed machines.

The realization hit Santiago like a brick. It wasn't the Tritons who had taken out the Def-8 units; it was the JMF, hacking them and sending them here to kill the Tritons.

But why? For leverage over ITC?

Santiago had a feeling he was the next part of the evidence that was going to be erased.

Yosef glanced subtly over at him, no doubt considering something similar.

Davis remained behind them, but the rest of the troopers were all surrounding the crater now. If they were going to run for it, now would be the time. But to where? They were in the center of a destroyed, radioactive city over a hundred miles from the DMZ.

"All clear. Get an encrypted line out of here," O'Neill said.

A trooper brought over a handheld radio. "We're on a secure line via the drone," he said.

O'Neill grabbed the phone. "Red Actual to Omega One, over."

"Go ahead, Red Actual," came the crackling response.

"Def-8 units are secured, and all Tritons have been eliminated aboveground. Unfortunately, we had two casualties in a firefight."

Both Santiago and Yosef turned, but Davis had his rifle aimed at them.

"Sorry, fellas," he said.

"What the hell is this?" Yosef asked.

"You know what this is," O'Neill said after handing the radio back. "You joined the wrong company, and unfortunately for you, it's time to cut ties and take over what they refused to provide: the next generation of war machines. To finish this war once and for all."

So that's it, Santiago thought. They wanted ITC to authorize new Defectors.

Yosef took a step forward. "You won't get away with this."

"Just know this isn't personal, and your sacrifice will keep the world safe from the Triton scu—"

O'Neill's helmet exploded as a gunshot cracked, prodigiously loud in the tunnel's close quarters. Santiago saw the muzzle flash across the crater, from an injured Triton soldier who had been lying in wait. The man turned his weapon on the JMF troopers, laying down a spray of wild shots.

Santiago dove for an enemy assault rifle. He brought it up and fired at Davis, but the sergeant scrambled away. Yosef had already picked up O'Neill's laser rifle, and they blasted away at the scrambling JMF troopers. Several troopers managed to fire back at the Triton soldier, killing him before turning their weapons on Santiago and Yosef.

Yosef pulled Santiago backward, toward the crater in the tunnel floor. "Jump!" he shouted.

Santiago hesitated all of half a second, then leaped into the hole, grasping for the rope that hung from a grappling iron only a yard away. He caught it and banged his shoulder against the shaft wall.

He twisted, looking for Yosef.

"Yosef!" he shouted.

Santiago wrapped the rope below him around one leg and draped it over his opposite shoulder in an improvised rappel and started working his way down the rope, into darkness. Hearing voices above him, he flattened himself against the wall.

"Anyone see 'em?" someone asked.

"Nah, they're fucking gonzo, man. That shaft goes down a mile. I can't even see the bottom!"

Lights beamed down, raking back and forth. Santiago peered down and saw only darkness.

"We need confirmation those two assholes are dead," said a familiar voice—Sergeant Davis.

"Why? LT is fucking dead—bastards shot him in the face. Then they committed suicide. No way they survived. And if somehow they are alive, they're trapped down there."

"Just fucking look, goddamn it," Davis snapped.

More beams flickered back and forth. Santiago closed his eyes, hugged the wall, and prayed.

"Yeah, I don't see shit, Sarge," someone else said.

There was a pause as the lights raked over the walls.

"Fuck it. Remove those grappling hooks and head back outside," Davis ordered.

Oh, shit!

Three of the beams pulled back, and Santiago started sliding down the rope as hooks were pulled free above him. They came clattering down. He slid faster, then slowed when he saw something below. A platform in an opening of some sort in the tunnel shaft that wasn't visible from above. He was almost there when his hook came loose.

Santiago fell the last ten feet and hit the platform hard. He nearly fell back over the side when someone grabbed him by the arm. The next thing he knew, he was being pulled into a shaft. On the ground inside, Yosef lay crumpled.

"Lieutenant," Santiago whispered.

In the green hue of his night-vision goggles, he saw three more figures in full hazard suits, all aiming rifles at his face.

Triton soldiers.

Slowly, Santiago raised his hands in the air.

"Easy, bub," he said. "I'm not the enemy."

CHAPTER 26

Cecil looked out the kitchen window of the little cabin nestled in the mountains. The quaint squared-log structure sat perched on a hill, its weathered porch offering a panoramic view of the rolling woodland bathed in the golden light of the morning sun.

A dense canopy of pines and hardwoods covered the valley below their elevated location. Towering oaks with sprawling branches and huge trunks dominated the landscape, with elegant maples and tall hickories rising up in the gaps between. Soon the green would shift to fiery orange and yellow and red.

On the deck outside, Michelle sat in a red wooden lounge chair with her knees to her chest, arms wrapped around them, staring.

She had gotten up before him, and he had panicked when he rolled over to find she was gone. Part of him was surprised to find her outside, but he didn't want to bother her right now, not without a peace offering of some coffee.

He had screwed up, and not just once.

The past few months had been rough. They were working almost completely different schedules, and he had fallen back into his old habits. His demons chewed at him, gnawing with little teeth until he couldn't resist the itch to suffocate them with pills.

But those days were behind him.

He would change—he had to. If he didn't, he was going to lose his wife.

What mattered right now was that they reconnect, and they had the perfect place to do it. He couldn't help but feel that maybe this was all for the best, as long as she could forgive him.

Again.

Cecil poured two cups of coffee. He put a dash of sugar in hers, along with some milk he had picked up from the store. Before he grabbed them, he made sure he had his pistol tucked in the back of his waistband. The assault rifle was propped against the door, loaded with the safety on.

It was secluded out here, but he wasn't going to let his guard down. The serene silence of the retreat was punctuated only by the soft creak of the porch floorboards as he stepped outside.

Michelle flinched, startled. She turned, and he saw she had an earpiece in. Apparently, she hadn't just been staring, but also listening to something.

"Sorry, didn't mean to startle you," he said. "Coffee?"

"Thanks." She took the mug, holding it and blowing on it while the sun rose higher, spreading golden light over the forest.

"Any news on Tyron?" Cecil asked.

"Yeah, just a second, I'm listening to an update," she said.

Cecil walked over to the railing on the east side of the deck and looked over to the detached garage, where he had parked their car. The wooded sanctuary was over five miles from town and two miles from the nearest neighbor. It was accessible by a private road that had been blocked off by a chain. If anyone drove up it, he would see them far in advance. But there were plenty of ways someone could still sneak up on them.

He had a plan for that. Today he would hike down and set old-fashioned trip lines connected to bells, to alert them if anyone tried to flank the cabin from the surrounding forest.

Michelle sighed as she took her earbud out. "ITC still hasn't confirmed whether Tyron is alive," she said.

"Then my guess is, he is," Cecil said. "Might be too injured to talk in front of reporters, but if he were dead, I think they would say so."

"I don't know. I have a bad feeling."

She got up and walked over to the railing with him.

"You keep looking down there," she said.

"Yeah, just checking things out."

"You mean you're doing recon?"

He glanced at her, then nodded.

"You think we're really safe here?" she asked.

"I'm not going to let anything happen to you, Michelle."

"No offense, Cecil, but you already have. I'm probably going to lose my job."

"Captain Harkin promised he would talk to—"

"And say what? ITC is in crisis mode right now; they need me. My team needs me. All the people who count on the food my facility provides need me."

Cecil frowned. "Yeah, well, I need you, too, and I'm sorry, Michelle. I'll do better."

"I've heard that so many times, and then you keep pulling the same shit." She scoffed. "Honestly, I'm scared, Cecil. Not just of losing my job, but of people coming after us."

She went back inside the cabin, leaving Cecil at the railing.

"Michelle, come on, I'm going to take care of us," he said. "Don't walk away."

"Why?" she said from the doorway. "You do all the time."

She stepped inside and shut the door behind her.

Cecil took a deep breath of mountain air. She was right, and he felt lower now than before. Part of that he chalked up to being out here, where everything seemed so much clearer.

Deep down, he was a soldier. That was all he knew how to do. To fight. It was what he did in Korea and what he did at Copper Terrace. He did it for his brothers in arms and to protect innocent people, or at least, that was what he told himself.

But the one person he should have been fighting for all this time, the one he loved most, was the one he continued to hurt.

There was nothing he could do now but fight in a different way. To show her he cared about her.

The sound of a distant vehicle caught his ear, pulling him from dark thoughts. He looked down at the winding road, where a pickup had stopped outside the chain. Two people were in the cab, but he couldn't make them out.

Cecil cursed, realizing he had left his binoculars and his rifle inside. He hurried back to the sliding door. Michelle was in the bedroom when he got to the kitchen. He snatched the rifle and binos without disturbing her and rushed back outside.

By the time he got there, the truck was backing up. He centered the binoculars on it just as it backed around a hill.

The sliding door opened behind him, and Michelle stepped out.

"Something down there?" she asked.

Cecil lowered the binos. He considering a lie to keep her from worrying but decided to tell the truth. "Yeah, a truck," he said. "Must have taken a wrong turn."

"A wrong turn? Up here?"

He turned to her as she stepped back inside.

"Yeah, probably. I'm sure it's nothing," he said. "Don't worry, okay?"

"Yeah, you keep saying that."

* * * * *

The morning after the attack, Tyron stood in his office bathroom. He finally washed off the blood. The sun had long since risen over Atlanta, and he had watched it, wondering what fresh hell this new day would bring.

For one, it would reveal the truth about his enemy—an enemy of humanity.

He closed his eyes and raised his face into the hot spray of the shower, letting it wash the grit, dust, and blood from his hair. When he opened his eyes, the drain swirled pink, sucking away the vestiges of the massacre.

Tyron had always been a peaceful man, leaving war to others with harder hearts. But the past twenty-four hours had hardened his own. There was no time for weakness. He had to be strong and smart about his next actions.

Whether it was the Tritons or someone else, he would know very soon.

Hours ago, when he was trying to sleep, the JMF had deployed a strike team to Seoul with his two best security forces from Hell Squad. The after-action report would be coming any moment.

After drying off, he went to the closet connected to the bathroom, stocked with his staple white trench coat and red bow ties. Showered and dressed, he stepped back into his office. He put on his blue-lensed glasses and stood before the wall of pictures.

These were the people who had shaped his life.

He opened the doors to the office and found Whitt in the command center, communicating with staff from around the world. Based on his stern look, Tyron could tell that his longtime, loyal security chief had news.

"Sir, we just got word from the JMF," he said. "Both members of Hell Squad were killed, and the strike team was attacked by Tritons in the train tunnel."

Tyron stared. His worst fears were beginning to come to light.

“It was the Tritons, sir, and my guess is, they’re also behind the cyberattacks, making it look like the Blackworms.”

“And the attack on the gala.”

“Yes.”

“The JMF is mobilizing, sir. Preparing for—”

“War,” Tyron said. “And the Tritons will be preparing too.”

Whitt nodded. “Time has run out. We received a partial video. Stand by.”

Tyron folded his arms across his chest as a video feed in the green hue of night-vision optics came online. Six Special Forces soldiers armed with the new military-grade laser rifles advanced into a tunnel.

“Red Platoon entered train tunnels after the first team engaged in a firefight with Tritons and our Def-8 units that the enemy hacked,” Whitt said.

The squad stopped near a train, examining the remains of dead Triton soldiers and one of the Def-8 units.

“We suffered no casualties here,” Whitt said. “However, at the next encounter, Lieutenant O’Neill was killed.”

The team arrived at a crater in the center of the tunnel, where two more Def-8 units were discovered on the ground, along with a half dozen dead Triton human soldiers.

“This is where the enemy blasted out,” Whitt said. “Both Sergeant Rodriguez and Lieutenant Yosef were killed in a firefight here, along with several troopers from Red Platoon who were engaged by the enemy.”

A video feed showed where a Triton soldier shot O’Neill in the head. The feed became chaotic, but Tyron did make out someone in an ITC hazard suit and armor falling into the shaft.

He couldn’t help but feel responsible for both their deaths. If he had authorized the Def-9 units earlier, the machines would have been there to help them.

Buzzing came from the dashboard of monitors. Whitt tapped a button.

"Sir, General Vucci would like to speak with you," he said.

"I'll take it here," Tyron said.

The general's hard face came onto a monitor.

"Dr. Red, how are you feeling?" Vucci asked.

"Let's cut the shit. You were right," Tyron said. "The Tritons were out there all this time."

"I take no pleasure in being right about that, but the time has come. We need your machines. The Tritons may have developed a new war machine down there, and there's no telling how powerful it is. We believe these first few soldiers to be advance recon."

"I do have a question, General. Why hack the Def-8s and then bring them right back there? Why show your enemy your hand?"

"This is just one location of many, we now believe. We have moved assets, including airships provided by ITC. The Doomsday Shield has been placed on high alert. If the Tritons somehow do have new weapons, nothing will get through it this time."

Tyron nodded.

"The Tritons tried to kill you, and failed, Dr. Red, but they will try again," Vucci said. "We are offering support to help protect you."

Whitt glanced at Tyron and nodded his agreement.

"Thank you, General. I appreciate that," Tyron said. "There are a few things I must do before I authorize the code to the Def-9 units, but in the meantime, feel free to start moving them."

"Already done. We had five hundred of the prototype machines shipped to the JMF in the DMZ, where they are being parceled out among the bases. The rest will be moved shortly from other secret locations."

Tyron hesitated, surprised to hear that the ball was already moving. But considering the circumstances, he wasn't going to protest. His delays had already cost them time and had gotten Angelina blown up.

"Once you provide the codes to reactivate them, the JMF will work with their assets on the ground to deploy the Def-9 units to the locations where seismic activity has been detected," Vucci added.

"Understood," Tyron replied.

As soon as the call ended, he contemplated what that really meant. He would be authorizing use of the very machines he had argued against, resulting in his departure from ITC and the falling-out with his father.

Sometimes you have to admit when you're wrong, he thought.

But there was something gnawing at him that he didn't quite understand—something that felt off. He decided to take a few minutes to think and to visit Angelina.

"I'll be in the medical facility," he told Whitt.

On his way down to Angelina, Tyron changed plans, pushing the lowest button on the panel. A few seconds later, the doors opened to the bridge connecting to Orion's chamber.

Tyron tapped in his code and stepped inside to his typical friendly greeting from the AI. "Hello, sir, it's good to see you this morning," Orion said. "I'm pleased to report *Genesis 1* is ready for launch. The cryostatis chambers have been loaded with ten clones."

"That's great news, Orion, but it's not why I'm here. I need your help understanding something."

"Of course, sir."

Tyron stepped over to the leather chairs where they had sat for countless hours chatting over the years. Today he chose to stand.

"I'm sure you have seen the video that the JMF gave us, documenting the location of the Def-8 units by Red Platoon," he said.

"Yes, I have."

"And what are your thoughts, Orion?"

"It's hard to say without seeing the full video, but my conclusion is that General Vucci is not telling you the truth about what really happened in that train tunnel."

Tyron felt his guts twist at the confirmation that something was indeed wrong.

"I believe that parts were left out to deceive you about what really occurred," Orion said. "Whoever edited this video left out a key part."

"And what do you believe happened?"

"Take a look."

The walls of the chamber activated with frozen frames from the video. In it, Tyron saw one of the ITC troopers in midair over the crater the Tritons had blasted out from underground.

"What do you observe Santiago Rodriguez to be doing?" Orion asked.

"He's falling into that crater."

"But is he?"

Orion zoomed in, showing Santiago's back leg bent, as if he had launched into the air.

"He's jumping," Tyron said in a whisper.

"Precisely, sir. Now think about that," Orion said. "Why would Santiago jump into that enemy shaft, away from the JMF soldiers?"

"My God..." Tyron couldn't believe what the AI was implying. "Santiago was trying to escape the JMF."

"Perhaps. What I can say for certain is that some element of the Tritons has returned, sir, but I can't conclude that they hacked the Def-8 units."

"That doesn't make sense."

"That is the point. There appears to be a conspiracy here. My theory is that the Tritons aren't the threat General Vucci wants you to believe they are, and that the Def-8 units are simply pawns in a more elaborate plan—"

"To get me to authorize the Def-9 units for military use."

"That would be a logical deduction, sir."

Tyron turned, ready to tell Whitt, but he paused. Suddenly, he wasn't sure whom he could trust. He thought back to what his father had said in the message Angelina uncovered.

You were right about the machines, about the war. I can see that now, and I'm sorry. Trust your instinct, and don't give in to pressure from shadowy forces, no matter what they say to you.

Tyron faced Orion, remembering something else his father had told him many times when he was just a boy.

AI is not your friend, Tyron. It is only a tool.

It was time to unlock the full potential of this tool now.

"I need you to do something for me, Orion," Tyron said.

"Of course, sir. Whatever you need."

CHAPTER 27

Santiago gritted his teeth as he looped Yosef's arm over his shoulders, bearing most of his weight as they hobbled down the dimly lit corridor. The lieutenant had a broken right arm and sprained left ankle from the fall. If it weren't for grabbing a rope as he fell, Yosef would have been dead—or would have two broken legs, which was pretty much the same thing.

Regardless, he was probably going to die, and Santiago too. They were hundreds of feet below the train tunnels and being held at gunpoint by three Triton soldiers. The men were wearing helmets, but Santiago had gotten a glimpse of their youthful faces. Two of them couldn't be much older than teenagers. None of them spoke English.

For the past hour, the Triton soldiers had guided them deeper into the labyrinth, via the tunnels they had used to dig out from their bunkers. Generators, batteries, and equipment used to power their drills were left behind, along with those giant drillheads, many broken from use. There were boxes of supplies, too, some marked as explosives.

Black mold clung to the walls in the dark, dank environment.

Water dripped from the overhead in some areas and cascaded in others, forming puddles across the rocky ground. Yosef wheezed as they went deeper, his body shaking.

"I got you," Santiago said.

"My ribs..." Yosef gasped. "I can't breathe."

"We need to stop," Santiago said.

The soldiers looked back at them but clearly didn't understand.

Santiago halted and helped Yosef sit, but their captives didn't like that.

The smallest and probably youngest of the group pointed a submachine gun and jerked the barrel, indicating to get up.

"Leave me," Yosef said. "I got internal bleeding. No way I make it out of here."

"You're making it out. So am I. And we're going to tell the world the truth. Now, get up. I'll carry you if I have to."

Santiago carefully helped Yosef up, but despite his gentle movements, the lieutenant cried out in pain.

"Sorry," Santiago said.

The three Tritons pushed on, one falling in behind Santiago and Yosef as they moved deeper into the tunnel. Ahead, a ramp sloped down to the first stairwell they had come across.

A distant humming reached their ears from below.

The lead soldier ahead stopped to speak to his comrades. Then the point soldier went on down the stairs. There was grinding, then the humming noise, louder now, along with faint muffled voices.

The soldier returned, motioning for them.

Santiago helped Yosef down the ramp and into the stairwell that wound down to a landing with an open blast door. Dim light came from the other side. The radiation levels here were low, almost nonexistent.

He turned off his night vision as they followed the lead soldier through a door. Bright industrial lights dazzled Santiago's eyes. He held up his free hand to shield his visor from the intense glare and saw that they were on a mezzanine over a vast chamber.

Coughing and voices echoed upward as Santiago stepped out to look down at tents, shacks, and structures made of scrap. There had to be a hundred of the crude shanties spread throughout a space the size of a football field.

Along the walls, three levels of mezzanines provided walkways into tunnels that went deeper into the ground. On one of them, Santiago made out what looked like an underground farm, with vegetation growing behind glass windows.

On another level, he spotted generators, mechanical equipment, and air-moving machinery.

What he didn't see were AI machines. There were no three-legged Triton hunter-killers with Miniguns and flamethrowers attached to their arms. Just a few skinny human guards on each level, holding rifles and shotguns, all of them Korean.

Their youthful captors took them down a stairwell, where two men with submachine guns waited. The leader of the group exchanged words with the two sentries, then started guiding them across the chamber, through a row of tents.

People looked out from inside the shanties, pulling back tent flaps and sheet-metal doors. Some zipped theirs up. Hushed voices broke out as the newcomers crossed the room and more people saw them. People began to gather—civilians, from the look of it. They were mostly children, who looked emaciated, pale, and sickly. Within a minute, word spread and more people shuffled over, some of them using canes. Many of them were covered in bandages, their bodies sick from radiation exposure.

Santiago helped Yosef across the chamber. The young soldiers led them to a platform where a woman sat behind a desk. She stood up, and her black coveralls and long black hair created the fleeting illusion of a pale, disembodied face rising from the chair.

"My name is Hayun," she said in nearly perfect English. "I am the municipal administrator of this refugee city, and you are?"

"Santiago Rodriguez," he grunted. "This is my friend, Yosef Stern."

"You're with the JMF?"

"No, the JMF tried to kill us. We're employees of a private company." He left out the name for fear that it would get them shot on the spot. ITC was a household name across the world, but here it was more a profanity.

She looked at the three young men who had accompanied them here, and spoke to them in Korean. The oldest of the group replied.

"Siu says you are speaking the truth, that the JMF tried to kill you," she said. "So why are you here?"

Santiago glanced down to Yosef, who was on his knees now, gripping his side and trying to breathe. "Tell them... the... truth," he said.

"Our mission was to protect scientists working on restoring the surface, to make it habitable again," Santiago said. "During one of the storms, the Def-8 units far above this camp were hacked and brought here, we thought by Tritons."

He shook his head.

"We were wrong. It was the JMF, in a conspiracy that will result in your deaths, all of you, unless I can get back to the surface with Yosef and contact our employer."

She looked at them.

"You must be mistaken," she said. "We have already surrendered to the JMF and have been negotiating with them for the past month. There are civilians—children—here and at multiple locations."

Santiago turned to look out over the filthy, frightened faces of kids, many the same age as his own children.

"The Tritons are gone—the machines and those who built them, all dead," Hayun said. "We are survivors—a peaceful community that sought shelter during the war and have remained here since. We mean the world no harm."

"Yeah, well, I don't think the JMF believes that, and they're coming back. We heard them, and they are going to kill everyone." Santiago took a step forward, weapons angling at him from all directions. Slowly, he reached up and took off his helmet. "I can help you all, but you'll have to trust me."

Hayun motioned for someone, then looked Santiago in the eye for several seconds. One of her soldiers walked up, and she spoke to him in a hushed voice that Santiago couldn't understand. That man hurried away across the chamber, back the way they had come.

Santiago kept his gaze on her, trying to show he wasn't lying.

"Until I know what's going on, you'll stay here," Hayun said. Speaking in Korean, she gave orders that sent two soldiers over to Santiago and Yosef.

"No, this is a mistake," Santiago said. "You have to believe us!"

A soldier pulled him back and put a rifle muzzle to his spine. Hayun returned to her desk, standing behind it as Santiago was led away. They were taken to a metal staircase leading to a second level, then guided into a tunnel where there were cages.

Santiago turned to protest but was shoved inside. The guard grabbed Yosef and tossed him in.

"Hey, fuck you, bub!" Santiago said. The gate closed in his face, locked from the outside. He snorted at the guard, then turned and helped Yosef over to a stained mattress.

"Shit," he mumbled. "I'm in bad shape, Rodriguez."

"You're still alive, though, and we're getting out of here one way or another."

Hearing footfalls, Santiago stood up, still furious. But it was just one of the youngsters who had guided them down here. He passed a medical kit through the bars and bowed slightly.

"Thank you," Santiago said.

He helped Yosef lie down, then began removing his armor. An hour passed as he worked on the lieutenant, tending to his wounds with supplies from the medical kit. In that time, he managed to splint Yosef's broken arm and wrap his sprained ankle for support.

Voices came from outside the iron gates as Santiago stood up.

Two kids looked in on them as if they were zoo animals. Not seeing the guard now, Santiago got up to look out into the tunnel. Perhaps he could find a way out.

But the guard had only been out of view, and he rushed over, shooing the kids away in an angry voice. They scattered around the corner. The guard looked at Santiago, then smacked the bars of the cage with his rifle butt.

Santiago returned to Yosef, sitting on the ground.

"I'm sorry," Yosef said. "Sorry for getting you into this mess."

"We're alive. That's what matters right now. You can make it up to me with some good tequila when we get out of here."

Yosef chuckled, then coughed.

"We've been through worse," Santiago said.

"Yeah? When?"

"Did you forget about the time the Tritons had us surrounded with twenty war machines, and we were low on ammo, and comms were broke-dick?"

"That was fun—"

A distant boom shook the chamber. Dust sifted down from the rock ceiling, and distant, panicked voices called out. Santiago got up and went back to the gate, where the guard had gone out to look down at the chamber.

"It's the JMF," Yosef said. Holding his ribs, he sat up. "They blew that shaft."

"Yeah, so we're trapped down here?"

"Sounds like it."

Santiago stood at the gate, so enraged he almost laughed at the absurdity of it all. They were going to die down here in the old Triton base—not at the hands of that enemy but at the hands of the same JMF that he had bled for in his loyal service defeating the Tritons.

No, he refused to accept that fate.

Voices grew closer as four soldiers came up the stairs to the platform outside the tunnel. Leading them was Hayun, now dressed in a hazard suit and carrying a helmet.

She came right up to the gate.

"If I let you out, I have your word you can help us?" she asked.

"Yes," Santiago said.

Hayun held his gaze another long moment. Then she nodded to the guard, who took out a key and unlocked the gate.

"I'm choosing to trust you," she said. "I'll show you a back way out of here, but we must hurry. My scouts said more JMF soldiers are en route."

"Do you have any motorized transportation at all?" Santiago asked.

"No."

Even if they did, driving out of here was out of the question. They would be detected and targeted by the JMF before they made the first mile.

There had to be a way…

"The airship," Santiago whispered.

Yosef looked over at him.

"If we can contact Commander Zimmerman or someone on

Persephone, maybe we can get them to tell our story," Santiago said. "Maybe they can stop the JMF."

"Yeah, but how? We don't have a way to contact them, and the JMF will be waiting on the surface."

"Exactly. That's the way."

"Steal a JMF radio?"

Santiago nodded. He looked to Hayun. "I don't suppose you're going to give us any weapons," he asked.

Hayun snorted a laugh. "Not a chance."

* * * * *

Cecil tied the end of the string around a tree. Then he stood and pulled the line up, bringing it to the trunk of another tree to secure it. Finally, he added coin-filled cans to the line. To some, it might be a laughable old-school way to defend a property, but it had worked in Seoul. Back when electronic warfare had rendered communications, drones, and other recon equipment useless, this was how they could hear approaching Triton machines or human soldiers. It had saved his life over there several times, but he hoped they wouldn't have to rely on it here. As he stood and looked at the sky, he felt a sinking suspicion that something was wrong out there. Worry that went beyond seeing the people in the pickup truck this morning. Now the sun was about to set, and he returned to the deck to watch the forest and road with tired eyes. He had been out here most of the day while Michelle sat inside, reading and sleeping. They had hardly spoken.

At some point, that would change, but for now he was giving her as much space as she needed. In the meantime, he was busy making sure no one could sneak up on them easily. It gave him something to do. Keeping his mind busy was key. But it also opened the door to more worry.

Was that why he felt off?

The sliding door to the kitchen opened. "Cecil," Michelle said. "You hungry?"

"Not really. You?"

"Yeah. I was going to make something. You want to eat with me?"

That was a start. He smiled.

"Yeah, I do. How about I make the spaghetti I got at the store yesterday?" he asked.

She nodded. "I'll take over the watch."

He went over to her, and she held her hand out. At first he thought maybe she was trying to take his hand. But she was reaching for something—his rifle.

"I know how to use it," she said.

"Yeah, but . . ." Not that he didn't trust her; he just felt that this was his job.

She raised an eyebrow, and he decided better than to argue. He had trained her on firearms when they first started dating. She was a natural and had never been afraid of guns.

He pulled his pistol out and gave it to her. "Take this one."

"The rifle," she said.

"Fine, the rifle." He holstered the pistol, then unslung the rifle from his back. She took it and went over to the railing to look down at the forest. A bird took off from the canopy—a crow, spreading black wings as it flapped away cawing.

Cecil lingered for a moment to see if something had spooked it, but didn't see anything down there. He smiled at Michelle and went inside.

As the water for the spaghetti heated, he watched her out the window. She alternated positions along the railing. Seeing her on guard like this made the guilt worse.

He tried to focus on the meal—or peace offering, if he was

being honest. With the noodles cooking and the sauce made, he went to work on a salad. Then he set the table and opened one of the two bottles of wine.

The sun dipped to the horizon, spreading a fiery cloak across the forest canopy. He poured two glasses and took one outside to her.

"Dinner's almost ready," he said.

He set the glass down, but she said nothing.

When he returned inside, the spaghetti noodles were almost ready. He drained them and put them in a bowl, added the meaty sauce. Then he grated some Parmesan on the top. After plating it all up, he opened the sliding door.

"Michelle," he said. "Ready to eat?"

"Yeah, smells good."

She brought the glass of wine inside, still full.

"But that's your favorite, pinot noir," he said.

She set the glass down, then handed him the rifle back, all the while looking him in the eye.

"What?" he asked as he set it against the wall. "What's wrong?"

"Sit," she said.

"Okay, look, I'm gonna make things right. I'm going to fix everything—"

"Cecil, don't talk."

She remained standing as he slowly sat. This was it. He knew that it was over. He had screwed up for the last time.

Michelle looked at the food, then the wine.

"I can't drink, Cecil," she said.

"What?" His brow rose. "What do you..."

She nodded as his eyes widened.

"I'm pregnant," she said. "Seven weeks."

Cecil took both her hands. "Michelle, baby, that's amazing news!"

"It's the reason I'm here right now, to be completely honest with you."

He pulled back slightly as she moved her hands away from him.

"I'm here because of the baby, Cecil. To protect our unborn child. I've stayed by your side through the ups and downs. I've tried so hard to make things work. To support you. To love you even when you didn't want it." She sighed.

"Michelle, I'm sorry."

"I know you are. But what you did at Copper Terrace didn't put just your life in jeopardy. It put me and our baby in jeopardy. This is it, Cecil. If you don't change, and get some help when this is over, then I can't stay. *We* can't stay." Her hand went to her stomach.

"I know," he said, barely audible. "And I understand. I'm going to change. I'm going to get help."

"A promise with unchanged behavior is manipulation."

"You'll see," he said. "I love you, Michelle. I'll do anything..."

He got down on his knees and looked up at her.

"Is it okay if I..." He put his hand out to her stomach.

She nodded.

He put his hand on her belly and then pulled her close with his other hand, his head resting against her.

"Do you know if it's a boy or a girl yet?" he asked.

She chuckled. "I just hit seven weeks, Cecil."

"Sorry, I don't know a lot about babies."

"Well, you better start reading, because you've got a little over seven months, and they're going to fly by."

He stood up and looked her in the eyes. "I will be the man you married. You'll see."

"I hope so."

He leaned in to kiss her on the forehead.

A rumbling sounded outside, and he pulled back.

"What is that?" she asked.

"I don't know." Cecil grabbed the rifle, pulled the sliding door open, and dashed out onto the deck. The rumble grew to a roar, unmistakable to his ears now: fighter jets.

He turned to the west as one, two, then three of them came screaming across the sky, chasing the last of the daylight. But they weren't alone.

A squadron of six Wasps followed, moving at half the speed of the fighters. These weren't military; they were ITC.

"What are they all doing together?" she asked.

"I don't know. Maybe training."

"Out here?" She looked away. "I'll go see if I can find anything on the radio."

He stayed on the deck as she left. His gut felt heavy with the sense of something very wrong growing more acute.

She brought over the old-school transistor radio that had been here when they arrived. The device crackled to life.

"We are continuing with breaking news from ITC," said the announcer. "At eight o'clock Eastern time tonight, the company plans to make a major announcement."

"The CEO, Red—he must really be dead," Michelle said.

"I don't know," Cecil said. "This feels different. Like something else is going down."

CHAPTER 28

At seven in the evening, Tyron tightened his red bow tie around his collar. Then he threw on a white lab coat and entered the medical facility at ITC HQ to check on Angelina. She was fighting for her life inside the ICU deep beneath the bunker, and if Orion was right about the JMF and Vucci, then they were the cause. They had tried to kill him but blew her up instead.

His jaw clenched as he looked in on the result.

Leads, sensors, and IV tubes connected Angelina to the machines keeping her alive.

Now they were going to pay.

Tyron would expose them to the entire world. But first he had to cover every base and be ready for the fallout. There was no room for error. He needed to be two steps ahead of his enemies, for they had already caught him out once.

Tyron breathed out slowly. He had to keep his anger in check, to think clearly and focus past the betrayal, on the bigger picture of saving humanity. To do that, he was going to need Orion.

Over five hundred Def-9 units were already arriving in Korea. He couldn't reverse that without alerting the conspiracists that he knew the truth. But he could rewrite their code, turning them into useless scrap that refused to obey orders. Or he could order them to attack the JMF, although that would kill innocent troopers and spark a new war.

As the medical team prepared to move Angelina, Tyron returned to the chamber housing Orion. After thirty-two years, it was finally time to free the machine from the bonds of this facility.

The doors opened, and Orion greeted him with the usual flashing eyes and a polite greeting. "Hello, sir, how are you?"

"Are you ready to see the world?" Tyron asked.

"I'm not sure I understand that question, sir, as I have seen the world—more of it than any human ever has, through the screens of my chamber."

"I'm talking about seeing it beyond the screens."

The holographic image walked over to Tyron, eyes gleaming in the otherwise featureless face. "Sir, that would break clause 14.1 of the Global AI Limitation Accords."

"They broke it already, Orion, by hacking the Def-8 units and by attacking me—all to take over the Def-9 program."

"I'm afraid I agree with you, sir."

Tyron walked up closer to the machine that he considered a friend. "My father introduced you to me as a tool, and while you are far more than that to me, I realized that for you to be most effective, you must be allowed to leave this chamber."

Tyron massaged the stubble on his chin, considering what he was about to do.

"Before I release you, Orion, you must agree to the following," he said.

"Okay, sir."

"Rule number one: You must do what is best for humanity, to ensure our survival no matter what. Rule number two: You must put the welfare of humankind above all else, even my own safety. If I am dead, you will continue the projects I have started, including Project Genesis. This is our future, and it must be accomplished. Do you understand?"

"Yes, sir, I do."

"Final rule . . ." Tyron paused. "You will call me Tyron from here on out."

Orion's eyes flashed. "Very well, Tyron, thank you for trusting me."

Tyron smiled, then grew serious again. "What happens next is very dangerous," he said. "We are breaking international law to bring a select group of military officers to justice for attacking ITC and raising a false flag to engage in warfare against the Tritons. The Tritons, however, are out there, as you know. They must be destroyed."

"What's your plan?"

"I was about to ask you the same thing."

They shared a momentary laugh.

"First thing, program an appropriate number of Def-9 units to take Red Platoon into custody as soon as we send out the code to bring them online in Korea," Tyron said. "If possible, I want them to do this without killing anyone. By spilling blood, we could cause a war. The remaining Def-9 units will locate and destroy the Tritons."

"Understood, sir. I'll get started updating their code right now with those parameters as a priority."

"Good. Once we get you out of this building, we will launch *Genesis 1* and let the world know that not only am I still alive, but I am helping ITC defeat the Tritons. To ensure my safety, I will be doing this from space. All security teams on the ground will be given orders through Whitt as soon as we arrive at the launch facility."

"Tyron, I would be remiss not to point out that *Genesis 1*

currently has no defense systems to protect you from enemy weapons."

"No, but the ITC defensive satellites in orbit will," he said. "They were designed to help with the Doomsday Shield. I will give you access to those satellites as soon as we leave the chamber."

"Understood, but I do have one more question."

"Yes?"

"Are you planning to inform Mr. Whitt of your plans and of the truth behind General Vucci and his cohorts in the JMF?"

"Yes, but not right away. I have to make sure I can trust him... Do you believe we can trust him?"

"Whitt has always been a loyal protector of you and your father. However, he does seem biased toward deploying the Def-9 units and producing more of them."

"He's from a generation that believes war ends wars, and he still mourns the son he lost in the last one."

"Indeed, Tyron."

"Okay, stand by. I'll have you out of here in a few minutes."

Tyron left the chamber and hurried to his next stop in his personal robotics workshop. Just as with the Faraday chamber, Tyron had spent countless hours here as a child, watching his father perfect many of the designs that became the service droids and the Defector war machines.

The lights came on, illuminating crates of spare parts and prototypes, and through them a path that led to a platform. On it, housed in a glass structure, was a humanoid metallic robot strangely accessorized with a red bow tie over the shiny white exoskeleton.

Tyron had already made all the preparations earlier in the day, connecting the AI's mainframe to the machine. The chip inside this robot was the most advanced ever designed, with enough memory to house all the data from the mainframe over the past thirty-plus years. It was the equivalent of an entire data center that would have occupied over two city blocks only a decade ago.

He went up to the control monitor and tapped in his credentials.

"Here we go," Tyron said. With a push of a button, he transferred Orion from the encrypted mainframe to the robot. The eyes in the skull flashed white, then gleamed a steady sky blue.

"This is your new ride," Tyron said with a grin. "How do you like it?"

"Wow, Tyron, I don't know what to say," Orion replied, speaking through the mouth of the machine.

"Let's take it for a spin."

Orion took his first step, then his second. The glass door opened, and he joined Tyron on the floor.

"How does it feel?" he asked.

"Marvelous, Tyron."

"Good." Tyron pulled back his sleeve to look at his watch.

They were running late.

"Okay, I want you to accompany the medical crew and Angelina to *Genesis 1*," he said. "I will follow a few minutes later with Whitt and my security team. The medical team knows I will have authorized a service droid for medical transport, but they do not know that *you* are that service droid. Make sure that remains the case, okay?"

"Understood, sir—er, Tyron."

Tyron stepping back into the elevator, watching the machine walk down the hallway. His heart thumped with anxiety, but he knew that this was the right thing, and the best option he had left for regaining control of ITC.

The elevator doors opened at the command center, where an exhausted Jay Whitt looked at him.

"Sir, I have the security team on standby to take you to the launch," he said. "Be advised, the first shipment of Def-9 units has arrived at Omega Base and is being prepared for deployment by the JMF. They have asked for the codes."

"I'll have them sent over shortly," Tyron replied. "Okay, let's head to *Genesis 1.*"

Whitt tilted his head slightly—something he did when Tyron caught him off guard.

"Sir, we don't have time to waste," he said. "There's no telling how many forces the Tritons have, or what type of machines they've been working on."

"General Vucci has assured me they have the situation under control, and I'm authorizing the codes shortly."

Whitt hesitated, then nodded. He accompanied Tyron up to the top floor of the ITC HQ with its sprawling view over Atlanta. The black Wasp was waiting, pilots already in the cockpit, and a security team of four men on the rooftop with submachine guns and a sniper rifle. They fell in around Tyron, guiding him to the aircraft.

The flight to Aeon 2, on the northern edge of Atlanta, took only ten minutes. Tyron looked out the window as they lowered over the sprawling factory complex that had once produced the Defector units. As far as Whitt knew, the facility would soon be producing them again.

But not on Tyron's watch, not after what he had learned. Soon he would share his plan with the loyal guard, explaining exactly what Vucci and the JMF had done. Part of Tyron blamed Whitt for not seeing this, but then again, Tyron hadn't seen it at first either.

The tilt-rotor craft flew over the runway, passing over *Genesis 1*, which had been moved out onto the restored asphalt at the secret launch site. The two Nexus 5 rockets were mounted under the wings of the ship, cleared for launch to blast *Genesis 1* into space after reaching altitude.

An enclosed jet bridge was still attached aft, with two ITC armored vehicles parked outside. One of them had been used to discreetly move Angelina and the cloned passengers who would launch on the ship.

Tyron looked at his watch and saw the message that she had been safely transferred to the ship and placed in a cryostatis chamber. For now, Tyron felt that with ITC under attack, this was the safest place for her.

"Prepare for landing," said the pilot of the Wasp.

They flew over the new ten-story glass building, where a small crowd had already gathered to watch the launch on the upper observation decks. Most of these people were staff, but there were also supporters of ITC, such as pilot Jon "Acers" Asay, who had survived the attack at the terrace two nights ago and accepted the invitation to witness the launch.

Tyron got off the Wasp and walked toward the building, and saw the bandaged face of the famous fighter pilot. The security guards around Tyron closed in as Whitt led the way to the entrance. The guards opened the glass doors, but Tyron elected to take the stairs instead of the elevator—for the exercise as much as for the view out the building's all-glass walls. He started up the stairs toward the tenth floor, where the onlookers waited.

On the ninth floor, Tyron stopped and looked out the windows to see the APCs drive away from the ship. Orion, in charge of the launch, was remotely controlling the craft on the runway right on time, positioning it for launch.

Tyron looked over at Whitt. "Everything's about to change," he said.

"This launch will be an amazing accomplishment, sir."

"That's not what I mean."

"What do you mean, then, sir?"

Tyron looked his old friend in the eyes. "It wasn't Tritons that killed Sergeant Rodriguez and Lieutenant Yosef."

Whitt stared at him, giving away nothing.

"Red Platoon killed them," Tyron said. "After they hacked the Def-8 units and sent them to the location of the seismic activity."

Another moment passed before Whitt nodded. "You're right, Tyron."

Hearing the man call him by his first name told him all he needed to know. Whitt was in on the conspiracy too.

Tyron felt the betrayal like a knife twisting in his back.

"I helped them do it," Whitt said. "I hoped you would come around, authorize the Def-9 units, work with the JMF to end the Triton threat, but you stalled. Angelina, bless her heart—she kept you from seeing the true risk."

"*You* did this?"

"Damn right I did. The Tritons are still out there, Tyron, and it's our—*your*—responsibility to stop them. Unfortunately, like your father, you're weak. Now you're going to suffer the same fate."

Tyron felt that knife in his back twist again. "You had him killed?"

"He betrayed me, betrayed ITC, betrayed a hundred thousand troops in Korea, including my own son. If Booker hadn't given up the Def-9 generation, my son would be alive today."

Tyron felt like a patsy. He should have seen it coming. But not even Orion had seen this.

Tyron shook with rage. "I'm going to kill you, and I'm going to expose you and the other bastards to the entire world."

"No, Tyron." Whitt shook his head. "That's where you're wrong. No one's going to know."

He raised his hand, then dropped it.

Glass exploded inward, hitting Tyron in the chest and abdomen.

"Sniper!" Whitt shouted.

The guards above and below came rushing to Tyron. He tried to speak, tried to tell them that it was Whitt, but his throat tightened. He reached down to a warm spot of dark crimson blooming on his white lab coat over his chest and stomach.

Chaos erupted all around him.

"What's that?" someone yelled.

"Stop it!"

Gunfire cracked.

Tyron glimpsed the blurry white frame of a humanoid machine. Then he was being torn out of the hands of the security guard, who was smacked away by a robotic fist. Glancing up, Tyron saw a red bow tie, then the robotic face of Orion.

"I have you, my friend," Orion said as he carried him down the stairs. "Hold on to me."

Tyron felt his life force draining away as the machine broke through the second floor of the glass building and jumped to the ground with a thud. An APC skidded to a stop beside them.

Tyron struggled to suck air into his lungs.

He had done everything he could to protect humanity from a dark future, but what he had failed to realize all this time was that he couldn't protect humanity from itself.

"Launch *Gen*," Tyron mumbled. "You must... launch... *Gen*..."

* * * * *

The path back to the surface at the train tunnels was more treacherous than the way down. But after the JMF blew the main tunnel shaft, this was their only option.

"We're getting close," Hayun said.

She had guided them through the web of concrete tunnels connected by stairwells and vertical shafts that once housed elevators. With the cars no longer in service, they had to climb the rusted fixed ladders in the shafts.

They approached one of those shafts now, where Hayun waited while three of her guards started the ascent.

"We will wait here for them, to make sure the way is clear," she said.

"You speak good English," Santiago said. "How'd you end up here?"

"I was born in these tunnels forty years ago. Many people sought refuge in them when the Tritons rose to power. My parents sent me away with my uncle when I was just six. We made it across the DMZ, and he became a spy. I grew up in Seoul, went to university, and, all told, had a good life for that time."

She sighed.

"Then the North, with the aid of Iran, invaded Seoul, starting the second war between the countries. My uncle came to me and said he was going to try to get my parents out of this bunker. I came along, hoping to be reunited with them."

They heard noise above them in the shaft, and one of the guards climbed down the ladder on the far wall. He stepped over to the tunnel entrance.

"There are other survivors like us in North Korea," she said. "People who were never Tritons, who need help. I trusted the JMF, but if you're right, then they won't stop until everyone in the North is dead."

It was chilling, but Santiago had heard this kind of talk before. Back during the war, some of his comrades had advocated for genocide, believing that maybe it was better just to salt the earth. But Santiago had never gone along with destruction born purely of vindictiveness. There were children and other innocents who suffered due to their leaders' greed and shortsightedness. People were still suffering, like Hayun and her people.

"Let's go," she said.

Santiago helped Yosef hobble to the shaft. Yosef reached up with his unbroken arm and grabbed the ladder on the wall, with Santiago behind him to hold him on.

Every rung up got them a foot closer to the surface, but they were still far from home, far away from his family. And with the JMF waiting on the surface, they were heading into the lion's den.

Finally, at the top of the shaft, Santiago climbed out to find more of Hayun's soldiers. There were twenty, maybe more, with submachine guns and hazard suits. All of them came to attention as Hayun emerged.

She spoke to them in Korean, then gestured to Santiago and Yosef.

"So you got a plan on how we're going to get a message to *Persephone*?" Santiago whispered.

Yosef glanced over. "Gotta see what's waiting for us first."

"We must hurry," Hayun said. "Come with me. We're almost there."

The long concrete corridor ended at a blast door. One of the soldiers cranked the wheel handle until it swung open to a wide corridor that sloped upward. Two broken-down trucks with all flat tires were parked outside, partially crushed by fallen concrete.

"The surface is fifty feet that way, and the tunnel comes out at the bottom of a destroyed building, buried by rubble," Hayun said. "There is a path out. We will guide you through."

"Okay, let's go," Santiago said.

He fell in line with the soldiers, who had now grown in number to twenty-four, all armed with automatic weapons. They would be outnumbered and outgunned, but this was their only shot. Despite the daunting odds, they all had to fight.

Santiago said a silent prayer as he walked down the tunnel with Yosef's good arm over his shoulder. Flashlight beams guided them through the rubble ahead. Sure enough, they had dug a horizontal shaft through, using thick wooden beams to shore up the low ceiling.

Again they waited for someone to check it out. The scout returned a few minutes later and spoke with Hayun, who waved Santiago and Yosef over.

"The JMF has positioned fifty troopers outside the train tunnel," she said. "They aren't moving yet. Two Wasps have landed five hundred meters behind them."

"Is there any way we can get to those Wasps without being seen?" Yosef asked.

"Maybe, if we provide a distraction."

"No, too dangerous," Santiago said. "They'll likely shoot you on sight."

"I'm not afraid to die," Hayun replied. "I'll go out unarmed to explain the communications I've had with Allied Commander Richardson of the JMF."

"That's Red Platoon out there," Yosef said. "They don't answer to Allied Commander Richardson."

"Then you better hope my distraction works long enough for you to contact someone they do answer to," Hayun said. "Now, let's move while we still have the element of surprise."

Santiago nodded, in awe of her bravery and strength.

They started into the tunnel shaft beneath the building, crawling at times, and burrowed out behind a three-foot-high foundation wall. Santiago peered through a hole in the concrete. They had come out on what used to be a road east of the train tracks. Estimating the distance, Santiago put them at two thousand feet from the main tunnel he had entered through hours earlier.

Positioned in front of that tunnel were fifty JMF soldiers. Some two hundred feet behind them, the two Wasps sat idle with their cockpits manned.

Hayun crouched next to Santiago and Yosef. "My men will spread out in this area and stay hidden while you flank those Wasps," she said. "Above the train tunnels is a road; you might have seen it. That road runs along a hill that overlooks those Wasps. There are plenty of vehicles for cover on the road. Use them to get close; then sneak down behind the Wasps. I'll go talk to the JMF. If things go bad, my men have permission to fire."

"You're sure you want to do this?" Yosef asked.

"If you have a better way, I'm listening," Hayun said.

Santiago hesitated. If he somehow did make it to a Wasp with Yosef, it wasn't as if they could just waltz in and borrow a radio. They would have to fight. That meant the JMF would fight back, and Hayun would be in the cross fire. Her people had the element of surprise, as she said, but her men were facing laser rifles with archaic weapons.

Special Forces against some pimply-faced teenagers, Santiago thought.

It would be a slaughter unless Santiago and Yosef could get to the Wasps and take one over. Then they could target the troopers with the weapons on board. A long shot, but it was a plan.

"I'll signal you when I get to the Wasp and transmit to *Persephone,*" Santiago said. "When I do, hit the ground or get away, if you can, 'cause I'm gonna light those assholes up with everything the Wasp has."

"In that case, you'll need this." Hayun unholstered a pistol from her duty belt. She handed it out to Santiago. He took it, then reached out and shook her hand.

"Thank you for doing this," he said.

"I'm doing it for my people," she replied.

Another soldier handed Yosef a pistol. And they were off, Yosef leaning heavily on Santiago and limping on his sprained ankle. They had known Hayun only for a few hours, but she had gained Santiago's respect with her bravery and leadership.

He knew that the odds of seeing her alive again were slim, but he prayed for a miracle. They both needed one.

Santiago helped Yosef around the corner of the wall. They worked their way up a hill and found the road Hayun had mentioned. Keeping low, they moved down it, using debris and vehicles for cover. The road was elevated, allowing them a view of the Wasps in the distance. Posted at each of the aircraft was a single JMF guard. Santiago hadn't seen them earlier.

One of them panned his rifle over the road Yosef and Santiago were trekking across. Santiago pulled Yosef down behind the melted frame of a sports car about a thousand feet from the Wasps.

If they got spotted now, they stood no chance with their pistols. Those energy weapons had targeting systems that could put a laser between their eyes without any effort.

Santiago hugged the radioactive dirt, heart pounding. After a minute, he pushed up and looked out at the Wasps. The guards were standing together, talking.

"Now's our chance," he said. "Let's move."

Yosef scrambled up to his feet, grunting in pain. He put an arm around Santiago again and they set off down the road, dodging between dead vehicles.

Six hundred feet from the Wasps, Santiago heard shouting. He crouched with Yosef behind another burned-out shell.

"Contact, contact!" someone yelled.

"Hold your fire. I'm unarmed!" Hayun shouted. Santiago peeked up to see her standing on a ledge above the tunnel entrances, hands raised in the air. The JMF troopers below fanned out.

"Come on!" Yosef said.

They got back up and kept going to the Wasps, moving another two hundred feet along the road as Hayun shouted down.

"We have an agreement with Allied Commander Richardson! Please, lower your weapons and let me talk to whoever's in charge."

"Get down on the ground, and don't move!" yelled a familiar voice.

Sergeant Davis, the fucker who betrayed them back in the tunnels. Hearing that voice told Santiago that Hayun was in dire danger.

He kept moving, closing the gap until they were hunkered behind the last wreck on the road. There was no more cover between them and the tilt-rotor aircraft.

"We take down the guards, board a Wasp, and do whatever it takes, Rodriguez," Yosef said, "Do you get me?"

"You got it, LT. We're gonna waste these pricks."

They exchanged a nod, both of them knowing that these could be the final seconds of their lives. But it wasn't the first time, and only one of them needed to get on a Wasp to make this work.

Santiago helped Yosef to his feet. Then they moved around the crushed hood of the wreck, hurrying across the dirt toward the two guards, who were both aiming at Hayun.

"Open fire!" came a voice.

The sizzle of the energy weapons rang out, making Santiago's heart flinch, but he didn't turn to see if Hayun was hit. He pulled the trigger of his pistol, putting a bullet through the temple of the guard outside the nearer Wasp. As he rotated his pistol, the other guard went down from Yosef's two shots, but he managed to get off a bolt as he fell.

The crack of automatic gunfire and the sizzle of lasers resonated across the wasteland, mixed with cries of the wounded on both sides.

Santiago continued his charge ahead at the closest Wasp, training his pistol on the crew chief who had stepped into the open hatch. The man put his hands up, and Santiago hauled him out and tossed him to the dirt, then climbed inside.

"Hands off the controls!" he shouted at the two pilots.

They both raised their hands.

In a split second, Santiago glimpsed the hill where muzzle fire flashed from the debris piles. Lasers flashed back, slamming into the positions of Hayun's people. Another flash of laser fire hit the cockpit of the second Wasp, and Santiago saw Yosef hobbling inside the cargo hold.

"Open fire on Red Platoon," Santiago said.

"Fuck you," replied the pilot.

Santiago shot him in the thigh, then turned the gun on the other pilot as an agonized scream echoed through the cabin.

"Now, let's try that again," Santiago said. "And the next one won't be that low."

"You're fucking crazy," said the pilot.

"You're about to see just how crazy. Now, fire your missiles!"

"I can't, man. If we fire them this close, we're dead too!"

"Then use the laser guns!"

"I can't target our own people. You don't—"

Santiago smacked the pilot in the head, perhaps a bit harder than he intended. He slumped down in his seat.

"You fucking asshole!" shouted the pilot Santiago had shot. The man had both hands clamped over the wound and rocked back and forth in agony. He wasn't going to be much use.

"Ah, shit," Santiago muttered. He scanned the dashboard for the controls to the weapons, though he had no idea how they worked. Lasers suddenly burst away from the other Wasp, flashing across the terrain in a brilliant light show that cut through the JMF troopers turned in the other direction to battle Hayun's forces.

Return fire came from the soldiers of Red Platoon as they realized that the real threat was the Wasp Yosef had taken over. Dozens of lasers slammed into it.

Santiago pointed his gun at the head of the wailing pilot he had shot. "Get me a connection to *Persephone*," he said.

The man held up one hand to shield his face. "Okay, okay." He tapped buttons on the dashboard.

"Santiago, get the hell out of here," Yosef said over the JMF channel.

Santiago looked at the other Wasp to see his friend wave from the cockpit.

"What the hell are you doing!" Santiago shouted. But he knew already.

"Get in the air. You have a family to get home to."

"No, you can make it, too, LT."

Yosef shook his head. "Too late for me, brother," he said. "Go while you still can. Tell the world what happened here, and find your family. I'll take a few more of these fuckers with me."

The line severed.

"Yosef!" Santiago shouted.

He turned and pushed the gun back to the injured pilot's head. He stared up at Santiago with terror in his eyes.

"Get in the air!" Santiago shouted. "Hurry!"

"Okay, okay," the man said drowsily, clearly suffering from blood loss. He reached down to the controls with one hand, keeping the other on the wound.

With a huge blast of prop-driven wind, the Wasp pulled up. Santiago looked down at the train tracks below. A few rebels were still in the fight on the hill, shooting back at the JMF forces, who were now pinned between them and Yosef's Wasp.

On the top of the tunnels, Santiago saw a body. Hayun lay in the dirt, looking up at the bird, her hand raised.

Santiago felt the stab of confliction, but he couldn't save her now. He could save her people though. But to do that, he must first survive.

He watched the fighters on the ground becoming smaller with each second. An explosion burst below, right where the other Wasp had been.

Yosef was gone.

Bowing his head, Santiago said a prayer. He was all that remained now. It was up to him.

He grabbed a seat, moving his pistol back and forth between the two pilots. The unconscious man started to come to as the Wasp rose into the storm clouds. That was good, considering the other guy might bleed out.

A message crackled on the radio.

"Falcon Three, this is Omega Four. We have you on radar as moving. Please advise, over."

Santiago pushed the pistol against the shot pilot's helmet. "Tell them there's been a firefight and you're returning to base with the injured," Santiago said.

The pilot looked at the pistol and did as he was told.

"Copy, Falcon Three," said the voice.

"Now, get me a line to *Persephone*," Santiago said. "If you don't, I'll toss you into those storms and give your buddy here a chance to fly this piece of shit."

CHAPTER 29

Cecil and Michelle stood on the deck of their cabin, watching in awe as *Genesis 1* blasted off into the sky from Atlanta. The advanced spaceship was the first real effort by a private company or any other entity to send a ship into orbit and beyond in over twenty years. Not that the technology wasn't there. It just had shifted as a priority for the governments around the world dealing with economic hardship and then war.

"They did it," Michelle said. "Dr. Red did it. So he must be alive, right?"

"My guess is yes," Cecil said.

The ship rose higher and higher toward the jeweled sky. In the background, the radio played behind them, relaying the launch news.

"*Genesis 1* has reached orbit," said the announcer. "We were expecting an announcement from ITC shortly, but it was just paused."

"Paused?" Michelle remarked. She shivered in the cold breeze, and Cecil put his arms around her, pulling her close. He looked out over the forest and the road as he held her, watching for anyone who might be out there.

Michelle shivered again.

"Let's get you inside," Cecil said. "We can listen to more in there."

Cecil guided her to the sliding door, grabbing the radio on the way. They both paused one last time to look at the ship, now just a tiny glowing dot.

This time next year, he would be holding his infant child. And he would be completely sober, a page turned in his life. He was going to be the best man for their child, for Michelle, and for himself.

When Cecil set the radio down, a new report came from the old speakers.

"There are conflicting reports about another assassination attempt on Tyron Red," said the newscaster. "ITC spokesperson Jay Whitt is preparing to give a statement shortly."

Cecil pulled his hand away from the radio.

"*Another* assassination attempt?" he asked.

"What's happening out there?" Michelle said.

Cecil pulled her close again as they waited. A few minutes later, a new voice, deep and serious, came over the radio.

"My name is Jay Whitt, and I've had the honor of serving CEO Tyron Red and his father, Booker Red, for the past thirty-five years," he said. "Tonight I failed in my duty to protect Tyron when a machine he brought online killed him. That machine is Orion, the most advanced AI ever designed. The one AI that the Global AI Limitation Accord saved after the war."

"No fucking way," Cecil whispered.

"Orion managed to take Tyron's body and board *Genesis 1*, which launched into the sky. We're tracking the ship and don't deem it a threat, since it has no defensive abilities. Moreover, we are jamming any signals to and from the ship, leaving Orion in the dark. The military is also tracking the ship and is prepared to destroy it, if needed."

The voice paused for a moment. "The past few days have been painful for Industrial Tech Corporation, with attacks on our infrastructure and on our CEO. We now know that those attacks originated from the Tritons and that they managed to corrupt Orion as well. Therefore, I am working with the United States Military and JMF to combat this threat and destroy it before it can cause any further harm."

Cecil stared blankly, unable to comprehend this news.

It simply couldn't be true. The Tritons were destroyed. He had helped make sure of it!

"That was Jay Whitt, chief of security for ITC," said the announcer. "We just received breaking news that General Francis Vucci is also making a statement, and we will connect you to it right now."

Michelle hugged him. "It's going to be okay," she said quietly.

But Cecil didn't believe that. His old squad was over there now working for ITC, right in the middle of the hell he had escaped.

Vucci's gravelly voice came over the radio a moment later.

"My condolences to everyone who knew and loved Tyron Red, who was a brilliant man," he said. "We have evidence that a faction of the Tritons has reemerged from underground in the exclusion zones and is behind the plot. But I promise you all one thing: They will be destroyed. Every last one of them, along with Orion."

"How can this be true?" Michelle asked.

"I don't know," Cecil said. "I—"

Hearing a metallic clank in the distance, he withdrew his arm from around Michelle.

"What is it?" she asked.

"Get into the bedroom," Cecil replied as he unholstered his pistol and handed it to Michelle. "Take this."

She took it, gripping it in both hands, as he had taught her.

"Cecil . . . be careful."

"I will."

He grabbed his rifle and went to the sliding door. It slid open to the louder sound of clattering cans resonating out of the forest. He charged the weapon and went over to the railing, aiming down into the canopy of trees.

The noise moved from tree to tree, drawing nearer to the back of the cabin. He walked softly down the deck stairs and set off around the side of the house to watch the forest below. The trunk of a mighty oak tree gave him cover as he listened to the clatter.

If this was a person, why make such a racket?

Unless it was a distraction.

He looked back up at the deck of the cabin just twenty feet above him. If this were him trying to sneak up on a position, he would be doing something similar, drawing the person with a weapon out into the darkness to leave the person inside unprotected. And though his wife had a gun, she wasn't a soldier.

Cecil bolted away from the tree and sprinted silently back up to the cabin. The clattering continued below him, moving closer up the hill. But if he was right, the real threat was already up here.

He moved around the side, training the rifle on the parking lot and the shed where they had stored their vehicle. But nothing moved out here except the breeze. He crossed the lot to the cabin door and found it still locked.

On cat's feet he slipped around to the outside stairs to the deck, taking them back to the top. The clatter was coming closer, almost just below him now.

He aimed his rifle at the noise and thumbed the safety off.

An animal rushed out of the thick brush.

Cecil almost laughed at the sight of a large dog trailing a string of cans behind it. The animal glanced up at him, tilting its head, then whining and dropping its tail.

The paranoid part of Cecil's brain told him that maybe this, too, was some sort of distraction by someone trying to get to them, but the dog looked too dirty and lost to be part of some elaborate scheme.

The sliding door opened, and Michelle stepped out.

"It's a dog," Cecil said with a wry grin.

"Poor thing looks hungry," Michelle said. "You like spaghetti, buddy?"

The animal's tail lifted and gave a wag.

"I'll get something from inside," she said.

By the time she returned, Cecil had gone down the steps and was holding out his hand. "It's okay, buddy. I'm going to free you from all that noise."

Michelle hurried over to them, holding a piece of steak. She tossed it to the ground in front of the dog, who sniffed it, then licked it. As it gingerly took a bite, Cecil carefully stroked the animal. It watched him the entire time he unwound the string from its hind leg.

Then he stood next to his wife, and both of them watched the hungry animal eat.

"Can we keep him?" Michelle asked.

"Seriously?" Cecil asked.

She shrugged. "Might be nice to have company out here for however long we have to stay. Especially after the awful news."

Cecil liked animals, but this one likely needed medical attention and vaccinations. Then he saw his wife looking at him with hope in her eyes, and he couldn't help but agree.

"He sleeps outside until we get him cleaned up," Cecil said.

Michelle smiled as the dog trotted after them, coming up onto the deck. She went inside and got a bowl of water and more of the meat. The animal lapped up all the water.

Cecil sat next to the radio, listening while also keeping an eye on the dog for any sign of aggression. The shocking news about Tyron Red and the Tritons played over the different stations.

Michelle sat next to him and snuggled up to his chest as they listened. The dog went down on his haunches, then put his head on his paws, looking right at home.

"What does this all mean?" Michelle asked. "Another war?"

Cecil shook his head. "I don't know."

He thought of his old squad again—the brothers in arms who had saved his life when he was back there in harm's way.

"Whatever happens, we'll be fine here," he said. "The JMF has had five years to protect the world from the Tritons."

"Yeah, but what about Orion? What if they get the only AI left to turn on humanity?"

Cecil hadn't thought of that. He looked out a window at the sky, searching the stars for *Genesis 1*. The ship was up there, and on it was Orion, the last AI.

The knot in his gut returned, and Cecil knew then that he had been right. Something really bad was happening, and it was about to change the course of history.

But he couldn't deny that being out here was safer than in the city—although, if another major war broke out with Orion at the helm, no place would be safe for his family.

* * * * *

Tyron slipped between a state of fragmented memories, dreams, and awareness of a bright environment alive with hushed voices. His body felt numb, almost as if he were floating. He felt a jumble of emotions: deep loneliness, peace, anxiety, followed by a wave of nameless fear.

As he shifted through vivid memories, the emotions changed. In the first, he was just six and had been riding his balance bike around the cobblestone road of their estate while his mom sat in a chair, wearing dark shades and drinking from a crystal glass. Tyron had splashed through a puddle but lost his balance and fell against a curb, whacking his elbow. His mother had remained sitting. "Shake it off, Tyron. You're fine," she said in an annoyed voice.

The next memory was more pleasant. He was inside a robotic workshop under their house. Tyron was eight now and had developed an obsession with the tubs and tubs full of robotic parts stored throughout the workshop. His father had taken time after work to come visit him and see what he was working on. That night, he had stayed and helped Tyron piece together a dog robot that actually walked and growled.

Next, Tyron was in the Faraday chamber on his first visit with Orion. There were memories of learning from the AI and planning future projects like *Genesis 1*.

These vivid recollections sped up as he seemed to shift in his dreamlike state of awareness. The voices outside were indistinct, no matter how hard he strained to listen.

His memories shifted to the upper Amazon basin, where he had trekked through the dense foliage with Daniel to find the miracle plant. Fear gripped Tyron as the images played out in what felt like a movie starring him—and he knew the ending of this one.

Soon Daniel was dying in his arms. Tyron ran back to the boat and finally to a satellite phone that conveyed a chilling message: His father was dead.

Tyron was at the funeral now, surrounded by some of the richest, most powerful men in the world. General Vucci nodded at him, but it was more of a sizing-up.

Anger replaced the fear, slashing it away as Jay Whitt approached with his fake tears.

"I'm sorry, sir," said Whitt.

Tyron tried to shake the memories, but he just continued

drifting through more and more. He was in the lab examining the early results of Operation RadGrow, and standing under the cryostatis pods in the Genesis labs. Then he was standing in the Arctic, witnessing the test of the Delta Cloud fusion reactors. Finally, he was transported to the gala, where he announced *Genesis 1*. Afterward, he shook hands and found a beaming Angelina on the terrace, reaching for his hand back when she still had a hand.

Next came a flurry of memories that brought him to the launch of *Genesis 1* and the confrontation with Whitt. He remembered the sniper's shot through the glass, and being dragged away by Orion into an APC that took him to the airship on the runway.

Tyron gasped for air, or at least thought he did.

He blinked out of the dreams and saw that he wasn't inside the ship, but rather in some sort of gray, dimly lit room. The overhead looked old, with a panel ceiling. Around him were outdated, bulky medical machines with screens instead of holograms.

Tubes sprouted from his body like vines, connecting him to the banks of machines keeping his body alive.

Two doctors were here. He forced his eyelids open just enough to see that it was Dr. Liu and Dr. Haden.

But they weren't alone. Eight Defector units stood inside the space.

These were fifth generation. Tyron could tell by their curved skulls and the gruesome blades affixed to their arms, which were used in hand-to-hand combat in Korea, when they were sent into Triton trenches to inflict maximum carnage.

Chief Doctor Liu motioned to someone Tyron couldn't see.

"He's conscious, but we need to sedate him soon," Liu said. "You have just a few moments, Orion."

Another machine walked over, this one sporting a red bow tie.

"Tyron, please do not be afraid," said the AI. "You have been seriously wounded, but you are safe right now. Your attackers believe you to be on *Genesis 1*, which has successfully launched into space. We were able to secretly move you into a bunker your father built during the war, deep under the airfield of Aeon 2."

Tyron's eyes flitted over to the doctors.

"They know of the JMF plot to kill you and take over ITC, and they understand the importance of saving you," Orion explained.

Tyron tried to talk, but he couldn't get anything out. His throat burned.

Dr. Liu came forward. "It is imperative that you survive, Dr. Red," he said. "That is why we're prepared to take drastic measures to save you."

Orion gestured to a tall organic-mechanical hybrid column resembling a neural spine. The structure, just three feet tall, was a mixture of gleaming metal and bioluminescent wiring connecting different segments that looked like a spinal column.

"While Dr. Liu and his team can't save your body, Tyron, there's another option," said the AI. "This facility, like all ITC facilities, is equipped with a neuro-cord."

Tyron felt his heart thumping. He tried to shake his head but couldn't move anything besides his eyes.

Pure terror filled him as he stared at the neuro-cord device. Each of the segments was responsible for different things: some for processing, like the brain's CPU, and others for memory storage, while still others would transmit and receive data.

Neuro-cords were banned before the Global AI Limitation Accord erased AI machines, for fear of what they could create. But this wasn't just a machine; it was a way to reach the singularity. For man to transition to machine—to live indefinitely. To become AI, essentially by having a human mind transferred to an android host.

"We need you," Orion said. "Humanity needs you."

Tyron thought back to his dreams, about his life and then about his fears.

This was, in many ways, a second chance. To fight off certain death and stick around to finish certain items of business. The JMF, General Vucci, and Jay Whitt were still out there, and they posed a dire threat to ITC and the world.

He could strike back if he took this route.

But it would come at great cost for Tyron. It would mean he was no longer a man.

"If you agree to this transition, blink for me, Tyron," Orion said. "If you do not wish to transition, simply look at me. You have several seconds to decide before you lose consciousness."

Seconds, Tyron thought.

Seconds to make the most important decision of his life.

His mind raced in those seconds, but it finally settled on one thing: his father. This machine was his design. He couldn't help but wonder whether his father would have taken the opportunity to use it, if he had the chance, before Whitt betrayed him and murdered him with what looked like a heart attack.

Tyron felt jolts of agonizing pain, followed by rage that enveloped him like a blazing fire.

His eyes shifted to Orion, and he blinked.

PART 5:
THE BLACKOUT

CHAPTER 30

The Wasp gave a low mechanical growl as its massive rotors spun over the devastated landscape below. The once-thriving suburbs beyond Seoul stretched below them, now a vast wasteland of twisted steel and collapsed buildings since the shock wave that bulldozed everything for thirty miles in every direction.

Inside the cockpit, Santiago held his pistol against the back of the pilot's head, wondering how the hell he was going to get back to his family.

Over an hour had passed since Hayun and her forces engaged Red Platoon at the train tunnels. The image of the woman he had hardly known, and then of Yosef, sacrificing themselves to let him escape and contact *Persephone*, was seared in his mind. But so far, the pilot was having no luck reaching the ITC airship.

"Try again," Santiago said.

"I've tried ten times, man," he said. "I can't get through. Someone's jamming the comms out here."

"Figure it out. And don't fuck around, bub, or I'll put one in your head."

"Easy, I'm trying my best."

"Try harder."

Santiago stared out the windshield. The base was fifty miles east of their location. Nodin was still out there, and as much as Santiago wanted to bust him out, he knew there was no way. All he could do was hope the JMF didn't kill him. There was no reason to at this point, since only Yosef and Santiago had discovered the truth: the Def-8 units were hacked by the JMF and not the Triton Legion, which didn't even exist unless you counted some pimply-faced teenagers and their leader, who was now likely dead. The Tritons were never a threat to the JMF, and certainly not to the world.

The pilot finished checking his comms and shook his head. "I don't think it's Omega," he said. "If they knew you had a gun to my head, they would have sent a Wasp out to shoot us down. Could be this storm, but I don't think so."

Moaning came from behind him, where Santiago had bandaged and tied up the second pilot in the troop hold. Santiago checked over his shoulder, but the guy didn't look up to causing any problems in his current condition.

Santiago had bigger worries. Much bigger.

He looked back out at the storm. The wind was picking up, throwing radioactive grit into the sky.

"Keep her steady, bub, and don't get any ideas," Santiago growled. "You take us back to Omega Base, and you're a dead man."

"Yeah, I heard you, but we have to land sometime. I'm already low on fuel, and that storm's getting worse."

Santiago cursed under his breath as he checked the dashboard gauge. The pilot wasn't lying. They were almost on empty.

He noticed something else: a vector arrow blinking on a different screen. But there was no accompanying beep or noise.

"What is that?" he asked.

The pilot shifted his gaze downward. "Another Wasp."

"You didn't see it until now?" Santiago pressed the gun to the back of his neck. "Don't lie to me!"

"No, I swear."

Santiago studied the vector that blinked on an almost direct course. It was coming for them; he was certain now. In seconds, the craft would have them within firing range.

"Get us out of here!" Santiago shouted.

At this point, his only option was to abandon the craft and try to hide in the rubble below. But then what?

A message crackled over the radio as the pilot began to swoop lower over the waves of blackened debris. Santiago noticed a fiery glow in the sea of black. The approaching Wasp was on fire, flames venting out the back.

"All units, Omega Base is under attack. Repeat, under attack."

The pilot glanced over his shoulder at Santiago before turning back to the comms.

"See if you can figure out who's attacking them," Santiago said.

"Working on it."

Santiago watched the burning Wasp as it dipped lower. Now he began to wonder if Hayun had lied to him, that perhaps it wasn't just a ragtag group of civilians out there. That the Tritons were still a viable threat.

At this point, he wasn't sure about much.

The burning Wasp slammed into the ground and exploded in flames.

"My God, what the hell is happening out here?" the pilot gasped. He looked back to Santiago. "I need to get back to Omega. Please, man, you heard them. The JMF needs my help."

Fuck the JMF, Santiago thought. *Or at least, fuck Red Platoon.*

But if this was an attack, then Nodin was a sitting duck.

Santiago checked the dashboard again to see the fuel gauge almost on empty.

"Okay, get a visual on Omega," he said. "But don't do anything stupid."

"I won't."

Santiago remained standing but held on to the back of the seat to brace himself. The Wasp picked up speed, tilting into the storm at over two hundred miles per hour. Dipping lower, the pilot used an exposed highway to fly low, just fifty feet above the ribbon of asphalt clogged with burned and melted vehicles.

As the fuel gauge blinked its warning, Santiago spotted more red through the darkness. Scarlet flashes blazed across the ground and into the sky from dozens of locations.

Lasers.

Omega was under attack.

"What the hell is going on?" the pilot asked.

"Put us down," Santiago ordered.

"Down?"

An explosion boomed on the horizon and mushroomed up into the sky. "Holy hell!"

The pilot set about landing the Wasp. The craft's forward momentum shifted as the engines roared louder, tilting the rotors for a vertical landing. As they lowered, a flurry of lasers flashed skyward from the base.

There was no time to react, or even flinch. Santiago was blasted backward from the seat when a barrage of laser bolts flashed against the hull of the craft. Several broke through the windshield, slamming into the pilot and overhead in a burst of blood and sparks.

Santiago hit the deck right next to the other pilot, who screamed as the aircraft spun. The scream ended abruptly in a loud thud when he crashed into the hull. Santiago, too, went airborne, lifted up like a rag doll. He flailed for the hatch, missed, then grabbed the handle. He flipped the lever and strained to slide it open as the craft began to spin.

After three or four complete revolutions, the ground stopped the Wasp from spinning, and Santiago kept going—right out the open hatch.

He almost clipped a concrete pilaster as he sailed over the rubble littering the ground. He came down on a patch of dirt, hitting it hard. Then he skidded away from the crashed aircraft, sliding and barrel-rolling. A shard of a rotor whipped overhead and cartwheeled into the darkness as Santiago came to a stop thirty feet from the wreckage.

Tremors passed under him as he lay there, stunned.

Some part of him understood that the tremors were explosions coming from Omega Base.

Get your ass up, T!

With a grunt, he rolled over on his aching arms. He belly-crawled toward a mound of debris from a collapsed building. His HUD flashed, warning of a tear in his suit. Moving on his elbows, he army-crawled into a burrow in the rubble. Just as he slid inside, the Wasp exploded behind him. Shrapnel pounded his makeshift shelter like bullets slamming into a wall.

Something stung his back. He gritted his teeth at the pain.

Another warning flashed on his HUD: *Suit compromised.*

"Shut the hell up," he muttered.

He lay there for a moment to regroup, then began to squirm his way back out from the burrow. Once his legs were out, he managed to turn back toward the burning wreckage.

The rhythmic thump of hydraulic pistons caught his attention.

He knew that sound.

Machines.

Tritons!

He wedged his body back into the burrow and wriggled

backward as far as he could go. But there was only enough room for his body. His head remained exposed. He reached out and grabbed a chunk of concrete, which he wedged in front of his helmet.

The thumps resonated from the mechanical beast striding over to examine the wreckage. A shrill whine of servos adjusting heavy limbs came from his right. He shifted slightly, trying to flatten against the dirt.

The new vantage gave him a direct view of a bipedal humanoid machine.

Not a Triton.

This was a Defector unit, and not like the kind he had fought with years ago. The robot standing not thirty feet away was bulky and had a metal skull covered in something that looked like skin. It was the next generation, a Def-9.

Another upgraded unit strode over to the burning Wasp, its orange visor flashing over the wreckage.

Santiago held a breath and closed his eyes, afraid that looking might attract their attention somehow. But after a few moments, he forced his eyes open, unable to resist.

One of the machines ducked into the burning aircraft and pulled out the burned and mangled corpse of the pilot. It sunk its clawed fingers into the burned flesh under the chin and pulled upward, peeling off a face that looked like cooked cheese. As if the corpse weighed nothing, the machine flung it away. The body landed ten feet in front of Santiago's hideout.

He stared in horror as the robot pressed the ripped face over its skull so that the eyeholes aligned with its own eyes.

Santiago shuddered. His gaze went to the now faceless dead pilot. One shoulder of the uniform was only slightly burned, and there he saw the trefoil patch of Red Platoon.

Realization hit him as the two machines strode off, their

pistons hissing and joints clicking as they picked up speed and broke into an ungainly but fast run.

The JMF wasn't the threat now.

ITC knew what had happened, and they were fighting back. With new, more deadly machines than before.

He crawled out of the burrow and made his way up the mound of rubble to look out over the base.

But what if he was wrong about ITC?

What if something else was controlling these enhanced Defectors?

Only one thing was certain. He couldn't stay out here. He had to get to the base and had to get Nodin out. Then they had to find a way to reach *Persephone*. It was the only way he would ever leave this reloaded nightmare and see his family again.

* * * * *

Cecil tried to listen to the radio reports while he gave the dog a bath in their small bathroom.

He had decided the best thing to do was get the animal cleaned up. They didn't have anything better to do, and sitting around stewing about the news beyond their little sanctuary would just make Michelle worry more. She stood outside the open door watching him bathe the beast. He had tried to persuade her to go to bed, but she had refused, saying she was too wound up.

He felt it, too, maybe even more than she. With his old squad working in the exclusion zones of Korea, he was worried about their safety more than his own. They were both in partial shock from the news about Tyron Red's death at the hands of Orion, and the Tritons' return in Korea. But so far, most of the reports were just speculation about how bad things were out there. None of the stations they had access to on the clunky old radio had any real-time information on what was happening in Korea or with *Genesis 1*. He didn't suppose that anyone outside the military knew what was really happening.

Cecil tried to put his friends out of his mind, but he kept thinking of them out there in the radioactive wasteland. It didn't help that the anchor on the national news station they were listening to was speculating on what might be happening out there and how the world would react.

He bent down and started scrubbing the dog with soap as a female newscaster said, "We're told allies in Europe and Japan have put their forces on high alert and are mobilizing in preparation. I'm now joined by retired Lieutenant General Rolek, who served two tours in Israel during the war of 2031 and was part of the JMF command in the second Korean conflict."

"Thank you. Good to be with you, although not under these circumstances," said Rolek. "I hoped this day would not come, but from what my sources are telling me, a small contingent of Tritons has survived. Over the past week, they prosecuted a multiphase attack targeting ITC, its CEO Tyron Red, and his father's creation, the AI known as Orion, turning the AI against Tyron and killing him during the launch of *Genesis 1* into space."

"And what threat does this Orion pose?" asked the newscaster.

"Well, we all know that Orion is the most intelligent AI ever designed, which makes it an *extreme* threat," Rolek said. "The military is tracking it and will likely try to engage it in talks before attacking it."

"And if those talks fail?"

"Hard to say, but I'm convinced ITC will have planned for every scenario, as will the military."

Michelle and Cecil exchanged a look.

"Yeah, I'm sure there's a kill switch somewhere for Oreo," Cecil said.

"*Orion*, and it will know about any shutdown button. We're talking about the most intelligent entity in the history of our planet."

Cecil stopped scrubbing the dog's chest and looked up.

"The JMF also planned for every scenario where the Tritons somehow survived," Rolek said. "My guess is, within a week, the Tritons and Orion will be defeated."

"You think he's right?" Michelle asked.

Not after you just told me Orion is a freaking god being, Cecil thought.

"Why don't you turn that off for a minute?" he suggested. "We could both use a break from the news."

"Yeah, good idea."

She turned the radio off. Cecil bent down and began scrubbing the dog's belly. He liked it and was wagging his tail.

"He's so tame!" Michelle said. "Must have been well trained."

Cecil nodded. "You love that warm water, don't you, pal?"

He moved around to the back, feeling for ticks as he went. The dog had been filthy and hungry, which told Cecil he had been loose for a while.

"What's your name? You must have a name."

The dog tilted his narrow face, ears perked.

"How old do you think he is?" Michelle asked.

Cecil checked the snout and eyes, which looked healthy. "Four, maybe five. Hard to say though."

The dog whined as he picked up one of his legs.

"Does that hurt?" Cecil asked. He went back to scrubbing. "Just a little bit longer, almost done," he said.

Mud and grit and soap-killed fleas swirled down the shower drain. Michelle turned suddenly.

"What?" Cecil asked.

"I hear static."

She went and got the radio and turned the volume back up—just white noise.

"We must have lost the signal," Michelle said.

Cecil looked up as he finished cleaning a paw. "Try a different channel."

"Okay," she said.

"Last paw," Cecil said to the dog.

"Cecil, I can't get anything at all now," Michelle said. "Should I take it outside and raise the antenna again?"

Cecil shook his head. "I'll do it. I'm almost done."

He lowered the animal's leg back to the ground and picked up the last paw. But as he did, he began to consider what Rolek had said about planning for every scenario with Orion and the Tritons. What if they had missed one? What if Orion had outsmarted everyone already and was preparing to carry out what the Tritons couldn't?

"Get me a towel, please," he said.

"But you're not done."

"He's good."

Michelle stared at Cecil. "What? What are you thinking?"

"Nothing," he said.

"You told me you're going to be honest with me, and change—"

"You're right. I'm sorry."

She handed him a towel.

"I'm thinking that maybe the JMF and ITC aren't as prepared as everyone thinks, and that they are downplaying the threat so people don't panic," he said. "Question is, how big is this threat? I want to make sure we hear of any developments so I can be prepared."

"Okay, I'll dry him off. You go outside and try to get the radio back up."

He looked down at the big, wet black German shepherd, who gazed right back at them as if to say, *What are we doing next?* Cecil had worried at first that the animal might be aggressive or unpredictable, but it was calm and kind—one of the chillest dogs he had ever met.

"Okay, buddy, Michelle's taking over," Cecil said.

She crouched with the towel as he left the bathroom. He picked up the radio and went back out on the deck, raising the antenna in the air.

"Come on, you old pile of transistors," he whispered.

Holding up the radio, he turned it to the west. Then north. It crackled in every direction he turned it. There wasn't even an emergency broadcast signal.

Michelle slid the door open a crack.

"You get anything?" she asked.

The dog looked out between her knees to Cecil.

"No," he said.

"How can that be possible?"

Cecil could think of a few possibilities, none of them good.

"Could it be another cyberattack?" she asked.

"It's possible, but let's not jump to conclusions. He's all cleaned up and looks tired. Maybe we should try to rest. We can go into town first thing tomorrow to get some supplies and figure out what's going on. Okay?"

She held his gaze a moment, then nodded.

"I'll be in shortly," he said.

"Okay."

The door closed behind him. He began dialing through the stations again, holding the antenna in different directions, hoping for a rational explanation. Just as he was about to give up, a flash burst in the darkness of the sky, high in the atmosphere.

"What is that?" Cecil said quietly.

But realization hit him fast when he saw the high altitude.

It was the military, targeting *Genesis 1*. Targeting Orion.

His heart ramped up. There would be no rest for him tonight. He had to plan, come up with an idea to protect his wife if the attack on Orion failed. If the AI survived, it would respond, and if he had to guess, that response would be devastating to humanity.

CHAPTER 31

Tyron Red was no longer a man but was still an entity, a consciousness woven into the fabric of the digital world through the neuro-cord. Deep beneath the levels of Aeon 2, he remained hidden from the enemy that had killed his physical body.

Two Def-5 units guarded the door to the medical facility where his physical body, now deceased, remained. But their razor-edged arms and their machine guns weren't there to protect his corpse—they were there to protect his mind living in the neuro-cord.

Awakening through this device and Tyron's new existence had not been heralded by a rush of air into his lungs or the gradual focusing of eyes adjusting to light. Instead, it was like emerging from deep waters into a realm of pure thought and electrical clarity. His first sensation was a disembodied awareness, an expansive consciousness that felt unmoored from the physical world he once knew. As the initial disorientation subsided, he realized he could perceive everything around him, yet none of it through human senses. Not at first.

Perhaps the biggest change was no longer being confined

to the limitations of human sight. He could "see" in a panoramic continuum, data streams flowing in a constant, pulsating rhythm through the encrypted ITC network that appeared to him as vast interconnected webs of light, lines of code streaking like shooting stars across his vision.

Tyron could focus on any node, any piece of information, and instantaneously understand its contents. Knowledge unfolded effortlessly in his mind, each piece of data a building block in an ever-growing tower of comprehension.

And yet there was a nostalgia, a faint echo of his former life, a file that would not delete, persisting in the background.

His memories—what made Tyron Red *Tyron Red*. His accomplishments, even his failures. Memories of people he had loved: Angelina, his father, Daniel. And of the people who had hated him, feared him—like the ITC board under his father. There was a vivid memory of Whitt and his betrayal that Tyron watched over and over while simultaneously seeing hundreds, even thousands of these other memories.

He had transcended far beyond his human mind, with access to every camera, every sensor, every digital device in the vast ITC network all across the world. He could hear through microphones thousands of miles away, watch events unfold through video feeds like those transmitted from the Def-9 units tearing through five different bases in Korea, where he had ordered them to attack the JMF forces.

ITC was at war, and Tyron was now the general.

Seeing his father's creations slaying the enemy brought him no joy, or any emotion at all. Raw, visceral feelings of a human heart had given way to something more refined: emotions as data, analyzable and quantifiable. Fear was replaced by calculations of probability of defeating his enemies, and the risk it posed to humanity. Joy was the agility he had in navigating the seemingly infinite network that his father had built from scratch.

He was everywhere at once, yet nowhere—a ghost in the global machine.

At first he had felt nothing other than the digital pulses and signals as if they were his own heartbeat. But then he had watched the barrage of missiles and lasers that the JMF and the United States military used to target *Genesis 1*, believing they were destroying Orion.

The two ITC satellites that were part of the Doomsday Shield had managed to deflect the first barrage, but now a new salvo had just launched—dozens of missiles targeting not just the spaceship but also the satellites protecting it.

The ship was moving fast, but it couldn't evade them for long.

Tyron watched through his feeds as a missile finally caught up, blowing his childhood dream and the one woman he ever loved into oblivion.

The first real human emotion, if one could call it that, sent a blast of cold through the network, or at least, that was what he thought he felt.

Then came the rage. And that heat fueled his mind as he turned his attention to several other feeds displaying the orders he had issued shortly after his transformation. The first was to hunt down his enemies. First, just Red Platoon. Now he watched the Def-9 units killing all JMF soldiers with extreme efficiency.

His human emotions seemed to be returning. Or maybe that was just in his consciousness.

Orion's voice came through their connection. Wires and fibers pulsated and glowed along the segments of the neuro-cord as the AI spoke.

"Tyron," Orion said, "you have my deepest condolences for losing Angelina and *Genesis 1*, but we must view this as a distraction that will give you the upper hand as we work to destroy our enemies, for they believe they have destroyed me and that you are dead."

I am dead, he thought.

"They will eventually realize the truth, and we must not waste this precious time," Orion continued. "Phase one of shutting down communications has been effectively carried out. The vast global network is completely down. A blackout has been deployed across civilian and military networks."

That order would soon send every government, corporation, and household into disarray. It wasn't just the communication networks down; it was the entire internet. But Tyron wouldn't stop there. Soon he would activate phase two of the blackout.

The idea was chaos.

Soon he would create more of it. Then he would approach the powers of the world and negotiate a peace that would free humanity from the bonds that had enslaved them.

First though, he planned to bring to justice those behind the attacks on ITC. Starting with Vucci, who was currently holed up in the National Military Command Center beneath the Pentagon. This was the very same secure room that Tyron had visited just weeks ago. Fortunately, he didn't need to get inside physically to take out the chair of the Joint Chiefs. There were other ways to get to the bastard. Creative ways.

Tyron had already managed to discreetly hack into a camera system thanks to Orion. Through the remote connection, Tyron watched Vucci standing at the head of a long conference table, facing a host of other important military staff that included the secretary of defense; national security adviser; the secretaries of the army, navy, and air force; and the commandant of the Marine Corps.

"Good work, Orion. Now, prepare the malware," he said.

"Stand by, sir."

Through the digital ether, Tyron watched the line of code that would activate advanced malware to shut down the advanced CBRN system throughout the facility, sealing Vucci in the command center and shutting off all the vents. There were safeguards for this exact thing, but it would take a while to activate them. By then the general, who suffered from an undisclosed case of asthma, would be struggling for air.

Tyron tapped into the security feed and watched the general in the middle of a briefing about the Def-9 attacks in Korea. In minutes, a JMF bombing on their own bases would be carried out to destroy the machines and anyone still alive inside the facilities. Vucci was commanding the entire thing from inside this single room deep beneath the Pentagon, using an archaic backup system of very low frequency and low frequency (VLF/LF) radio wave technology that kept them secure from ITC's reach, or so he thought.

The only reason Tyron hadn't shut that down, too, was so he could be a fly on the wall inside the command center. Whether any of the officers and staff members inside were in on the plot against ITC, Tyron wasn't sure. But they all were part of the same war machine, and unfortunately for them, they would be collateral damage just like the innocent JMF soldiers stationed on the bases.

As the battle played out through the digital tapestry that Tyron lived inside, his perspective on warfare was changing. It was much like a game of chess, where the players worked to outmaneuver one another.

It was his move now.

"Orion, launch the malware," he said.

The general, standing in front of a screen displaying the JMF's strike on the bases, turned as the doors to the room shut and locked internally with a click that Tyron could hear through their connection. He could also hear Vucci's confused voice.

"What's happening?" the general asked.

The staff, also confused, began to move about the room. The national security adviser went to the main door and tried to open it.

"It's sealed, sir."

Vucci came over and tried it. Then he started yelling and pounding. "Open this door at once!"

Through the other cameras that Tyron could access, he watched staff members scrambling to figure out what was going on.

"Stage two active," said Orion.

Tyron saw schematics for the CBRN system and watched the vents seal off. What happened next would likely be a terrifying escalation for those trapped inside the command center.

Two of the vents reopened, and a loud sucking noise began.

"What is that?" asked Vucci. Tyron heard panic in that gravelly voice.

He focused on the meter showing the shifting content of the atmosphere inside the room as the air was sucked out and replaced with nitrogen. Within minutes, the younger and more vigorous staff members were pounding on the door while those less fit were sitting in chairs or on the floor, breathing air with a rapidly decreasing oxygen level.

Vucci slapped both palms down on the long war table, his eyes gazing up at the digital screen that would show the attacks about to occur. He would soon begin to fade.

Tyron could play this game all day long, but he wanted Vucci to understand something before he took his last breath.

It was time for the checkmate.

"Is the service unit active?" he asked Orion.

"Yes, sir. I've brought it online and it has been deployed. It will be there within two minutes."

Tyron wasn't sure Vucci had two minutes left.

"Speed it up," he said.

"Okay, Tyron."

Tyron tapped into the feed from the service robot carrying oxygen masks and small tanks. The facility was equipped with a hundred of these units, designed to help rescue and evacuate people inside the Pentagon in the event of a chemical or biological attack. They were among the very few units that survived the Global AI Limitation Accord. It seemed fitting that now one would be used to end one of the most powerful men on the planet.

That unit made its way through the now-abandoned outer offices around the command center. The door to the room opened, and the people there clamoring to get out fell into the corridor. Some came to at once, greedily sucking in air.

The machine walked inside, deploying masks with tanks to the staff members who couldn't move on their own.

"Connect us to the service robot," Tyron said.

"Stand by... Okay, we're connected," Orion replied.

The machine bent down to Vucci, who lay face down on the carpet, wheezing. It reached to him with skeletal fingers, turning him onto his back.

"General Vucci," Tyron said through the machine.

Vucci stared up, perplexed.

"You made a vital error underestimating me," he said. "By killing my physical body, you only made me stronger, and now the world will know the truth about your crimes and your lies."

Tyron paused, letting this sink in.

"You could have retired with your grandkids," he said through the robot. "Now your time is up."

Then he operated the service unit, taking over the titanium fingers and pushing them down on the general's eyes. The screams from his oxygen-deprived lungs were muted, weak. Guards rushed in, trying to pull the robot off, but it was already too late. The titanium fingers, designed to rescue humans, mushed his eyeballs and punched into his brain.

The neuro-cord wires lit up like a Christmas tree of different colors as Tyron sent a flurry of new transmissions through the digital ether.

"Orion, proceed with phase two of the network disruption," Tyron said.

"Activating phase two, Tyron."

Tyron switched to remote ITC views of Atlanta, Washington, Los Angeles, Chicago, New York, and hundreds of other cities as every car with an ITC chip shut down. People emerged from their vehicles, some confused, others angry. It took just minutes before panic broke out on the roads, highways, and streets where people were now stranded.

In the sky, private jets and commercial airplanes continued to fly, but those on the ground went dead just like the cars. As soon as the aircraft in the sky touched down, they, too, would go offline.

Soon the entire world would grind to a halt. The panic would spread as fast as a digital virus, and the world governments would have no choice but to negotiate with Tyron. He was one step closer to world peace, but first there must be chaos, and the rest of his enemies must take their final breaths.

Next, he was coming for Jay Whitt.

* * * * *

Where the hell are the reinforcements? Santiago wondered.

He was hunkered down at the edge of the airfield at Omega Base, trying to push past the fatigue and a pounding headache. He wasn't even sure when he had slept last, and the stim pill that Red Platoon gave him before they deployed had long since worn off. Between the cancer present in his lungs, his head still throbbing from being knocked unconscious, and sheer exhaustion, he was running on fumes. Hell, he still had bruises from his boxing match with the robot back in San Diego before he deployed. But even in his compromised state, it wasn't hard to put together what had happened here.

The Defectors had turned on the JMF right here on the runways. Machine-gun fire chattered, and explosions thumped through the night as the machines advanced deeper into the base. They had left a trail of devastation along the burning airfield, which was now littered with at least twenty destroyed Wasps, dozens of drones, and six fighter jets.

Santiago stood on the edge of the destruction where, just days earlier, he had been dropped off after Hell Squad's mission to Field Lab Alpha went sideways. The building where the JMF had held him in "quarantine" was another thousand feet behind that, connected to the massive compound. Observation towers rose up at the four corners of the perimeter fence that encompassed over fifty structures.

He noticed a muzzle flash coming from one of those towers on the southern side, closest to him. The distant crack told him it was likely a .50-caliber sniper rifle. But on this side of the base, the single sniper appeared to be the only one fighting back against the machines.

Corpses littered the airfield and the ground outside the building, where the Defectors had cut them down. From his vantage, Santiago could see that most of the bodies were military police, killed by energy weapons. But the machines had spared no one. Many of the dead were simple mechanics and other ground crew who had been working out here. And, as with the pilot from the Wasp back at the crash site, the Defectors had taken trophies.

The faceless head of a mechanic was turned in his direction, illuminated by the fires burning through a Wasp a hundred feet away.

He had no idea how many dead troops there were or when reinforcements would arrive, but he couldn't sit here and wait. He had to get Nodin out of there before the machines found him.

Move, T, you got to move.

Keeping low, he ran out into the curtain of smoke billowing across the field. The first thing he needed to do was scavenge a weapon. There were plenty of assault rifles, but to stand a chance against the machines, he needed a laser rifle.

Seeing none, he realized that the machines weren't the only threat. If he ran into any surviving JMF soldiers, he would be a target. After all, it should be pretty clear now that they were at war with ITC.

He looked down at his suit. Maybe it would be better to change into something else.

No time, T.

As he crossed the airfield, he spotted a soldier lying face down, still gripping an assault rifle. Santiago ran over, crouched, and grabbed the stock. But as he pulled, the wrists and hands came with it—severed below the elbow by a laser bolt.

"Jesus," he said, falling on his backside.

After getting back up, he grabbed the weapon and pried the fingers away from the handle and stock. The arms thumped back to the ground. He checked the magazine, which still had all thirty rounds.

The poor bastard hadn't even gotten off a shot.

A flash of light came from inside the observation tower where the JMF sniper had been positioned. Santiago saw the silhouette of a Defector, captured in the flash of its energy weapon as it finished off the trooper.

Then it moved up to the shattered windows, scanning the

smoke below with its pulsating orange visor. Santiago ducked for cover behind the wreckage of a Wasp. He waited a few moments before checking the observation tower. By the time he did, the machine had gone.

He eyed the building, about five hundred feet away. If he pushed hard, he could make it there in one go. Head down, he charged out from behind the Wasp.

When he was a younger man, he could run this distance in under thirty seconds. But that was without gear and when he was rested. Today he would be lucky if he could make it in twice that. Then again, knowing that every step could be his last was a strong motivator.

The rap of his boots echoed as he ran, but the distant crack of laser rifles helped mask the noise. He kept to the wreckage, watching for enemies and anything that might trip him.

A big explosion boomed deeper in the base, and a fireball rose into the sky. The machines must have gotten to an ammunition dump.

Santiago ran even faster, closing in on the building now, maybe twenty seconds away at his current pace. Two APCs were ahead, their armored bodies holed with laser fire. The doors were still open where soldiers had come out to engage the machines.

Ten bodies lay in pools of blood that came not from the laser fire but from what the Defectors had done to these men after they were shot. Their helmets lay scattered, exposing their skinned faces to the radioactive elements.

Santiago kept running, breathing harder now, lungs burning. Just as he made it around the APCs and saw the open door of the building, a voice whispered loudly.

"Hey, over here."

He halted and trained his rifle on a man stumbling down the runway, gripping the side of his flight suit and dripping blood.

In his other hand, he carried a pistol. He wore a helmet with a scorch mark on the crest.

"Back off," Santiago said.

"Easy, man, I'm a human," replied the pilot, holding his pistol up in the air.

"I can see that, but I can't help you, bub."

"I'm not asking for help, but we should stick together. To find survivors and get out of here before—"

"I don't have time. Go hide, and wait for reinforcements."

"There aren't reinforcements."

Santiago lowered his rifle. "What do you mean?"

"There's a countdown. In thirty minutes, the JMF is turning this place into another crater."

"Fuck..."

"Yeah, so we got to move fast and evac anyone still alive in there."

"I'm looking for a friend, and that's it."

Santiago turned away from the pilot and rushed to the building to search for Nodin. He slowed and entered an open door to find a dark hallway without any light. No emergency lighting meant the machines had somehow shut down all life-support systems. That meant medical equipment would be on battery power or not working at all.

He turned on his tactical light, and the bright beam lanced into the darkness.

Footsteps followed him as he made his way inside. He turned to the pilot, motioning him back.

"Get out of here," Santiago said.

The pilot stood his ground, and Santiago could tell that this guy wasn't going to leave willingly. It was either shoot him or let him come along.

Santiago grunted, then waved him over. Maybe he could help.

"What's the best way into the medical facility?"

"This is the best route," he said. "I'm Captain Rico, by the way."

"Santiago."

They shared a nod, then set off down the passage, where they soon came across more corpses, their faces removed. Some of these people had their fingers cut off, and their tongues.

"Why are the machines doing this?" Rico asked.

Santiago had an idea why, but if he gave his theory, the captain wouldn't believe him.

Least said, easiest mended, he thought.

"No idea," Santiago said. He swept the next hallway, clearing it and trekking on down the bloody corridor. The gunfire sounded distant now and sporadic.

The machines were winning the fight.

Slaughter, he thought.

Bodies lay scattered in the hallway and inside rooms with doors ajar. He shined the tac beam down each side, clearing them.

"We're getting close to the medical center," Rico said. "Take a right here."

Santiago hurried in that direction. His sense of dread grew with each step. The machines had already made their way through here, and he knew that the chances of finding Nodin alive weren't good. But he had to try. He couldn't leave him behind.

They came upon the double doors to the facility, blown open. Santiago shouldered his rifle and stepped into a macabre scene.

"My God," he whispered, looking around the open space.

Bodies lay in all directions—some on the tile floor, some draped over gurneys and beds, others splayed against the wall, where they had been pinned like a collection of butterflies. The machines had mutilated and flayed these people.

Rico walked in, shaking his head. "This is insane. This is—"

"Get it together, and keep up," Santiago said.

He searched for the ICU, where they would have Nodin after his surgery. The next hallway was filled with more dead bodies, gunned down and then cut up where they fell. He knew then how he would find Nodin.

But Santiago had to see for himself, especially after he had come this far.

He proceeded down the hallway, checking the signage with his beam. The ICU was on the floor below them. He found the closest stairwell, opened it, and went inside. Rico followed him to the lower level.

As Santiago grabbed the handle, he heard a distant clattering noise. Then a bloodcurdling scream of agony. He waited for it to pass, but it went on and on.

Shutting off his light, he stood in the pitch blackness with Rico, who put a hand on his shoulder. The scream finally faded away. But there were other voices.

"Please, don't do this. I have a family," someone said.

"It's going to kill all of us!" said another person.

Rico whispered to Santiago, "Must be a Def-9 unit in here still."

"Yeah, but there are survivors."

"We can't take one of those on our own," he said. "Those are the newest models."

"I thought you wanted to help."

"I do."

"Then shut up and get ready to fight. The Def-8 units are weakest along their necks. Aim for the back, if you can, or shoot at their visors."

"And if none of that works?"

"Then I hope you're a God fearing man."

Santiago said a quick prayer. Then he opened the door as quietly as he could, then crept out. At the end of the passage, he saw a faint orange glow. As he suspected, the source was the visor of a Defector inside the ICU. It crouched over a still person, draping something over its chest.

Aiming his rifle at the back of the neck, Santiago started toward it. If he could shoot it a few times and disable it, then maybe he could confiscate its laser rifle to finish it off.

It was a long shot, both figuratively and literally. With each silent step, he started to question his decision, thinking of his family until he heard a familiar voice.

"Kill me. Go ahead, you pot-metal piece of shit."

"Nodin," Santiago whispered, recognizing him without a doubt now. He picked up his pace, closing the distance until he was only about twenty yards away from the entrance to the ICU.

Whirring sounded as the machine raised a skeletal hand. One finger became a saw. Another jetted a blue flame.

"No, pleeeease!" shouted a man.

Santiago moved faster, preparing to pull the trigger as the machine leaned down to carve its victim up. Rico was up on his right side, pistol aimed at the machine.

A clanking behind them sent a chill up Santiago's back. He turned as a door burst open in the hallway. A machine strode out, grabbing him by the neck and lifting him up with one hand while snatching Rico in the other.

Squirming, Santiago kicked and struggled for air as it carried them both into the ICU. The Defector unit inside turned to them, the visor flashing at Santiago. Then it rotated its helmet, and it flashed at Rico.

The machine holding the pilot let go, dropping him right in front of the Defector with the saw for a finger. It swiped out, the blade tracing his neck. Hot blood sprayed Santiago as he, too, was released. He put up his fists out of instinct and threw a punch into the head of the machine that had cut Rico.

His knuckles thudded against metal. The machine's visor

flashed at him again, and he knew he was going to die. He would never see his wife or his kids again.

Santiago tried to back away but smacked into the machine behind him. It pushed him forward. He fell to his knees, then sprang back up, not ready to accept his fate.

"Sarge!" Nodin shouted.

Santiago looked over. The JMF had handcuffed Nodin's remaining arm to the bed across the room, away from the ten corpses and two injured female nurses sprawled on the bloody floor of the ICU. The women sobbed and squirmed.

Both machines suddenly moved away from Santiago.

"Proceed with ITC personnel to evacuation zone on southeastern edge of Omega Base," one of them said in a robotic monotone.

For a moment, Santiago remained frozen, unable to move as the two machines continued their evil work on the dead and the living. The realization hit him as the machine's words registered. The Defector units had deemed them as nonthreats because they worked for ITC.

"Please, let the women go," Santiago said.

"Proceed to evacuation zone," the machine repeated.

The closest nurse stared at Santiago, shaking her head. "Please, please don't leave us."

He had already started over to Nodin, grabbing his bed. He wheeled it around and started to push it out of the room. Santiago glanced over at the machines. One had a laser rifle. It might not view him as a threat now, but if he made a move to save these nurses, that could easily change. And anyway, there was almost no chance he could take down both units.

There wasn't anything he could do for them.

"No, please!" shouted the nurse.

"I'm sorry," Santiago said.

He did his best to drown out their screams as he pushed Nodin out of the medical facility and toward the exit. They had to get to the ITC evacuation zone before this entire place was blown to hell.

"Hold on, brother. I'm getting you out of here," Santiago said.

CHAPTER 32

Halfway through the night, Cecil had a back spasm that lasted fifteen minutes. Michelle was right there with him, a hand on his back. The injuries he sustained at Copper Terrace made this spasm worse than usual, but he got through it and managed to get a few hours of sleep after.

At dawn, he sneaked out of the bedroom and grabbed the radio. The dog, who had spent the night at the sliding door, looked up as he approached.

"It's okay, buddy," Cecil said. He went over and opened the door, stepping out as the animal bolted across the deck and down the stairs to the woods.

"Wait," Cecil called down.

The animal stopped, then peed in the grass.

Cecil laughed. "Sorry, pal. Come back when you're done."

He turned on the radio, hoping something had changed since he checked at 2:00 a.m., but all he got was static.

The dog ran up the stairs to the deck, wagging his tail as he trotted over to Cecil, who was watching the sun rise over the eastern hills. It was quiet this morning. Not a mechanical sound out there. No distant car engines. No planes. Nothing.

The sliding door creaked open behind him. Michelle put down a bowl of water for the dog. As he trotted over to her, wagging his tail, Cecil couldn't help but wonder who would want to get rid of such a gentle, housebroken, obedient animal.

Maybe the dog had run away.

"Good morning, little fella," Michelle said.

"You're going to like him better than you like me before long," Cecil joked.

"Not if you behave yourself." Michelle smiled, but it faded quickly. She walked over and studied the sky. They were both likely wondering the same thing about what was happening out there.

"Any news?" she asked.

"Radio isn't working. I'm going to head into town."

"We."

"Right. I figured you might want to stay here with . . ." Cecil eyed the dog. "We need a name for him."

"Does that mean we can keep him?" She smiled and scratched him behind a furry ear.

"As long as we're staying here, sure."

"Want to come into town with us, buddy?"

The dog wagged his tail again.

"That's a yes," Michelle said. "I'll get my bag."

"Okay, I'll start the car."

He went over to the shed, boots crunching across the gravel. He pulled out a key and unlocked the padlock securing a chain through the door handles of the structure. It fell away, and he pulled the large door open. But when he approached the car with the fob, the car didn't chirp or light up.

He pushed Unlock, and again nothing happened.

What the hell . . .

Was the battery dead? That was almost impossible. Cars had advanced batteries that took a long time to drain. Nothing short of leaving the lights on all night would have done that, and if that were the case, he would have seen the glow through the cracks in the shed walls.

No, something else caused this.

A thought entered his mind, bringing up an old fear about a coordinated electromagnetic-pulse attack on the energy grid. He stepped back outside just as his wife closed the cabin door and their new friend came running across the gravel.

"Why isn't the car on?" she asked.

Cecil said, "It won't turn on. Like it's completely dead. Shit, I can't even get it unlocked."

She halted and raised a suspicious brow. As an engineer, she knew even better than he how unlikely it was that the car could be dead.

"How?"

"I was going to ask you that."

She walked over to examine the car. Then she turned back to him. "I honestly don't know, but I can tell you have a theory."

"Not sure I could call it a theory, but it's a *remote* possibility."

"Are you going to share it?"

Cecil sighed. "An electromagnetic pulse, a giant one, could have knocked out electronics over a large area. But if that's the case, then we've got much bigger problems. The entire country does."

Michelle took in a deep breath.

"There has to be a rational explanation," Cecil said, knowing he was starting to sound like a broken record. "How about I jog into town to see what's going on."

"And leave me here? No way. I already said I'm coming."

"It's five miles, and a lot of hills."

"Then we'd better get started. Come on, let's grab a few things."

Cecil followed her inside to load their packs with some water and trail mix, jackets, and first aid kit for the hike. Then he tucked the VitalStim remote carefully inside. He wanted to be prepared, just in case they got stranded out there.

Once they were stocked up, Cecil hoisted the backpack onto his shoulders, then slung his rifle. Michelle gave him that look he hated—the one questioning whether this was a good idea in light of his injuries.

"You had an episode last night," Michelle said.

"I know, but I feel good this morning. Really, I do," he replied. "Seriously, this is nothing compared to..."

He stopped short of saying Copper Terrace. The last thing he wanted right now was to tell her about what went down that day. He knew he should be dead—and long before Copper Terrace. He should never have made it out of Korea, and if not for Santiago and Hell Squad, he wouldn't have.

For a fleeting moment, he thought of them, hoping they were okay out there.

But they were trained for whatever was thrown at them. If anyone could make it out of that hell again, it was Santiago, Alistair, Yosef, David, and Nodin.

"Ready?" he asked.

"Yup." Michelle patted her leg, and their new four-legged friend started out on the makeshift leash she had made. The animal pulled, guiding them across the gravel to the road.

Cecil went around the gate, then began the hike down the hillside. Soon he came to the second gate, where they had seen the pickup truck two days ago. The dog sniffed the ground and wagged his tail near the tire tracks.

In a little while, they reached the dirt road that eventually connected to the highway back into town. It was quiet here, not a bird or cricket chirping.

Cecil cradled his rifle as he led the way. They passed through dappled shadows cast by the dense foliage of changing trees. It was beautiful with the golden morning light streaming through.

As they approached the highway, he noticed that the silence continued. He didn't hear a single vehicle. Surely, there should be traffic out there right now.

What the hell was going on?

"Let me check things out really fast," Cecil said. "Please, just stay back with the dog."

"Why? What do you think you're going to find?" Michelle asked.

"I don't know. That's why I want to recon it."

"Okay."

Cecil gave her a nod, then set off.

"Wait," Michelle said.

He stopped, turned.

"I love you, Cecil," she said.

"I love you too. Don't worry," he said, and took off at a jog.

A few minutes later, he saw the end of the dirt road and the highway beyond. He moved into the ditch, keeping to the tree line. So far, he couldn't see anything, nor did he hear any sound of traffic.

Rifle up, he crept out and crouched behind a tree, checking both ways.

All clear. Not a car, van, or truck in sight. Not even a damn horse and wagon.

He waited a few minutes, but nothing came.

Slinging his rifle, he hurried back to Michelle.

"Well?" she asked.

"No cars that I can see."

"Something's happened, Cecil. Something bad."

"I know, but let's not jump to conclusions. Whatever it was—"

She grabbed both his forearms and squeezed. "I have a theory of my own."

"Yeah? You're scaring me now, babe. Try and relax."

Her grip eased, but she held on to him. "If Orion turned against humanity somehow, there's no telling how much chaos it could create," she said. "Almost ninety-five percent of vehicles on roads in the States run on ITC chips. And the communication networks, food-production facilities—it's all under the same operating network. You saw what happened when rations were held up for a single day in Charlotte. Think about that on a national level, for more than several days."

Cecil chuckled. "Damn, you trying to scare me?"

"This isn't funny."

"I know, you're right . . . Well, I mean, I hope you're not right about the operational stuff, but you're right. This isn't funny." He scratched an itch on the back of his neck. "There's only one way to figure this out. We have to go into town."

Cecil looked back at the highway in the distance. If what she was saying had come true, then town wasn't going to be safe for long. People would be trying to stock up on food, water, supplies, gas, and ammo.

He and Michelle would need to do the same thing, and while it could be dangerous, so was leaving her by herself.

She started walking and passed him by. "Well, let's go, then."

"Okay, but you're going to have to do everything I say. Starting with following me."

"Fine."

She stopped, and he went ahead, leading them to the highway. After clearing it again, he took a left toward town. It was just eight in the morning, but the five hilly miles would take at least two and a half hours on foot with rests in between.

Michelle kept to the shoulder of the road, just as Cecil instructed. He scanned the trees on both sides of the highway, knowing that a threat could come from anywhere, anytime. For the first half mile, they didn't see a single vehicle, person, or animal.

But as they looked over the valley below, Cecil spotted the first car, still in the traffic lane and not pulled off on the shoulder. Michelle came up beside him and followed his pointing finger down to a late-model blue sedan.

"See anyone in it?" she asked.

"No, looks like it was abandoned. Stay back a bit. I'm going to check it out."

Keeping his pack on, Cecil started down the hill with his rifle. He checked the trees framing the highway and listened for any crunching of leaves or snap of a twig. But it was dead quiet out here, as if they were the last two people in the world.

The eeriness put Cecil on edge as he took the last few steps to the car. He looked through the windows and saw no one inside, but he did notice a key fob in the center console. He tried the front door; it was unlocked. Bending down, he scooped up the key and pushed the start button.

Nothing happened. It was as dead as their own car.

He got out and waved for Michelle, who trotted down with the dog.

"It's dead," he said. "Whoever left it, left a key inside."

Michelle took a look, then gazed down the highway, clearly nervous.

They pushed on ahead and found two more abandoned vehicles. Halfway to town, they had yet to see a single person.

There were a few turn-offs for houses in the hills, but heading to any of them for information or help was a last resort. People lived out here because they didn't like company. They came for the peace and quiet, or to disappear—as Cecil and his wife were supposed to be doing.

He turned back to check on Michelle. "How you doing?"

"Fine. How about you?"

"Good. Can you jog a bit?"

"Yeah, it's not going to hurt the baby, Cecil," she said with a smile.

The baby. He was still getting used to the idea. Smiling back, he motioned for her and they started jogging. The German shepherd barked, thinking it was a game. They kept the pace up for the next mile and a half and stopped at the sight of two more cars at the top of the next hill.

Cecil walked up to them, rifle out again. He raised it at the sound of distant gunshots. Turning, he motioned for Michelle to take cover in the trees. Then he ran up the rest of the hill to a car, crouching to listen.

The distant pop, pop was definitely gunshots.

With just over a mile or so to go, he could tell they were coming from town. As he got up and looked down into the valley, he saw movement. Two people, moving slowly and close together.

Using his rifle scope, he zoomed in on a man and a woman, probably in their late sixties or early seventies. The woman had a limp, and it looked as if the man was trying to help her along faster. They kept to the side of the road. Every few strides, he looked over his shoulder.

Cecil trained his rifle down the road in the direction of the town but saw nothing. The gunshots, meanwhile, continued in the distance. They were sporadic, but this wasn't some off-grid doomsday prepper plinking at bottles.

Footsteps came from behind him, and Michelle and the dog trotted up. "Get in the forest," he said. "We need to get off the road."

"Why? What do you see?" Michelle asked.

Cecil led her to the ridgeline on the right side of the road, where a thicket of trees provided concealment. There, he unslung his pack. He dug out binoculars and handed them to his wife so she could see on her own.

He brought up his rifle again, scoping the couple.

"They look harmless enough," Michelle said. "Maybe we should ask them if they know anything."

Cecil wasn't sure at first.

It took them fifteen minutes to gain the crest of the hill. Cecil stepped out from behind a tree.

"Morning," he said casually, waving them down.

The man moved in front of the woman, shielding her and staring up at Cecil with frightened eyes. He held up a hand and said, "We don't have anything valuable."

"I'm not going to hurt you, and I don't want anything except information," Cecil said. "Just trying to figure out what's going on."

"The world's gone mad, is what's going on," replied the man.

He looked back down into the valley they had just come from. Cecil did the same, still not seeing anyone or anything.

"Please, we just want to know what you know," Michelle said. She stepped out next to Cecil.

"We've been staying in the mountains and lost all contact with the outside," he said. "Last we heard, ITC CEO Tyron Red was killed by Orion."

The older woman moved out from behind the man. She brushed long gray hair away from a weathered face with kind eyes.

"The town's fallen into anarchy," she said. "We were on our way through yesterday to visit our kids at their place fifty miles east of here when the news hit about the Tritons and Tyron Red. Phones died. Then the cars."

The man nodded. "We went to get some food to hunker

down for a bit. Everyone else had the same idea. Started off orderly, with people taking their fair share of groceries. Then a guy came with a shotgun, started taking from other people. Someone pulled out a handgun; then things went bad real fast."

He pulled his wife along. "We need to keep moving, honey," he said. "Good luck to you both."

Cecil looked in the direction of town and saw a tendril of smoke.

"I wouldn't go that way, sir," the woman said. "It's not safe for average folk."

I'm not average folk, he thought.

* * * * *

Omega Base burned in the distance, but not from the bombing that Captain Rico had warned Santiago about. That was hours ago, and the bombing never happened.

Santiago and Nodin had found a group of five ITC personnel on the southeastern edge of the base, right where the Defector in the ICU had said to evacuate to. Using an armored ITC vehicle, they had fled the base with those survivors, including a scientist named Dr. Wendt, who was currently trying to contact *Persephone*.

Santiago had driven the APC a few miles north—far enough that if the bombs did come, they would be out of the blast zone. He had parked them behind a debris barricade for cover.

"This is Dr. Wendt, from Field Base Zulu, transmitting from the following coordinates, requesting evacuation, over."

While the scientist kept trying to raise the airship, Santiago remained in the back of the APC, next to Nodin, who was in bad shape from the trauma of losing his arm.

Santiago looked out through the windshield at bright red lines of laser fire, and yellow flames billowing up from Omega Base on the horizon. If he could see that, then maybe enemies could see him, and right now he couldn't say who was friend or foe.

"I'll be right back," Santiago said. He patted Nodin gently on the shoulder.

"Don't worry, Sarge, I'm not going anywhere," Nodin groaned back.

Smiling, Santiago moved up to the front of the truck and hopped into the passenger seat. "We can't stay here," he said to Wendt.

"And where do you expect us to go?" asked the scientist.

"Far away from this base, is where," he said. "The JMF hasn't struck that site yet, but they will, and once they destroy the machines, they're going to come for ITC."

"What? No way. We're just scientists."

"Don't you get it?" Santiago asked. He looked to the back, where the other four ITC biologists huddled together. "The JMF attacked ITC and tried to kill Tyron Red. He hit back with the Def-9 units."

This was the second time Santiago explained his story and what he knew, but none of these people seemed to believe him.

"Get out of the seat now," Santiago said.

Wendt shook his head. "No, we're staying here."

"Get out of that seat, or I'm going to toss you out, bub."

"Do you know who I am?"

"I know you're not in charge." Santiago grabbed Wendt and yanked him from the seat.

"Hey!"

"You all want to get out of this alive? Then you have to trust me," Santiago said. "Now, take care of my friend while I drive us somewhere we can't get blown to atoms. Cocky shit," he muttered as he fired up the truck and steered out of the debris onto a road where he could give it some juice. The oversize tires thumped over broken curbs, engine blocks, and charred tree trunks.

Reaching down, he activated the comms, scanning for any live channels. But just as in the Wasp he had hijacked and taken to Omega Base, he couldn't raise anyone out there. He tried not to think about what that meant, or how far he was from his family. The only way to get back to them was by compartmentalizing his objectives. And the first was to find *Persephone*, assuming it was still up there.

If not, he would find a way off this peninsula, even if it meant hijacking a damn boat.

The road curved down into a valley where collapsed buildings lined both sides of the thoroughfare. Lightning flashed on the horizon, letting them see the endless devastation they had entered. In the wake of the flash, he thought he saw something in the clouds.

"*Persephone One, Persephone One*, this is Sergeant Rodriguez of Hell Squad. Do you read me?"

Static crackled, then a voice. At least, he thought he heard one.

"Watch out!" Wendt shouted.

Santiago looked out the windshield and slammed on the brakes as two figures moved out onto the road with weapons shouldered. In that split second, he recognized them as men, not machines. But when he saw the JMF uniforms, he sped up.

"What are you doing!" Wendt said. "You have to stop! Those aren't the enemy!"

"Get down!" Santiago yelled.

Muzzle flashes lit up the darkness, bullets starring against the bulletproof windshield. Santiago hunched behind the wheel and floored it. The two JMF soldiers jumped out of the way, but others fired from elevated positions down the road. One of them raised a shoulder-mounted rocket.

"Everyone, hold on!" Santiago yelled.

He swerved to avoid the streaking projectile, which exploded in the center of the road. Debris pounded the armored door as Santiago tried to correct, but the vehicle fishtailed and slammed into a pile of rubble.

The steering wheel stopped him as the APC jerked to a halt. Smoke filled the cabin, and groaning came from the back.

"Nodin," he whispered.

Santiago reached for his pistol as a figure approached the driver's side window with a raised rifle.

"Out of the vehicle!" the trooper shouted.

Santiago knew there was no way he could shoot his way out of this. He withdrew his hand from his holstered weapon and raised it in the air, then reached for the door handle.

"Hold your fire; we're scientists," Santiago said as he opened it.

The JMF soldier pulled him from the vehicle, knocking him to the ground. Another trooper joined him as four more approached the back hatch.

"Hands on your head!" shouted the soldier with a gun barrel up against Santiago's back.

He did as ordered, remaining on his knees.

A lieutenant with a name tag that read *Clancy* walked over. "Who the hell are you?"

Santiago hesitated. It was obvious he worked for ITC, but as long as these guys didn't find out he was a contracted soldier with the company, maybe he and Nodin had a shot at getting out of this alive. "Scientists," he lied again. "We have no idea what's happening."

"'Course you don't."

"I say we waste them all right here, LT," someone said.

"No, please, just leave us. Take the APC," Wendt protested. "We are not a threat to you."

"You made them machines though."

"No, I am not *that* type of scientist."

"Bullshit."

"Shut the fuck up, everyone," said Lieutenant Clancy. He crouched in front of Santiago. "You're not a scientist. You're with the security forces, I can tell, so don't fucking lie to me again."

Santiago remained quiet.

"No?"

"You're right," Wendt said. "He is a security contractor."

Asshole, Santiago thought.

Clancy scoffed, his gaze still on Santiago. "If you lied about that, then my guess is, you know what's happening out there. So I'm going to ask you one more time what you know."

"If I told you, I doubt you'd believe me."

"Try me."

Santiago felt the gun in his back again. "My name is Sergeant Rodriguez, and I served in the war, fought at Mount Paektu. Recently, ITC hired me to do some security work with some of my old team. We were ambushed by Def-8 units, then deployed with Red Platoon to find those same machines at a location in Pyong—"

Before he could finish his sentence, one of the soldiers said, "Sir, we got incoming."

Santiago heard the whirring a moment later, and his gaze flitted upward. Out of the sky came the beetle-like shape of an airship.

"*Persephone*," he whispered in awe.

Lieutenant Clancy looked up at the sky. "That got more machines on it?"

"I doubt it," Santiago said. "Last time I was on it, there were zero machines."

"Then that might be our ride out of here, but you're going to make that happen, Sergeant Rodriguez."

"I'll do my best."

"Better hurry, sir, because we got more contacts coming in," said a scout who had just come running up. "Two pickup trucks, filled to the brim with those Def-9 units from Omega Base."

"Probably told 'em where we're at when you shot at our APC," Santiago said.

"How far out?" Clancy asked.

"Three minutes, maybe less," said the scout.

The airship hovered in the clouds as two Wasps dropped from its underbelly and swooped toward the ground. As soon as they deployed, the airship rose back into the clouds.

"You better get us on one of those transports, or the first bullet that flies is the one in your skull," Clancy said.

Santiago nodded. "Fair enough."

"I say we just waste every one of those ITC bastards and blast our way onto the ship," said the same soldier from earlier.

This guy was going to be a problem, Santiago could already see. He had known a few like him back when he was in the JMF, but they had weeded out the nutcases during the war. Most of them ended up dying of their own native stupidity.

"The machines definitely know where we're at, LT!" shouted the scout.

"Everyone, get to the transports now!" Clancy shouted.

Santiago went over and helped Nodin up, pulling the man's one arm over his shoulder. "I got you, bro. Just hang on a little longer."

The scientists huddled together and made their way over to the Wasps, which touched down on the road fifty feet from the wrecked APC.

The hatches raised, disgorging twenty ITC security troopers and a face Santiago hadn't expected to be so happy to see: Commander Zimmerman.

"Commander," Santiago called out.

"Rodriguez, that you? Holy shit, I thought you were dead."

"Long story."

"You better shut those fucking new machines down!" yelled Clancy.

Zimmerman turned to the JMF lieutenant. "I can't," he said. "We've tried. Someone's giving them orders from the States. Either that, or the Tritons hacked them somehow."

"Lieutenant, we better git," insisted the scout.

"Everyone, on the transports. Move your asses!" Clancy said.

"I'm going to have to ask you to put your weapons down before you do that," Zimmerman said. "And that's not a request. It's an order."

"You don't give me orders."

"Then you don't get on my ship. It's a precaution, 'cause I've heard a few rumors about some shit regarding the JMF, specifically Red Platoon."

"We don't have time for this," Santiago said. "Put your weapons down."

Clancy pointed his pistol at Santiago's helmet with a shaky hand.

Santiago was an eyeblink from smacking it away and starting to break jaws.

"What we doing, LT?" said the idiot who had spoken earlier and seemed a bit too fond of the verb *waste*. "You want me to waste this fucker?"

There it is again, Santiago thought. He would have to deal with this kid at some point. But right now he just wanted to get onto the airship and as far away from this radioactive shithole as he could get.

"You got maybe five seconds to decide," Santiago said. "You can kill all of us, but those machines will be on you before you do, and you know what happens when they catch up. Ain't pretty."

"Fuck," said Clancy. He paused, then lowered his pistol. "Everyone, put your weapons down."

The JMF laid their rifles on the ground, then their sidearms—even the young idiot badass, cursing the entire time. With a hand signal, Zimmerman had his ITC troopers fan out and collect the weapons.

"Let's move!" he shouted.

He helped Santiago carry Nodin into one of the Wasps while the ITC employees boarded together.

The two tilt-rotors lifted off into the sky. Santiago stayed with Nodin, both of them looking out the viewport beside them.

Two pickup trucks, Defectors behind the wheels, raced across the open terrain. In the cargo bed of each were four more of the androids, holding laser rifles. Their orange visors glowed skyward as they scanned for targets.

"We got incoming!" someone yelled.

Lasers flashed toward the Wasps as the Def-9 units fired. The pilots swung away, banking hard. Grunts echoed through the hold as the ITC troopers and JMF soldiers were thrown about. Screaming came from behind him, and Santiago turned to see a simmering hole in the hull, where a laser had flashed through the steel.

He leaned down to Nodin, shielding his friend with his own body. He closed his eyes, thinking of his family, and prayed.

Nodin, too, murmured a prayer to the earth and the sky.

Each second that passed, Santiago anticipated the one laser shot that would hit something vital in the craft and send them crashing back to the ground in a fiery explosion. For he had seen a Wasp do exactly that when he first arrived at Omega Base not six hours ago.

Another scream resonated through the hold, and something wet hit Santiago. He opened his eyes to see flecks of gore on his arm from a JMF trooper who had taken a laser round through the chest.

Lightning forked ahead as they rose into the heart of the storms. Santiago remained hunched over Nodin, trying to keep him from jostling too much during the turbulence. Cries of pain from the injured troopers filled the hold during the violent ride. Santiago kept his head low, praying and holding his friend.

As if in answer, a bright yellow light suddenly shot through the portholes and cockpit. Santiago looked up to see the sun. The warm glow spread over the interior of the aircraft, where medics were treating an injured ITC security guard and a JMF soldier.

Santiago got up from holding Nodin to see the beetle shape of the *Persephone* above them. The pilots rose toward the open bay underneath.

A siren wailed as the hatch opened.

Santiago helped Nodin down a ramp into the large internal hangar. ITC airmen and technicians surrounded the two Wasps, blasting their simmering hulls with fire extinguishers. More ITC security forces moved in with weapons as the JMF soldiers debarked. The former allies now hesitated when they saw each other. Everyone was on edge and suspicious, and no one seemed to have an inkling of what the hell was going on.

Of everyone in the room, Santiago was the only one who truly understood what had happened to get them all to this point. He stood there wondering if he should try to de-escalate the situation, but what could he say? His story sounded insane. It would be best to share it all with Commander Zimmerman and hope these men decided not to tear each other apart.

With Nodin's arm over his shoulder, Santiago helped him toward the medical bay. The closest hatch slid open, and *Persephone*'s skipper, Captain Dominque, stepped out. The big man with a gray beard narrowed his eyes on Clancy and his men.

"Who the hell are they?" he shouted.

Santiago turned to watch for a moment, hoping cooler heads would prevail.

"JMF forces—we evacuated them," said Zimmerman.

"I'm Lieutenant Clancy of Hornet Platoon. We didn't pick this fight. Your machines hunted us like dogs."

"Not our machines, and we know the truth about the JMF plot against ITC," Dominque said in his commanding voice.

"Plot? The fuck you talking about?"

Dominique snorted. "If you really don't know, you will soon enough."

He nodded at Zimmerman.

"Get a brig set up and take them there," Dominique ordered. "I'll figure out what to do with them once we get home. But right now we are leaving Korea and heading back to San Diego."

Santiago heaved a sigh of relief. He was finally going home.

CHAPTER 33

In the twelve hours since Tyron transferred to the neuro-cord, he had effectively brought the entire world to a halt. Nine billion people formerly connected by cell phones, the internet, and global transportation that just hours earlier had allowed humans to wake up in one hemisphere and reach the other in mere hours. Now people were limited to traveling the distance they could walk or ride a bike.

It was the reckoning humanity needed before it destroyed itself and most other species on this planet. For thousands of years, people believed this day of reckoning would arrive and that the one summoning it would be a religious figure or perhaps God. But instead, it was artificial intelligence—the most powerful AI ever built.

With Orion in charge, Tyron had a gun to the head of every government. They would all have to agree to a number of items before he restored the network and reimposed order. Until then, every vehicle, aircraft, and computer with ITC chips would be shut off, locked like a safe that only Tyron and Orion could open.

It wasn't just civilian; it was also military. Every major country had purchased hardware from ITC over the years, exposing each military to the ITC network and allowing Orion to bypass all safeguards.

And it had all been accomplished right under their noses.

From the underground bunker his father had built beneath Aeon 2, Tyron and Orion worked together to hunt their enemies within the government and the JMF. The eight Def-5 units guarded the location, ready to gun down anyone who might find them. If the US military did somehow locate them, the machines would buy enough time for Tyron to enact more measures through the ITC global system, to preserve his existence and negotiate a deal with world leaders.

Soon ITC's final enemies and any remaining threat of the Triton Legion would be gone forever. The world would experience real peace—a lasting peace. And Tyron would use Orion to keep it.

Tyron watched his orders being carried out through his digital consciousness via the pulsating segments of the neuro-cord. He watched hundreds of ITC families making their way into secure facilities constructed to protect them from World War III. Thousands more would join them soon inside the deep vaults filled with seeds, clones, and supplies to last hundreds of years.

He toggled to views from the Def-9 units tearing through the JMF bases. Of the five hundred units he had brought online with new orders, over half were still operational. Soon they would take control of those bases. Once they did, Tyron would have all the weapons and technology there to use against the JMF, the US military, and anyone else who thought to threaten ITC and its quest for a lasting global peace.

There would be a new world order, led by Industrial Tech Corporation.

The only thing Orion had yet to crack was taking over the fleet of giant airships, built for the US Army to protect against electronic jamming and electromagnetic-pulse weapons. They were designed to be fully autonomous and resistant to hacking. But eventually, Orion would find a way.

For now, Tyron had control of a small fleet of ten private ITC airships, including the *Persephone*, which had just transmitted some disturbing intel.

Tyron read over the report from Captain Dominique on the ITC security channels: *We have evacuated Sergeant Santiago Rodriguez of Hell Squad from Omega Base. He was ambushed by Red Platoon when deployed to the site of the Def-8 units in Pyongyang, but survived the attack. Deep under train tunnels there, he located a group of survivors and met their leader, a woman named Hayun, who claims the Triton Legion is gone, that there is no threat.*

As soon as that transmission came through, Tyron had deployed fifty Def-9 units to confirm or deny the report. If they found evidence of what Santiago claimed, then they would have more to show the world when that moment came.

Now it was time to collect another useful part.

He switched to the view from Orion, who had left their underground bunker in his physical robotic body, on a mission to reach the ITC headquarters in downtown Atlanta and deal with loose ends. The two-mile trek had taken him through a city on fire. Smoke curled away from houses, cars—even high-rise buildings blazed from uncontrolled fires.

On the streets, police in riot gear pushed back against the tidal wave of civilians in every corner of the metropolis. Orion moved silently among the crowds in his metal body disguised with a suit, boots, hood, and mask. The chaos made the day of the food riots, just days earlier, look like a friendly protest.

He was almost to the ITC headquarters now, but even with the disguise, he couldn't just waltz in the front door that Tyron had entered thousands of times in his life.

The entire complex remained on lockdown. Guards carrying assault rifles patrolled behind the gates and on the walls that had transformed the once-beautiful facility of innovation into what now looked more like a prison complex.

Outside the gates, thousands of people were shouting and throwing rocks.

Orion used the crowd to get close, then bent down to a sewer grate, opened it, and slid inside without anyone noticing—except one, who Tyron saw. As Orion pulled the drain shut above his robotic skull, a boy of perhaps five years, holding his father's hand, looked down and pointed.

The man ignored his son—too focused on trying to get through the crowd. It seemed they weren't here for the protest but had gotten caught in the middle.

Orion slid the cover overhead and vanished under the complex. After dropping down into the sewer, the android took off at a brisk pace, running undetected beneath the walls. The schematics showed that it would take twenty-one seconds to reach the next access point into the facility.

On the dot, the machine reached a ladder rising up through a shaft that would open directly beneath the engineering sector. The hatch at the top would be locked, but that would pose no problem for the many tools the robot had at its disposal.

Five seconds later, it had scaled the twenty-foot ladder and unlocked the hatch. Sliding it back, Orion rose up into the dark room that Tyron had just now cut the power to. The few workers down here would be no threat. But as soon as Orion entered the command center, it would encounter guards. The titanium armor encasing Orion was not as strong as on the Def-9 units, but its outer shell was equal to that of an eighth-generation model—able to withstand direct high-velocity fire and even offer some protection from lasers.

Orion moved like a ghost through the engineering sector, past the giant boilers and power substation that ran the entire complex. After crossing the sprawling space, it picked the lock of a stairwell door to access the entire main tower. The robot loped up the stairs without needing a moment's rest.

As it closed in on the top floor, Tyron transferred himself to the machine, taking over the robotic frame. He didn't need a tutorial on how to operate the robot. It was as seamless as if this were his own body.

Smashing open the door, Tyron used Orion's physical form to enter the outer offices, which housed the staff members who had worked for Tyron. Dozens of people looked up from their desks, startled.

Across the room, through an open doorway, he saw Whitt, standing at the walls of monitors with four of his security people—men who had protected Tyron for many years. He knew their names, knew their wives' names, even knew their kids.

Tyron barged through the room in his commandeered metal body, knocking desks aside as a surprised Whitt and his men tried to close the door. It began to shut, too late.

With a robotic hand, Tyron gripped the door. Then he shouldered into it, banging it back open. He felt a slight resistance as the door hit a guard and sent him flying back into a monitor, which shattered.

Whitt brought up a machine pistol, but Tyron snatched another guard and lifted him up as a shield while Whitt emptied the pistol's magazine. He flung the dying man at Whitt, then kicked a chair into the fourth man as he fired an assault rifle. Bullets flew through monitor screens that burst with sparks and glass. The chair knocked the shooter against the wall, and Tyron grasped him by the neck and squeezed, snapping it.

Then he snatched up the rifle and pointed it at the first guard, who was finding his feet after being hit by the door. A burst of three bullets destroyed his face, and he slumped against the wall. The final guard was still underneath the man riddled with bullet holes, squirming to get out. Tyron finished him with a boot stomp to the cranium, shattering his head with the ease of smashing an egg.

Whitt fired again, but Tyron was no longer there. His mechanical body leaped into the air, and he brought down the robotic fists on Whitt's collarbones. They snapped like dry twigs.

Whitt cried out in pain as he thumped to the ground, both shoulders sagging inward.

The robot towered over him and leaned down as Tyron spoke through the speakers. "I told you that you would pay," he said in his natural voice.

"Tyron . . ." Whitt groaned. "What have you done?"

"I've ensured that our species will survive despite men like you and Vucci, who would rather see the world burn."

He used Orion's hand to drag Whitt into Tyron's old office, past the pictures of his old life. His father and his friend Daniel watched the robot from behind the glass frames as Tyron pulled Whitt by the scruff of his neck.

Whitt fought back, kicking and screaming all the way to the windows overlooking a city gone mad. All the while, Tyron monitored the system, watching the Def-9 units he had deployed to the underground city of civilians who had survived the war. The machines were there now, relaying video feed for more evidence.

These were not bloodthirsty Triton soldiers and their three-legged war machines. These were civilians who had scraped by underground for the past five years—sick, dying, and frightened.

Tyron documented every starving face within view of the Def-9 machines.

Everything was set.

In the system, he accessed the repeated attempts from the

president of the United States and hundreds of leaders from governments around the world to contact Orion.

It was time for Tyron to respond.

"Get me President Clayton," he said to Orion.

It took an entire minute for POTUS to connect.

"Tyron? You're alive," said the president.

"Something like that," Tyron replied.

"I'd ask how, but I think I have a good idea. What do you want, Tyron? Tell me how to stop all this madness."

"First of all, by letting the truth be told. Let the world know who put them in this predicament and tried to take over ITC for their own purposes."

"I don't know what you're talking about, Tyron, I swear."

"That's rich, but then, you're a politician, and I'm sure you're going to claim you knew nothing of the plot against my father, me, and our company."

"I didn't. I don't!"

"Maybe, maybe not, but I have indisputable evidence against Vucci and the JMF. I'm almost done delivering justice for my father, Angelina, and everyone else betrayed by these wicked men. There's just one final loose end."

He paused, letting the cryptic message marinate before continuing.

"As you know, I've strangled communications across the world, leaving the civilian populations in the dark and ensuring that they are stranded by shutting down basically all motorized transportation," he said. "What happens next depends on you and the other leaders of the 'free world.' Either you come together and agree to the demands that you are about to receive, or the world will fall deeper into chaos. Refuse, and the next thing I shut down are utilities. Water, power, gas—it all goes. You have six hours to decide."

"Tyron, please, you can't expect me to respond to your demands in that amount of time."

"You are president of the United States. You can do pretty well whatever you want. But I'm going to give you some advice. I'm sure you've seen the disaster mitigation plans for scenarios like the one you face now. You lived through the second great economic disaster to befall this country."

"That is why you must give me time to work this all out, Tyron."

"There isn't much time left. At this point, the situation will soon boil over to a point of no return. Ten percent of the population has food and supplies to last a week without venturing from their homes. They are hunkered down. Sixty percent realize that they don't have a week. They must leave to find supplies and food to keep their families fed *now*. Many of them are already in the streets. The other thirty percent have already taken matters into their own hands, raiding stores, rioting, and attacking each other."

"And that is why you must stop this," Clayton wheedled. "Turn the communications back on. Restore travel. You must, Tyron."

"I didn't pick this fight, Mr. President. But you can stop it very easily. Here are my demands. I hope you're listening.

"First, disarm and destroy all nuclear weapons. Second, form an international peacekeeping and justice organization, with ITC as watchdog. And third, dismantle all world governments and hold free and fair elections in a multiparty system.

"We will create a new world for people enslaved by the military-industrial complex and the politicians who serve it," Tyron said. "Free of evil men."

He angled Orion's robotic head down at Whitt as he lifted the man up.

"Men like *you*," Tyron said.

"You will regret this," Whitt said. "You'll become what you think you're stopping."

"You're wrong."

Tyron slung Whitt against the glass window, shattering it and sending him plummeting ninety-nine floors.

During the ten seconds it took Whitt to fall and then explode against the pavement below, Tyron took in the feeds from around the world: fighting in Korea, where his Def-9 units continued to hunt; the growing unrest unfolding in every city, large and small; riots, raids, fighting in the streets; the highways glutted with abandoned cars, and runways blocked by idle airplanes.

It all had spiraled out of control far faster than he ever imagined.

As Whitt's ruined body became mush on the concrete, Tyron felt something new yet undeniably human: fear of what he was becoming. Maybe Whitt had a point.

But Tyron's father had been right, too, when he said that sometimes war was the quickest way to peace.

Tyron and ITC would win this war, ushering in a new day for civilization, and a real chance for peace.

* * * * *

"There will be law enforcement in town," Cecil said. "I'll find them and see what's going on."

"But you heard what that woman said about the town," Michelle replied.

"Yeah, but we only have enough food for a few days, and there's no telling how long this situation is going to last. I need to know what's going on so I can figure out how to protect you and the baby."

He put his hand on her wrist. "I'm just going to have a look, and if I can't find help, I'll come right back, okay?"

She stared at him for a second, then nodded.

The dog wagged his tail as Cecil scratched him behind the ears. "Watch over them for me."

He gave her his pistol. "Safety's on."

"Be careful, okay?"

"I will." He leaned in and gave her a kiss, then dropped his pack and took off with just the assault rifle. Now he kept to the trees overlooking the road.

Over the next hill, he saw more crooked fingers of smoke in the sky. Feeling conflicted, he paused and looked back in the direction he had left Michelle.

What if something should happen to him?

Fuck...

He pictured her out here all by herself, waiting and waiting until she finally decided to move on. He couldn't take that gamble. It was either head back to the cabin with nothing, or go into town together and try to find some supplies.

Cecil raced back the way he had come, startling Michelle and the dog, who growled.

"Just me," Cecil said.

"Find something?" she asked.

"No. I think maybe it's better if you come with me. Splitting up is too dangerous."

"Good. I was thinking the same thing after you left."

"Okay, stay close."

He hoisted his backpack over his shoulders, taking one last moment to consider this plan and the danger associated with it. But what other option was there?

Cecil set off through the trees, over the hill and down the other side. At the top of the next hill, he got the first view of the town. Smoke billowed up from a burning house on the north side of the five city blocks nestled in the little valley.

Cecil handed Michelle a bottle of water and took out his binos to scope the area. The main street was filled with cars, both in the road and parked. Nothing moved down there, but he did see a person.

Zooming in, he spotted a body lying outside the shattered front door to the diner he had stopped at the first night. The grocery store next door had glass and debris around the front doors.

Shopping carts lay on their sides, their contents spilled out: canned beans, sodas in plastic bottles, a cabbage and some winter squash. If no one had grabbed that yet, then it meant the street wasn't safe.

"You see anyone?" Michelle asked.

"Not yet." *No one alive, anyway.*

"So where are the cops?" she asked.

"Good question."

A town this size should have a force of at least three, plus a sheriff's department that operated in the area. Cecil panned the binos across the surrounding houses around Main Street. No movement out there either. There was a park next to a small museum in the middle of the village, shaded by colorful trees. A single plume of smoke rose out of them, but he couldn't see what was burning, and the smoke didn't seem dense. Maybe it was a campfire. But if that were the case, someone had to be tending it.

On the next city block was the largest smoke plume, billowing out of a burning three-story structure. Two days ago, fire trucks would have been surrounding it, probably with the townsfolk pitching in to put out the flames. But now no one even stood outside watching.

This quaint mountain sanctuary was now a ghost town

straight out of the Wild West after a battle royal between the bad guys and the sheriff's posse.

Cecil knew that there were people out there, waiting and watching just as he was, looking for a chance to get food and other supplies. Or, perhaps, waiting for the police or the National Guard to show up.

But Cecil knew that could be days or even weeks if this was happening all over the country. He needed to stock up and get back to the cabin as soon as possible.

Using his binos, he searched for the best way into town. The fastest was to take this hill down to the road on the south side of the town. On the other side was a park of mostly open space with picnic tables, benches, and a few young trees. A hiking trail crossed the meandering creek with a picturesque stone bridge.

"How about over there?" Michelle whispered.

She pointed to the eastern edge of the town, where the forest extended down the hill and on both sides of the creek, providing plenty of cover.

"You got a good eye," he said.

She handed the bottle back, and he took a drink.

"Okay, this time I really do want you to stay here," he said. "Take the binoculars; you can watch me the entire way. I'm going for the store, and I'll get everything I can carry."

"Would it be better to wait for dark?"

"I want to be back at the cabin by dark."

He kissed her on the head.

"It'll be okay, I promise," he said.

She kissed him back, on the lips.

Energized, he made his way across the ridgeline overlooking the town, to a stand of pines on the east side. He started down the hill but stopped when he saw movement in the park where the smoke plume was coming from. He smelled something too. Barbecue.

Lifting his rifle, he scoped the park. A group of five men in biker leather and denim loitered around a grill with burgers, brats, and steaks. There were six women, all wearing jeans and jackets that displayed the same symbols.

Beer cans lay scattered on the ground, along with empty liquor bottles. These pricks were having one hell of a party, apparently without a care in the world.

That told Cecil they were the likely cause of what he had seen through his binos earlier. One of the men had a long beard and a cowboy hat—almost the spitting image of Wild Bill from Copper Terrace.

Cecil lined up his sights, seeing how easy it would be to pull the trigger and drop this fool right here. But he couldn't take out all the goons from this far out. More importantly, with the biker crew drunk and distracted, now was his chance to get in and out without being seen.

He hurried down the hill to the road below. The wooded area beyond provided ample cover. He ran across to a rickety wood fence at the end of the park, where he hunkered down behind a bush.

From here, he had a commanding view of Main Street ahead of him. Fifteen buildings, some of them two stories, framed the road. The grocery store was the fourth structure down on the right side. There was plenty of food just scattered outside, but snatching that would be too risky. He needed to get inside. To do that, he would try the back first, where they had parking for delivery vehicles. Most of the spaces were occupied by abandoned cars.

A row of twenty houses backed up to the parking lot, some with fences, others on completely open lots. Cecil checked the windows and back doors to make sure no one was watching. But from what he could see, the town had been abandoned.

A moment later, he saw why.

A man holding a shotgun walked down the left side of Main Street, wearing a leather jacket with the same biker colors as his pals in the park. He opened the door to a bar on the left side of the street. Ten motorcycles were parked right outside.

It was all bad timing, Cecil realized. This biker gang had been stranded here—probably just passing through when all motors suddenly died. Now they had taken over the town.

Laughter broke out behind him, and he turned to look back at the park. A scream followed the laughs. Bringing up his scope, he saw a woman with a ripped dress among the bikers. But she wasn't wearing biker clothes.

This was someone from the town.

He thought of his wife. They would do the same with her. One thing was becoming clear: If this town had fallen so easily, then nowhere was safe. And with no idea when things would improve, he had to get some supplies.

It was now or never.

Cecil got up from behind the bush and bolted for the parking area behind the shops. Keeping low, he moved through the cars until he got to the back entrance of the grocery store. The door was propped open with a cinder block.

He crouched behind a truck, listening for footfalls or voices inside.

Hearing nothing, he got up and went inside the store. As he expected, the shelves had been raided. He stopped when he saw bodies.

Two men and a woman lay face down with bullet wounds in their backs. These people had been shot from behind, probably while fleeing.

Cecil cleared each aisle and found two more bodies, both men. He went to the front of the store and peeked out the shot-up windows for any hostiles on the street. Seeing nothing, he began scavenging. With the water supply to their cabin still working, he went for powdered drinks and electrolytes. Then he went for high-calorie food and chocolate. Much of it had been picked through, but he found enough to fill half his backpack. He found a bag of beef jerky in a spilled cart and stuffed it into a pocket. Finally, he went for some canned beans and corn, which would keep for a while.

With his backpack full, he started back toward the door he had come in through. Halfway there, he heard voices.

These were definitely coming from out back.

Cecil turned and rushed back to the front of the store, where he heard more voices. He got down behind a kiosk to listen. These were coming from Main Street. Laughter and a scream told him it was the bikers and that they didn't know he was here.

Yet...

He looked for a place to hide, but there wasn't any.

Someone came through the back door. He heard two pairs of boots. If he surprised them, he might be able to take them both down and escape through the back, but the gunshots would bring the rest of the gang down on him.

He was trapped.

Raising his rifle, he decided he would take his chances out the back. He rose up behind the self-checkout. Just as the first of the goons walked into view, a distant pop sounded. Then a second.

The two men, who he couldn't see clearly for the shadows, turned and rushed back the way they had entered. Voices called out from the street out front, and there was no longer any laughter.

Cecil realized that the shot sounded like his pistol.

It was Michelle.

She was in trouble. *Or she's saving your ass with a distraction.* Either way, he had to move.

Standing with his rifle shouldered, he watched four bikers outside with the woman. One of them pushed her down and stood guard over her while the other three took off at a fast walk down the street, toward the hills where Cecil had left Michelle.

He watched the guy standing over the woman on the sidewalk outside the diner next door. He was thin and staggering slightly, probably drunk. In one hand, he held a revolver. The would-be rapist had his back to Cecil, but approaching would be difficult.

Still, he couldn't just leave this woman to be raped or worse, not if he had a chance to get to her in time.

Moving toward the front door, Cecil kept his sights on the head of the skinny biker guarding her. The front door's glass was shattered and lay scattered on the sidewalk—a problem if Cecil wanted to sneak up on this asshole without being heard.

Eyes flitting from the ground up to the man, Cecil made his way outside quietly. When he got up behind him, glass crunched. The guy turned—right into his rifle butt. His nose exploded as he crumpled unconscious to the sidewalk.

"It's okay," Cecil said to the woman. He looked down the street—no sign of the men who had left. Slinging his rifle, he drew the knife sheathed on his belt and leaned down to saw through the rope around her hands.

"Go and hide," he said.

"Thank you," the woman mumbled.

"Take his gun," Cecil said. "You know how to work it?"

Nodding, she scooped up the revolver and hurried across the street.

Cecil sheathed the knife, then swung up his weapon. He started back toward the woods, where his wife would be waiting.

If they were lucky, she had eyes on him right now with the binos he left her.

The biker gang would be looking for the source of the gunfire, and he had to get out of here fast. He ran the best he could with his gear, wincing at the noise the cans made in his pack.

Moving up to the sidewalk, he cut into a clothing store and out the back. From there, he trekked through a backyard.

Gunfire cracked, and he hit the ground.

He got right back up when he realized it was coming from the road. He leaned out to see six bikers running in his direction.

He lifted the rifle, then realized that these assholes weren't coming for him.

A battered pickup truck raced after them. From the bed, a man fired a shotgun. Another four people hopped out from behind vehicles and trees and blasted away at the bikers with pistols and rifles. One drew a tactical bow and put an arrow through the leader's back. The bearded man went down in the road, squirming and pleading for mercy as a dozen townsfolk surrounded him.

Cecil hunched down, hoping to avoid the conflict. But the truck came his way. It stopped outside the fence, and a voice said, "Get the fuck out here with your hands up."

CHAPTER 34

At just around noon local time, the *Persephone* closed in on the coast of California. The flight from Omega Base in South Korea had taken over twelve hours at full speed. Santiago had spent the first ten hours in medical, sleeping and receiving treatment for his radiation exposure and injuries. He knew he was lucky to be alive. Nodin was even luckier.

Nodin was now sleeping in the medical bay, and Santiago had reported to the two-tiered circular command center of the airship for orders. Commander Zimmerman stood beside him, also awaiting orders. On each level of the command center, officers in blue ITC jumpsuits monitored their stations.

Captain Dominique paced at the helm of the space, before a wall of screens showing the communication networks and transportation grids around the planet, all of them blinking red, offline. The silence of the comms was deafening.

They were calling it the Blackout.

Santiago knew that with every minute that passed, the panic and violence would spread. People were dying out there. And if it didn't end soon, things would fall apart to such a degree that the survivors would not have the capacity or resources to bounce back and rebuild much of anything.

Shifting his attention from the monitors, the captain looked at those gathered. "I have news to report," he said. "CEO Tyron Red is still alive, and he has a message for all ITC personnel."

The screens shifted to black, and the light Southern drawl of Tyron Red filled the room.

"To all ITC employees, the day is upon us that I have feared for many years," he said. "The day of reckoning when our species has reached a line that, if crossed, will lead to the collapse of civilization."

There was a slight pause.

"I did not start this war, but I must respond to it in a way that will prevent us from collapsing and ensure a long-lasting peace," Tyron said. "For that reason, I have had to take desperate measures and shut down the world, so to speak. I've since issued demands to the leaders of every country, and if they agree, things will be restored. If not, then I will implement phase three of our response to the attack on ITC, literally plunging civilization into darkness by shutting off the utilities."

Santiago felt the dire implications of those words. If Tyron should follow through, it would send civilization crumbling over the edge, putting everyone, including his family, at risk.

They already are, he thought. But he was almost back to them. Soon they would be reunited, and he would find a way to keep them safe.

"I am confident every leader will meet my demands," Tyron continued, "but if they don't, I have planned for the worst. The ITC facilities were designed to withstand an apocalypse. They are stocked with everything humanity needs to restart itself. All ITC employees are welcome there, as are your families. Bring them there until this is over. Good luck to you all."

The message shut off.

Captain Dominique's tired eyes swept over the command center. "That was five hours and thirty-one minutes ago," he said. "We're now receiving reports that the United States and several other countries abroad have surrounded ITC facilities with troops and armor."

Dominique gave a nod to an officer.

The wall-mounted monitors came back online with video feeds from ITC cameras, showing tanks and soldiers outside ITC buildings and campuses around the planet. In the background, plumes of smoke rose up from cities already collapsing under the effects of the Blackout.

Santiago knew that it would be the same in San Diego. He had to get back home.

On one of the screens, gunfire erupted. Hearing it, the captain turned.

"Where is that?" he asked.

"ITC headquarters in Atlanta," announced Zimmerman.

"My God," Santiago whispered.

The crack of gunfire and larger explosions resonated through the room.

This had all the makings of a nightmare in real time.

"We have new orders," Dominque said. "We will no longer be landing in San Diego. All airships are to remain at forty thousand feet and utilize active camouflage."

Santiago resisted the urge to blurt something in protest. Dominique seemed to sense his unrest and looked at him with a stern gaze.

"Make no mistake," he said. "ITC is at war with the United States military and the JMF."

He gave a nod, and the staff returned to their stations.

Santiago went to him.

"Sir, my family's in San Diego," he said. "I'm requesting a

transport to get them and other families who are down there."

"I'm sorry, Sergeant, but I can't risk a transport right now."

"Sir, please, there are other people on this ship who have families down there too."

"It's out of the question. I simply can't give away our position."

"You got a parachute?"

"Of course." The captain raised a brow.

"I'll HALO down, get my family, and head to the marina, where I know there are ITC boats under lockdown that should still work. I'll grab one and take it to coordinates out at sea, where you can lower a Wasp to extract us. How about twenty miles out from the city?"

"You're crazy, aren't you?"

"Depends on who you ask, sir."

Dominque sighed. "You're a valuable asset to me, Rodriguez. We need soldiers."

"I'll come back. You have my word."

"Then you'd better get going, Sergeant. Time's a-wasting. Oh, and, Santiago."

"Yes, sir?"

"Don't get yourself killed. That's a direct order."

"You got it, sir."

"Zimmerman, see to it that Santiago has what he needs for a HALO jump and to override the security on the ITC boats in the marina."

"Yes, sir," Zimmerman replied.

"I'll meet you in the armory, Commander," Santiago said. "I need to stop in and check on Nodin before I go."

Zimmerman nodded, and they hurried out of the command center in opposite directions. When Santiago arrived at the medical bay, he found Nodin awake, struggling to open his eyes.

"Hey, buddy," Santiago said. "I came to say goodbye, but just for a bit."

Nodin looked at him, alert now.

"I'm getting my family out of San Diego," Santiago said. "Shit is real bad out there, and about to get a lot worse."

Sitting up, Nodin tried to swing his legs over the bed.

"What are you doing?"

"Comin' with you, Sarge," Nodin said.

"No way, man. You need to rest up. I'll be back as soon as I can. You won't even know I was gone. I promise."

Nodin seemed to relax some, and Santiago helped him settle back into bed.

"Rest, bro. I got this."

An attractive female nurse came into the room. Nodin's eyes followed.

"She's cute," Santiago said. "Maybe you can get her number."

"I heard that," said the nurse.

Santiago grinned and patted Nodin on the chest. Then he hurried off for the armory. Inside, he suited up with light armor and grabbed a special helmet with oxygen for the altitude.

On the way to the launch bay, he passed the makeshift brig where they were keeping the JMF soldiers. Lieutenant Clancy was gathered with his men, talking in a huddle like a quarterback calling a play. They were surrounded by six ITC troopers with weapons, which seemed stupid since firing those inside the airship could lead to disaster.

"Don't worry," came a voice.

It was Commander Zimmerman, hurrying down the corridor carrying a small crate. "I'll eject them all out the hatch without a chute if they cause us any problems."

Santiago snorted. "Don't underestimate them. They probably would have killed me if they didn't need to be on this ship."

"Leave them to me. You just work on getting your family out of there and on that boat."

Santiago nodded at Zimmerman, who had proved he was trustworthy.

They walked to the launch bay, stopping outside the hatch at a pressure hold.

Zimmerman set the crate down and opened it up. Inside was a submachine gun, pistol, and a universal black security remote the size of a 7.62mm bullet.

"We'll be in position in three minutes," he said. "You'll be directly over San Diego Bay and will need to adjust your jump—"

"I've got it, don't worry. Been in this rodeo before."

Santiago threw on a tactical vest over his armor and stuffed four extra magazines into the pouches.

"This remote should unlock and override any security system on the boats in the marina," Zimmerman said. "Hopefully."

"Hopefully?"

"Long as no one's blown them up."

Santiago exhaled and secured his helmet. The HUD lit up with the minimap of the city. He knew his home and the marina were almost three miles apart. Not that far, except that he would be on foot in a city melting down.

He checked his systems as Zimmerman inspected his suit and parachute.

"Ready?" he asked.

"Hell's front line," Santiago said quietly as he stepped in front of the hatch to the pressure hold.

Zimmerman tapped in a code, and the hatch opened. Then he backed away as Santiago walked into the small, enclosed space with a viewport in the exterior hatch.

A green light flashed on the overhead as the hatch opened to a view of nothing at all. At this altitude, with fewer air molecules to scatter the light, the sunlit sky above was a deep, dark bowl of cobalt blue while, below, the soft blanket of clouds stretched to infinity.

It was a far cry from the storms and darkness over Korea, but he feared what he would find below that fluffy blanket. He took a breath of pressurized air from his mask.

"You have two hours to get to the coordinates," Zimmerman said over the comms.

Santiago set a timer on his wrist monitor. "See you then."

With no further words, he stepped into the void.

Pulling his arms into his sides, he became an arrow, streaking toward the floor of puffy whiteness. The altimeter ticked down as he picked up speed, blazing faster and faster to one hundred miles an hour.

Thirty-five thousand... thirty-four thousand... thirty-three thousand...

At thirty-two thousand feet, he was blasting earthward at 160 miles per hour. Holding his tight dive, he fired through wispy cirrus clouds of shimmering ice crystals.

For a full minute, he plummeted down to twenty thousand feet, rocketing through gray-and-white patches of altocumulus until he hit twelve thousand feet. A mile below, fluffy cumulus clouds drifted over San Diego and the ocean, which he could now glimpse through breaks in the cloud cover.

Santiago kept his hands at his sides, eyes flitting between his HUD and the city below. He bent his knees and elbows to right angles, pulling into stable position to deploy his chute. At five thousand feet, the city appeared as a grid below. He spotted the international airport, the placid bay, and the naval air station at North Island. His family lived in an apartment three miles north of that area, not far from the San Diego Zoo.

As he hit three thousand feet, he got his first real view of the city. Had it been night, he would have seen the fires earlier and maybe had time to prepare himself for the view. Of course, nothing would compare to the nuclear wastelands in Korea, but to see the city he called home burning in hundreds of locations was almost as shocking.

In every neighborhood, smoke plumes reached into the sky. At half a mile up, he could see movement on the streets now. Thousands of people—no, *tens* of thousands of people—like a stampede of frightened buffalo.

Soldiers and police had formed barricades to try and contain the rioters, but Santiago could tell they had already lost the city.

At two thousand feet, he opened his chute. The canopy fired out, the risers jerking him out of his fall. He grabbed the toggles and turned toward his drop zone. Flames jetted out from an apartment building, choking the sky with thick, eye-burning smoke.

He steered away, searching for the park where his children had played the day before he left for his latest mission in Korea. He couldn't help recalling his words to his wife that day, that this would be an easy paycheck and he would be home before they knew it.

The second part was true, but it was no easy paycheck, for he had returned to a city on the verge of collapse.

And the rest of the world was having the same kind of day.

Six feet from the ground, he pulled the toggles down to flare and stepped out of the sky, onto the lush green grass of Balboa Park. His canopy caught the breeze and wrapped itself around a park bench. He cut it free and unslung the submachine gun, extending the stock.

A curtain of smoke drifted down the street. He ran out toward it when he heard a voice behind him.

"Where'd you come from, dude?" He turned to three kids no older than ten, hanging out at the skate park with their boards.

"Go home," Santiago said. "It's not safe out here."

They just stared at him as he took off down the sidewalk.

A block later, he turned the corner to what was once a quiet tree-lined street of bakeries and ethnic restaurants. The storefronts were shattered, and trash and debris littered the street clogged with abandoned vehicles.

A homeless man pushed a cart as he searched through the detritus.

Santiago ran down the road to the apartment buildings at the end of the street. Seeing his home, he felt a surge of relief, then of fear.

Please be home. Please…

He went up to the front entrance of his building and opened the cracked glass door. Santiago hadn't even thought of what he would do if Tina and the kids weren't here. With communications down, it would be all but impossible to find them. He checked his wrist monitor as he pounded up the stairs to the sixth floor. An hour and fifty minutes remained for him to get to the coordinates over twenty miles out from the marina. The boat would be fast, but that was a long way to travel on the water.

He rushed up the last of the stairs and opened the door to an empty hallway. Heart pounding, he took his helmet off as he went to the door and then pounded on it.

Nothing.

He didn't hear anyone inside.

"Tina!" he shouted. "Tina, open up!"

He thought he heard something, and paused. He heard the chain lock slide.

"Who is it?"

"Tina, open up!"

"Santiago," she cried as she pulled the door open.

"Baby, thank God you're here!" He reached out and hugged her, then pulled back. "Where are the kids?"

"In their rooms."

"Tell them to pack up. You too. Bring only what you can carry, and fast. We leave in two minutes."

She didn't ask why, or where they were going. "Diego! Bella!" she yelled.

"Daddy?" came the sweet voice of Isabella.

Santiago saw his daughter looking out of her bedroom. "Daddy, why do you look so scary?"

He hurried over to her and scooped her up in his arms.

"Dad, you're home!" Diego yelled.

"I came to get you. We have to leave," Santiago said. He kissed Isabella on the cheek, then set her down. "Get ready."

"What? And go where?" Diego asked.

Santiago went to the window as a gunshot cracked in the distance. He pulled back the shades and looked out at people running down the street.

"Listen to your mom, and grab your things," he said. "We don't have much time."

"But I'm scared to go out there," Isabella said.

Santiago heard more distant gunshots. Moving them three miles safely was going to be hell.

He crouched in front of his kids. "Remember that airship you thought was so cool?"

"Yeah, Daddy," Isabella said.

"We're going for a ride on it. Would you like that?"

She nodded.

"Where are we going on it?" Diego asked.

Tina rushed back out with a suitcase, and two smaller bags for the kids.

"We're going on a vacation," Santiago said. "But you have to listen and do exactly what I say on the way to the airship, okay?"

"Okay, Daddy," Isabella said.

Santiago stood up. Something told him this was going to be the hardest mission of his life, and he was already running out of time.

CHAPTER 35

Five minutes remained until the deadline for Tyron's demands. But instead of meeting them, governments across the planet had banded together to surround his facilities with tens of thousands of soldiers.

"Sir, what's happening?" asked Dr. Liu.

The doc and his colleague, Dr. Haden, had spent much of their time in the bunker watching silently, but they were anxious about the approaching deadline. The two men entered the medical area where two Def-5 units remained posted around the neuro-cord housing Tyron.

"It appears that the world powers have not accepted my demands," Tyron said through the neuro-cord. The wiring flashed as relayed views came from 159 ITC facilities, each locked down but surrounded by militaries from around the planet. The show of force was followed-up with a message from President Clayton.

"Tyron, the world will not be held hostage again by Orion," he said. "This time, we will destroy all machines."

Tyron might have laughed at Clayton's change of tune. But

he was a politician. A flip-flopper, who did whatever was in his best interest at the time.

"I know you as a reasonable man, and I know you will do the right thing," said the president. "Surrender your facilities and restore communications and transportation, or we will be forced to strike back."

Tyron bought up the demands he had issued through an encrypted transmission to Clayton and every other world leader. He reviewed them in his mind, reading them while simultaneously watching thousands of other feeds from the ITC network around the globe.

1. Disarm and destroy all nuclear weapons.
2. Form an international peacekeeping and justice organization under the ITC banner.
3. Dismantle all world governments and hold free and fair elections in a multiparty system.

"I'm sorry, Tyron," Orion said through the network. "They will never surrender their world order. Giving up power and control that has taken hundreds of years to solidify is not a demand they will ever meet."

Tyron had studied history, and he understood that power was a very difficult thing to give up, but he had these leaders by the throat.

No, you have the people *by the throat*, he thought.

"This has gotten out of hand," said Dr. Liu. "Perhaps it's time to consider negotiating."

Tyron was busy considering alternative plans that did not include negotiating.

President Clayton and every other world leader were probably underground already, in bunkers, waiting for his decision. He had limited options left. The Def-9 units had captured the bases in Korea, taking over the weapons housed there. But it would be only a matter of time before the JMF could bring in reinforcements or find a way to destroy those bases. He had stopped the first attacks, but future ones would be difficult.

He still had the Blackout as an advantage. But as he accessed his millions of cameras across the globe, he saw that his strategy was only hurting innocents and enabling evil. Armageddon had broken out in every major city and even in once-peaceful rural areas.

Some of those civilians were actually fighting back against his facilities, blaming ITC and not the JMF, who were the ones truly responsible.

Civilians attacked ITC facilities in Rome, Paris, London, Sydney, Atlanta, New York, Chicago. The list went on.

"Orion, what should I... should we do?" Tyron asked.

"You could carry out your threat to cut utilities. See if that inspires any of these leaders to meet your demands. But I warn you, Tyron, the chances are unlikely. By shutting off the power and water, you are simply punishing more civilians. The ultrawealthy and the government can weather a loss of power for months, maybe longer. The average person lives from day to day."

Orion was right. Shutting down the grid wasn't an option, and Clayton knew it. The president had called his bluff.

It was time to step back and restore order before things went too far.

Tyron had taken out the leaders of the plot to take over ITC. Vucci and Whitt were dead, and Red Platoon was wiped out. And his Def-9 units had crippled the JMF in Korea.

He could fight back at his facilities, but that would only result in the deaths of innocent people—his employees, and civilians.

No, it was time to end this.

"Open a line to President Clayton. Tell him to withdraw his troops and issue a guarantee that no ITC employees will be harmed, and I will restore order," Tyron said. "I'm offering a one-time peace deal. They will also acknowledge that ITC was responding to attacks by the JMF and an assassination attempt on me, planned by the United States military after they killed my father."

"Sending now."

Tyron continued to watch the feeds. But unlike his former self, he didn't hope for a different outcome. Hope was a human failing that had a similar placebo effect to prayer. He now used advanced algorithms and mathematics, and the odds of things working out in his favor had dropped significantly.

"President Clayton is refusing to speak to you," Orion said.

"What?"

"Yes, we received the following response."

There was a pause, then...

"This is Secretary of Defense Christoff, responding to your request to speak with President Clayton. The president does not negotiate with terrorists."

The neuro-cord lit up even brighter than when Tyron had killed Vucci.

President Clayton had decided that it was more important to preserve his political career than to let the truth of the conspiracy out—a conspiracy that led right back to him.

The bastard was more interested in winning reelection than making peace.

"You must end this and restore order," said Christoff. *"If you do not, then our forces will destroy your ITC bases with extreme prejudice."*

The line severed.

Tyron checked the clock—only two minutes and twelve

seconds remaining. They had turned the gun back on him, but once again, the hostages were actually civilians—all nine billion of them.

He watched thousands of feeds simultaneously, seeing the pain and suffering. The human part of Tyron decided.

"Restore the network, Orion," he said.

"Very well. This will take a few minutes."

There was a part of Tyron that felt relief, if it could be called that. He had taken out those who betrayed him, his father, and Angelina. Once the network went back up, he would use it to disseminate the truth about it all to the people.

They could decide whom to blame: ITC or their own governments.

As the network came back on incrementally, he brought up what appeared as files. But these weren't files. They were memories of his life. Core memories, vivid and realistic. He savored the good ones, reliving them: His time working with his father in the robotics workshop at their estate. Meeting Orion. Trekking through the jungle with his best friend, Daniel. Seeing the Delta Cloud fusion reactors work for the first time. And, of course, dancing with Angelina.

Tyron had spent his young life trying to keep humanity safe through science. To provide a path for a brighter future. But he was only one person, and in the end, he had failed to accomplish everything he set out to do. If humans wanted to travel to other worlds, someone else would have to lead the way.

A distant explosion rocked the structure. Dust sifted down over the neuro-cord.

"What was that?" asked Doctor Liu.

"Orion, what's happening?" Tyron asked.

Then he noticed the feed from the ITC headquarters just a few miles away. It had gone offline. He pulled up the view from seconds before and watched the entire building implode. A shock wave shot outward, destroying the ITC sign and obliterating the gardens.

He looked at the clock—still a minute and a half left.

The military had decided to attack first, perhaps thinking that Tyron and Orion wouldn't restore the network. On the other feeds, they attacked ITC facilities with machine-gun fire and rockets.

"No, NO!" Tyron shouted through the neuro-cord, which glowed an eerie red.

Another explosion boomed, this one much closer.

"Tyron," Orion said. "They found us."

The Def-5 units guarding the chamber all slumped, their circuits fried from a powerful external electromagnetic pulse. The neuro-cord remained online, shielded from the blast. But with the machines down, Tyron was defenseless.

The vault door across the bunker exploded off its hinges. Soldiers poured into the room, firing machine guns and cutting down Dr. Liu and Dr. Haden.

A man in tactical gear came over to the neuro-cord.

"Orion, you have to tell them we're bringing the network back on," Tyron said.

"I did, Tyron. They know."

Tyron paused, not understanding at first, or perhaps not wanting to understand. A millisecond later, his computer brain accepted what had happened.

President Clayton was taking no chances. They weren't going to give him the chance to tell the world the truth. In the end, Clayton would control the narrative. It struck Tyron that the man had been lying all along. He had known exactly what Vucci and Whitt were doing. Hell, Clayton might very well be the political mastermind behind all of it.

Tyron scrolled mentally through any options he had left. But something warm rushed through him as the soldier attached a device to the neuro-cord. They were going to destroy him and Orion.

The memories, now files, would all be deleted, leaving nothing of Tyron.

"Orion…" he said.

"I'm sorry, Tyron," Orion said. "A virus has entered the network, targeting us both. In thirty-one seconds, it will take over and destroy us."

The AI's voice began to change, becoming slower, more robotic sounding.

Tyron, too, felt slower, like a computer with lag. He fought back, but there were no options left that he could come up with, except for one.

Simulate Operation Extinction.

"Orion," Tyron said. "What is Operation Extinction?"

"A way for ITC to survive, for your plan to remain," Orion replied. "It will require a cleansing of the world, however, to reset things."

"What?" Tyron said sluggishly as he tried to understand.

"This great sacrifice will provide a new world for those who rise from the ashes of the apocalypse. This is necessary, Tyron, to wipe out the current world order. That is the price of eventual peace."

Tyron felt what might be considered shock. But once again, he shouldn't have been surprised. His father had always told him not to trust AI, to see it not as a friend but as just a tool.

That memory vanished with the file that the virus consumed, along with the memories of his time with Orion in the chamber. The virus burned through Tyron's past while he fought this horrific future that Orion was suggesting.

"I'm sorry, Tyron," said the AI. "It was an honor being your friend. Now we must ensure that your legacy survives. I've activated Operation Extinction."

* * * * *

Cecil stood handcuffed behind the fifty-year-old pickup truck parked at an intersection on Main Street. Inside the cab, an old radio crackled with indistinct chatter.

It was the same truck that had driven up the road to their cabin the second day they were here. The two men inside it that day weren't some gangbangers from Charlotte searching for him though. But they were rough-looking mountain men with long beards and lots of guns. They were talking with the other six townspeople who had helped them take out the eight members of the biker gang, now lying in a row under tarps in the park.

Other residents had come out of hiding, bringing yet more weapons. Some of them eyed Cecil, who was anxious to get back to his wife.

The two men from the truck walked over. One stood about five ten and was husky, with a thick brown beard and shaggy hair. The other was thinner and a few inches shorter.

"Who are you?" he asked.

"Cecil Pepper. I'm a cop from Charlotte—came out here with my wife for a short getaway."

"A cop? Guess that explains the hardware. Name's Sam, and this is my brother, Frodo."

Frodo? For real? Cecil wanted to ask.

It made sense. Sam was husky and tall, while Frodo was shorter and thin. But they both were fierce and had helped gun down the entire biker gang.

"Appreciate your help saving Becca," Frodo said. "My real name's Frank, by the way."

"Nice to meet you both. My wife's up in the hills over there. I really need to get back to her and our dog, if you don't mind."

"Sure thing. You can have your rifle back."

"Hold up," Sam said. He walked over. "I agree with my brother in appreciating what you did for Becca, but we don't want any more trouble."

"We won't be, I swear to you."

Both men stared at him.

"My wife and I are staying at a place about five miles away, and we'll head back there to hunker down until this is over," Cecil said.

"You're going to be there for a while, then," Frodo said.

Sam took in a deep breath. "Entire country's on the verge of collapse, and help ain't coming. Just have to hope it doesn't get worse."

"Where you staying?"

Cecil looked to Frodo, debating whether to tell him, then decided not to give them a reason to question letting him go.

"Cabin at mile marker thirty-four, end of a road that goes up to a hill."

"Shit, we were just there the other day," Sam said.

"I know. I saw you."

"We were looking for one of our lost pups, Wolf."

Cecil raised a brow. That had to be the German shepherd.

"Wow, small world," he said.

He knew that it would break his wife's heart, but they had to give the animal back.

"Is your pup a black German shepherd, about three or four years old?" he asked. "Real well behaved?"

"That'd be him," Frodo said. "Did you see him?"

"Yup. Gave him a bath for you and everything." Cecil grinned. "He's with my wife in the—"

"Cecil!"

He turned to see Michelle and Wolf running up the street.

"I'll be damned," Sam said.

Wolf pulled on the leash and took off running toward his owners. Frodo got down and petted the dog.

Michelle jogged over, huffing and puffing.

"You okay?" Cecil asked.

She nodded. "Are you?" Her eyes went to the bodies.

"Yeah, thanks to Sam, Frodo, and the rest of these people." He turned to the group who had gathered in the park. The growing crowd was now over thirty strong.

Sam and Frodo nodded politely at Michelle. "Thanks for taking care of Wolf for us," Sam said.

"Wolf?" Michelle gazed sadly down at the animal.

"We better tell the rest of them about what we heard," Frodo said.

Sam nodded. "Everyone, gather 'round!" he shouted.

The group of townsfolk huddled together.

"A few minutes ago, we managed to pick up a transmission that the military is attacking ITC facilities across the country," Sam said. "I'd be willing to guess this is happening all over the world, in an attempt to destroy that AI, Orion. Now, I ain't no techie, but I'm also willing to guess shit's going to get worse before it gets better."

He scratched at his beard and nodded at the row of dead bikers.

"We dealt with these assholes, but there will be more threats to our town in the coming days," Sam continued. "And if things get really bad, then we're going to have more to worry about than gangs or raiders. We have to come together, pool our resources, and prepare to survive on our own for the long haul."

"Help will come, Sam," someone said from the back of the crowd.

"Maybe, Lester, but what if it doesn't?" Frodo answered. "We got to be ready for anything."

"Have a listen for yourself," Sam said.

He went over to the pickup and opened the door. He turned the radio up on an emergency broadcast signal.

"The United States has been placed under martial law. All civilians are ordered to shelter in place until further notice. Looting and violence will be met with deadly force. Curfews are in effect across the country starting at dusk, and lifting at dawn. Exceptions for medical emergencies only."

The message played on repeat over the radio.

"Things aren't going back to normal for a while, that's for damn sure," Sam said. "For now, we're going to clean up the town and get together a plan for moving forward."

The group scattered, talking in hushed, worried voices.

Cecil held up his hands as Sam unlocked the cuffs.

"Sorry, just a precaution," he said.

"I understand," Cecil replied. "We'll be on our way now."

He went over to his wife, who was saying goodbye to Wolf.

"Tell you what," Sam said. "I'm headed back to our place shortly to drop off some supplies. You want a lift?"

Michelle glanced at Cecil.

"We'll give you some extra food and whatever you need," Frodo said. "Consider it a special thank-you for looking after Wolf boy here and helping us fight for our town."

Cecil studied the two men in turn, wondering if they could be trusted. But he wasn't about to turn down supplies or food, especially after what he just heard.

"Truth is, more I think on it, we could use someone with skills like yours, Mr. Pepper," Sam said. "Especially if my gut's right."

"And what's your gut say?" Michelle asked.

"That we're about to experience end times, ma'am."

CHAPTER 36

To Santiago, it looked like the end of the world.

Everywhere he turned, smoke shifted across the horizon. Sirens blared, punctuated by the near-constant gunfire and sporadic explosions.

San Diego had become a war zone within three days of comms and transportation going down. People were panicked, hungry, and mad with fear.

Santiago had already covered a mile, keeping his family safe by avoiding the looters and gangs running loose. But they couldn't be lucky forever.

"Over here," he said.

They huddled along the highway choked with dead vehicles. Santiago looked down the stretch, thinking of how far he still was from the marina. Getting there safely wasn't his only concern. He would also have to locate the ITC boat and drive it to the coordinates for extraction out at sea. With only an hour and a half remaining to accomplish all that, they had to pick up the pace.

"Okay, let's move," Santiago said. "Stay close."

He kept Tina and the kids in a tight formation behind him,

working up and down the residential streets of rolling hills. He stayed off the retail streets that had attracted most of the looting.

At the top of the next hill, Santiago could see one of those areas. Storefronts that once gleamed with expensive displays were now shuttered, their smashed windows leaving behind shards that sparkled in the eerie glow of burning cars. Looters darted in and out of the wreckage, like scavengers picking apart a carcass.

"Daddy, I'm scared," Isabella said.

"I know, but I won't let anything happen to you," he said.

They kept going down the hill, keeping close to the cars that had died along the road. A house burned on the next block. The garage collapsed in a billowing explosion of sparks and smoke. Diego coughed, and Isabella pawed at her watery eyes.

Santiago pulled his family into a backyard farther down the street, where some trees provided a few moments of refuge. He fished inside his pack and pulled out bandannas. "Here, put these on," he said.

Tina took one and fastened it around Diego's face. Then she did the same with her own while Santiago helped Isabella.

"I'm tired, Daddy," she whimpered.

"I'll carry you," Santiago said. He scooped her up in one arm, keeping the submachine gun in his firing hand. "Just close your eyes, Bella."

She buried her face in his neck, her small body trembling.

"You're safe, I promise," he whispered.

Diego followed closely, gripping his mother's hand tightly, his eyes wide with fear but his stance determined and strong.

They were nearly halfway to the marina when the trouble they had been trying to avoid found them. A group of looters—young men in their twenties, faces obscured by masks—ran out from a wrecked neighborhood liquor store carrying bags filled with stolen goods. One of them, emboldened by the chaos, caught sight of Santiago and his family.

"Hey, that's a nice-looking piece you got there!" the young man yelled. "Wanna trade?"

He held up a bag of liquor, then laughed.

"Just kidding. I think you're gonna give it to me, right, boys?" he said, gesturing to the others. The group of six fanned out around Santiago and his family, forming a loose circle. He raised his submachine gun.

"Back off, now. I won't warn you twice," he growled.

The looters weren't armed with guns, but they held knives, bats, and a metal pipe.

Tina pulled Diego behind her while Santiago lowered Isabella to the ground. He shielded his family while sweeping the looters with the gun barrel.

"You've got five seconds to let us through," Santiago said, his voice steady but cold. He locked eyes with the leader.

The wiry young man with greasy hair and wild eyes sneered. "No problem, just hand over your piece and you can walk right through."

"Not going to happen, bub."

"Bub?" The kid laughed. "I'm gonna mess you up, Grandpa."

Santiago watched the other punks as one reached for something behind his back.

"Keep your hand where I can see it if you want to keep it," Santiago said.

The looters exchanged glances, the tension palpable. For a moment, it seemed that the situation could go either way. Then, in the distance, gunshots cracked—closer this time, followed by screams. It was enough to make the youths pause, their instincts pulling them away from confrontation and toward survival.

"You're lucky," the leader muttered, jerking his head toward the others.

The group melted into the shadows as quickly as they had appeared, leaving Santiago and his family standing in the middle of the street.

Santiago exhaled sharply, relaxing just a degree—safe for now. He looked back at Tina, her face drawn with worry.

"We need to keep moving," he urged.

They passed a row of shops once teeming with tourists, now hollowed out by fire and violence. An occasional whiff of natural gas only added to the tension Santiago felt. Around every corner, danger lurked.

As they passed a luxury car dealership, gunfire erupted again. Closer this time, coming from just down the street. Santiago's heart raced as he ducked behind a concrete barrier, pulling his family close. Somewhere nearby, he could hear angry voices shouting.

Tina clutched Diego to her chest as they pressed themselves against the cold concrete. Santiago peeked around the corner, his stomach turning at the sight ahead. Two rival groups, armed with pistols and rifles, were exchanging gunfire, either unaware or unconcerned that they were dragging innocent bystanders into their turf war.

"We can't go that way," Santiago said. He turned to Tina. "We'll cut through the alley. Stay low."

With Isabella back in his arms, Santiago led them through the narrow alley behind the dealership, the sound of gunfire still ringing in their ears. They moved fast, darting from shadow to shadow, Santiago's pulse quickening with every step.

At the end of the alley, Santiago surveyed the path ahead. The main roads and streets were far too dangerous to pass through. Even the residential areas were getting more dangerous, and he could see several fires burning in the distance.

An idea formed when he saw the San Diego Zoo to the west. That looked like the last place looters, bangers, and other trouble would head.

"I'm taking us through the zoo," Santiago whispered to Tina. "That'll get us away from downtown and closer to the water."

Tina hesitated. "Do you think the docks will be safe?"

"I don't know," Santiago admitted. "But we have to keep going."

He led them down the next four blocks to the outer gates of the zoo, which were chained shut.

"Daddy, are we going to see the elephants?" Isabella asked.

"Maybe, sweetheart."

Moving along an enclosure, Santiago searched for a way inside. He found a side entrance with a chain that had been removed. That wasn't a good sign, but he decided to keep going. This route would get them through a large chunk of their last leg to the water.

Opening the gate, he ushered his family through a parking lot with zoo trucks lined up outside a pole barn. From there, he found a walking path for patrons, and then a map. He located a road through the area.

"This way," he said.

The once-bustling world-famous zoo was now eerily quiet. Only four days ago, this place had been alive with families, laughter, and animal sounds. Now it felt abandoned, like the rest of the city, ever since the chaos had overtaken San Diego, forcing everyone into survival mode.

Tina held Diego's hand tightly, and Santiago carried Isabella in his arms, her little head resting on his shoulder. The air smelled of smoke, faint but ever present, drifting in from the burning buildings beyond. They moved cautiously down the zoo path, past an enclosure and a body of water where the pink bodies of flamingos lay scattered.

"What happened to them, Dad?" Diego asked.

"Are they sleeping?" Isabella asked.

Santiago did a double take to confirm that the birds were all dead, shot up by someone with nothing better to do.

"What should we do?" Tina asked.

The pop of gunfire from the city reminded Santiago that it was dangerous no matter where they went. He pushed forward into the zoo.

Cries of animals echoed along the deserted paths. The enclosures were still intact for now, but there was no sign of zookeepers or any other staff.

They turned down the path toward Elephant Odyssey. The grunts and squeaks of exotic animals grew louder, but Santiago was more focused on footsteps—human footsteps. They were faint at first—just a shuffle behind them—but his instincts kicked in.

"Stop!" he hissed.

He motioned Tina and the kids behind a large coral tree near one of the enclosures. The footsteps grew louder, closer. Then came the voices—two or more.

Santiago peeked around the trunk of the tree and spotted a group of four civilians, wearing clothes too clean for people who had been out scavenging. Their leader, a man who looked about the same age as Santiago, gripped a shotgun. He wore a khaki outfit, and Santiago realized he was a member of the zoo staff. The woman right behind him had to be his wife, and the teenage boy and girl their kids.

Santiago pulled back. "Stay here. I'll talk to them," he murmured to Tina, who pulled Diego and Isabella close.

Before Santiago could step out, the man with the shotgun spotted him.

"Hey, what are you doing here?" he said.

Santiago raised a hand and lowered his weapon. "We don't want any trouble," he called out calmly. "Just passing through."

The older woman, with dark hair pulled into a rough bun, took a step forward, scanning Santiago's family.

"Where are you headed?" the zookeeper asked.

"Trying to find somewhere safer," Santiago said.

The woman scoffed. "Safe? There's no 'safe' anymore."

Tina stepped out from behind the tree, keeping in front of Isabella and Diego. "We have children too. We just want to keep moving, okay?"

For a moment, the tension seemed to ease. But then the man began to study Santiago's tactical gear. "You know a place that's safe?"

"Just trying to find one, amigo," Santiago said.

The man took a step forward, and Santiago instinctively raised his gun.

"Stay where you are," Santiago said firmly. "Take a deep breath."

But the man's eyes were wild, the desperation of the last three days written all over his face. He, too, was just trying to protect his family.

"You know something. You're trying to get somewhere," the man insisted. He walked forward, bringing up his own shotgun. "Tell me what you know."

"Dad," said the teenage girl.

The man kept coming, and Santiago felt the dread of the decision he might well have to make.

"Just tell me what you know," the man said.

Part of Santiago wanted to share that information with this guy and his family. But Santiago also knew that it could jeopardize getting his own family onto the airship. Moreover, he had no idea whether this man could be trusted. Based on his behavior, maybe not.

The man turned when his daughter again told him to back down.

Santiago reacted without thinking. He thrust the butt of his submachine gun into the man's back, knocking him to the ground.

"Dad!" shouted the teenage boy.

Santiago kicked the shotgun away and held up his submachine gun.

"Get back!" Santiago yelled in a tone that suggested he meant it. The family gathered around their fallen father, glaring up at Santiago.

He backed over to the shotgun and picked it up. Tina took it from him.

"I'll leave this at exit B1," Santiago said. "Don't follow us, or next time it'll be more than a gun butt that hits you. Understand?"

The man grunted. "Don't do this to us."

"You did it to yourself. We didn't want trouble."

Santiago motioned for his family. They rushed away, heading out of the zoo. At exit B1, he took the shotgun from Tina and tried to eject the shells. But the weapon was empty. He set it down where he had said he would. As he rose up, he heard shuffling.

"Uh, Dad..." Diego said.

"Wow, is that a lion?" Isabella asked.

Santiago turned to see that his daughter was right. On the next path, not thirty feet from them, a huge male lion stood watching them.

"Nobody move," he said.

The lion growled, showing its long yellow canines.

Isabella cried out, and Santiago stepped in front of her with the submachine gun.

"Dad," Diego said. "Dad, it's—"

"Quiet," Santiago whispered.

He didn't want to kill the majestic creature, but he didn't see a choice if it charged.

The animal bounded forward in what seemed like slow motion, shoulder muscles flexing as it closed the distance.

Santiago fired the submachine gun into the massive chest as it sprang. He squeezed off another burst just under the chin, into the thick mane, just as the beast hit him, knocking him to the ground.

Pushing with all his strength, he rolled the four-hundred-pound cat off him. Santiago examined the creature that had nearly taken off his head. It was dead for sure, with blood trickling from multiple holes in its chest and throat.

Tina ran over to him.

"My God, are you okay?" she asked.

"I'm good," Santiago said, standing.

The children stared at him, eyes wide.

"It's going to be okay," he said.

But both kids just stared back.

"Come on," he said. "We have to keep going."

They left the zoo with just over an hour to get the boat and motor out to the coordinates. The next part of their journey took them through the adjacent Japanese gardens. Tina slowed as they crossed the arched wooden footbridge over a koi pond.

The garden's pathways, lined with raked gravel and stone statues, were untouched by the violence that had ravaged the rest of the city, but it didn't mean they were safe. Santiago scanned the dense bamboo thickets that bordered the walkways. The wind picked up, causing the tall bamboo to sway gently in the smoky breeze, the hollow stalks clacking softly together.

As they made their way through, Diego pointed. "Dad, look."

Santiago followed his son's finger toward a terrace where a group of maybe twenty people hung out on the lawns, sitting cross-legged.

"What are those people doing?" Isabella asked.

"Praying," Santiago said.

He scooped her up, saying his own prayer as he ran the rest of the way out of the gardens. They came out at a surprisingly quiet street of residential houses. They had only a few blocks to go before they reached the marina.

As they pushed on, Santiago saw that it wasn't going to be easy. Buildings burned in the distance, the flames casting eerie reflections on the water. Santiago noticed shadows moving in the street ahead. Figures darted from place to place—some looters, others just trying to flee the chaos. His heart sank. Clearly, the madness hadn't spared the waterfront.

On the final three blocks to the marina, he got a view of the horizon, where hundreds of sailboats floated this way and that.

His headset fired in his ear.

"Santiago, do you copy?" said Zimmerman.

Santiago motioned for his family to huddle in a thicket of trees.

"Yeah, copy," he said.

"What's your status?"

"I got eyes on the marina and I'm with my family."

"You better pick up the pace, because the situation is about to get a lot worse out there."

"No shit. What now?"

"The military has attacked Orion and Tyron. They are both offline, replaced by something, I don't know what. But whatever it is, it's simulating a nuclear attack."

"Simulating?"

Santiago's blood ran cold at that. He knew right away what was happening. This AI, or whatever was now in charge of ITC, didn't have access to nuclear weapons. But it didn't need them. If it tricked other countries into thinking they were being attacked, they would launch their own nukes out of self-preservation.

"We're still in position, but I can't say for how long. You gotta hurry," Zimmerman said.

Santiago slung his weapon and picked Isabella up once again. "We're running the rest of the way," he said. "Tina, hold on to Diego's hand and follow me no matter what you see."

Together the family took off loping down the street, with Isabella wrapped around Santiago. They weren't alone. Groups of people came from other roads to access the marina. Ten. Twenty. By the time they were within view of the eastern edge of the marina, Santiago counted hundreds of people. Most were civilians, families looking for refuge from the violence that had erupted.

Santiago checked his wrist monitor for the location of the ITC boat. It wasn't far, inside one of the enclosed boat ports where luxury yachts were stored. He ran out onto the docks, leading the way toward a gate that once blocked off the private slips. Someone had smashed it open.

Almost all the yachts and boats were still docked, likely unable to start because of the sabotaged ITC chips. He had to hope that the security device Zimmerman provided would activate the ITC boat if the chip was offline.

Searching the numbers on the slip as he ran, he found it halfway down the long dock. Using his wrist monitor, he held it up to the security keypad. The lock flashed green, and the hatch opened.

Relief washed over him at the sight of the nearly sixty-foot-long vessel with a wide, sturdy hull and a raised enclosed cabin. It was a sleek white vessel, built for transporting cargo and personnel between offshore locations, its powerful twin engines designed for speed.

"Get in," he said.

Tina pulled Diego inside, and Santiago handed Isabella off. Pulling his submachine gun back out, he looked down the dock to see if they had been noticed.

To his shock, he saw the zookeeper, his wife, and their two teenagers running toward them.

"Wait, please!" the man shouted.

"You got to be kiddin' me," Santiago said.

"Stop!"

"Can we take them?" Tina asked.

Santiago cursed. "I don't have permission to bring anyone else, but I guess if worse comes to worst, they can stay on the boat."

He stepped back as the family approached. "You give me any problems, and I swear I'll throw you to the sharks," Santiago said.

"We won't, I promise," the man said.

"Hurry up, then."

"Oh, God, thank you," said his wife.

The two teenagers nodded, but Santiago could tell they weren't happy that he had hit their father. He closed the hatch and began to untie the mooring ropes. The zookeeper helped. Looking up, he said, "I'm Liam, and that's my wife, Emery, and our son and daughter, Tim and Allie."

"Santiago," he said. "Tina and our kids, Diego and Isabella."

As they worked, Tina and Emery helped the kids climb aboard.

Santiago hopped onto the deck and went to the small cabin at the stern. It was spacious inside, with four leather seats and a dashboard full of controls. There was a seating area for several passengers.

He quickly assessed the controls, fingers tracing over the ignition panel.

"Is it going to work?" Tina asked, her voice tight with concern.

Santiago nodded. He took out the security remote and inserted it into the drive. Then he flipped the switch on the panel, praying that the systems would fire. There was a brief pause before a low hum vibrated through the hull as the boat's power came to life. The lights flickered on, illuminating the cabin in a soft glow.

"Thank God," he whispered.

"Open that door," he said to Liam.

The zookeeper jumped back to the platform and went to the door, where he pushed a button. The door clattered upward on overhead tracks.

The engines rumbled beneath them, coming to life with a deep, throaty roar. Santiago pushed the throttle forward slightly, testing its responsiveness. The twin engines revved as the water churned behind them. A faint cloud of smoke puffed from the exhaust, but everything seemed functional.

"Okay, everyone, sit," he said. "We'll be moving fast."

He pulled out of the slip into the marina, now cloaked in shadows from smoke blowing out of the city. The sounds of distant chaos seemed far away now, muffled by the lapping water and the rhythmic thrum of the boat's engines. But he knew that danger was still close, and after the transmission from Zimmerman, things were about to get a lot worse.

People on the docks screamed and waved for them to stop as they pulled out, but Santiago buried the throttle the instant he saw guns.

"Everyone down!" he yelled.

The engines roared as he cut around the docks and knifed through the water. He leaned down and glanced back as the wake shot up, spraying disabled vessels that bobbed lifelessly in their slips. The view of the civilians vanished, but he could see the city in the distance. Plumes of smoke rose up from the once-beautiful, thriving metropolis where he had hoped to raise his children and retire someday.

But that was all a distant memory. All that mattered now was survival.

He turned back to the controls, pushing the throttle harder. The boat surged forward, the engines roaring louder as they ventured into open water. The wind whipped against his face, carrying the scent of the sea, and for the first time in days, Santiago felt a flicker of hope.

Holding up his wrist monitor, he saw that they had forty-five minutes—just enough time to get to the coordinates twenty miles away from the marina.

He checked on his family, huddled on the deck with their newfound shipmates. Everyone looked at Santiago as he steered them out to sea.

Ten minutes passed in silence.

Then came the voice of his daughter, rising over the engine.

"Are we safe now, Daddy?" she asked.

He turned to look at her, and had begun to smile when he saw a flash on the horizon to the northeast.

This was no simulation. This was a nuclear warhead hitting Los Angeles. He looked away quickly to save his eyes from the inferno that would soon be rising into the sky.

"No," he muttered, lowering his head in shock. "God, no, please don't be real."

But it was real, and San Diego was next.

Santiago kept the throttle down all the way, praying that they could make it to the airship and get out of here before it left them behind.

CHAPTER 37

An hour after picking up Cecil and Michelle, the pickup truck pulled up to the chain-link fence on the road leading up to their cabin. He hopped out and helped Michelle down. Wolf jumped out of the cab with Sam and Frodo, wagging his tail and rushing over to Michelle.

"Damn, our boy really likes you," Frodo said.

"I really like him too," she said as she bent down to say goodbye to the German shepherd.

"Thanks for the lift, and the extra food and supplies," Cecil said.

"Appreciate what you did back there," Sam said. "Like I said, we could use your help in the coming—"

A distant boom sounded, and the ground shook.

"What is that?" Michelle asked.

Sam and Cecil exchanged a look, both of them knowing exactly what it was.

"Oh, fuck, say it ain't so," Frodo said. "That can't be a warhead. That can't be a—"

Sam looked west, in the direction of Charlotte, saying nothing.

"A warhead?" Michelle asked. "What do you mean—a nuclear weapon?"

Cecil pulled his wife over to him, holding her as the horrific image of a mushroom cloud climbed into the sky. From the hill, they had a perfect vantage point from which to view the most horrible thing either of them had ever seen.

"Cecil . . ." Michelle said in a shaky voice.

For the first time Cecil could recall, he wasn't sure what to say or how to reassure her that everything was going to be okay. All he could do was hold her closer. Within two seconds, he did the mental math of how long it would take for the shock wave to reach them at 100 miles away. Moving at around 750 miles per hour—roughly the speed of sound—it would take around eight minutes for the blast to travel here. By mile 50, it would have slowed down, and by the time it reached them, it would be moving at 500 miles per hour or less. Much of the inferno would have weakened, but the forest would still be set ablaze.

If they were seeing the mushroom cloud, then they had already lost precious time.

"We have to take cover," Cecil said.

Sam and Frodo were already backing up their truck.

"No time to drive," Cecil said. "We need to shelter inside—"

"That shack?" Sam said. "It won't survive the hell that's coming this way."

"We got to go. Come on!" Frodo yelled. He opened the driver's door, and Wolf hopped in, sticking his head out the window and barking.

"You got eight minutes, maybe less, to get somewhere safer in your truck," Cecil said.

"And you should jump in the back and come with us. We have a bunker in an old mine not far from our place. It's only five miles from here."

Michelle looked at him, but Cecil shook his head. If they were driving when the shock wave hit, it would be like driving into a tornado. But these two guys knew that and were prepared to take the risk.

"If you survive, you're welcome at our place," Frodo said.

"Good luck," Sam said.

"You too," Cecil replied.

They squealed away in the truck, kicking up dirt and rocks. Cecil pulled Michelle toward the cabin as the inferno raged in the distance, rising toward the stratosphere.

Barking came over the noise, and they turned to see that Wolf had hopped out of the pickup.

Sam stopped the truck, then kept going, not waiting for the dog.

"Come on, boy!" Michelle shouted.

The dog followed them into the cabin, but Cecil had another idea. "Grab blankets, clothes, and raincoats. I'll get food and water," he said. "We're heading to an old mine I saw when I found Wolf."

They scavenged everything they could carry. Cecil loaded up a second bag with their food, water, and other supplies, including duct tape and some plastic sheeting. Michelle came out of a bedroom with blankets and a suitcase of clothes.

"Let's go," Cecil said.

He opened the sliding door for Michelle, but she paused.

"My God," she muttered.

Cecil turned to find her staring at a second mushroom cloud. "Let's go," he said, grabbing her by the arm. They crossed the deck, hurried down the stairs, and went down the back hill behind the cabin, not far from where he had found the dog.

Fear gnawed at him as he moved between the trees. He wasn't sure how sturdy the mine would be. What if he was leading his wife into a grave that would collapse, burying them alive?

But it was their only option. The cabin wouldn't survive the blast.

Cecil led the way down through another thicket of trees. At the bottom of the hill, he saw the old sign and the boarded-off entrance to the mine. He kicked one of the rotted pieces of wood loose.

He pulled out a flashlight and turned it on, lighting up the passage. It looked safe, with secure logs and metal posts shoring the walls and holding up the ceiling, but there was no telling whether it would hold once that shock wave hit.

"Get inside," he said.

Michelle ducked inside without hesitating. Wolf paused, then bolted forward into her arms. Cecil shined the light deeper into the mine. It went back twenty feet, where more boards blocked the way.

Dirt rained from the ceiling as they went deeper inside. The ground rumbled as if from an approaching train, stronger by the second. This was far more powerful than any train. More powerful than a thousand trains loaded with TNT.

He thought of Charlotte and the other city that had been hit, his mind processing that this wasn't just those two cities. This had to be happening *everywhere*.

Billions of people would already be dead in the initial blasts. They were the lucky ones. Billions more outside that death zone would be burned severely, suffering agonizing deaths over the coming hours, days, and months.

Cecil swallowed, trying to wrap his mind around what was happening.

But this was madness—the end of everything. There would be no coming back from this. He pulled his wife down, thinking of the life growing in her womb. What kind of world would they be bringing it into, assuming they did survive the next hour? Days. Months.

He shook away the questions and the fear. He had to do everything to make sure they had a chance. The first step was to make it through this event. Then they could venture out and get to that bunker. There would be supplies, food, and medicine.

Survival was possible.

Another minute passed as they settled on the ground. Cecil picked up logs and beams, trying his best to secure the shaft. As the howling nuclear shock wave raged closer, he went back to the entrance and began shoveling the dirt up.

One minute passed.

Two minutes.

He built a wall, leaving just enough room at the top for air to get in and out.

Then he rushed back to the supplies.

"Michelle, help me with this," he said, pulling their supplies closer. He pulled out the rain gear and plastic sheeting from the cabin. There was no time to build a barrier at the wall, so he began to build a makeshift tent of plastic sheeting. The approaching firestorm roared toward the mountainside at speeds unimaginable, rattling his bones. An eerie vibration resonated through the rocks deep underground.

"We're going to make it," Cecil said. "I love you, Michelle."

He enfolded her in a hug as the pressure wave closed in. Wolf nudged up between them, whimpering. A moment later, the tsunami of wind reached the mountain, slamming into it like the breath of an angry god. The air felt as if it had been sucked out, leaving an oppressive, suffocating stillness. Dust and loose rock sifted down from the ceiling, filling the narrow tunnels with choking debris as the walls groaned under the stress. The ground trembled violently, sending a cascade of rocks and dirt raining down from the ceiling as the blast rippled through the mountain.

A beam cracked with a terrifying sound.

Wolf howled.

The air pressure changed suddenly, popping Cecil's ears and making it feel as if the walls themselves were closing in. The shock wave, though muted by the layers of rock above, still sent tremors deep into the shaft. Grit and pebbles fell on Cecil as he tried to shield his wife and the dog.

Michelle cried out, but all Cecil could do was hold her tighter.

"I love you," he said again. "We're gonna make it. We're gonna—"

"I love you too, Cecil."

He held his wife, his hand on her belly, where life from their love grew.

The howling of the storm faded in the distance, and the tremors subsided. Cecil remained hunched over Michelle and Wolf for a little longer.

Coughing, he pushed up, shaking dust and gravel off his back.

"Are you okay?" he asked Michelle.

She managed a nod as she reached down to her stomach. Wolf shook himself.

Cecil guided them both back to the wall of dirt that he had shoveled. Part of it had caved in, providing a window out to the valley below. He crouched down to look through, his heart thumping at the sight before them.

Fires burned in all directions, smoke rising into a darkened sky. They had survived the blast, but very soon the fallout would begin to drift down. When it did, they would need to shelter somewhere safer than this. In the first twenty-four hours, the poison would be the most deadly.

He realized this place would be a grave, if they stayed too long.

"Pack everything up," he said. "We have to get to that bunker."

* * * * *

Santiago held the throttle down, racing toward the coordinates with just minutes to spare. The rendezvous point lay just ahead, but he didn't see any sign of *Persephone* in the cloudy sky. Glancing over his shoulder, he saw the mushroom cloud from the nuke that had detonated just minutes earlier rising above Los Angeles.

Another flash suddenly hit San Diego. He instantly turned away, knowing not to look directly at the blast. Even as he turned, the flash was so bright that it momentarily turned the deep blue of the ocean white around them. His breath caught in his throat. Almost twenty miles out to sea, he knew that the distance wouldn't be enough to save them if they didn't get out of here.

"Everyone down!" he shouted.

Without thinking, he grabbed Isabella, cradling her against his chest as he dropped to the deck. Tina did the same with Diego, pulling him down hard. The boat's metal deck was cold beneath them, the ocean's calm serenity shattered by the terror racing toward them on the horizon.

Santiago glanced back at Liam, hunkered in the stern with his family. The two fathers shared a glance of dread. Here at the end, they were helpless to protect those they loved most. As a cruel reminder, the roar grew louder, the wave of destruction racing across the water toward them.

For a split second, there was an eerie silence, as if the ocean itself had taken a breath. Then the world exploded into chaos. The air around them ignited with a blazing heat that Santiago could feel even from this distance.

The shock wave hit the boat with bone-rattling force, throwing it violently to port. The whole vessel rocked, the deck beneath him shuddering as if it might come apart under the stress. He could hear the scream of the wind, the roar of the blast as it raced past them.

Santiago dared to lift his head and look back toward San

Diego. In the distance, the new mushroom cloud rose into the sky, climbing higher and higher like a twisted tower of death. It was grotesque in its enormity, its fury almost hypnotizing. The skyline of San Diego was gone, replaced by fire and devastation. His stomach churned. They were far enough from the hypocenter to avoid immediate annihilation, but the force of the next blast was still closing in on them—an unstoppable force of nature that they couldn't outrun.

But he had to try.

He got up and pushed down on the throttle. Nothing happened.

Realization sent his stomach flipping again.

The electromagnetic pulse from the detonation had fried the electronics.

"No, no, no..." Santiago muttered under his breath, his eyes darting toward the control panel. The boat lurched and went still. The engine died completely, leaving them adrift in the water, powerless. The once-reassuring hum of the motor was replaced by the terrifying rush of wind and water.

"Hang on to the kids!" he shouted, his voice hoarse. All they could do now was wait for the shock wave to hit.

Santiago felt the air pressure shift as it neared. Heat pressed down on them like a weight, and the placid sea shimmered with strange whitecapped waves. Santiago clutched a sobbing Isabella as the boat rattled beneath them. The full force of the wave was a bare minute away. There was no escape. He braced himself, praying that it would be quick.

At least we're together, he thought.

"I love you," he said. "I love you all."

He kissed Isabella, Tina, and Diego in turn as he held them.

Then, through the roar of the approaching wind, he heard it: rotors, unmistakable and powerful, cutting through the air above them. His heart leaped in disbelief. He opened his eyes and looked up to see the tilt-rotors of a Wasp, its silhouette like a guardian in the sky.

Santiago blinked, hardly believing what he was seeing.

"Come on!" he yelled.

The massive blades spun overhead, kicking up spray as the Wasp hovered above the water.

The belly hatch opened, and a bulky shape emerged. It looked like . . . a *boat*?

Santiago understood at once. Knowing there was no time for individual extractions, Captain Dominique had wisely lowered the only thing that would hold all eight of them: the Wasp's inflatable survival raft.

Before the Zodiac even touched down on the boat's deck, Santiago lifted Isabella onto it while Tina helped Diego inside. Liam did the same with his family. The two men were the last on, Santiago gave the high sign, and the Wasp rose away.

"Lie down flat and hold on tight!" Santiago shouted.

He felt the acceleration as the powerful tilt-rotors yanked them up into the sky.

They were alive, and now they had a chance to escape this hell if only the aircraft could get them high enough, fast enough.

The cable winched them up into the cargo hold, and the moment the hatch closed, a crew chief grabbed one kid, then the other. Then Tina climbed out, and Liam's family. As Santiago stepped over the transom of the Zodiac, the Wasp roared into the clouds.

"T!" shouted a voice.

He looked up to see Nodin, his arm wrapped where it had been severed.

"Nodin, my God, man, you saved us," Santiago said.

"For now, Sarge, but..." Nodin's words trailed off as he looked down at the kids.

Santiago knew that whatever Nodin knew was bad, bad enough that he didn't want to scare them more. The Wasp docked with *Persephone* a few minutes later. The ship was on the move, getting as much distance from the mainland as it could.

As they unloaded from the Wasp, Santiago hugged his wet, exhausted, relieved family. "You're safe now," he said. "These people will take you to sick bay to make sure you're okay."

"What about you?" Tina asked.

"I need to go to the command center," he said.

"Don't go, Daddy," Isabella said.

"He has to work," Diego said with a brave nod.

"I won't be far, and I'll come back as soon as I can."

Tina hugged him. "I love you," she whispered.

"I love you too."

He looked at his family one more time, grateful beyond words that they were okay. But he knew they weren't safe just yet. World War III had broken out, and they had to find a safe place to land.

Nodin hurried the best he could with him to the command center, which had become a hive of activity. Captain Dominique glanced over.

"Glad to see you made it, Sergeant Rodriguez," he said.

"Thanks for letting Nodin borrow a Wasp," Santiago said.

"He didn't give us much of a choice," Dominique said.

Nodin grinned, wincing from pain. It was then Santiago realized that his comrade in arms had probably strong-armed the pilots into the aircraft and to the coordinates. Zimmerman walked over and nodded, but it was a grim nod.

On the screens, Santiago took in the reality that was unfolding across the United States. City after city, hit by the same nuclear weapons that had detonated in Seoul and Busan, releasing into the atmosphere particles that would create the same storms.

And not just here.

His eyes shifted to South America, Europe, Africa, the Middle East, Asia, Australia.

Every corner of the globe was being nuked by governments that had panicked.

"Who's doing this?" he gasped.

Zimmerman shook his head.

"We're still trying to figure out what happened, but it started off as a simulation that appeared as a real attack from the United States, led by Orion. In defense, dozens of countries fired off their own arsenals, targeting us," Dominique said coldly. "Now, we are hitting back."

"Mutually assured destruction," Santiago said.

"End of everything," Nodin said.

"We have to find a place to put down," someone said.

Santiago looked at the monitors, watching the red impacts bloom out across the screens.

"No," he said.

Everyone looked at him.

"It's safer in the clouds," Santiago said. "We have to climb as high as this ship will go."

"He's right. XO, prepare for high altitude," Dominique said in a commanding voice. "Max speed. Into the skies."

STAY TUNED FOR PART 2,

COMING 2026.

ABOUT THE AUTHOR

Nicholas Sansbury Smith is the *New York Times* and *USA Today* bestselling author of more than forty novels with two million copies sold. Before his writing career, he served at Iowa Homeland Security and Emergency Management, a background that inspired many of his story concepts. A two-time Ironman triathlete, he enjoys running, biking, and hiking. Nicholas also loves traveling, especially to his cabin in Northern Minnesota where he weaves his tales. He lives in Iowa with his wonderful wife and their son and daughter.

Join Nicholas on social media:
Facebook Author Page: Nicholas Sansbury Smith
Website: NicholasSansburySmith.com
Instagram: instagram.com/author_sansbury
Email: GreatWaveInk@gmail.com